BY JAY BONANSINGA

Frozen

Twisted

Available from Pinnacle Books

TWISTED

Jay Bonansinga

PINNACLE BOOKS
Kensington Publishing Corp.
www.kensingtonbooks.com

PINNACLE BOOKS are published by

Kensington Publishing Corp.
850 Third Avenue
New York, NY 10022

All Kensington titles, imprints, and distributed lines are available at special quantity discounts for bulk purchases for sales promotions, premiums, fund-raising, educational, or institutional use.

Special book excerpts or customized printings can also be created to fit specific needs. For details, write or phone the office of the Kensington special sales manager: Kensington Publishing Corp., 850 Third Avenue, New York, NY 10022, attn: Special Sales Department; phone 1-800-221-2647.

ISBN 0-7860-1724-4

First printing: July 2006

10 9 8 7 6 5 4 3 2 1

Printed in the United States of America

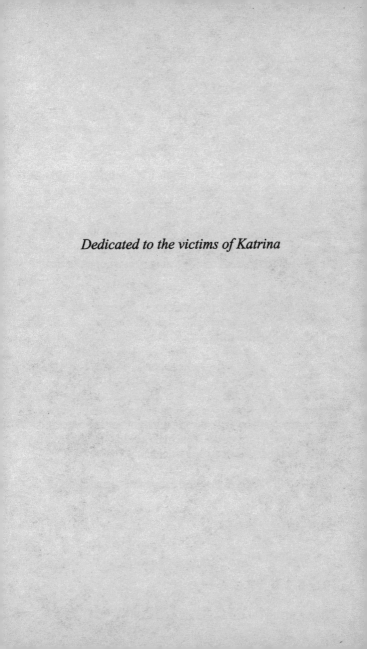

Dedicated to the victims of Katrina

Foreword

In August of 2005, an unprecedented storm hit the Gulf Coast of America, wreaking havoc across three states. The city of New Orleans was especially hard-hit. The ensuing floods brought about devastation on a biblical scale, resulting in loss of life and property damage that are, at this book's press time, still being tabulated.

In July of 2005, I turned in the first draft of a book about an epochal hurricane hitting New Orleans, including scenes of deadly flooding, levees giving way, and the whole gamut of heart-wrenching human behavior in extremis—all of this written months before it happened in real life.

For an author of commercial fiction, this presented a major dilemma—albeit one that paled in comparison with the misery and heartache experienced by Katrina's victims. Still, I had a difficult decision to make. Should I scrap the whole thing out of respect for the dead and dispossessed? Or should I "Katrina-ize" the existing story?

Ultimately I decided—along with Michaela Hamilton, my sage and patient editor at Pinnacle Books—to stick with New Orleans. And stick with the hurricane.

Novels take place in a "parallel present" and our current present will forever be affected by Katrina. But

I'm sticking with New Orleans because you do not abandon those you love. Because New Orleans should have *libraries* of books written about it. Because New Orleans is us.

Long live the Crescent City!

PROLOGUE:
City of Ghosts, City of Martyrs

New Orleans
Present day

That night, as the latest storm closed in on the old man's row house on Dumaine Street, the world seemed to turn inside out. The black rain, coming down in sheets, strafed across the professor's ruined tile roof. The Spanish windows rattled and thrummed. The wrought-iron galleries moaned and whistled. Every few moments lightning flickered, filling the cozy bachelor's lair with the glare of a photographer's strobe.

Hunkered down in his cluttered living room, surrounded by his beloved books and wax 78s, the old man tried to ignore the overwhelming feeling that the imminent hurricane was the least of his problems. Nowadays, he and his fellow New Orleanians had become practically inured to—if not downright contemptuous of—hurricane warnings. Besides, the old man had bigger catastrophes on his personal horizon. He had made troubling discoveries over the past few months, as well as grave mistakes. Dreadful mistakes. Mistakes that were just now coming back to torment him through terrifying permutations.

He put his book down, unread, on the side table, the

winds continuing to rage against the window glass. He rose to his full height and tried to decide what to do: evacuate or wait out the storm in the reinforced garage behind the building? How many people had asked themselves that very question last year when Katrina was bearing down on the Gulf Coast? How many lives were snuffed out in '05 in the fury of those floodwaters because of a single poor decision? And how many more perished because of the simple, inexorable fact of poverty?

For a man in his late seventies, Professor Moses Andrew Jackson De Lourde, PhD, was not the type to ruminate on such matters. He was a robust old coot of impressive stature—both figuratively and literally. Nearly six feet tall in his stocking feet, with long, storklike legs and a little oval paunch, he wore the garb of a nineteenth-century aristocrat. Evening jacket, silk cravat, and riding boots. His long iron-gray mane was swept back off his lined, leathery face, and the single delicate gold loop piercing his flabby left earlobe only hinted at his bohemian lifestyle, not to mention his proud gayness.

So how had he sunken to this point? How had he botched his affairs so completely? Moses De Lourde was supposed to be a man of measured judgement, one of the Old Lions of Academia, an authority in arcane corners of history, anthropology, and archaeology. Now look at him: alone, afraid, reduced to the level of a Neanderthal huddling horror-stricken in his cave, waiting for the angry nature gods to subside. Like so many folks in this town, De Lourde seemed to suffer from post-hurricane stress disorder, a form of manic depression punctuated by periods of debilitating pessimism. Pessimism about the future, about God and country. But all this merely served to bolster the professor's stubbornness and pride, and insistence on staying put—like most of his heartier fellow denizens. The city had weathered three centuries of turmoil. No goddamned hurricane was going to shut them down now.

He heard another noise from down the hall, maybe from the bedroom. It was a flinty, scraping noise, followed by a series of clicks.

He had been hearing these noises all evening, and had initially thought them simply figments of his imagination or merely the palmetto branches scraping the windows. But now he was convinced they were the sounds of a human intruder. Someone was trying to get inside!

"The nastiness seems to be commencin' a trifle early this time around," he muttered to himself, reaching down into the pocket of his coat. He pulled out a small can of pepper spray, a precautionary purchase that he had made last year during the days marshal law ruled the Quarter. In those awful weeks after Katrina had flooded the entire metro area—when the French Quarter, the only high and dry area for miles, had been reduced to the wild west—De Lourde had cowered, day in and day out, behind his second-floor gallery like Gloria Swanson in *Sunset Boulevard*.

The little aerosol bottle felt reassuring in his gnarled, liver-spotted hand as he started down the back hall toward the noise.

His bedroom was empty. The French doors latched. The windows locked securely. A single bedside lamp threw a dull, yellow cone of light across the Persian rug. Nothing out of the ordinary here.

The bathroom was also as he had left it. Shower curtain drawn back. Rusty water dripping perpetually into an old claw-foot bathtub.

But just as he was about to turn away and make his exit, he paused suddenly, noticing something peculiar on the outer surface of the window above the toilet. The little porthole-style pane overlooked the rear alley two stories down. No human being could reach the outside of that window. The drop was at least thirty feet. A person would have to have wings.

"Sweet Jesus on the cross," De Lourde uttered, staring at the symbol scrawled there, his southern drawl barely a whisper.

He began backing away, moving almost involuntarily, until his back bumped the opposite wall of the corridor. He kept gaping at that window, and the strange characters drawn across it in red paint. The more he stared at it—especially the way it was streaking and blurring in the rain—the more he realized it was not red paint at all.

"This cannot be happenin'," he murmured, his voice drowned by the sound of the rain, as he turned and staggered back down the hallway toward the living room.

An old princess model phone sat on a French provincial table by the fireplace. He grabbed it and tried to dial the nonemergency number for the Orleans Parish Detective Squad. He knew a good old boy over there who might listen to the ravings of a crazed old queen.

The phone was dead.

"Damn, damn, *damn.*"

He hobbled over to the hat rack by the door. His London Fog slicker hung there, next to his walking cane and Panama hat. He quickly shrugged on the coat, then grabbed the Panama, and the cane, and a large umbrella.

Then he awkwardly whirled around, searching for his cell phone. It sat perched in its charger by the bookshelf. He went over, snatched up the cell, then made his exit.

Quickly . . . down the rickety back stairs. Across an iron platform greasy with rain. Past his new tomato plants, past his ragged bougainvillea trellis, still bearing the scars of Katrina's winds. The tip of his old lion-head cane slipped and squeaked as he trundled through a narrow gate and into the storm-swept back alley.

Rain lashed his face as he hobbled across slimy cobblestones. Lightning flashed again, turning the scene into a silent movie flicker show. The old man turned up his collar, lowered his hat, and squinted up at the gray shrouds. What in God's name did he think he was going to see? And what did he think he was going to *do* if he saw something?

The storm pressed down on him as he gazed up at the back of his place and tried to figure out how someone could draw an ancient symbol on his bathroom window. He saw nothing but tangled power lines and rainwater streaming down cracked, weathered timbers.

He made a decision then. He would skip the parish detective squad, and he would make a call to the one man who might take all this nonsense seriously.

The professor took a deep, pained breath then and headed for the mouth of the alley . . .

. . . completely unaware that he was being followed.

The dark figure tracked the old man with amazing stealth and skill, moving from shadow to shadow, keeping just enough distance between the twosome to remain undetected.

Tall and rawboned and sinewy, this impressive figure possessed preternatural hearing and vision, and blended into the battered, wounded cityscape, and the veils of rain, and the swirling salt winds, like a graceful black chameleon. This was a deadly predator—newly born, newly minted—and he moved with a singular purpose.

Up ahead, the old man stumbled slightly, fiddling with his umbrella and cell phone, trying to find the entrance to the garage's storm shelter, trying to be heard above the wind and rain. "—dreadfully sorry to call at this hour—hello?—Ulysses!"

The dark figure paused, shivering now with anticipation, crouching just inside the alley's shadowy threshold. Clad in black ceremonial garb, draped in ritual implements, the figure coiled itself there with cobra stillness.

Several things were happening all at once: the hurricane approaching, the first sequence beginning, the bloodlust rising, and the voice, the voice, its words hollered into a cell phone, barely audible in the roar of the rain.

"Ulysses, can you hear me? Hello! I'm frightfully sorry, dear heart, but I believe I have a situation on my hands—I said a situation!—*Hello*!"

Thunder boomed.

Lightning crackled.

The figure crept—cautiously, smoothly under the cover of darkness—toward the professor. Fifteen feet. Ten. Eight. The old man was now trying to open the garage shelter door, grunting with effort, the phone wedged against his ear as he wheezed at the top of his lungs: "Ulysses? Ulysses!"

The figure pounced, and the old man jerked.

Something flashed in the momentary strobe of lightning like tinsel in the dark.

It was over before the old man hit the ground.

Over the course of the next hour and forty-five minutes, Hurricane Cassandra roared into town, battering the French Quarter, strafing Jackson Square, and taking the tops of trees off like an angry, petulant god. It was nowhere near Katrina-sized, of course, but it was deadly just the same.

By that point, most of the residents of New Orleans— or at least those lucky enough to possess the proper conveyances—were either evacuated somewhere up-state, waiting out this category-one blowhard, or safely tucked away in storm shelters. Very few—if any—on-lookers witnessed the furious winds that reigned across the Quarter and into the Garden District for several hours that night. Nobody saw the ancient rows of live oaks being shredded once again like sickly stalks of wheat chewed up in a cosmic combine. And nobody saw the dark figure dragging the limp form from doorstep to doorstep, from alcove to underhang, fighting the horizontal rain and seventy-five-mile-an-hour winds.

Nobody realized that this dark figure had been transformed by the weather, a force of nature *himself*. He thought of himself as the Holy Ghost now, and the title suited him. He was a glorious visitor from another realm, here to equalize a universe in turmoil.

He dragged the professor's flaccid body down the ramp and into the shadows of the scarred and shambled Riverfront, into the dark, swaying palmettos of the Toulouse Street wharf. The sky was changing. That was good.

It was nearly time.

In the churning blackness under the festering Toulouse Street steamboat slip, the Holy Ghost laid the body in the rancid mud and prepared for the ritual. The Great Process was about to begin. The summoning. And this old man was merely the beginning. A prelude to the main event.

The ultimate sacrifice.

PART I
Offerings

If a sane dog fights a mad dog, it's the sane dog's ear that is bitten off.

—Burmese proverb

1

"Y'all been down to the Big Easy before?"

The old man behind the wheel of the dented minivan was attempting small talk in order to lighten the mood, which hung like a pall over the vehicle's interior as the van rattled over the dark, bombed-out interstate. A brown-skinned Cuban gentleman of indeterminate age, he kept throwing sidelong glances at the man sitting in the shotgun seat.

From the moment he had arrived in New Orleans, the dapper, handsome African-American man on the passenger side hadn't said much. Dressed in his sharp Burberry topcoat and charcoal silk scarf, he was as stony as a department store mannequin, clearly still in shock over the professor's death, clearly being buffeted by the sudden and unexpected loss. You could see that much in his eyes. In fact, the man's eyes were dead giveaways. The almond-shaped, cappuccino-colored eyes were set off by almost feminine lashes and arched brows. The eyes of a movie star—at least superficially. Upon closer scrutiny, however, the man's eyes revealed deeper anxieties, rougher times about which the driver could only speculate.

"Once," Ulysses Grove replied, gazing wistfully

through the rain-jeweled window. They had just left the airport (much of which was still under repair), and the terrain looked like a desolate, uncharted planet in the outer reaches of some uninhabitable solar system. Illuminated only by sporadic sodium light, the scars left behind by the floodwaters were still apparent everywhere. Before Katrina, or BK as the natives referred to places and things that had survived the disaster—sadly, much of what occured in New Orleans these days was given the suffix AK or After Katrina— the district along Highway 10 once looked like a vast, innocuous industrial park. Now the waterlogged warehouses and abandoned factories were mostly dark, and the interstitial roadways and vegetation had mostly been eaten away with rot, suffocated by flood damage—some of it still underwater. "Years ago I came down here," Grove added softly, "when I was in the service."

The army, to be exact. He had been an investigator in the CID Unit in the eighties, and had come here for a few days to ferret information from the family of a deserter. The case had been a routine job for Grove, but he had gotten to know the city fairly well on that trip, and found it fascinating in spite of his aversion to its more voluptuous pleasures. New Orleans had always been a big flirtatious harlot of a town, and still was, bless her heart, despite her recent miseries and endless months of cosmetic surgery. But during that routine trip back in 1987, the place had touched some deeply repressed part of Grove's psyche.

Of course, repression was di rigueur for Grove. It was how he did his job. It was how he lived with the terrible images that stained his mind's eye. It was also how he dealt with his grief and sorrow. It was how he was dealing with De Lourde's death, and it was how he had carried on after his wife, Hannah, had succumbed to cancer a little over five years ago. Maybe that was why Grove felt so adrift in melancholia now. The post-Katrina New Orleans mirrored his wounded soul.

"A military man!" the driver exclaimed, raising his bushy graying eyebrows with histrionic relish. Miguel Lafountant, a music instructor at Tulane, was an old friend and colleague of De Lourde's. In the glow of the dashboard lights, clad in his leopard-print sport coat, he looked more like a pimp than a professor. He had a thick, soft physique and ancient, wrinkled brown hands—hands that gestured dramatically as he spoke in his odd Creole accent. "Sweet Lawd, Delilah," he commented with a lascivious chuckle, glancing in the rearview mirror at the figure riding in the backseat. "I'll just betcha he still looks stunnin' in that old uniform . . . whattya think?"

"Oh Lordy, I'd give my eyetooth to see that!" laughed the figure in the rear. Obscured in shadow, she had a big, husky, smoke-cured laugh.

It was difficult for Grove to make out the woman's features in the dark van, but every few moments a flash of sodium vapor light would illuminate her statuesque form. A big-boned black amazon, Delilah Debuke wore a sequined top, a feather boa, and a big bouffant of crow-black hair. It took more than a few furtive glances at the rear seat for Grove to realize that she was not a *she* but a *he*.

Grove smiled to himself. Over the years, as an overworked criminal profiler for the FBI, he had become so accustomed to the far boundaries of human behavior that he found most of the harmless, eccentric varieties—drag queens, cross-dressers, transsexuals—almost quaint in their requisite delicacies. In fact, he always took a gay man's flirtation as a compliment. Besides, Grove was immersed in the professor's world now: a place where ruined marble tombs vie for space with strip clubs, and the spirits ooze from the cracks in the moldy cobblestones like absinthe, and the stains of Katrina's floodwaters tattoo the sides of buildings like the ghosts of some ancient holocaust burned into the sediment. It all had begun to wrench at Grove's heart.

"So y'all worked together on cases?"

The smoky voice from the backseat pierced Grove's thoughts, and he said, "Yes, as a matter of fact . . . last year, right before Katrina. The professor helped me on a tough one."

"Did y'all catch the guy?"

"Actually, we did."

"That's good."

It seemed odd, when Grove thought about it—and he *did* think of it often—how Katrina had come only days after the resolution of the Sun City case. It was as though the heavens had opened up and purged some kind of malevolent force that had been festering up there in the upper atmosphere. And the subsequent, tragic aftermath, claiming the lives of so many innocent and poor, would prove to be America's deepest wound, her greatest natural disaster. But for Grove, the Sun City case had been a *personal* disaster, a turning point in his life and career, and even in his belief system.

It had started simply enough—a series of motiveless murders across the Midwest, all the victims posed postmortem, taken down by a sharp trauma wound to the neck. But the case had taken a bizarre and unexpected turn when a vacationing Grove had happened to visit a remote laboratory in Alaska to view an archaeo-

logical discovery. The six-thousand-year-old mummy
had been found in a glacier by some hikers in 1993 . . .
but the weird part, the absolutely *inexplicable* part, was
that the mummy, a victim of foul play itself, bore the
exact same pose—the same modus operandi, the same
signature, the same *everything*—as the victims of the
current at-large killer Grove had been hunting.

From that point on, there was nothing ordinary
about the Sun City case.

Grove remembered the first time Professor De
Lourde had come on board the case. It was in a hotel
banquet room in San Francisco a year and a half ago—
during the Sun City Killer's final spree. De Lourde had
been one of a handful of anthropologists who had provided expert background on the connection between
the current killings and the cycles of similar homicides
down through the ages. In many ways the professor's
analysis had helped Grove catch Richard Ackerman.

Ackerman had been an accountant in "civilian" life,
a secretly deranged man who might or might not have
been possessed by an alternate personality as ancient
as the mummy itself. But ultimately, in the course of
apprehending Ackerman on the side of a jagged precipice
in the Alaskan wilderness, Grove might very well have
absorbed the entity *himself.*

To this day, the profiler was not certain about what
had happened in that remote mountain cabin in the
woods after Ackerman had been killed. All that malig-
nant energy had seemingly transferred itself into Grove.
But all Grove knew for sure was that De Lourde had
been there during the so-called cleansing ceremony that
had saved Grove's life. Professor De Lourde had helped
save Grove's soul, if not his sanity.

"He helped me in ways I'll probably never know,"

Grove mused finally, staring at the rain-streaked windshield. "He was an amazing character."

"He was always quite proud he had survived Katrina's floods," the drag queen commented.

Grove asked whether Miguel and Delilah had evacuated or stayed in town.

The drag queen waved her painted nails. "I got the hell out of Dodge, thank you very much. I didn't need no mayor telling me to skedaddle."

"I fled the scene as well," the driver said, not without a trace of shame in his heavily accented voice. "I still remember Camille in '69. I was just an adjunct at Tulane at the time . . . it was just awful. And *this* one made Camille look like a gentle summer rain."

Delilah's voice broke a little. "Of course, when we came back there was nothing. Nothing left. My place on Napoleon Avenue was reduced to a couple of chimneys stickin' outta the water. Roof collapsed like a toy. They found my landlady in the rafters, nothin' much left of her."

Grove said he was sorry.

"But old Moses, he stayed put," Delilah went on. "Right in the Quarter. Like Joan of Arc. He was such a drama queen. Said he didn't care, he would ride the gallery into the gulf if it came down to that."

"What happened?" Grove asked.

A shrug from the drag queen. "Lucky for Moses, the Quarter's always been smack dab on a sandbar, highest point in town, and most of them old Spanish galleries survived Katrina."

Miguel Lafountant let out a sad chuckle. "I remember comin' back a couple of months later, when they got the bridge back up and running. Found Moses right where I left him, down at Jack Riley's bar on Bourbon

Street, sittin' there just as pretty as you please. Still decked out in his seersucker and silk, sipping a finger of sour mash. I understand Riley's stayed open the whole damn time, even during the floods."

Grove sighed. "I just can't believe he's gone. Still doesn't seem real."

They drove in silence for a while.

As they neared the Central Business District, the lights of old New Orleans began to spangle the horizon. After months of heartache, lawlessness, disease, rebuilding, drying out, more lawlessness, more disease, and more rebuilding, the old Crescent City still clung to its fetid concavity between Lake Ponchartrain and the Mississippi like a stubborn barnacle. Some of the old sections of town were still flooded or still in transition, the cranes rising up and vanishing in the dark heavens, the ruined tops of crumbling gothic cathedrals truncated like old, twisted, deforested trees. A putrid odor pervaded everything: the air, the ground, the sodden buildings still musty from the cleanup. It was the mingled stench of rot and mold—a mixture of stagnant, polluted waterways and the methane and swamp gas from all the decay—most of it thinly masked by the sickly sweet scent of commerce, a smell of grease, malt, and burning sugar.

They turned south down Canal Street, a vast expanse of trolley tracks and traffic lanes strewn with branches and papers and sundry storm detritus. It was hard to tell which of the litter was from recent storms, and which was from Katrina. Now they headed east into the French Quarter, their tires growling on centuries-old wet cobbles. The streets narrowed, and the buildings closed in, their gaslit promenades flickering and sputtering behind veils of mist. Grove rolled down his window and breathed the air, which was so musty-smelling it brought to mind the inside of an old clothes hamper. The sidewalks were strewn with trash stirred up from the storm.

Grove finally broke the silence. "Really appreciate you picking me up. Especially during such a—"

Grove stopped abruptly when he noticed the old Cuban was softly crying. Tears glistened on his lined, leathery cheeks. His shoulders trembled.

"—sad time," Grove said, completing the thought. It was all he could think of saying. It was the night before the professor's funeral, and the pall that seemed to hang over this city only added to Grove's sense of loss, sense of hopelessness.

The drag queen in back was fighting his own tears. "Damn fishy time, y'all ask me!" he blurted.

Now that's *an interesting thing to say at a time like this,* Grove thought, and all at once he noticed something about Delilah Debuke that he hadn't seen initially. It was apparent in the flashes of passing light, the way her watery gaze kept shifting from the window, to Grove, to the floor. Grove knew that look well. Over the years, he had seen it on the faces of witnesses, the faces of suspects, the faces of victims' families. It was the look of someone who had something to set straight.

"I'm sorry, did you say 'fishy'?" Grove turned to face the back now.

"I'm making a play on words, in case you hadn't noticed," the drag queen murmured, the passing lights of a car gleaming like two pinpoints of flame in the centers of his painted eyes. "I mean, sure, poor ol' Moses met a *fishy* end out there on the point, but at the same time the whole thing stinks of rotten fish, if y'all know what I mean."

Grove cocked his head at her. "I'm not following. The news reports said he died from flying debris. From the storm. Did they get it wrong?"

"What was he doin' in Algiers?" Delilah said with a little rhetorical flick of his brow.

Miguel spoke up then in a ragged voice: "Delilah, this is not the time!"

"Shush up, Miguel. I'm just talkin' to our handsome, illustrious friend here." He looked at Grove. "The truth is, Mr. Grove, our dear rebellious Moses would not have been caught dead in Algiers."

"Why's that?"

"Because he was allergic to Jefferson Parish."

Grove still didn't get it and said so.

Miguel spoke up. "He had a nasty-ass experience out there one time. Back when he was a young associate professor at Tulane. Tell him the story, Delilah."

Delilah sighed. "S'pose he *was* still working out the ways of the world for queers down here. Place he came from, Old Birmingham, they was a lot more closed down for faggots. Especially back in the 1960s. Hell, round here Black folks were still contending with Jim Crow laws. And you don't even want to *know* what it was like to be a queer little Black boy. But that's another story."

"Tell him about the muggin'," Miguel urged.

"*You* tell him, *cheri*, I ain't got the energy."

The Cuban shrugged sadly. "Ain't much to tell. One night Moses took a walk on the wrong side of the tracks—or should I say, wrong side of the *river*? I remember it was a swelterin' spring night, and we was holdin' court down at Old Napoleon's Saloon, havin' our customary evening tonics. I was tired that night and decided to go home early. But Moses, he wanted to stroll some. He loved to walk with that silly cane, like some kind of French nobleman. Anyhow . . . that night, he walked all the way down to Spanish Plaza, then decided to ride the last ferry across the river into Algiers. To this day, I ain't real clear on why he went over there. He did, though, he sure enough did. And he wound up in exactly the wrong place at the wrong time for a man of Moses De Lourde's . . . *propensities*."

Lafountant shook his head a little as he drove, as though the memory itself weighed down on him.

Delilah spoke up from the back in a low, outraged tone: "Truck full of crackers coming home late from a drunk nearly ran him off the sidewalk. They circled around and jumped him. But they didn't just rough him up and steal his money. They beat him pretty near to death. All on account of him being queer and all."

"Maybe Moses said something that set 'em off," the Cuban mused. "He was like that, bless his heart—he could make a cutting remark as quick and easy as spit."

"That's nonsense, Miguel, and you know it!" Delilah flicked the back of his hand at the Cuban. "Them rednecks was just out for some fun that night, and poor Mose was *it*." Then the drag queen fixed his makeup-caked eyes on Grove. "They found him in an alley the next morning, pants around his ankles, word 'fag' spray-painted on his ass. Had about a dozen broken bones and he pretty near bled to death."

Grove asked if the attackers were ever caught.

"Moses never pressed charges," Delilah said with an exhausted sigh.

Now Grove was turning something over in his mind. He looked at Delilah. "So this all happened in roughly the same place they found him on Sunday?"

"That's right."

"Hmm."

"What is it?" Miguel asked Grove.

"Excuse me?"

The Cuban smiled. "You said '*Hmm*.'"

"Did I?"

"Yessir, you surely did."

"I'm sorry, it's nothing."

"That's funny, it didn't sound like nothin'," he murmured, pulling the van over to the curb in front of the Hotel Philippe de Champaigne on Dauphine Street. He put it in park and stared down at his lap. "Anyway . . . whatever happened, old Moses's number done come up and that's all there is to it."

And with that, the old Cuban grabbed his ivory cane, got out of the car, and hobbled around to the rear hatchback to began the business of helping Grove with his luggage.

That night, well into the small hours, Grove sat in his dark hotel room, staring out the rattling, rain-dappled windowpane, thinking about the late, great Moses De Lourde.

The old man had been a true character in the Old South style, a sort of academic Oscar Wilde, and a veritable institution on the lecture circuit. He had enjoyed teaching positions at several venerable institutions of higher learning across the South. But to the intelligentsia, De Lourde would become known primarily for his *avocation*: the obsessive study of "foul play" through the ages. Through his mysterious fieldwork, the occasional macabre article in scientific journals, and his investigations of the occult, the professor became both controversial and renowned. Which was precisely why

Professor Moses De Lourde had been destined to cross paths with Ulysses Grove.

Pacing that lonely motel room, turning all this over in his mind, Grove finally decided to do a little impromptu Web search for any further information about De Lourde's death. He plugged his laptop into the hotel's DSL and found two new links under De Lourde's name. One of them was a straightforward news item from the *Times-Picayune:*

Esteemed Professor: A Likely Victim of Cassandra

NEW ORLEANS—The body of a New Orleans man found on Algiers Point near Seguin Street Sunday morning has been identified as Tulane Professor Emeritus Moses A.J. De Lourde of 748 Dumaine Street.

"It appears the storm caught the victim by surprise," said Captain Grayson Capps of the Jefferson Parish Police Department at a press conference held yesterday. "Flying debris from the wharf combined with high water can be a deadly combination." The captain went on to remind reporters that the medical examiner is withholding the official cause of death pending notification of next of kin.

De Lourde's lifeless remains were found by a dockworker some time before dawn on Sunday— only hours after Cassandra's eye passed over central New Orleans. The professor may be the first official death in Cassandra's wake. There are already 73 reported injuries directly connected with the category-one hurricane. Damage estimates range from two to four million dollars. A mere gulley-washer compared to Katrina. But not without its own deadly irony when the lives of Katrina survivor's such as De Lourde are lost.

Grove wondered about an autopsy. The article left many questions unanswered.

The second item was from what Grove assumed was a college Web site, an underground arts and culture e-zine called *Synapse* whose home page was now emblazoned with a photograph of a dashing young De Lourde from decades ago:

ONE OF TU'S TREASURES PASSES

Tulane lost an institution on Sunday. Whether you passed him in the dreary halls of the anthropology building . . . or saw him holding court down at Antoine's . . . or witnessed him playing his clarinet (badly) with the Dixie Jammers in front of St. Louis Cathedral . . . he was always one of kind. Sui generis. A true American original. Professor Moses De Lourde—sustaining a fatal injury Sunday in the hurricane—leaves us in body only. His spirit lives on in the late-night bull sessions over at Dinwiddie Hall, or the endless discussions over cheeseburgers at the Camellia Grill, or the drunken reveries of "graddies" down at Jimmy's. De Lourde had that one ineffable thing that students require to be inspired—mystery. You never knew what outlandish theory he was going to postulate next. With apologies to Steinbeck, Professor Moses De Lourde will never truly leave us. Whenever some pothead babbles some cosmic theory into the wee hours . . .

he'll be there. Or whenever some underclassman is on fire with intellectual curiosity . . . he'll be there. Rest in peace, Moses, we love ya!

Grove's eyes got a little wet at that one. But the questions lingered, nagged at him. Why would the old man go back to that hated place? What was he doing in Algiers in the middle of a hurricane? And what was the significance of that mysterious last phone call?

It had come late last Saturday night, while Grove was dozing fitfully on the couch of his log cabin in the Virginia woods. The remote A-frame belonged to Tom Geisel, Grove's section chief and best friend at the bureau. Grove had been living there for the past year while he recuperated from the wounds—both external and internal—sustained during the Sun City case. For many months the cabin had been a welcome refuge, but lately Grove had been getting restless. Restless to get back on the job. Restless to see that journalist, Maura County, again. Restless to rekindle his relationship with her.

Maybe this was why Grove had been having trouble sleeping lately. He had been having nightmares of that deranged accountant from the Sun City case, Richard Ackerman, and the way he had metamorphosed into ghastly permutations. There also had been dreams of Africa, dreams of his own birth. In fact, Grove had been dreaming of his mother the very night his cell phone chirped so unexpectedly on the coffee table next to him, displaying the Orleans Parish area code: *Fffffft!* "Dreadfully sorry to call at this hour"—*zzzzzht!*— "Hello? Ulysses!"

The voice had been instantly recognizable to Grove, even in his drowzy stupor, and he had tried and tried to hear what the problem was, but the connection had been miserable, wrought with crackling interference and lightning bursts. "Ulysses, can you hear me?"—*zzzsssshht!*—"Hello! Frightfully sorry, dear heart, but I believe I have a situation on my hands"—*ffhhht!*—"need your help!"—*ffssshhhhhtt!*

The call had suddenly crapped out then, like a switch being thrown, leaving Grove to wonder for the rest of that week what the hell the "situation" was, and why the professor needed his help. These were questions that would probably never be answered, and maybe that was a fitting legacy for a man such as De Lourde, a man so inextricably linked with—

Grove looked up.

A noise.

Outside his hotel window, just under the sound of the rain, a metal clicking noise had pierced his ruminations, raising the hackles on the back of his neck like the arched spine of a cat. Grove was hypersensitive to certain noises—the cocking mechanism on a gun, the creak of a floorboard. But *this*. For some reason this noise was just . . . wrong. Right outside his window—which he had raised a few inches earlier that night to let in the breeze—in the middle of the night, in the rain: a hollow metal *click!*

Grove rose slowly, all his defensive instincts kicking in now. He reached over and turned off the desk lamp, plunging the room into utter darkness. He moved cautiously toward the window. The streetlamps outside filtered through the mist, painting watery shadows on the walls behind him. He paused and considered going for his weapon.

Why so tense right now? It was just a noise, for God's sake. Why all the nerves?

The truth was, Grove had felt this vague undercurrent of tension from the moment he had arrived in New Orleans, tension that had only been magnified by Miguel's and Delilah's odd story. It sounded corny but Grove actually felt as though he were being watched. He got that feeling sometimes. He had a sixth sense for this kind of thing. And now his inner voice was screaming, *Houston, we have a problem!*

He looked out the window.

Several things flickered through the rain—a metal ring bouncing on the cobblestone sidewalk three stories down, directly below his window, and a flash of something falling to the left, on the hotel's outer wall. But it was only when Grove heard the accompanying sound of feet landing with a muffled thud on the ground, followed by the blur of a shadowy human form darting away, that he realized somebody had been scaling the wall outside his window.

He whirled back toward his room, his heart jumping now in his chest. His Charter Arms .357 Tracker was nestled inside his coat, snug in its case. Safety on. Chamber empty. He moved quickly, silently, with a dancer's grace. His brown face and bare legs shimmered with sweat as he grabbed the gun and the speed-loader.

He was out the door and halfway down the hall before he realized he was in his ratty sweatpants.

It didn't matter. His heart thumped with nerves as he took the stairs at the end of the corridor, barefoot, two at a time, down the antique runner, the risers creaking like crazy. It took him less than a minute to reach the lobby level, which was musky with mold and water damage. Less than sixty seconds: all the while calculating how far the intruder could have gotten down Dauphine Street, or the adjacent alley, while he slammed six rounds into the cylinder—*Bam*! *Ssnap!*—hollow-point loads, liquid tip.

Then he was outside in the stink.

Hands cradling the weapon, the barrel raised and ready, he scanned the shadows north and south, east and west. His bare feet on the cold, slimy, wet cobbles. The fishy-rotten mist in his face. Who the hell was that? How far could they have gotten? He made his way down the walk to the mouth of the alley. A pause. Then . . . *whap!* Swung the barrel around the corner. Aimed it at the empty darkness.

Nobody there.

Grove paused for a second. Breathing hard. Cocking his head and listening. The patter of rain, and the occasional wet gust rattling the street signs—and that was it. No footsteps. No shadowy movement. It was as though the ghostly intruder had beamed back on board the *Enterprise*.

The rain had already soaked through Grove's sweatpants, his sleeveless T-shirt adhering to his shiny brown shoulders. He wiped his face and turned, and regarded the facade of the Hotel Philippe de Champaigne. The leprous stucco wall rose above the front awning, crowded with scores of stained glass windows, many of them cracked or broken out from wind damage. It looked like a vandalized church.

Grove's window was on the third floor, right in the center of the building. Very few hand- or footholds existed. A flagpole about ten feet to the left of it, and half a story down. A few window-unit air conditioners. Squinting to see through the misty darkness, Grove noticed scuff marks six feet below his window, and twenty feet below that, a series of diagonal scratches. He looked back at the deserted street.

Something shiny lay on the sidewalk at his feet.

He knelt down and carefully picked it up with the barrel of the gun. He recognized the dull gleam of an aluminum carabineer. An oval ring about the size of a half dollar with a clip on one side, it was a piece of mountain climbing gear designed for quickly snapping together ropes during ascents or rappelling. It screamed significance at him.

Time to get inside.

He dropped the carabineer in the pocket of his sweatpants and went back inside the hotel. The lobby was deserted. A light burned near the front desk, and soft Muzak droned from some inner office, but nobody stirred at the muffled sounds of Grove crossing the carpeted lobby in his soaked skivvies. *Thank God*, he thought, *thank God nobody saw that*.

It was nearly dawn. He needed to get some sleep—at least an hour or two—before the funeral. He changed into dry underwear and lay down on the king-sized bed without even turning down the covers, and he lay there for endless minutes in the dark, thinking about what had just happened, thinking about De Lourde's mysterious death and the things that did not add up. The dull metal carabineer sat on the desk across the room, gleaming in the darkness.

Grove kept staring at that thing, and listening to the rain outside, and the endless sluicing of water running down the gutters of ancient paving stones. He could not sleep, and he could not take his eyes off that metal ring.

He didn't realize it then but a strange and deadly game had already begun.

2

The wake was held in the Garden District, a couple of miles upriver from the French Quarter, in a small Unitarian chapel on Magazine Street. Grove arrived at five minutes to eight and stood in line for nearly twenty minutes in the rain with the other mourners.

The modest little Georgian building—a stubborn survivor of Katrina, with its cracked faux-marble columns, its canopy of tattered live oaks, and its water-stained clapboards—could not begin to accommodate the eclectic throngs that had turned out for the beloved professor's send-off. There were distinguished professors with their blue-haired wives looking pained and regal under lacy Laura Ashley umbrellas. There were tattooed street punks in combat boots and leather, disheveled grad students in shopworn tweed jackets, and nattily dressed old queens from the gay enclaves along Bourbon Street. There were somber clergymen, obese politicians, and a gaggle of cherubic little black children splashing through puddles and darting under people's legs. There was even a heavyset Hispanic woman in spandex and feather boas who looked to be either a stripper or a prostitute.

Grove searched the crowd for one particular mourner.

He wasn't sure if she would be there. She lived in San Francisco, and had spent very little time with the professor over the last year, and was also busy working on a book. But there was a slight chance she would be there. She was the type to show up to things such as this. It would be just like her to travel all those miles simply to honor a good and decent man such as De Lourde.

By the time Grove reached the doorway, he was as damp as a wrung-out rag from the rain and emotions.

The chapel smelled vaguely of mildew and body odor, the central aisle completely clogged with mourners. A small jazz combo was playing a slow blues up by the altar, the sniffling sound of a snare drum mingling with the whispered sobbing, the massive tarnished brass bell of a tuba reflecting the sad promenade. Grove glanced across the front of the room and saw familiar faces hovering beside the open casket.

Edith Endicott, the matronly Scottish scientist who had helped build a case against the Sun City Killer, now stood in her black mourning dress, her gray, wrinkled face downturned. Father Carrigan, another friend and mentor from the Sun City debacle, stood between her and the coffin. The old priest was hunched over with grief, his gnarled hands clasped respectfully as he gazed down at the coffin's pathetic contents.

Grove gently pushed his way forward.

"Ulysses," Dr. Endicott whispered, her sad, hound-dog eyes brightening.

"Dame Edith," Grove said as he approached the woman. They embraced. Grove could smell the woman's fatigue, the acrid tang of her sweat and perfume. This woman had come a great distance to be here, to say good-bye to a man she hardly knew. Grove realized right then that De Lourde had bonded with Edith Endicott the same way he bonded with all his friends: instantly and permanently.

Grove turned to Father Carrigan. "Hello, Padre."

The old man raised his grizzled face toward Grove and managed an anguished smile. "Young man."

Grove put an arm around the priest. Carrigan's body was trembling faintly. Grove's eyes filled up. "I wish I knew what to say."

"We'll all see him again someday, Ulysses," Carrigan said, his milky eyes twinkling suddenly, and all at once Grove saw the true man inside the old Irish priest—the mercurial demon hunter, the man who had sparred with the Vatican, and, more recently, the one who had helped exorcise Grove's own demons at the culmination of the Sun City case. This same charismatic figure had now somehow reverted to his natural state: a loving, fatherly, neighborhood clergyman, equally at ease counseling an alcoholic father as he was baptizing an immigrant baby. A scalding tear tracked down Grove's chiseled brown features as he turned reluctantly, inexorably, toward the open casket.

He was just about to look down at the professor's remains when a familiar figure shuffled awkwardly toward him in his peripheral vision. He glanced up and saw her, his stomach immediately clenching with emotion. "Hey," he whispered at her, hardly getting the word out.

"Hey, stranger," Maura County whispered back at him, an inscrutable little smile on her face as she approached with her arms outstretched. Her eyes were hollow and wet. A small, pale, girlish woman in her late thirties, the journalist wore a black dress with sedate pearls, and her mousy blond hair was pulled back in a French braid.

They embraced, only inches away from the coffin, both of them shaking slightly.

She still smokes, Grove thought as he hugged her. *Still smokes, and I still feel terrible about losing her.*

They clung to each other as the air around them filled with sniffling sounds and the low shuffling drums of funeral blues. They hadn't seen each other since the Sun City case, and had only talked on the phone once—and *that* was simply to confirm that their relationship would never work—but now it felt to Grove that their time together had never ended.

It was hard for Grove to believe that they had yet to consummate *anything*, had yet to even kiss, but that didn't matter to him. The way she felt to him right then—the way her diminutive five-foot-two-inch frame fit into the center of his chest like a nesting doll—seemed good and true.

Their embrace lasted for an absurdly long time, like the embrace of two old veterans of foreign wars reuniting after a long convalescence. Grove had dreamed of this moment. For weeks he'd anticipated this very greeting. Would they kiss? Would they shake hands? Would the tension and awkwardness sour the moment? It turned out that the truth was none of the above. In the wake of all the unexpected sorrow, this simple hug was a salve, a balm on his soul. It lasted maybe sixty seconds in real time—at the most—but for Grove it passed in a single heartbeat. He had not felt this happy to see a woman since he lost Hannah.

"God, it's good to see you," he murmured when they finally stepped back and looked at each other at arm's length.

"You too, Uly."

"Wish it could have been—" He stopped, feeling

ridiculous, feeling as though every word was a cliché now.

"I know." She looked at the casket. "I know, he was . . . what can you say?"

"He was a pain in the ass . . . and I guess I loved him. I can't believe I only knew him for . . . what? A year?" Grove glanced at the coffin. He didn't know if he was ready to take a closer look. He didn't know if he was ready for that.

The sound of whispering tugged at Grove's attention, and he looked up.

Behind Maura, along the front of the choir nave, a motley assortment of De Lourde's old cronies stood side by side like a formation of colorful, exotic birds. Some of them, like Delilah, looked like old silent movie stars decked out in their black regalia and dark Joan Crawford sunglasses. Others wore eccentric, southern dandy mourning coats and top hats as though garbed for a parade.

Miguel Lafountant, the stout little Cuban, stood at the end of the row, nodding a tearful greeting at Grove. "Hello, Mr. Ulysses," he uttered in a broken voice.

Grove turned to Maura and gently offered his hand. "Some people you should meet."

They went over to the Cuban.

"Miguel, this is Maura County." Grove spoke in a low, respectful tone. "She worked with the professor off and on. She was writing a book with him. Maura, this is Miguel Lafountant, a fellow professor at Tulane."

"Pleasure, *cheri*," Miguel said with a sad little nod.

"We'll miss him a lot," Maura said.

"That's a fact."

A painful pause as the Cuban looked down, a single

tear dripping off his swarthy cheek. Then he looked up. "Where's my manners?" He nodded to a young man next to him. "This handsome young man is Michael Doerr, one of Professor De Lourde's star graduate students. Michael, say hello to a couple of Moses's illustrious associates."

An effeminate young man of mixed race stepped forward and gave a little bow. He wore a crisp tuxedo shirt under his velveteen jacket, and his sculpted caramel face was runny with tears. "Pleasure, ma'am . . . sir," he murmured in a soft, deep southern accent, his voice trembling slightly. He was painfully shy and refused to even look at Grove.

Miguel gazed at the young man like a proud father. "Michael was part of the team that went to the Yucatan with Moses, smack dab in the middle of that *other* terrible hurricane."

Grove's ears perked. "No kidding."

"Yes, it was quite an expedition."

Grove was confused. "This was recently?"

Miguel shrugged. "Couple of years ago . . . March of '04, I believe. Is that correct, Michael?"

The shy young man nodded, gazing down, wringing a shredded Kleenex in his hands.

Miguel then gestured at the tall, willowy young woman next to Michael Doerr. "And this lovely specimen is Ms. Sandi Loper-Herzog, the Queen of Darkness and all things metaphysical. Another one of Moses's star pupils."

The girl was draped in goth finery, all gangly arms and legs, her dark, sunken eyes stained with lampblack. "How ya doin'?" she croaked, her voice saturated with grief.

"Pleasure," Grove said and then found himself suddenly at a loss for words, his mouth feeling as though it were cast in concrete. What could he say? What can anybody say at a funeral other than empty, pathetic platitudes? Grove let out a pained breath as he looked at the floor for a moment. In his peripheral vision he sensed the young man in the tuxedo, Michael Doerr, fighting a wave of sobs.

Grove wanted to say something but could not muster a single word. He turned and looked at the coffin. Almost imperceptibly, Maura County stepped back to a respectable distance. Miguel Lafountant stepped back as well, and Grove felt an inexorable tug drawing him toward the coffin.

At last he went over, and he spent one last moment with his friend.

That's not Moses De Lourde.

That was the first impression that struck Grove as he stared down at the shriveled husk of a human being that lay nestled in the elaborate sarcophagus, wrapped in seersucker and silk, painted in grease pencil and rouge. But of course, it *was* De Lourde, or at least what was left of him. Offerings of all sorts had been tucked around the slender remains—a package of pastel cigarettes, a small volume of Rilke poems, a packet of chickory coffee, a broken 78 rpm recording of Louis Armstrong's "Basin Street Blues." But the professor's kind, regal face—still full of cavernous wrinkles and baggy flesh—now looked empty, barren, antithetical to the vigorous De Lourde whom Grove had known and loved. Caked with so much concealing powder and reconstructive putty that it looked papery and hollow, the faux face simply broke Grove's heart. The real De

Lourde would have been appalled at such a mediocre makeup job. It would not even have been worthy of an after-hours Mardi Gras party.

A wave of sorrow sliced through Grove, as sudden and sharp as a blade thrust through him. How could they do this to him? How could they take him to his final soiree looking so déclassé? Tears burned Grove's eyes, and he took out his handkerchief and held it to his mouth, when the second impression struck him: *His eye is gone.*

Sure enough, the old man's papery, wrinkled left eyelid—upon closer scrutiny—appeared *concave*. It was a detail most people would certainly have missed. But Grove was not most people. To Grove, the missing eyeball was as glaring as if they had put his nose on his forehead. The other eye was clearly apparent beneath its drawn lid. But the left was conspicuously absent, which led Grove to make a third observation: *Those bumps on the professor's chin and forehead look suspicious.*

The sad fact was, Grove could not shut off his forensic mind, his morbid expertise. He knew death the way a botanist knows the rings of a tree trunk, and now he began to profile the poor bundle of remains.

Grove had initially thought the bumps were moles but now realized they were wounds—appearing like small bubbles spackled over with heavy mortician's powder—and they combined with the missing eye to begin to strum the chords of Grove's nervous system. The regularity of the abrasions under the makeup—especially the fissures around his mouth and brow—called out to Grove, screamed in his brain, and sent high-voltage signals across his synapses.

Without even knowing it, Grove was doing what he always did, what he was *born* to do: sniffing something out, adding up seemingly disparate facts of an event or a situation to form the early skeletal outlines of a deduction. Over the last twenty-four hours he had absorbed enough random detail to fill an entire file.

But there was something *else* now adding to his frisson of suspicion. Grove had first noticed it when he had entered the chapel. Initially he had written it off as mere nervous tension, perhaps some kind of residual angst from attending Hannah's funeral. But he noticed it again when he had approached the coffin for his final communion with De Lourde's remains—a powerful feeling of being watched.

Ordinarily he would have ignored it. After all, this was a funeral. People watched. Mourners kept tabs on other mourners. But after the events of the previous night—the thwarted intruder, and the carabineer left at the scene—Grove was hyperattuned to such feelings. And he could not remember ever having such a strong sense of being watched. It bored into the back of his skull like drill holes, raising gooseflesh on his scalp and neck.

He turned away from the casket, and he searched the huddled mourners for Maura.

She was standing over by the Cuban, holding a paper program, fanning herself with it, gazing at the floor. She looked so small and sad and beautiful to Grove right then, she nearly stole his breath away. He almost hated to tell her what he was feeling. It would most certainly put up another wall between them, maybe even scare her away once and for all. He wanted so badly to tell her he was getting out of the game. But he couldn't. He couldn't change who he was.

He went over to her and whispered in her ear, "I need to take care of something at the professor's place. After the burial. Can you come with me?"

A slight pause, a subtle knot over her eyebrows as she thought it over. "I guess . . . I mean. Yeah, sure. My flight's not till tomorrow."

"Perfect."

Grove took her hand, then led her through the crowded chapel to the entrance vestibule, where they stood waiting for the funeral procession to form.

After a series of eulogies, poetry readings, and eccentric musical numbers—including a performance by an obese drag queen singing "What a Friend We Have in Jesus" to the accompaniment of an accordion and a musical saw—the casket was finally sealed and carried out into the overcast day by pallbearers representing both Tulane's distinguished faculty and the finer drag clubs of Bourbon Street.

A horse-drawn hearse-carriage waited at the curb, flanked by the "grand marshal"—an old dapper black gentleman in a Salvation Army uniform. The coffin was loaded under a low, greasy sky. Then the procession made its way down Magazine Street—which still looked like a war zone, complete with boarded, swamp-stained buildings and empty shells of looted stores—creating an undulating snake of garish multicolored umbrellas sprouting like exotic blossoms in the mist.

LaFayette Cemetery Number 1 is a New Orleans landmark, one of the great Cities of the Dead. Encompassing an entire square block from Prytania to Coliseum, and from Washington to Sixth, it is bordered by a high rampart of ancient marble the color of weathered gunmetal. All the grave sites are aboveground due to the vagaries of living below sea level, not to mention the shifting mud of a river delta. Inside Lafayette's walls, the rows and rows of squat marble tombs and decorative family crypts—many of them containing remains dating back to the early nineteenth century—now lay in disarray like discarded dominoes. Last year, Katrina had had her way with Lafayette Number 1, ripping the tops off the sarcophagi and sending coffins sprawling every which way on the furious currents. The cemetery now resembled an ancient Greek ruin, a stony acropolis of broken stone markers, most of them beyond repair, a few scaffolds here and there where the NOLA Friends of the Cemeteries Association had been reconstructing historic tombs.

Today a new resident was moving in.

Professor De Lourde was laid to rest in a grand vault at the end of row seven. The band played "Amazing Grace" while the pallbearers slid the great steel coffin off the carriage runners and into the darkness of a gleaming marble crypt erected just six months ago by the Benevolent Society on the former plot of the orphans and homeless tomb. It was over within minutes.

After a few hushed good-byes, Grove and Maura made their exit and took a trolley back into the French Quarter. En route, as the rickety streetcar snapped and sifted over ancient petrified rails, Maura looked at Grove, who was staring out the grimy window, deep in thought. "What's wrong, Ulysses? What's going on?"

He looked at her, licked his lips, measured his words, and finally decided to tell her the truth. "Moses De Lourde was murdered, Maura."

She stared at him for a moment, then gazed out her window with a pained expression, her murmur barely audible above the clack of the streetcar. "Oh Jesus . . . here we go again."

3

The professor's little shabby-chic apartment had always impressed Grove as being like a set in a stage play, maybe some traveling road show of *A Streetcar Named Desire*. Situated above a sheet music store at the corner of Dumaine and Bourbon, the building had been a typical Spanish double-gallery with ivy-clogged wrought-iron balconies and chipped, pastel-colored trim . . . before Katrina. The hurricane had literally denuded the storefront exterior, as though it were sandblasted. The street-level window was now a moldering slab of plywood with graffiti scrawled across it, and the outlines on the siding where sconces, gaslights, and signs once hung were now merely tangles of wires.

Inside, the place was a virtual curio emporium, with all manner of antiques, folk art, knickknacks, bric-a-brac, and various and sundry tchotchkies. But very few gadgets. No CD player. No TV. Nothing but an old rotary phone, an ancient Norge icebox, and an antique Apple computer dating back to the first Bush administration. His files, including his notes and journals—De Lourde had been a compulsive diarist—were either saved on old floppy diskettes or scattered throughout the place, tucked into drawers, shelves, nooks, and crannies in every room. The details that Grove needed right now were hidden somewhere—he was convinced—in these journals.

Which is why Grove was currently hunched over the keyboard of the old Apple SE, opening files, looking at documents and notes, trying to find something, anything, that might hint at a connection to the suspicious way the professor had died. Still clad in his Armani dress shirt, his tie undone, his sleeves rolled up, his caramel skin shiny with perspiration, Grove was especially interested in that expedition to the Yucatan that Miguel had mentioned at the funeral.

"Okay, here's something about him planning an expedition to South America," Grove was reporting aloud to Maura, who was in the kitchen, brewing tea with the contents of a dead man's pantry. Miguel had given them the keys, but what they were doing was probably illegal. "Unfortunately," Grove added with a shrug, "it's dated in the midnineties."

"What's the connection?" her voice called back.

"I'm not sure yet."

There was an old dial-up modem on the table next to the Apple, and on a whim Grove decided go online. He tapped into a local AOL server, listened for the trademark toots and squeaks, then used the bureau account and Googled the following: de lourde + archeologist + expeditions.

Grove waited for the list to display itself. Within seconds a scroll of entries appeared, and Grove's eye fell on one particular item:

From Professor M. De Lourde's journal: ". . . made base camp near *Los Manos Negro* . . . all grad students and instructors back at TU . . . learning more than we bargained for about the ancients and their nature gods."

—Similar pages

Grove stared at the entry. The word *hurricane* struck his eye like a beacon.

He couldn't resist double-clicking the heading. The screen flickered for a moment as the home page for some obscure academic journal unfurled across the screen. Nothing fancy. A few logos for charitable foundations at the top, and a menu of subjects ranging from offshore geological surveys to paranormal investigations. But at the bottom was a box with abstracts from Mose De Lourde's Yucatan expedition journals.

Pulse quickening a little, Grove quickly scanned the first few entries. The basic information could be gleaned fairly quickly: In early 2004, De Lourde had led an expedition of archaeologists and students to the Yucatan to establish a dig and study artifacts from the ancient Toltec civilization. But when Grove read the entry from day sixteen, the linkage started engaging in his brain:

DAY 16: Helena hit at around five this evening, and she is a royal bitch. I must say, the Greek allusion is a canard. Helena flooded the lowlands, and decimated both the dig and the camp. Most of our specimen tables washed away. All is lost. Perhaps it's appropriate. The only saving grace is the fact that the whole team made it back to high ground at Merida City. All accounted for. Looks like we all shall make it back to the States with our skins intact. Although I'm not so sure about our sanity. Will certainly have plenty to discuss at the Royal Society symposia this autumn! More later.

Grove's scalp crawled. He knew in his bones he was onto something. He felt this way whenever the opaque aspects of a case began to clear. The crawling scalp, the dry mouth, heart rate speeding up—it was practically neurophysical. The fur standing up on a cat. Three years . . . and three hurricanes?

"This feels wrong, Ulysses," Maura's voice called from the kitchen. "Us poking around in here."

"Wrong how?"

She came back out with two steaming teacups, handed one to Grove, and stood looking over his shoulder for a moment. She still wore her little black dress. "Wrong like creepy."

"Listen, the old man would have *wanted* us to dig, believe me, he was the champion digger."

"How can you be so sure he was murdered?" she asked then, sipping her tea.

He looked up at her. "Accumulation of detail." He started to say something else, to amplify, but he realized there were aspects of all this, cognitive leaps that he was making, that he didn't understand himself.

"Excuse me?" Maura was looking incredulous.

Grove smiled. "Call it intuition."

"Didn't the coroner deem it an accidental death? Officially, I mean?"

"Yes, and he may be right, but it looks hinkty to me."

She looked at him. "Hinkty?"

He nodded. "In the words of Delilah Debuke . . . *fishy.*"

"Why?"

A pause here as Grove considered how much he should tell her. Even though Maura County was tough as nails, and ambitious as hell, and smart, too—smart enough to crack open the strange connections between a six-thousand-year-old mummy and a modern-day serial killer on the Sun City case a year ago—she was still pure civilian. She had been scarred permanently by her flirtation with Sun City. Kidnapped by Ackerman in the final throes of his spree, beaten to within an inch of her life, left for dead in the Alaskan wilderness, the young journalist had experienced trauma that would have destroyed most psyches. But now, in a strange way, she seemed more grounded than ever. It was as though the experience had galvanized her. Grove saw it in her level stare, in the way she carried herself, that stubborn sort of vigor.

"Because of a lot of things," Grove finally said, blowing on his tea. "But mostly because of what happened last night, at my hotel."

"What happened at your hotel?"

He told her everything. Told her about the carabineer, about the shadowy figure trying the scale his wall. He told her about the suspicious wound patterns on the professor's body. He even told her what Delilah and Miguel had said about De Lourde inexplicably turning up dead in a place he vowed never again to visit.

When he was done, Maura looked ashen. "You're telling me whoever's responsible for this is after *you*?"

"It's too early to tell, actually . . . and besides, I didn't say he was *after* me. That's not exactly what I'm talking about."

"Then what exactly *are* you talking about?"

"I've seen this kind of thing before."

"What do you mean? What kind of thing?"

Grove sipped his tea. "Look, sometimes I get in the newspapers. That's all I'm saying. I get into the press, and that leads to certain stuff."

She thought about it for a moment. "You mean like last time . . . with the *Weekly World News*?"

He gave her a look. "You had to bring *that* up, didn't you?"

She was referring to an article that had appeared in the sleazy tabloid during the Sun City case, the headlines crowing: EXCLUSIVE: BEHIND-THE-SCENES PHOTOGRAPHS OF A MONSTER HUNT. The lurid copy had introduced readers to "Ulysses Grove, the mysterious manhunter from the FBI, and his mystical methods." A few lines farther down the page, the article had promised readers a hair-raising story of "a monster on the loose, possessed by the spirit of an ancient mummy." As usual, they'd gotten most of the facts wrong, but they had also gotten just enough right to avoid a lawsuit. But it wasn't the copy that had bothered Grove. What had bothered him was the accompanying photograph, rendered in grainy paparazzi-style shadows, showing Maura and Grove having a private moment outside the lobby of an Anchorage Marriott.

That was the day he had gotten up the nerve to ask her out, and was in the process of doing just that when the photo was taken. They had almost kissed at that point. But not quite. She had agreed to go out with him, though, and all had seemed to be well with their budding relationship . . . until the trauma of Sun City had curdled both their enthusiasm, and they had agreed to part ways.

Now Grove was trying to figure out how to breathe life back into their stillborn relationship.

"What are you telling me, Ulysses?" Maura wanted to know. "You've been stalked before?"

"Not *stalked* exactly." He put his tea down, got up, and paced across the room. "After the Keith Jesperson trial, for instance, I did a profile for the Seattle police. Tried to figure out this random series of murders, people getting killed in their homes. What happened was, the perp started writing me."

"You've got to be kidding."

Grove waved off her skepticism. "It's not as uncommon as you might think. The BTK Killer in Kansas, for instance. He loved to write the press, loved to toy with the investigators. Son of Sam, Jack the Ripper. It's all part of the sociopathy, part of the sickness. But this suspect up in Seattle, he had a thing for *me*, for some reason. He'd send me mementoes."

Maura looked aghast at him. "Oh Jesus . . . you don't mean . . . ?"

"No, no . . . nothing grisly, nothing wet. I'm talking about the drivers' licenses of known victims, articles of clothing. That kind of thing."

She let out a sigh, and said nothing. Her eyes clouded over for a moment with bad memories. She looked like a passenger on an unsteady ship.

"He was using an industrial postal meter," Grove went on. "It's what finally led us to him. Turned out he was a letter carrier. Which was how he was gaining entrance."

Maura shook her head then. "You know what? This is too much information."

Grove felt a pang in his gut. "I'm sorry. Maura . . . I'm sorry. I never should have—"

"No, it's okay."

"But I really shouldn't be talking about—"

"No. It's all right. I'm here, aren't I?" She laughed bitterly. "I'm back for more punishment. More death and mayhem and sick shit."

He took a step toward her, then paused. "Maura—"

"No, it's okay. I'm a big girl, Ulysses, I can handle it. I can handle this." She reached over to her purse and dug out a cigarette. She lit it with shaking hands. "I'm smelling another great story here. Okay? I'm totally cool with it."

It was very clear to Grove that she was not totally cool with it, and he had made a big mistake, talking about this stuff in front of her. "I'm sorry I dragged you over here," he said finally.

"You don't get it, do ya?" She angrily puffed her unfiltered Camel. "I *chose* to come here."

He looked at her then. He was close enough to smell her hair, which was still damp from the rain. "If you don't mind my asking . . . why? Why did you come here in the first place?"

"To say good-bye to Moses, whattya think?"

"No, I mean now. Back here. Why did you come back here with me?"

She looked away, her voice softening. "I don't know . . . maybe because I miss you."

Grove was speechless. A long pause, as she looked at him, and they studied each other.

Maura was still shivering. "Okay, I confess I came here because I miss you. Because I'm a pathetic, lonely workaholic with no life. Because I'm a hopeless piece of—"

"Okay, stop."

He reached over and took her cigarette out of her hand, then snuffed it out in a nearby ashtray. Then he took her by the arms and looked squarely into her eyes, and he spoke in a low, hushed tone: "I give you my word, my solemn word, as an agent of the federal government and a former Boy Scout . . . I will never let what happened on Sun City happen to you again." He suddenly burned with the urge to kiss her, and the timing felt right. He leaned down slowly, tenderly reaching up to her face, but before he had a chance to lock lips with her she pulled back suddenly.

"No." She looked faint, the blood draining. "No, this is not right."

"Maura, I didn't mean to—"

"No, I'm sorry." She was shaking her head now. "We just can't pick it up right where we left off."

He felt as though he'd been punched in the solar plexus. "But why not?"

"Because too much has happened . . . because this is just . . . this is not going to work."

"I swear to you, Maura, you will never, *ever* be in the line of fire again."

"I'm sorry. Ulysses . . . I'm sorry." She was looking around the room, looking for something. "I should probably go."

"No way."

"I should get back."

"Wait a minute, just wait. The old man would've whupped your ass. Leave here on a night like this? I can sleep on the couch, you can take the bed."

She chewed on a fingernail while she thought it over.

Grove gave her a sad smile. "You can trust me, kiddo, I work for the government."

Maura grinned. "Oh, that's a relief."

"Please," Grove said. "Please stay the night, I'll take you to the airport in the morning."

Another long pause, and then she said, "Okay, but I get the couch."

His grin warmed.

Maura heard the sound first. Alone in the living room, curled up on the sofa, wrapped in an old afghan, she stirred now, trembling from the chill of cooled sweat. She sat up and looked around the dark room, trying to get her bearings. Through the teak blinds a pale membrane of light shone down on the rug.

The sound of bare feet padding across hardwood behind her made her jerk with a start. She twisted around and saw Grove coming out of the bedroom, pulling on a pair of sweatpants. "You okay?" he asked. "I heard a noise."

Maura spoke softly, hoarsely, under her breath. "It wasn't me, I heard it too."

"What was it?"

She pointed at the door across the room. "Out in the hall. Might have been the wind or it might have been—"

"Ssshh."

Ulysses put a fingertip to his lips, cocked his head, and listened closely.

Just beneath the noise of the rain came another creak. And not merely a creak from a gust of wind, which sounded more like the yawing bulwark of an old ship. This was a shorter, more furtive creak. The creak of a footstep crossing the landing at the top of the stairs.

"The door to the sheet music place—did you notice which side of the building it's on? It's on Dumaine, right?" Grove was frantically tying the waist string of his sweatpants. He wore a sleeveless T-shirt, damp at the armpits.

Maura wore only her panties, but modestly kept the afghan around her midsection. "I have no idea," she whispered, pulling her black dress over her shoulders.

"There's a back way up, but there's only one door up here, and that's the professor's."

"You know this place better than *me*. You're the one who's stayed here before."

"Are you expecting anyone?"

Her whisper rose an octave: "No—I mean, it could be anybody. Might be Miguel. Or the mailman."

"It's six in the morning."

"I don't know who the hell it is, Ulysses. What do you want me to say?"

"Stay here."

"No way."

Grove was slipping his feet into his loafers. He pulled on his oxford shirt, not bothering to button it. "There's no other way in," he assured her. "Don't worry, you're safe in here."

"Jesus Christ, Ulysses." She watched him pull the .357 from inside his hanging overcoat. "Jesus *Christ*!"

"Ssshhhhhh, it's all right. Just stay put." He turned toward the door. "It's probably nothing." But he knew it was *not* nothing.

He assumed the "Weaver" position, which had first been drummed into him back at the bureau academy—feet spread shoulder-width, one hand around the grip, the other underneath, cradling, stabilizing—and he moved toward the door, ready for anything. He crossed the twenty feet of Persian rug in seconds, and reached the door just as a thin shadow flickered under it, visible for a brief moment through the space at the bottom.

Grove took a quick breath, then with his free hand suddenly threw the door open.

"Hey!"

He almost fired but let up on the trigger when he realized the figure had already vanished around the corner of the narrow ten-foot-wide vestibule. Something skittered across the floor. Grove froze for a second, paralyzed with sensory overload, pointing the barrel at the staircase to his immediate left—down which the muffled sounds of frenzied footsteps were rapidly descending—and then at the object spidering across the welcome mat on the floor before him.

He frowned at the tiny little marble that had come to rest at his feet. His scalp crawled as he instinctively aimed the barrel at it. He recognized what it was. "Holy Christ," he uttered in shock.

"What is it?"

Maura's voice was like a slap in his face, and Grove whirled toward the apartment.

"*Stay down!*"

Then he turned and lurched out the door, vaulting over the tiny orb, then hurling toward the staircase, his gun raised and cocked.

The figure had already reached the bottom of the stairs. Grove leaned over the banister and caught just a fleeting glimpse of the dark assailant darting toward the exit. Grove aimed the .357 and fired.

The blast lit up the dark hallway, a chink of plaster dust erupting down on the first floor, just missing the figure, who had already lunged through the doorway. Grove's ears rang as he leaped down the stairs—two at a time—his brain screaming that this might be his only chance.

He reached the dark lobby of crown molding, damp carpet, and old brass sconce lamps. The door was swinging free in the wind. Grove barreled through the exit and into the overcast, misty morning.

The pale light and rain assaulted him as he spun north, then south, then north again. A shadow flashed at the end of the block, lurching behind a wrought-iron gallery. Grove raised the gun and got off three more shots.

The bullets chewed through the newel post at the end of a gate, one of them ricocheting off the iron in a bloom of sparks, but none of them hitting their target. The shadowy figure had vanished once again into the veils of rain.

Grove stood there in front of De Lourde's for a moment, his heart thumping, the back of his shirt sticking to him. He tried to memorize every detail like a walking camera. Like a recording device. This was all significant. This was all feeding the psychological profile, which had already begun in earnest. He was part of the pathology on this one.

Somehow Grove was at the center of this profile.

The gun fell to his side as he turned, then made his way back inside. Grove could smell cordite emanating from his gun as he ascended the stairs and strode down the hall toward the professor's doorway.

The police would be here soon enough. The details of this private little game of cat and mouse would become public. Geisel would find out about all this. But Grove felt something more than nervous tension now. He ached with that weird hunger that usually accompanied an imminent breakthrough. It tingled at the back of his neck, at the cusp of his spine. He was about to make another huge intuitive leap. He could taste it on the back of his tongue as if he were sucking an old penny.

Maura was trembling in the doorway, now clad in her black dress, her slender arms holding herself as though she might fall apart at any moment waiting for him to return.

"It's all right," he said as he approached. He gently urged her back inside the apartment, shoving the gun inside the back of his belt.

"Was it him?"

"Who?"

"The guy—the guy you think killed the professor."

Grove shrugged. "Chances are good, yeah. Wait for me inside for a second."

"The hell is *that*?" Maura was pointing at the object on the floor, the tiny ball about the size of a jawbreaker. "What *is* that?"

"Wait for me inside, Maura, please," Grove said and gestured toward the living room.

Maura reluctantly backed away, then turned and marched across the room toward her purse, toward her pack of cigarettes. The distant sound of sirens was rising on the wind, the cops on their way, most likely summoned by a complaint of gunfire (sadly, a not uncommon phenomenon now in the Quarter).

Grove turned back to the shiny object on the floor. A thin leech trail glistened behind it like a translucent ribbon. He knelt down, dug in his pocket for his handkerchief, found it, and snapped it open.

He was carefully picking the thing up when he noticed something else out of the corner of his eye on the floor of the alcove, shoved into a corner. Yesterday's *Times-Picayune*. It was still in its plastic wrapping, a forlorn sight if ever there was one. A newspaper subscription that would never be renewed. But it was the front-page graphic that caught Grove's attention: the swirling multicolored satellite photo of a new tropical storm out in the Atlantic.

DARLENE BUILDING STEAM, warned the headline, and it looked as though *this* storm was heading up the eastern edge of the gulf, on a direct path for Florida. Maybe Pensacola, maybe Panama City Beach. But all this information merely streamed into Grove's midbrain and evaporated as quickly as it had entered. What truly held his attention for that single, intense, revelatory split second was the graphic.

He stared at that swirling mass of color, the brighter oranges and reds spinning toward the middle, the tiny black nucleus like a seed or a pit. He stared and stared until the sound of Maura's voice snapped him out of his sudden momentary paralysis.

"What the hell was that thing on the floor?" she called from the living room.

Grove snatched up the newspaper and went inside the apartment, pausing to latch and secure the door. He threw the dead bolt, turned the lock, and jiggled it just to make sure. The sirens were closing in. Somebody was hollering something outside the building.

"The key to everything," Grove muttered as he looked down at the gelatinous ball in his hankie.

"What?" Maura was madly smoking now, trying to control her trembling.

"I don't want you to freak out here," Grove said, looking up at her, sounding almost apologetic. He had the newspaper tucked under one arm, and he held the specimen from the hallway floor like a wounded bird in his handkerchief.

"It's too late for that, Ulysses, I'm already in the throes of a major freak-out."

"I'm going to need you to stay calm."

"I'm calm. What is it?"

He told her.

"Oh my God."

"Maura—"

"I need to go."

"Hold on a second—"

"I need to get back, I got a deadline." She started gathering up her things, her purse, her coat, her umbrella. "I need to go, I need to get out of here."

"Maura, it's okay, calm down. This is a breakthrough, we're going to catch this guy."

"Not with me," she said, heading for the door. The sirens were outside the building now. The squad cars screeching to a halt one by one, radio voices crackling.

"Maura, wait—"

"I'll call you. Good luck with the case and everything, take care, bye-bye."

She left, slamming the door behind her, leaving Grove standing there, alone, yet galvanized, staring down at De Lourde's missing eyeball nestled in his hankie.

4

The statuesque blond woman in the diaphanous linen top and thong bikini crouched against the raging salt winds, grimacing, struggling with a loop of nylon rope, completely unaware that it was the last time she would secure a storm tarp over her beloved little motel's swimming pool.

The sky had turned black, and now the winds were bull-whipping wildly across the cement pool deck and the granite breakwater just beyond the southern edge of the Sea Ray's property. Flagpoles rang and pinged hysterically. The furled Cinzano umbrellas flapped, and every few moments another wave would crash against the granite wall, sending particle bombs of water thirty feet in the air.

Hurricane Darlene was coming, her outer rings sending sheets of horizontal rain across the Florida panhandle, her eye bearing down on Panama City Beach.

Frantically the flaxen-haired amazon yanked the corner of the olive drab tarp with her long, slender, manicured hands, trying to get it onto the cleat. She had already broken two nails, and chipped another one, and *that* was really pissing her off. The wind bellowed over her head, a jolt of sea mist lashing her perfectly sculpted face. A deck chair cartwheeled past her like a tumbleweed.

Suzanne Kennerly braced herself against the cleat. A willowy woman in her late thirties with diamond-hard gray eyes and exquisite cheekbones, she had once been a top model at Ford's in New York, but that was ancient history now. Nowadays she was stuck down here on the Redneck Riviera with this roach motel and nothing but old men in black socks and sandals to keep her company. All because of two simple mistakes made at the peak of her career, the two biggest mistakes in her life: She had gotten knocked up, and had married the prick who did it to her.

In the subsequent divorce proceedings, her ex-husband, Hamptons real estate mogul Jerry Ruckman—he of the small prick and huge ego—had made her a deal she couldn't refuse: her daughter for the Sea Ray Motel. It seemed like a good idea at the time. Suzanne could conquer new territory in Florida without the yoke of a child tugging at her, and in time she could work her way down to Miami, where she could rekindle her modeling career and get back to a normal life. But that was nearly three years ago. And in that time, all Suzanne had gotten was mounting debts, an addiction to Xanax, and chronic sun poisoning. But no goddamned hurricane was going to change her game plan. She was going to ride this thing out just like she had ridden out every other hideous thing that had happened to her.

Another wave surged against the breakwater, the whitecap swirling up into the winds and exploding. Suzanne wiped the moisture from her face and tried to make her way across the deck toward the opposite corner of the pool, using the chain-link fence poles as leverage, but it wasn't easy. She could only move a few tentative inches now with each step. The wind was like an invisible anchor mooring her to the cement. The collar of her linen cover-up was flapping so hard it felt as though someone were slapping her.

Finally the blouse literally blew off her back like a papery skin shed into the wind, revealing her meticulously tanned, surgically enhanced bosoms nestled in a revealing leopard-print bikini top.

Another surge erupted over the breakwater.

Suzanne froze, gaping up at the enormous white monolith rising into the sky. It looked like a huge albino dinosaur climbing up over the breakwater, coming for her. Suzanne's heart rose in her throat. The monster suddenly burst apart in the wind, sending a wave of wet sand spraying across the pool deck. The wave struck Suzanne's legs with the force of a battering ram, knocking her feet out from under her.

She fell then, sprawling across the deck, skidding sideways, her oiled body as slick as a slug, skating across the sand-lashed cement until she smashed into the side of the cabana. The impact sent pain bolting up her back, and she gasped for breath, trying to get her bearings. Slowly, agonizingly, she began crawling toward the office, toward the safety of the side screen door, which was hanging open, banging wildly in the wind. She got maybe five or six feet closer when another great spasm of white sand roared over the breakwater.

The wave flung her against the building, slamming her into the bricks with enough force to crack her lovely capped molars. She let out an involuntary yelp, the pain was so sudden, so searing, so sharp in her ribs. It knifed up her side and seized her left arm. *Not yet, not yet, NOT YET!* her brain screamed at the storm.

Now Suzanne was crawling on her tummy toward the flapping door. It was only about ten feet away. *Just ten feet.* But her left leg was deadweight now, as if she were dragging a huge sandbar, and the wind was a freight train, and the deck was shifting beneath her, shifting and seething with soupy waves of sand. Suzanne could barely see.

Eight feet now.

Another gusher of sand levitated off the beach and crashed down on the deck, shoving Suzanne Kennerly sideways. She howled in pain, but somehow she kept going, kept crawling toward that flapping screen door and the safety behind it.

Six feet now.

Five now.

Four.

Three.

Two—and all at once Suzanne grabbed hold of the jamb with her cold, stiff, manicured fingers.

With every last shred of strength she pulled himself inside the doorway, dragging her numb leg behind her. Pain burned up her left side. Her vision blurred. But she ignored it all and managed to crawl inside the office.

She slammed the door with her one good leg, then collapsed. The office was dark.

Lying there, dripping wet, gasping for breath, Suzanne could not for the life of her remember if she had forgotten to turn on the office lights or if the power had flared out due to the storm. It was the middle of the day yet it was so dark. Like night. What was happening? The pain in her hip was disorienting her, making it hard to figure anything out.

A noise behind her, something shifting in the shadows of the office.

Suzanne managed to twist around enough to see a shape lurking in the corner. Was it that asshole Koz's German shepherd? Keven Koz owned the Gulf Breeze Motor Court a hundred yards south of the Sea Ray, and his fleabag of a dog would sometimes slip into unattended offices to wait out storms. But wait . . . no . . . this silhouette was human. Tall and dark and slender and silent, and *human*, and holding something that dangled like a pendulum.

"Who the hell are you?" Suzanne's voice was strained above the muffled roar the hurricane.

The shadowy figure pounced.

Suzanne tried to call out but something struck her hard, a roundhouse thump to the left side of her head, making her ear ring, and then there was something cold and reeking of ammonia pressing down on her mouth, and then the light dimmed.

And then there was nothing.

"This guy's on an escalating spree, believe me, De Lourde's murder was just the beginning."

Ulysses Grove stood at the dry-erase board in the fluorescent-drenched conference room at the Louisiana Bureau of Investigation's Baton Rouge field office. He wore his sedate, pin-striped, double-breasted Bill Blass suit with his charcoal-gray power tie—the uniform of a CEO addressing his rank and file, or perhaps a dean of education giving a valedictory speech. In fact that was exactly what an FBI profiler was: a teacher, a highly trained consultant.

But over the past few years, Special Agent Ulysses Grove had become much more than a mere consultant; among bureau insiders he'd become a rock star. He was the man who had chased Richard Ackerman into the frozen tundra, the man who had faced off with the Happy Face Killer in a squalid truck stop restroom. But rock stars can also be flakes, and a lot of guys want to shove rock stars off their pedestals. Grove certainly had his share of detractors in the law enforcement community. Right now, in fact, he was having a hard time convincing the grizzled veterans sitting in front of him.

"All due respect, I'm hearing a lot of *extrapolation* here, a whole lotta *theory*," said a portly man in a seersucker jacket in the front row, his southern drawl dripping with skepticism. His named was Marvin Pilch, and he was an LBI section chief in charge of the Orleans and Jefferson Parish region. "I mean, assuming De Lourde was murdered, I don't even see a series here yet."

The other men, all seated around the oval conference table, each holding a report folder that Grove had prepared for this very meeting, offered various nods and grunts of agreement. These men included Lieutenant Harry Brenniman, a skinny black detective with the New Orleans PD detective squad; Special Agent Arliss Simms, a heavyset bureau lifer who had worked the back alleys of the French Quarter for most of his adult life; and Dr. Maynard Nesbitt, the balding Orleans Parish coroner, who had a special aversion to Grove since it was Grove's profile that was calling into question Nesbitt's original autopsy conclusions. In other words, this was a tough crowd.

A voice crackled out of the squawk box on the center of the table: "Gentlemen, I think it might be best if we just hear Grove out before we comment."

The disembodied voice belonged to Tom Geisel, avuncular head of the Behavioral Science Unit at Quantico; Grove's friend, boss, and mentor for nearly fifteen years. Thank God for Geisel. Thank God for that deep, stentorian tone coming out of that speaker. Grove didn't know where he would be without Geisel. Probably locked up in a rubber hotel somewhere.

"Believe me, guys, I understand your concerns," Grove told the room, glancing at each man, one at a time. "I had the same concerns when I started down this road, but a lot of times a break like this starts with intuition. Connections. A chain of inconsistencies. De Lourde would never have gone to that place, and he was calling me for help that night. I could be wrong about all this, but I don't think so. I think De Lourde was murdered, and I think he knew his murderer."

Marvin Pilch stifled a burp. "So . . . explain to me again how the man's eyeball got into your possession."

Grove sighed and glanced up for a moment at the dry-erase board that he had positioned at the front of the room. Clipped to the top edge of the board was a forensic black-and-white blowup of the errant eyeball, which was currently sitting in a pathology lab at the parish morgue.

In extreme close-ups the human eye looks like an overdone hard-boiled egg, with a corona of gelatinous color—the iris—and a fuzz of tiny white cilia around its milky spherical retina. Like a little tulip bulb, De Lourde's severed eye also sported a purple stem—the optic nerve—that snaked off the side of each photograph. Most human eyeballs, when viewed outside their owner's cranium, have a sheen and a weight to them, which is apparent in photographs. De Lourde's was no different. Billions of vitreous cells inside the sclerotic shell are ever coiled to translate visual information down the optic canal to the brain. Images take on meaning.

Profiles begin to take shape.

Also clipped to the board were close-ups from De Lourde's autopsy, highlighted by lavish microphotography of the strange ridged wounds on the professor's upper lip, chin, and soft palate. On the far edge of the conference table sat a row of Zip-Loc evidence bags, each one filled with a crucial item such as the metal carabineer that Grove had found outside his hotel, or shavings from the cobblestones. The rest of the blackboards and flip charts around the room were plastered with graphics and satellite images of *another* kind of eye, a far larger and more elusive one.

"It was delivered to me," Grove finally said in a flat, unaffected tone.

"By the perp, you mean?"

Grove shrugged. "Could have been the perp, could have been an intermediary. But it was meant for *me*, it's fueling the fantasy here. It's a symbol, a talisman. For some reason, our guy *wants* me to break this thing."

"Shades of the BTK Killer?"

"Something like that."

Pilch frowned. "I gotta tell ya, I got nothin' but respect for you Behavioral Science boys . . . but this one just doesn't add up."

Grove looked at Pilch. "I would agree with you, Chief. It *doesn't* add up. Not yet."

Pilch was about to respond when Detective Brenniman

spoke up. "We're sure this here eyeball belongs to the victim, to the professor?"

All heads turned toward Dr. Nesbitt, the coroner, who sat perched on a windowsill in the rear, his bald pate shiny with nerves, his scowl reflecting his disgust. "Yes, well . . . preliminary blood-typing and DNA analysis show a match, although the *manner* in which the eyeball was lost is still undetermined. Now maybe it's just me, but I just don't see how y'all can call that *irrefutable* evidence of a wrongful death. Hell, after Katrina, we had people impaled on parking meters, lobotomized by slivers of glass. Shoot, there were some eaten by *gators*. That don't mean there was serial killers roaming around."

Grove had expected this from the coroner, and didn't say anything right away. Instead, he calmly went over to his briefcase, which sat open on the corner of the table. He dug inside a flap and pulled out a sheaf of Xeroxes faxed earlier that morning from the Okaloosa County medical examiner down in Fort Walton Beach, Florida.

"These were DOAs that came into the Okaloosa Morgue yesterday," Grove explained, holding the photographs up for all to see. "They came in only hours after Hurricane Darlene had moved through the area—about two hundred miles from here."

The room got a lot quieter then. The sounds of shifting feet under the table, throats being cleared. The photographs were stark, ghastly close-ups of faces. Bloodless, dead faces. A woman named Suzanne Kennerly. An octogenarian named Barney Kettlekamp. A thirtyish businessman named David Stohlp. Each face was toothless, and each featured a hideous, livid, purplish socket from which a missing eye had been extracted.

"Tom, you should have copies," Grove said to the speaker box on the table.

"Got 'em," the voice crackled. "So tell me what we're looking at here."

"Let's start with the MO," Grove began, walking slowly around the table, around the backs of the investigators who were glancing over their shoulders at Grove's Xeroxes, each grainy photograph looking pretty darn irrefutable. "At roughly 5 o'clock last night, Hurricane Darlene hit the Gulf Coast around Panama City, with winds of maybe a hundred miles an hour or so, which would make it a category-two storm. Satellite images tracked the storm's eye across the Choctawatchee Bay and into—"

"Beg your pardon, sir?" Nesbitt interrupted. "But what in heaven's name does this have to do with modus operandi? Are you referring to *God's* modus operandi?"

Grove offered the coroner a cold smile. "Time of death on each body, and the location of each dump, correlated perfectly with the position of the eye."

"Okay, hold your horses a second," Pilch chimed in. "I want to make sure I'm following this. You're telling us *all* these murders occurred *inside* the eye of a storm."

Grove did look away from Nesbitt. "Different storms, different eyes . . . but yeah."

"How do you know they didn't happen somewhere else and just *blew* into the path of the eye after the fact?"

"It's possible . . . but I think they *happened* in the eye," Grove asserted. "I went back and checked the illustrious Dr. Nesbitt's time of death on Moses De Lourde. The official record states the professor died between midnight and two o'clock that evening, which tracks perfectly with the moment the eye passed directly over Algiers."

Another tense beat of silence. Pilch looked at Brenniman, and Brenniman looked at Arliss, and Arliss looked at the rainbow-colored spiral taped to the blackboard: Hurricane Darlene viewed from space, her dark nucleus like a bullet hole in a pristine blanket of gray.

Grove knew they all thought he was crazy, but he didn't care. He was no longer interested in the MO. The modus operandi was the least critical part of any psychological profile, and it was the only part that was fluid and could change according to opportunity. Far more interesting were the *patterns* and *signatures* of the killings—those uniquely personal compulsions that always remained static. The imagery of the eye, the ritualistic fetish of hurricanes, and the obsessive flirtation with Grove himself. Sooner or later, the accumulation of these patterns and details would reveal something far deeper here, far more savage, far more intricate: the purpose.

To the criminologist, *purpose* is the finest edge you can put on a profile. It reveals the raison d'etre of the act. Often the only purpose of a psychopathic killer is to derive sadistic pleasure. But once in a while—and these cases are as rare as albino tigers—a case is so complex and mysterious and seemingly motiveless that the purpose becomes the final touchstone by which the killer will ultimately be caught. That seemed to be a real possibility here: The eyeballs and teeth being removed, the systematic wounds, the murders happening *inside* hurricanes—it would all ultimately reveal purpose. It always did. Take Jeffrey Dahmer, for instance. It would turn out to be his collection of "mementoes" of "souvenirs" ranging from victims' belongings to their actual severed body parts that would ultimately lead profilers to conclude that Dahmer's purpose was to fill an agonizing, bottomless pit of loneliness. In *this* case, Grove suspected a purpose far more ritualistic and obscure. But he didn't have it yet.

Not yet.

"The caribineer is all smooth glove," Grove went on. "No latent prints. The perp is A-positive, size eleven double-E shoe. Lab results also indicate that the killer may very well have disabled the victims before killing them. Traces of sodium pentobarbital were found in the victims' bloodstream, as well as indications they were tortured before they lost their lives."

"How do we know this?" Detective Brenniman asked in a smoky baritone.

Grove pointed to one of the forensic shots of De Lourde's upper palate, then indicated a lab report thumbtacked to a bulletin board on the wall. "These ridged wounds here, I'm convinced, were all man-made, the teeth removed by an instrument, and the increase in serotonin and free histamine levels in the wound sites indicates that the victims lived for at least fifteen minutes after the teeth and eyeballs were extracted."

Stony silence in the room.

A long pause.

"Let me jump in here for a second, gentlemen," Geisel's voice crackled from the squawk box.

Grove looked at the speaker. "Go ahead, Tom."

"For the sake of argument here, let's say we were going to allocate resources on this thing—"

"Whoa there, Tonto," Chief Marvin Pilch broke in, glaring at the talk box. "LBI is pretty near tapped out, and we have been since Katrina. . . . I mean, shit, we got dozens of active case files right now screamin' for attention."

"I understand that, Chief." Geisel's voice was monumentally patient. "I'm not saying we're going to funnel anything away from state or local. I'm just trying to figure out where we stand here. Ulysses, hypothetically speaking, what exactly would you need from us on this situation?"

Grove's chest tightened with nervous tension as he measured his words. He needed Geisel right now. He needed the section chief to be on his side on this thing. It had been over a year since Grove had worked on an active case, and now he was being drawn into one whether he liked it or not. His gut burned with urgency as he said, "I'm not asking for resources, I'm just asking for access. Access to files, to crime scenes, to databases. Basically, Tom, I'm asking to be put back on active duty here. That's all."

Now there was a long, agonizing silence, during which throats were cleared and gazes were averted.

Grove knew he had developed a reputation over the years as a flake. And his last case had only cemented this image in people's minds—this notion of Grove as an eccentric egghead who had been pushed over the edge by too many scuffles with the monster. Rumor had it that Grove was damaged goods now, a shell-shocked head case who should just retire and write books or teach abnormal psychology at some junior college in the sticks. But what nobody at the bureau knew was that Grove had been changed by the Sun City debacle.

The mysterious sickness that had overtaken Grove at the end of Sun City—the strange "psychosis" that could only be cured, ultimately, by ancient ritual—had somehow launched Grove on a new trajectory. He was now being tugged along by something unseen, something unspoken, some kind of secret conflict that he had yet to figure out. But it was there, it was present at all times now, in the shadows around him, in the clues being left behind, *purposely*, by this bizarre lurker in the wind.

"I'm going to have to get back to you on this," Geisel's voice finally informed the room.

"Fine, fine . . . *whatever.*" Grove slammed his briefcase shut, his face stinging as though it had been slapped. His life was on the line here. Hundreds of future victims of this escalating murder machine . . . and Geisel was *going to have to get back to him on this?*

"Ulysses—"

"No, that's okay. I understand where you're coming from, Tom. I do."

Then Grove strode across the room to the door. He paused before leaving, turning back to the others. "Gentlemen . . . I thank you for your time."

Then he walked out.

Grove got halfway across the parking lot, the edges of which bordered a swampy landfill, the sky low and dark above it, when his cell phone began chirping. He dug it out of his pocket and looked at the display. It was a Virginia prefix. Grove snapped it open. "What, Tom?"

The section chief's gravelly voice: "I can't think of too many other profilers who would storm out of a meeting on me like that."

"What do you want from me, Tom?"

"You really think this perp is trying to lure you into a trap of some kind?"

Grove sighed. "What do you want me to say?"

"And you don't think it's too early for you to be traipsing off on a case?"

Grove climbed into his rental car and sat behind the wheel for a moment with the phone pressed against his ear. "Like I said, I don't have a choice. This case chose *me*."

Geisel was silent a moment. "You're going to use yourself as bait, aren't you?"

"Tom—"

"Don't answer. I don't want to know, I don't."

"I'm going to find this guy, Tom, and when I do, I'm going to take him down. Simple as that."

After another pause: "Ulysses . . . this perp . . . first of all, he killed your friend. That's a conflict of interest, and that's grounds for reassignment."

Grove gripped the phone a little tighter. "Is this conversation coming to an end?"

"I didn't say I was going to reassign you. But this thing has got to be kept off the books. I don't assign my profilers to vengeance jobs. Besides, you're a consultant, you're not Tactical. How many times do I have to tell you that?"

Grove stared at the windshield, the water droplets on the outside surface looking like diamonds in the pale light. "What do you want me to do?"

"It's up to you. We never had this conversation. This is your deal."

"I hear ya."

Geisel's voice got sharp and hard then. "And if I find out you found this guy, and you didn't call in Tac for backup, I will personally see to it that you spend the autumn of your career as a traffic guard. Comprendé?"

"Anything else?"

"Nope."

"I gotta go, Tom." Grove started the car. "I'll call you at home in a couple of days."

"Uly, wait!"

Grove paused before snapping the phone shut. "What is it?"

The longest pause of them all now.

Geisel's voice returned at last, soft and low: "Go catch this son of a bitch."

PART II

The Killing Jar

These who sow the wind shall reap the whirlwind.

—Old Testament, Hosea 8:7

5

At O'Hare, Maura County bought a ticket to San Francisco, then waited in one of airport's innumerable coffee kiosks, perching herself on a sad little plastic stool, composing a note to Ulysses Grove in her head. It wasn't going to be easy. There was so much she wanted to say to him, so many bittersweet feelings. She had started the note a dozen times in her head on the flight from New Orleans to Chicago but simply had not been able to come up with the right words.

She didn't want to hurt him.

At last, she opened the little spiral notebook that she carried with her at all times. It was the same dog-eared, salmon-colored Mead notebook in which she had recorded her nightmares at the behest of her therapist. She had been keeping the dream journal ever since the Sun City fiasco.

Getting kidnapped by a deranged, psychotic serial killer was bad enough. The physical trauma alone had necessitated weeks of treatments and convalescence. Maura had been subjected to three full-blown blood transfusions, countless stitches, and a metal pin surgically inserted into her knee where the cartilage had been violently torn away. She had walked with a cane for nearly three months. But that stuff had been the easy part. It gave her something to write about in her articles and books, and something to talk about in interviews.

The hard part was the *psychological* scarring. It seemed to come out of nowhere—months after the fact—just when she thought she was truly over the ordeal. It started with sudden and chronic insomnia. Every creak in her apartment, every whisper of her air conditioner, every flutter of the breeze through her blinds started sounding more and more sinister and started pegging her eyes open like an electrical jolt. But whenever she closed her eyes she saw the *face*: the gaunt, stoic, pasty face of the killer Richard Ackerman.

Phase two was even harder to take. She started seeing Ackerman's ghostly face everywhere she went. In cars at stoplights, in crowds at train stations, behind store windows. That was when she finally broke down and sought out help from a Napa Valley stress specialist named Dr. Herbert Ford. The shrink helped her immensely by letting her vent, and prescribing some decent medication.

But one thing that remained unresolved in her life was her relationship with Grove. Dr. Ford thought it went far deeper than mere romantic attraction. He thought there was a part of Maura that was attracted to Grove's world, even attracted to the danger of it. But Maura maintained that it was exactly that—the grisly aspect of Grove's profession—that was keeping her from consummating anything.

Which was precisely why she was now sitting in a busy airport, trying to compose a proper note to the man. She turned to a blank page and started in earnest:

Dear Ulysses,

Where to begin? Okay . . . what I wanted to tell you . . . well, let me just blurt it out: I can't handle you and me. I just can't manage it. I love you, Ulysses, and I think I always will, but I'm writing this letter because it's easier to articulate my feelings and thoughts on paper than doing it while staring into your big brown eyes. You know, those amazing eyes can be intimidating, kiddo. But never fear: This is no "Dear John" letter. Okay? It's not going to be one of those "it's not you, it's me" type things, because the truth is, it's both of us. For my part, I don't have the stomach for your avenging angel routine. I just don't. I know I've said it a million times before, but I just can't handle all the excitement. But I've also come to the conclusion that I can't ask you to change just for my own selfish purposes. I can't ask you to shed that part of your life like a dead skin or something. This is who you are. You are a person who lives to chase down evil fucking freaks (pardon my French). But I also think you might want to take a long, hard look at yourself. Like the twelve-steppers say: Take a searching moral inventory . . . because your behavior is becoming a compulsion, and when it becomes a compulsion it's a problem. I really believe this. Your profiler thing is becoming a problem. Or maybe I should say your obsession with it is the problem. It's not just because of the dangers involved (although, God knows, there's plenty of those), but it's more because you seem to have this weird tunnel vision that blocks out any other

*part of your life. It's kind of hard to explain. But
the truth is, I'm worried about you. Really I am.
Maybe you could see somebody. Maybe you
should*

"Christ, this is ridiculous." She hissed the words
under her breath, tore out the page, and wadded it into
a ball. Then she tossed it into the trash receptacle next
to the coffee counter. The acne-scarred teenager behind the counter stared at her, and she offered him an
exasperated smile.

She just could not put her feelings into words. Was it
because she still wanted to be with Grove? Was it because she was a born journalist, and was too ambitious
to let this amazing relationship go? She closed the
notebook and let out a pained sigh, sitting back in the
stool and watching the ebb and flow of passengers
passing through the terminal.

Maura found airports oddly comforting: all the
hurly-burly action, all the transient noise and cross-
sections of middle-class travelers bustling silently back
and forth across desolate corridors—all of it hermeti-
cally sealed in air-conditioned, single-serving stasis. It
reminded her of her childhood, growing up on Long
Island. Her father, who had been a sportswriter for
the *Daily News*, would take her down to Penn Station,
and they would get ice cream cones and sit on one of
the burnished oak benches and just watch the passers-
by.

Now, thirty-odd years later, her beloved father long
ago claimed by lung cancer, she found herself sitting
next to a Cinna-Bunz, craving a cigarette (she was trying to quit for the third time in as many years), and ba-

sically doing the same thing her father and she used to do.

She watched it all. She watched the harried businessmen hustling toward their gates, murmuring compulsively into cell phones. She watched frazzled mothers lugging children and strollers and equipment toward exits. She watched lithe and shapely flight attendants effortlessly pulling neat little overnight cases on little wheels, walking two or three abreast, idly chatting, looking like android soldiers marching toward some silent conflict.

Finally she got up to get a cup of coffee and passed a newspaper vending machine, when she saw a headline that caught her eye.

She stopped. And stared. It wasn't really the headline per se that gave her such pause: WORST HURRICANE SEASON ON RECORD: IS THE EAST COAST NEXT? That was mildly attention-getting, considering it was ostensibly a hurricane that had apparently broken the back of her relationship with Grove. But that's not what sent the little *zing* of electricity through her memory circuits. It was the accompanying graphic: a huge, multicolored swirl of aerial thermophotography.

The whirlwind from space.

For a moment, Maura just stood there, staring at that little squat, glass case with the *Chicago Tribune* logo on the side, trying to figure out why that sinister rainbow-colored image was giving her the jimjams.

All at once, she remembered the article she had written for *Discover* so many years ago. It had been a spec job, about six thousand words of investigative prose. She remembered poring through those thermographic aerial shots of hurricanes for endless hours at the Smithsonian, and scouring the National Archives, and the Library of Congress, and even the great European libraries like the Biblioteca Pasolini and the Karlsruh Bibliothek. This was in the dark ages of the late 1980s, while Maura was still a freelancer, and the Internet was still a few years away, still merely cocktail conversation among computer geeks. But what had sunk a hook into Maura back then and had gotten her a cover byline—in fact, what had truly spooked the hell out of her—was now bleating in her brain like a clarion horn.

"Oh my God, the *other* one."

The words blurted out of Maura, almost unconsciously, startling an elderly woman standing next to her, who was searching through a little rubber coin purse. The old blue-haired woman looked up with a thunderstruck expression on her face. Maura blinked and backed away, thinking to herself: *No way . . . no way. But Jesus, what if?*

She hurried back to the bench where her carry-on bag sat on the floor next to her chair. It was a little nylon rucksack containing her purse, a few magazines, an emergency pack of Marlboro Greens, a notebook, and her cell phone. She fished in it and grabbed the phone.

She dialed Grove's cell phone number on the off chance she might get through. She expected to hear the obnoxious recording from AT&T or Southern Bell or whoever it was these days that controlled the airwaves or the satellite or whatever it was out there that connected wireless communications. She was surprised, after only a few rings, to hear a click and then Grove's comforting, silky baritone: "Hi, this is Ulysses, you've reached my personal voice mail, and I'm away right now, but leave a message and I'll get right back to you."

After the beep, Maura tried to keep her voice steady and casual: "Ulysses, it's me, Maura, I'm . . . well, it's a long story. I need to talk to you about something. It's too complicated to leave on your voice mail but it's very important, Ulysses, it's about your theory that people are getting murdered during hurricanes. It's about an article I wrote for *Discover* a long time ago."

She paused and thought about it for a moment. "Tell you what . . . I don't know when you'll get this, but I'm in Chicago now, and I think I'll page you. Call me as soon as you can. Hope you're okay and you didn't get eaten by an alligator in those woods. Anyway . . . call me."

She thumbed the End button, then called him back and tried paging him.

Grove was heading east on Highway 10 in a rented Chevy Geo, chasing the next hurricane, when her page came through. He had left Baton Rouge earlier that day, and now, as darkness rolled over the Florida panhandle, he reached down with his free hand, dug his phone out of the map case, and checked the display. A 415 area code told him it was Maura, and he grinned in spite of his nerves.

"There she is," he muttered and quickly punched in her wireless number.

He got a recording.

"Shit," Grove whispered under his breath, and then, at the sound of the beep, he raised his voice loud enough to be heard over the whine of the wheels: "It's me, it's Ulysses, trying to reach you, call me back as soon as you can, I'm in Florida, and I'm heading east, toward the East Coast, where the next big storm is heading. I'm gonna try and get inside the eye, if possible, because I have a feeling that's where this guy wants me, because that's where he operates, so that's where I gotta go. Anyway . . . I'm sorry I dragged you into all this. Please call as soon as you get this."

He thumbed off the phone and put it back in the map case, then let out a sigh.

He had been on the road for five hours now without a break, all the revelations swirling through his brain—*this freak is on a spree now, the death toll rising with each storm, De Lourde in New Orleans, three separate victims back in Panama City, so how many next time? And why? Why! Just to lure me into the storm? It doesn't make any kind of sense yet! Yet! Yet! YET!*

The stress was starting to get to Grove. He was sore and hungry and tired and covered with all manner of road grime. He badly needed food and rest and maybe even a little medication. He had forgotten to take his antidepressant and antianxiety meds that morning, and he felt that terrible tightness in his gut that signaled a panic attack coming on. Unbeknownst to any of his colleagues or friends, he had been having the momentary attacks since his tribulations on Sun City, and he had almost gotten used to them.

Almost.

But now there was a counterpoint to the dark dread stirring in his solar plexus, almost like an undertow deep down inside him, a strange mixture of restlessness and exhilaration. He was on that investigative "vector" again, relentlessly following leads, working a case. He started tapping his foot, and tapped it ceaselessly throughout the next hundred miles.

He drove east through the misty, waning light, trying in vain to reach Maura on her cell phone.

Around Pensacola, as darkness set in, he managed to retrieve Maura's message about her being in Chicago—O'Hare Airport, to be exact—and having something terribly important to tell Grove about people getting killed in hurricanes. Nothing about walking out on him in such a state of agitation in New Orleans, though, nothing about their tattered relationship. Grove wondered if she was really done with him. But repeated attempts to reconnect with Maura's cell phone had been futile.

In the shifting bands of storms rolling across Florida, cellular connections were miserable.

By midnight Grove had reached Georgia, and was starting to drift intermittently across the center lines. His fatigue was catching up with him. He needed to find a roadside motel and rest his eyes, maybe have something to eat. Just for a few hours. Maybe take his medication. Then he'd be good as new. Then he'd finally be able to get his notebook full of disparate forensic details laid out in the logical order.

He started searching for a suitable fleabag motel in which he could replenish himself.

Moments later a shimmering mirage appeared in the dark, misty distance about a half mile away, a nimbus of brilliant sodium light just east of the highway, smack dab in the middle of a peanut field. A massive neon sign, veiled in rain, rose on two pillars proclaiming in blurry magenta letters: ROOMS HERE—STARLIGHT MOTEL—FREE CABLE. . . .

The blue flicker of television news filled Grove's motel room that night with up-to-date bulletins on the next great storm of the season. Reports of Hurricane Eve, her birth out in the mid-Atlantic, and her subsequent march toward the northern edge of the Caribbean Sea, dominated CNN's headline channel. Raincoat-clad reporters, bracing themselves against the lash of wind-driven rain, stood on vibrating piers and shouted at the camera. High-tech graphics illustrated the ominous rainbow-spiral thermography of this new invader. Each utterance of that single-syllable name touched off dark, biblical connections in Grove's brain: Eve . . . the original sinner . . . Eve . . . taster of knowledge . . . Eve . . . the destroyer of men. Grove watched all the reports, pacing the length of his cramped, airless motel room that smelled of burnt coffee and urine-impregnated rubber shower curtains.

Forecasters had plotted Eve's course across the upper edge of the Caribbean, and then about forty-five degrees northwest, straight toward the outer banks of Cape Hatteras. Experts predicted that she would hit the mainland, somewhere between Wilmington, North Carolina, and Norfolk, Virginia, at around five o'clock eastern standard time the next day.

Now Grove watched and listened and paced that tawdry little room with those two tiny pills melting in his palm. The Effexor was an aqua-blue two-milligram oval about the size of a Tic Tac, the Xanax a one-milligram pellet of egg-yolk yellow—his little colorful, cozy security blankets. But he could not bring himself to take either one. He was worried they would make him sleepy and he no longer wanted to sleep. He no longer wanted to rest. He calculated the amount of time left before Eve reached the U.S., and he calculated what he had to do before that happened, and all that had to be done afterward.

In forensic circles, there's a phenomenon known as

the "evidence clock"—the critical time immediately following a crime, during which evidence is at its freshest. Unfortunately, each passing minute degrades the evidence further and further, until latent prints fade, DNA washes away, and even the psychological staging of a victim is lost in the clumsy shuffle of investigators and emergency personnel. Grove knew he had to try to get to the coast of North Carolina by five the next day, especially if his instinct about this killer was correct. Grove knew it wouldn't be easy, and he knew he would need help. He also knew that help would not be readily available from the bureau since he was basically working on his own time now, just another poor bastard in the private sector.

Grove went over to the window and looked out. Cones of sodium light shone down through the rain, reflecting off the flooded gravel lot. The tops of the tupelo trees and scrub palms flanking the property were bent over in the winds. Vast thunderclouds of mist rose off the distant peanut fields and erupted in the whirling atmosphere. Grove felt nerves knotting in his stomach. Something was happening to him. Something spurred on by the storm.

All at once he recognized the early warning signs of another full-blown panic attack, another paralyzing wave of anxiety. It felt as though a truck were parked on his chest now. His scalp bristled, and a cool trickle of inexplicable terror ran down his spine.

He fought the urge to anesthetize himself. He fought it by thinking about his dear friend Moses De Lourde. Most violent crime investigators and psychological profilers keep themselves focused and motivated by thinking about the victims, by working up that righteous rage. But Grove had a lot more to think about than one wrongful death. He had that mysterious, fractured cell phone call.

"*. . I believe I have a situation on my hands . . . I said a situation! . . .*"

It wasn't just guilt that Grove felt festering in his guts. If it was possible for Grove to feel love for another man he hardly knew, he had certainly felt love for De Lourde, genuine love. The professor had become Grove's adopted father. And now some freak obsessed with hurricanes had ended De Lourde's great life in the ugliest of fashions. The monster had mutilated Grove's best friend, tortured him, made him suffer.

You ruined his face, you motherfucking freak. Grove's hot breath fogged the window glass as he focused his thoughts on the unknown subject—the "Un-Sub." *It was a good and noble face, and you ruined it, and now I'm going to stop you. That's what you want, isn't it? That's what you're gonna get.*

Grove spun around suddenly and hurled his medication at the wall. The pills bounced off the TV and the baseboard and the desk. Then Grove went over to the telephone, practically ripping the receiver off the cradle.

He made two calls in quick succession.

All of it accompanied by the tinny sounds of raincoat-clad reporters shouting to be heard, their pitiful monotones drowned by the mounting winds.

6

The Holy Ghost came from the south, from the train yards, slipping into town right before dawn on a tramp freighter as Hurricane Eve approached. He hopped off the train, then strode along the edge of the massive breakwater that bordered the town from the aging boatyards of Pamlico Sound, the rain enveloping the Holy Ghost's slender, muscular body like a silver sheath. He used the iron rail for purchase in the excruciating wind. He wore a long black coat that billowed regally behind him. His ropes and metal hooks and instruments of death dangled beneath his cloak, some of them flagging in the winds. He held his dark head proudly, upturned against the fierce waves of rain. He watched the last of the mortals scurry for cover all around him like parasitic insects fleeing down holes in the wasted earth.

A few reckless souls remained outside, their rain slickers flapping. Some were frantically stacking sandbags, others nailing sheets of plywood over windows and doors. Eve was bearing down on the quaint little village of Ulmer's Folly—an enclave of Colonial-style cottages, antebellum rooming houses, and steepled churches. Only a few hundred miles offshore now, the hurricane was closing fast, turning the sky the color of charred lampblack. Soon the storm surge would push over the breakwaters and bury the town in waves of brine.

The Holy Ghost paused near a worm-eaten piling, grasping the salt-weathered wood with one powerful hand. He was virtually invisible to the mortals, his dark form melding with the darkening horizon.

He pulled a cable from his belt with his rubber-gloved hands and looped it around the piling, mooring himself to the dock with the click of a rusty old carabiner. Then he watched with amusement the pathetic struggles of his prey, his storm bait. They meant nothing to him. They were *less* than nothing. In the grand scheme of things, they were strictly fuel for the machine. Merely fodder to draw the Last Manhunter into the eye.

That was the Holy Ghost's ultimate purpose. To lure the hunter into the sacred space where the Holy Ghost could complete a cycle that had started many millennia ago. It was a battle that had consumed many hosts, many bodies, many spirits over the years. But it was an eternal battle, a conflict that would continue to rage until the Last Manhunter was vanquished. It would take an enormous trap, and such a trap would require an enormous amount of bait.

A sudden sound pierced the seventy-mile-an-hour winds, and the Holy Ghost became very still. Ears preternaturally attuned to the mewling of his prey, he heard the dog barking before he saw it. Scanning the adjacent streets, he searched for the source of the sound until finally locking his gaze onto a small hound scurrying down a narrow side street.

It looked like a mutt, a spaniel-foxhound mix, with a

dappled coat and a long little snout, darting in and out
of the storefront shadows. A middle-aged man and two
teenagers were half a block behind the animal, pursu-
ing it through the deluge, their brightly colored nylon
raincoats blurring in the downpour, their flashlight
beams scissoring through the gloom. "Mitzie!" Their
frenzied voices strained against the roaring sky:
"Mitzie, come!"

The Holy Ghost loosened the cable, then slipped it
off the piling.

The wind came in great heaving gusts now as the
stranger lunged nimbly across the dock, then lowered
himself down to street level and made his way through
a grove of pecan trees. He had to stay low, hugging
equipment close to him, creeping across a gully thick
with weeds, moving silently toward the narrow side
street. The noise all around him was tremendous—a jet
engine bearing down on the land, wrenching the trees
sideways, swirling loose trash up into the air in great
whirling dervishes. But just under the roar came the
desperate voices.

"Mitzieeeeeeeeeeee!"

In one leaping stride the great Holy Ghost crossed
Seafront Street, then slammed against a boarded-up
barbershop with its charming little candy-striped pole
and wrought-iron bench out front (now chained to a
U-bolt in the sidewalk). He edged his way around the
corner of the building and saw the father and two teenage sons chasing the dog into a blind cobblestone alley
a block away. The Holy Ghost darted across the street
and then crept through shadows under weathered cop-
per awnings.

*"Come, Mitzie stay! Bad dog! Stay! Mitzie, stay!
Mitzie, you stay right there!"*

The angry, disembodied voices, barely audible now over the storm, were homing beacons for the Holy Ghost. He moved toward the mouth of the alley with panther certainty, his heart rate a steady sixty beats per minute, his ropy, wiry muscles flexing under his long coat, his gaze dilating and fixing itself on the alley with the precision of a falcon.

"Grab her! There! There! Hold her, Brian, and don't let go whatever you do!"

The Holy Ghost reached the mouth of the alley, peered around the corner, and saw the three figures about forty yards away, near the end of the brick and mortar passageway, huddling close to the ground under an iron loading dock, wrestling with the errant dog. They were too distracted, too occupied with their task, to notice the tall, thin figure silently slip into the alley and approach them. The father was trying to get a leash on the wriggling, frightened animal.

"Hold her still, Brian!"

Cautiously, stealthily, unseen in the gauzy mist swirling through the wind tunnel of the alley, the Holy Ghost approached, reaching inside his coat for the metal flask in his inner breast pocket, the one with the specially designed cotton stopper. Sodium pentobarbital—the colorless, odorless liquid that sedated his subjects, made them manageable. With one easy motion the intruder tipped and squeezed the flask, saturating the cotton. His other hand busied itself with a home-made blackjack.

"Got her! Pick her up! Let's guhhhh—"

The sap came down hard on the father's cranium, cracking his skull through the hood of his rain slicker. The man flopped to the pavement, landing directly on the dog, which let out a stunned yelp. Lightning flickered overhead as the Holy Ghost whirled toward the sons.

It happened so abruptly, so decisively, and yet so *impassively*, that the two boys—both big kids, both varsity athletes—had little time to react. One of them looked up and gasped. The other boy simply reared back, shielding his face as though the very sky had started falling.

"Nnooo!"

The Holy Ghost lashed out again with the sap—a leather sock filled with steel slugs and lead sinkers—striking the older boy on the bridge of the nose as he tried to rise. The boy staggered, letting out a garbled cry—"Unh!"—right before his knees started buckling.

The younger brother, crying out now, tried to flee, but the Holy One grabbed him around the waist as though grabbing a squealing, rain-slick piglet trying to escape the slaughter. The flask came out, rose to the boy's contorted face, pressed down on his upper lip, and muffled his screams.

The father was starting to move again, writhing on the ground in rivulets of rain and blood, the dog still pinned and whining under him. By this point the younger brother had sagged into unconsciousness in the Holy Ghost's arms. The assailant let the boy sink to the cobblestones, then reached over and pressed the soggy stopper of sodium pentobarbital against the father's face, disabling him, silencing him.

As thunder boomed and waves of mist furled through the alley, the Holy Ghost dragged the father's limp body into an alcove behind a loading dock for safekeeping. The two boys were left in the alley; the Holy Ghost had no use for children. But the father's body would remain untouched in the alcove until the hour of transformation. And *he* was only the beginning!

Trembling with emotion, the Holy Ghost paused and looked up at the sky.

The black ceiling churned, lightning flickering like phosphorous veins. The hurricane was approaching. It would only be a matter of hours now. But there were many more subjects to harvest before the hour of transformation. The Holy Ghost turned his face to the angry heavens and let out a joyful howl until something unexpected caught his attention.

A noise to his immediate left: a faint whimpering sound. He looked down and saw the wounded dog. Panting and whining in agony, it was trying to limp away toward the mouth of the alley. Its hindquarters had been shattered.

The Holy Ghost went over to the animal, effortlessly scooping it up, then twisting its neck until cartilage and bone snapped. The dog expired instantly. Then the Holy One reached inside his pocket, found a spring-loaded blade, pulled it out, gave it a flick, and plunged it into the animal's underside between its teats. Blood bubbled and fizzed in the rain, a pink stringer momentarily swirling up into the wind.

The Holy Ghost reached into the dog's steaming carcass, plucked out its heart, and ate it.

"Grove, Grove, Grove . . . have you finally gone . . . what is the American phrase? Over the hill?" Shaking his enormous head, the Russian could not believe what he was hearing on the other end of the line. "I cannot scramble the aircraft in one hour, Grove, I cannot even get a single roll of toilet paper for the men's room in this place of the godforsaken."

"'Over the hill' means *old*, Kaminsky," the voice informed him. "I think you meant to say 'Around the bend.' Right? Meaning crazy? Nuts?"

"Yes, that is it, most definitely, you have gone around the bend with the crazy nuts." Kaminsky nodded profusely. He sat in his little electronic nest at the National Security Agency's Plum Tree Island Experimental Station, chewing a soggy cheroot cigarillo, the phone propped into the crook of his thick neck as he kept an eye on three separate cathode-ray screens in front of him displaying three separate satellite views of Hurricane Eve as she approached the East Coast.

Ivan Kaminsky had been a weather analyst for the U.S. government for nearly two decades now, ever since he had defected in the mid-1980s during Reagan's "tear down this wall" period. Before that, Kaminsky had been in the Soviet military, working in a top-secret branch of the KGB dedicated to studying global climate changes. At the time, rumors had circulated in the intelligence community that the Soviets were trying to *control* the weather, not just study it, but Kaminsky had always laughed that off as a folktale. The truth was, nobody could control the weather, but men like Kaminsky could certainly get inside it, ride the tiger for a while, get to know its most ferocious moods. And that's essentially what Ivan Kaminsky did for the NSA: He chased storms. He was practically a legend among the wags at the National Weather Service. In 2005 he flew a Lockheed four-engine prop job into the eye of Hurricane Katrina as it passed over Gulf Port, Mississippi, and he won a Pulitzer for his photographs, as well as a Distinguished Service Medal for his report to the NWS. In fact, the only thing that had kept Kaminsky from getting a top government desk job was the vodka.

Kaminsky loved his Stolichnaya more than life itself, and over the years this love affair had taken its toll on the Russian's mind and body. A massive bear of a man with a great, frizzy, iron-gray beard, he had expanded at a geometric rate over the last decade. His huge hooked nose now looked like a road map of busted capillaries, and his memory had blown out like a bad fuse. He could still quote the wind speeds of storms from the 1970s, but he couldn't remember what he had had for breakfast that morning. All of which was why he had been exiled by the feds to this rat-infested lighthouse overlooking a wild corner of the Chesapeake Bay.

"Look, Kay, I know it's short notice, but this freak's on a spree, an upward spiral," the voice of Ulysses Grove explained after an agonizing pause. "And like I said, it has something to do with me, so whatever you can do to get me up there, in the eye, in a hurry, would make a huge difference."

"But why? This one is already up to a category three, and she is still just north of Nassau. She will be category four by the time she reaches the cape, you realize this, I assume?"

"I realize this, and it's not like I'm dying to fly into the eye of a hurricane, but I have no choice."

"Why though? Why do you not have the choice in this matter? Please explain."

A sigh on the other end. "Because I believe the eye of the storm is the key to catching this guy."

"The key? The key—what does this mean, the key?"

"The only way I'm going to catch him is in the act,

in the eye, in the middle of a storm. He wants me there."

"Ah . . . now I *know* you are 'around the hill.'"

"Around the *bend*, get it right, Kay, for Chrissake, it's 'around the bend.'"

"This is impossible, what you are asking, it is . . . How did you come up with this?"

Grove told him about the details surrounding De Lourde's murder, the shadowy figure who delivered the missing eyeball, the murders down in Florida during Hurricane Darlene, all the missing eyes, all the weird little circumstantial clues. "Trust me on this, Kay," the voice went on, "the clock is ticking for people up around Cape Hatteras. More people are going to die unless I can get up there and take this guy down. I need you to get me right in the middle of the shit."

Kaminsky laughed out loud, then stubbed the cheroot out in an ashtray. He reached over and filled a paper cup with another inch of Stolie, then took a sip. "You can rest assured, my friend, you will get plenty of 'shit' coming at you at precisely a hundred and seventy-five miles per hour."

"I understand that—"

"No, my friend, I do not think you understand, I do not think that you are hearing me at all." Kaminsky took another slug and let it burn the back of his throat. His voice lowered an octave as he stared at the TV screen projecting satellite images of Eve. "Have you ever seen what a category five eye wall can do to a telephone pole?"

"Kay—"

"Let me finish, Grove. Please. In 1992, during Hurricane Andrew, I witnessed a telephone pole jump out of the ground and impale a fireman to a barn, Grove. It drilled itself right through his chest cavity, pinning him to the barn like an insect, Grove, like a butterfly." Kaminsky stifled a belch, and Grove started to say something but the Russian would not let him interrupt. "One year ago . . . Hurricane Katrina . . . we found a severed hand, Grove, in Slidell, Louisiana, in a vacant lot next to an overturned tractor. Police could not identify this hand, which had a Spanish signet ring on it. Do you know where this hand came from, Grove?"

No answer.

Kaminsky asked again if Grove knew where this severed hand came from.

"No, I don't, Kay, I don't know where it came from," the voice said with a sigh. "But I'm sure you're going to tell me."

"Cuba, my friend. The hand, it came from Cuba, a thousand miles away."

After a pause, the voice said, "Are you finished?"

Kaminsky grinned. "I simply offer this word of warning as a service to the public."

"You mean a 'public service,' it's called a 'public service.'"

"Right, yes. Precisely."

"I appreciate the thought, Kay, but I still want you to fly me into Eve's eye today."

Kaminsky shook his head. He had known Ulysses Grove ever since the Happy Face Killer case back in 1990. At that time, Grove was still a young turk, pissing off the brass at the bureau on a regular basis with his controversial theories regarding lunar cycles and weather, and their effect on the psychopathology of serial killers. During the hunt for the murderous truck driver, Keith Hunter Jesperson, Grove had come to Kaminsky for expertise on the moon and its effect on tides and weather. The twosome instantly clicked, notwithstanding their vast personality differences. Kaminsky had always admired Grove's methodical, relentless professionalism. Kaminsky had known young men like Grove back in Moscow, men who invariably clashed with the Central Committee and were often exiled to Siberia. *Men with balls.* Kaminsky looked up to these men—mostly because Kaminsky never had the courage to stay in his homeland and fight. Instead, he defected, and ran away from his problems. But Ulysses Grove had never been the type to defect from anything. Even now, this very moment, Kaminsky could sense this iron spirit radiating over the wires. "Still the same old Grove," Kaminsky said finally, taking one last sip of vodka.

"Whattya say, Kay? You gonna help me out here or what?"

Kaminsky glanced at the clock, then shot a glance over at the wall map that hung above the coffee machine. "Tell me where it is that you are again?"

"Let's see, I'm about forty miles south of Savannah, in a little fleabag just off I-95."

"Hold on, I am putting you on speaker." Kaminsky dropped the phone, poked the Speaker button, then quickly rolled his swivel chair across the tile floor to the topographical map of the eastern seaboard. Color-coded stick pins denoted the coastal "entry points" of past hurricanes: Elena, 1985. Gilbert, 1988. Hugo, 1989. Emily, 1993. Opal, Michelle, Lily, Isabel, Jeanne, Cassandra, and . . . of course . . . the mother of all hurricanes, Katrina. Other colored pins showed federal disaster facilities, military bases, and quick-response centers. Kaminsky traced his long, nicotine-stained finger down the coast of South Carolina. "You and I are apparently equal distances from the cape," Kaminsky bellowed at the room.

Grove's voice, filtered now through the tiny speaker: "Sounds about right."

"How quickly can you get to Seymour Johnson Air Force Base in Goldsboro, North Carolina?"

Through the speaker: "Goldsboro . . . is that near Wilmington?"

Kaminsy yelled back that it was about forty miles southeast of Raleigh/Durham, and it was also a high-security base so Grove would probably have to answer a lot of questions.

"That's about two hundred miles away," the voice sizzled through the speaker. "So basically if I get moving, I could get there around noon today. Is that going to work for you?"

Kaminsky glanced at the monitors displaying Eve's progress across the Atlantic. "It does not leave us much of a margin of contingency," he said with a sigh, "but yes, all right, I will tell you what I will do. But I must also warn you if you tell anyone at the NSA that I helped you today I will tell them I have never met you, and that you are insane and should be locked up, do you understand what I am telling to you?"

Grove said he understood, and then Kaminsky told the profiler where to meet him.

Grove left the Starlight Motel at 7:00 a.m. in his rented Geo, which had begun to reek of body odor and stale fast food. He stopped at a Dixie Boy Truck Stop and got a muffin and a large coffee, then topped off the gas tank. The wind whipped fishtails of mist under the overhang roof, soaking Grove's long coat, rattling his pant legs. Grove welcomed it. He needed to wake up, needed a bracing slap in the face.

Inside the truck stop, while paying the tab, he noticed a display of little white "diet" pills on a spinner rack by the cash register—Truckers' Friends, they were called, chock-full of ephedrine—and he considered buying some. He knew the last thing he needed right then was speed, but he also knew he was going to be useless in a few hours without either a couple of hours of sleep, or some heavy-duty pharmaceutical stimulants.

Ultimately he decided against the Truckers' Friends, paid his bill, and hurriedly got back on the road.

He pushed the little Chevy as hard as he could through the rain, up Interstate 95, scooting around Savannah, then tooling across the state line and up into the eastern sand hills of South Carolina. The landscape got bigger and more ruggedly beautiful the farther north he got—even in the storm—now stretching in all directions over endless forested dells and limestone cliffs rising up into the black sky like alabaster monuments. The gusts toyed with the little sedan, every few moments giving it a violent nudge.

When Grove finally got Maura on the phone, he had to press the wireless hard against his ear in order to hear her over the noise. "Finally, finally we connect," he said into the cell phone. "I've tried getting through at least a dozen times."

Her voice sounded as though it were underwater. "God, how I hate cell phones."

"Where are you?"

Ffffhhhzzzt—"on my way ba"—*fffht*.

"What?"

"Atlanta . . . I'm in Atlanta."

Grove frowned. "*What* are you doing in Atlanta?"

"I'm"—*fffht*—"back to New Orleans"—*fffzzzt*—"had a stopover in Atlanta."

"Did you just say you're heading back to New Orleans? Did I hear you right?"

The voice informed him that he had indeed heard her correctly, she was heading back to the Crescent City. "Got halfway home," she said, her voice softening, "then started feeling guilty for bailing out on you. Figured you could use some help."

Grove's gut clenched with emotion for a moment. He had underestimated how much he needed this woman, how much he wanted a relationship with her.

For the last five years, Ulysses Grove had been living in a shell of grief and repression, consumed by his work, ignoring his needs. But something had happened to him—something unspoken and inchoate—on that Alaskan mountainside last year, when he had grappled with the madman named Richard Ackerman. Whether or not there had been an actual demonic entity inside Ackerman—and regardless of whether that entity had projected itself into Grove—there *had* been a change within Grove that day. He had faced his true self. He had come to terms with who he was: the latest in a long line of manhunters. It was there in the DNA of a six-thousand-year-old mummy, a paleolithic bounty hunter, and it was there in Grove's blood chemistry. He was the genetic descendent of those ancient manhunters, the shamans and medicine men who had ferreted out evil from the tribes and villages. This epiphany had changed the way Grove looked at himself. This was *who he was*, and there was nothing he could do about it—even if he wanted to. This sense of self, this sense of peace with himself, had made him want Maura all the more. No more lies, no more shame. He wanted a companion who was an equal—a strong, feisty, brilliant, soulful woman.

"Maura . . ." Grove began, then paused when he heard a shuffling sound coming through the earpiece. He realized it was the sound of Maura lighting a cigarette. "Are you smoking again? I can hear you puffing away."

"Okay, yes . . . yes, I'm smoking again," she confessed. "Look at me, smoking again, and back for more murder and mayhem. Pathetic, huh?"

Grove smiled to himself. Outside the car, the wind was raging so hard now the rain was sheeting *up* the windshield, and he had to grip the wheel with both hands to keep the Geo in the fast lane. He had the speedometer practically pinned at ninety miles an hour. "I'm glad you're back, Maura, I really am."

Her voice had a grin in it. "Don't get cocky, smart aleck."

"I won't, believe me . . . but what's all this about an old article on hurricanes?"

A brief pause, then Maura's voice changed, becoming soft and grave: "I was at O'Hare last night and I saw this picture of Hurricane Eve out at sea, and all of sudden it hit me like a ton of bricks: *the first global warming.*"

"The what?"

Another pause, then this: "I did this piece for *Discover* years ago on ancient climate change, and it turns out there was this period of global warming about fifty thousand years ago that was a lot like our current situation . . . and I remember digging this stuff up about hurricanes."

"Go on."

"In the fossil record they found, there was just this

amazing number of hurricanes back then. It was like the apocalypse or something. But that's not the weirdest part. You want to hear the weirdest part?"

"I do, yes."

"Unexplained"—*ffffzzzzt*—"Ulysses."

"Say again, I didn't hear that last bit."

"*Unexplained deaths,* I said. That's how Leakey put it in 1972 right before he died—Louis Leakey, the great anthropologist. He uncovered these huge mortality rates, and all these unexplained human and animal remains at the ground-zero sites of these hurricanes."

Grove shrugged. "Sounds like you're just talking about basic storm fatalities. I mean, these primitive villages would have just gotten chewed up by the hurricanes. Right?"

The voice crackled: "This is something else. This is Louis Leakey we're talking about here, this is the guy who discovered the missing link. I remember he had perfect fossil evidence of these bizarre deaths that were always directly in the path of these ancient storms . . . but were not accidental deaths."

"What do you mean—'not accidental'?"

A surge of static obscured her voice for a moment. *Fffht*—"down their throats or"—*ffffzzzhht!*

Grove gripped the steering wheel tighter. "You're breaking up again."

More static. "I said. Some of them. Had *spears.* Rammed down their throats. Others were dismembered, or decapitated. Cows mutilated and dismembered. Stuff like that. Really disturbing shit."

"I suppose the wind could do that." Grove didn't believe his own words any more than she did.

"Now you sound like that medical examiner down in New Orleans, what's-his-name."

"Nesbitt."

"Right. Nesbitt. C'mon, Ulysses. You're telling me the wind can drive a stake down a person's throat? I just remembered running across all that stuff and being so, you know, like repulsed and fascinated at the same time. I guess for quite a few years this was one of the big mysteries in the archaeology field that Louis Leakey basically took to his grave with him."

Grove drove in silence for a moment.

He found himself gazing through the layers of rain at the distant horizon. The muffled, percussive tattoo of the wipers combined with the rhythmic waves of rain striking the windshield, creating a hypnotic drone that held his gaze for a moment. His eyes stung, watering from lack of sleep. *Scan, don't stare*, his old high school driving instructor used to admonish him. But Grove had always been a daydreamer, a gazer, and now he found himself staring at the bleary gray distance and thinking of tornadoes from his childhood in Illinois. Then he found himself thinking of his mother, thinking of Africa, thinking of the place he was born and the great siroccos that used to blow across the dusty wastelands of southeastern Kenya.

Something pale and indistinct loomed in Grove's peripheral vision, and Grove's heart leaped into his throat. *"What the fuhhhh—"*

He yanked the wheel. The car zigged across the parallel lane, and Grove shot a glance through the passenger-side window. At first he thought another vehicle was trying to pass him on the right—*on the shoulder, for God's sake!*—and then he realized it wasn't a vehicle at all. It was a great white whirlwind of dust, rising up from the sand hills a hundred yards away, coming at him like that old Warner Brothers cartoon character, the Tasmanian Devil, only *this* one was a thousand times bigger, the size of a massive pyramid in the shape of a funnel cloud.

"Ulysses? You okay? Ulysses!"

All at once the sound of Maura's voice in his ear, as well as the sound of another car behind him honking furiously, made the white whirlwind abruptly vanish, and Grove uttered something inarticulate under his breath as he steered the Geo back into the proper lane. He swallowed hard, realizing instantly that he had gone into a temporary trance state and had seen a vision, and just as suddenly as it had appeared, it had disappeared. Grove took deep breaths, steadying himself, clenching and unclenching his cold, sweaty hands around the steering wheel.

Maura's voice was in his ear again. "What happened? What's wrong?"

"Nothing, nothing . . . just a little wind. It's getting a little dicey up here."

"Probably ought to think about pulling over, don't ya think? If it's getting that bad?"

"I'm fine, Maura, really . . . I'm all right," Grove lied, breathing deep breaths and gripping the wheel. It had been months since he had experienced any significant visions. In fact, in the weeks before De Lourde's death, Grove had thought that perhaps he was over them. But the truth was, deep down, a part of him knew he would never be completely free of the damned things.

He had been having visions, off and on, his whole life. Sometimes in dreams. Sometimes during dizzy spells or these weird temporary "fugue" states that afflicted him during moments of stress or physical exhaustion. His mother, Vida, a tough, spirited Kenyan woman who had immigrated to America when Grove was only a toddler, had always attributed Grove's visions to some mystical source. According to Vida they were prophesies, portents, glimpses of the future or some message from the spiritual realm.

But these dusty whirlwinds were not mere figments of Grove's overheated imagination. He remembered seeing these weird white storms as a kid, just after his thirteenth birthday. Visiting Africa with his mother and uncle, he had returned to his birthplace that summer: Kibuyu, the small Kenyan village on the Ethiopian border. They stayed there for a week, ostensibly to teach young Ulysses his heritage, but on a deeper level, it had terrified him down to his bones. It wasn't merely the brutal, primitive nature of the town—part village, part military base, Kibuyu had become, after decades of draught, a refugee camp of baked mud houses and goatskin tents. It was also the weather, and those strange early morning phantoms known as "dust devils."

Formed when the savage sun first beats down on those arid, poorly conducting desert plains, dust devils are basically ten-to-twenty-foot-high whirlwinds of sand that travel with a macabre jerking motion across the barrens. They look like ghosts, especially the small ones, which are alarmingly *human*-sized funnels of swirling, gauzy white cobwebs. They're self-perpetuating, too, which adds to their haunting quality. Grove witnessed one travel through a wire fence and over the backs of emaciated cattle before vanishing *into* the side of a broken-down thatched barn.

But why now? Why today? Why had the dust devil reared its eerie, diaphanous head in Grove's imagination? Was it because he had cut off his medication? Or was there a deeper reason it had loomed for one brief, thunderstruck instant outside his window?

"Listen," Grove said finally into the wireless. "Here's the thing. I need you to head back to the professor's place. Dig up anything you can find on this Yucatan expedition."

"What am I looking for?"

Grove took a deep breath. "I don't know . . . anything and everything. Names, places."

After the most agonizing pause Grove had ever heard, the sound of Maura's voice returned. It sounded almost tender in his ear. "Watch your back, hotshot . . . and your front and sides, too."

Grove made it across the North Carolina border by ten, which meant he was an hour ahead of schedule, which was good, because he was so tired by that point he could barely keep the Chevy on the road. Between the wind shears and the mounting rain, not to mention the virtual whiteouts from passing semis, driving had become nearly impossible. Grove's eyes burned. His head felt as though it were filled with concrete. Soon he realized if he didn't stop and rest, he would never make it to Goldsboro.

He found a suitable spot under an overpass about fifteen miles south of Fayetteville, in the shadows of sacred Civil War battlefields, the surrounding hills still haunted by General Sherman's bloodiest campaign. Grove pulled over to the shoulder and put on his emergency blinkers, then put his seat back all the way. He set the alarm on his watch to go off in an hour. In the steady white noise of rain and strafing winds, he was fast asleep within minutes.

Without the tether of his medication, the recurring dream ran amok in his midbrain in full Technicolor, more vivid than ever before.

7

The last voice the elderly Kenyan woman had expected to hear that morning when she answered the phone was that of her son; but on a deeper, unconscious level she had also been expecting this call, *dreading* it.

"Are you not well, *Mwana?* Where are you?" She snubbed out her cigarette in an oyster shell on the dust-coated yellow windowsill.

Vida Grove had been standing at the kitchen sink in the rear of her little Chicago bungalow, skinning sweet potatoes with a rusty metal peeler, an L&M filter cigarette dangling from her lips. She wore a housedress and slippers, and her ashen skin had the leathery, scuffed color of a tortoise. To the neighborhood kids up and down Lawrence Avenue, she was the old, feeble African crone, the crazy lady with the weird outfits. But if you looked closer, all her delicate eccentricities were belied by the diamond-sharp glint in her ancient eyes.

"Mom, I'm fine, I'm fine, I'm fine," said the harried voice on the other end, the sound of it nearly drowned by a rushing noise that reminded Vida of a thousand Hoover vacuums.

"Then why must you need to know this thing?" she

asked. "Why with so much urgent need? What is wrong? Something is wrong. I can hear it in your voice."

The voice said he was sorry, but he didn't have much time right now to talk, he was catching a plane in a few minutes, and he just needed to know this one thing, and he promised he would call in a couple of days and explain everything.

"But why, Ulysses?"

After a brief pause the voice said: "I've been having this recurring dream. It's so real, Mom. In the dream I always start out in total darkness, and then I'm pulled toward this strange light. Now I realize what it is, I'm dreaming of my own birth. It happens. Sometimes people remember their own births in their dreams. But the really weird part is, in the dream, when I'm finally born, there's this tremendous noise and light and—"

The voice cut out for a moment, and Vida said, "*Mwana*? Are you there?"

"—and then I'm lifted up by the *tabibu*, this midwife, and I see the sky. I see this horrible black sky. I know it's just a dream, Mom. But this one feels different, vivid, like a memory. People *do* sometimes have memories of their own birth. Was I born outside, Mom?"

A long pause.

"You *were* born outside, Ulysses," she finally told him. "We had troubles with the generator. So many bugs. But yes, the sky could have been the first thing that you saw."

"What was it *doing*, Mom?"

Vida frowned, confused. "I do not understand."

"The sky. What was it *doing*? Was there a storm? I know it sounds nuts, but I need to know if I was born in a cyclone, a hurricane. Or was it just a dream?"

A sudden cold feeling of dread trickled down Vida's swayback spine, and she chewed on her lip for a moment, thinking about how to answer. In all her years of motherhood, the question had never come up—even on the rare occasions that she had talked about his birth. She had told him about her diabetes, and the doctors telling her that her child might not make it. She had even told young Ulysses about the Sudanese fortune-teller who had said the boy would grow up to be a prophet, and would walk with world leaders. But she had never mentioned the vision of a whirlwind that had stricken her. To this day, she was not certain whether that strange and horrifying dust storm that had appeared out of nowhere was real or imaginary.

Semiconscious at the time, Vida remembered seeing it at virtually the same moment her baby had crowned. In a daze of pain and excruciating pressure, she had cried out, bug-eyed, gazing off at the distant white twister on the horizon, coming straight for the village, coming from the distant border of Ethiopia. Later, she reckoned that she was simply hallucinating from the pain and emotion of giving birth to her first and only child, but right then, as the *tabibu* rooted out the writhing, bloody, caterwauling infant from her womb, the village had started levitating on the swirling winds. Clothes flapped and whipped and flew off clotheslines. Animal-hide tents were ripped from their moorings, swirling up into the sky. Chickens scurried in all directions, many lifted up into the chaos as though filled with helium. And it had come out of *nowhere*—as though it were heralding the arrival of this new, still nameless baby boy. The *tabibu* finally wrapped a swaddling cloth around the newborn and ushered both mother and child to the relative calm of their small shack of a house, where the whirlwind finally seemed to dissipate. But now, many years later, a dream had shown Ulysses the same storm. The gods had shown him the vision for some reason that Vida would never be able to understand. "Yes, it is true, Ulysses . . . in a *way*," she finally said, gazing out the window at a crow lighting on a telephone wire. "You *were* born in a kind of a storm."

"What do you mean, Mom—what *kind* of a storm?"

In a low voice Vida told him the whole story—her weird spontaneous vision of chickens floating through the air, and the sand forming bizarre shapes. She didn't tell him what had happened immediately after the phantom storm . . . she didn't tell him any of *that* part of the story, the strange and troubling events that *followed* the dust devil.

"Mom, thanks . . . thank you," his voice said at last when she had finished her story. "Listen, I gotta go. My plane just arrived. I'll call you next week. I promise."

"Wait, Ulysses, wait."

"What, Mom?"

She chewed her lip some more. "Whether you are born in a storm or not . . . what difference does it make?"

After a long pause the voice said, "I promise I'll call you next week."

"*Mwana*—"

"I gotta go, Mom. I love you. Thank you. Take care of yourself."

The line clicked.

Vida stood there for a moment, holding the phone like a dead bird in her hand. Then she carefully replaced the phone on its wall cradle. She thought about what her son had said, the disconcerting tone in his voice, and she thought about where he said he was: *North Carolina*.

Filled with a vague, inexplicable dread, Vida went into the living room and turned on the small, portable TV set that sat on her imitation oak bookcase. She flipped through the channels until she found the cable weather channel. It wasn't long before they were showing a graphic of the eastern seaboard, the familiar Day-Glo spiral of Hurricane Eve now within a hundred miles of Cape Hatteras.

"Dear merciful Allah," she uttered under her breath, putting her ashy brown fingers to her lips.

Ulysses Grove slid his cell phone back in his pocket and watched the battered Jeep Cherokee approach through curtains of hard, steel-gray rain. He felt woozy from the catnap, and a little dizzy with nerves. Why had he bothered calling his mom? It was just a dream, for Christ's sake—why had it bothered him so much?

His trench coat collar raised and buttoned against his neck, his eyes stinging from the razor-wet winds, Grove started pacing under a corrugated tin awning that fronted a deserted hangar on the edge of Seymour Johnson Air Force Base. To Grove's right was the labyrinth of rusted-out Quonset huts and hangars that made up the eastern edge of the base. To his left, the vast crisscrossing tarmacs of weathered runways, looking ghostly and shapeless in the rain. It was a miracle that Grove had gotten past the guard shack on Highway 117. A flash of an inactive bureau tag and some fancy talking had gotten him through. Just barely.

Now he watched the Jeep coming toward him from the north, down a pea-gravel road that wove through a copse of thick live oaks shrouded in fog, about a hundred yards away and closing. Grove knew it was Kaminsky from the tangle of instruments on the vehicle's roof, the fog lamps, the satellite dish, the barometric instruments like the gleaming works of a great Rube Goldberg machine.

"The people you meet at air force bases," Ivan Kaminsky hollered out his window as the Jeep pulled up to the deserted hangar.

"How much time do we have?" Grove asked as he circled around the front of the Jeep.

"Not enough! Get in and do exactly as I say, and we might even get airborne!"

Grove got in and Kaminsky gunned the Jeep before the passenger door was even shut.

The four-wheeler lurched past the hangar, made a hairpin to the right, then started down the rain-slick access road that ran along the remote runway. Gales of rain hammered down on the roof. Grove bounced around on the passenger seat, ignoring the empty bottle rolling around at his feet, or the odors of dried sweat and stale cigar smoke thinly veiled by sickly sweet wintergreen deodorizer.

In his booming Russian accent Kaminsky explained that there were only five planes on the eastern seaboard that he would even consider flying into a hurricane, and two of them belonged to NASA and thus were off-limits to a cowboy like Kaminsky. Of the other three, one was a tricked-out U2 spy plane hangared in Alexandria that belonged to the CIA, and one was a retro-fitted DC-8 down in Miami that belonged to the National Oceanic and Atmospheric Administration, and one was here—a Lockheed WP-3 that had seen better days. Kaminsky would have preferred the U2, but he had burned too many bridges at the company, and besides, Goldsboro was closer to the epicenter.

"What's the problem with the Lockheed?" Grove asked, gazing out the window at the standing water on the pocked runways, the surface dimpled by the wind.

"Suffice it to say it is old," Kaminsky said, a crooked little smile creasing his salt-and-pepper beard. "The less said the better, I think."

"Just get me up there, and get me into the eye," Grove murmured.

His voice had lost much of its vigor.

Due to rapidly changing weather conditions on the eastern seaboard, Maura had to hustle through security in Atlanta in order to catch the last flight south that day. The plane pulled away from the Jetway at around eleven o'clock that morning, just as Hurricane Eve was crossing international waters north of the Bahamas. By 12:30 p.m.—right around the time that Grove was climbing into Kaminsky's rickety Jeep—Maura's flight was entering southern Louisiana airspace.

Just before landing, as the airliner careened through furious turbulence, a portly businessman sitting next to Maura muttered something about another tropical storm developing off the southern coast of Jamaica.

"They're callin' her Fiona," the fat guy drawled out of the side of his phlegmy mouth, as though he were imparting some dirty little secret. "Can ya believe it? Sixth goddamn hurricane in two weeks, and they're saying it might very well be headin' straight for N'awlunz."

Maura felt a tension headache pressing on the back of her eyelids. "Did they say when it'll hit?"

"They don't know shit, as usual, but I'll tell ya this,

if it's another big one, I'll betcha Bush'll be down there the next day in a rowboat."

The big man laughed so hard he spewed spittle across the seat back.

A few agonizing minutes later, Maura was on the ground at Louis Armstrong International.

She went through the same ticket agent that she had used the night before, and the stately black woman jokingly asked if Maura was trying to rack up enough free miles to get to Hawaii. Maura managed a feeble laugh and explained it was "her boyfriend's fault," which sounded strange coming off her tongue, but on some level it was the truth. She was doing this for love. And also for something a little thornier, a little more complicated—and maybe even subconscious—tweaking her, driving her to step back into Grove's macabre circus.

Call it naked ambition.

She still remembered how it felt to sell something like "The Unexplained Plagues of Ancient Climate Change" to *Discover* magazine. That piece put her on the map as a science journalist. Not only had *Discover* put her article on the cover, but the offers had started rolling in for assignments and speaking engagements. She had never bothered to follow up on the climate change piece, but she would always remember the feeling that it brought her. The only other time she had felt anything even remotely like that was back in Alaska last year when Ulysses Grove had first seen a connection between the death pattern of the Mount Cairn mummy and the Sun City Killer's modern victims. Immersing herself in that world had been like a dangerous, addictive board game. It had brought her a temporary excitement, even euphoria, followed by a long period of agony, capped off by a near-death experience.

She hoped she could avoid that last part this time.

"There she is, the old whore," Kaminsky blurted from behind the wheel, squinting to see the massive shape dead ahead of the Jeep. Ahead of them, out of the curtains of rain, a ghostly shape had become visible at the end of the runway. The huge aircraft sat off by itself, tethered to the pavement like a great beast captured in battle. Other than the enormous antenna housing rising off its forward cockpit like the horn of some prehistoric rhino, it looked to the untrained eye like an ordinary—albeit *mammoth*—prop plane. In fact, as Kaminsky pulled up to its tail, Grove found himself marveling at how *unremarkable* the thing looked.

About the only thing that struck Grove as exceptional was the span of the Lockheed's wings. They spread at least a hundred feet across the tarmac, and supported four massive turboprops—a pair on each wing—each the size of a Volkswagen Beetle.

Kaminsky parked about twenty feet off the airplane's starboard hindquarter, and the two men climbed out of the Jeep. Wind rustled across the empty tarmac, making an eerie whistling noise. Grove found the lack of activity a little strange. One would think there would be ground crew around, maybe other members of the flight team. But the place was deserted. It did not give Grove a warm feeling.

The rain had picked up now, coming in gray waves, and Kaminsky had to hold his duffel in front of his face as he led Grove across the cracked tarmac and around the gigantic landing gear.

Squinting to see what he was doing, Kaminsky kicked the blocks out from under the wheels with his muddy, black jackboots, then quickly unsnapped the mooring cables one at a time with his huge callused fingers. Cables pinged. Rusty fasteners clattered into puddles. Then Kaminsky led Grove over to the nose. An iron ladder rose up to the cockpit doors, which towered more than twenty feet above the runway. The Russian helped Grove up the cleats, then through the cockpit door.

The sudden muffled silence, the chalky-chemical odors, and the dim light made Grove a little queasy.

"Now, Grove, I am going to need you to sit right there in the middle, in the seat of the flight engineer—quickly now, quickly!" Kaminsky ordered, pointing to a battered upholstered chair mounted to the floor. The walls and ceiling were lined with instrument racks. The air reeked of old leather and something cold and acrid like butane. "Right there you will help me with the stick."

Grove glanced over his shoulder and gazed down the center of the cabin. It took his breath away—the narrow corridor, the seats long ago removed and replaced by a virtual laboratory's worth of experimental gear. Computers, radio gear, cameras, centrifuges, all manner of meteorological instruments. "Did you say 'help with the stick'?" Grove marveled as he turned back to his seat, settling in and fastening his shoulder harness.

Kaminsky was digging in his duffel bag, putting a headset on, plugging jacks into the panel, and tapping his curved mouthpiece. "Tower-Huey, this is Three-Delta, do you copy?"

A voice crackled from the console. "Three-D, this is Tower-H, copy that, confirm status."

"Coming on line, Tower, requesting clearance."

"Three-Delta, you got clearance on Baker-one-nine," the radio said. "Better put the spurs to her, Ivan. Skipper's due any minute."

"There is no worry, Tower," Kaminsky said and started moving levers. "We are out of town."

Lightning flickered outside, a sheet of rain whipping along the top of the fuselage, and now lots of things began to happen simultaneously, and Grove tried to take it all in and keep his heart from punching a hole in his sternum. A high-pitched humming noise had started as Kaminsky flipped switches, and something started vibrating low and deep in the floor and Grove realized he was hearing engines igniting. He looked around and noticed odd little things like Hostess Twinkie wrappers on the corrugated iron deck and a small stuffed Garfield toy, its suction cup paws stuck to a portal.

The aircraft began to move. *Backward.* Grove instinctively gripped his armrests while Kaminsky taxied the monster back across the apron, nearly clipping the Jeep Cherokee with the outboard stabilizer. When the plane finally came to rest in the center of the northernmost runway, which was currently deserted, bordered by flashing silver strobes, Kaminsky pulled some more levers. The craft jerked, and Grove held his breath as they started rolling forward toward the gray horizon.

Thunder rumbled as the behemoth gained speed, and Grove felt the massive turbines growling, the vibrations traveling up his bones, the noise so loud now it made his ears pop. Kaminsky was yelling into the headset, but Grove could hear nothing but the cacophony of engines. The g-forces pushed him into his seat as the plane levitated off the runway—

—and just like that they were airborne, arcing up

through layers of turbulence. Grove twisted to see down through Garfield's portal, which was now streaked with angry rains. Like a dream, the rolling patchwork of deep green tobacco fields and crisscrossing arteries of rutted roads fell away under the giant craft as it bounced upward and upward. Grove started frantically looking around the cockpit.

"What in the devil's name are you looking for!" Kaminsky yelled over the chorus of engines.

"Oh, I don't know . . . maybe parachutes?" Grove's stomach was already in his throat, his gut smoldering. A cold sweat had broken across his brow. He could control his conscious fear for the moment, but his body was another matter.

Kaminsky's booming, incongruous laughter pierced the noise. "Parachutes? Parachutes! Parachutes are useless in a hurricane, my friend."

"What are you talking about?"

"In hurricane conditions a parachute goes *up*!" More phlegmy laughter from Kaminsky as he gripped the control yoke, his gaze everywhere at once, on the altimeter, on the air-speed indicator, on the trim levers, on the radar monitor, and especially on the narrow windshield that spanned the bulwark, its wiper beating a rhythmic march as the plane climbed. "Unless that is what you *want* to do, which I would not advise in a hurricane if you want to come back down."

Grove could not force even a smile. "How long is it gonna take us to get there?"

Kaminsky glanced at the GPS screen. "Assuming we can maintain a rate of two hundred knots, we will reach the outer bands in approximately forty-minutes."

The plane careened through another layer of turbulence, slamming down hard on the unstable slipstream, the rivets complaining and creaking. Grove clutched at the armrests. Wind shears moaned below them, above them.

"Two hundred knots!" Grove was confused. "That sounds slow."

"Slow is good when you are flying into the eye of a hurricane!" Kaminsky yelled back over the din. "That is why we use prop planes. A jet would come out the other side with its wings torn off."

"Did you say *into* it?" Grove looked at him. "That was just a figure of speech, right?"

Kaminsky looked over at him. "I am not following."

"I asked you to fly me *into* the eye, yeah, but I figured you would fly *over* it."

"*Over* it?" Kaminsky laughed again, both hands on the control yoke now. The planed shuddered, violent turbulence rocking the fuselage. It sounded like an enormous animal in its death throes. "What gave you that idea?" More laughter. "'Over it,' the man says . . . *over* it!"

Grove glanced nervously down past the Garfield toy at the veins of lightning marbling the scorched clouds.

He tightened his harness.

8

"Here, help me with these! Throw 'em in the back! Hurry! Please!"

The emaciated girl with the chartreuse hair and raccoon eyes was lugging a stack of vintage vinyl record albums in her spindly arms as she hurried across the windy street corner toward her battered, rust-pocked panel van. The van was idling, rear door gaping open, parallel-parked under one of the Garden District's few intact pre-Katrina live oaks. On her way around the rear of the van, Sandi Loper-Herzog stumbled on a broken bottle, and the records went flying, pinwheeling in all directions, skidding across the wet cobblestones.

"Oops—let me help you with that." Maura County went over, knelt down, and hurriedly helped the girl pick the records up, noting the homogenous genre of music in the collection: Bauhaus, The Cure, Black Sabbath, Souxie and the Banshees, The Cure, Dead Can Dance, and some more Cure. These goth types had always slayed Maura; they were almost quaint in their monochromatic worldview. Obsessed with death, always with the Stevie Nix black veils and coal-black lining their eyes, they were practically nerdlike in their fixation with necrophilic romance. But what better place to practice the lifestyle than the festering, ghostly, cryptic sinkhole of New Orleans, the former home of Anne Rice and the spirit of Tennessee Williams?

"I'm sorry if I seem, you know, a little, whattyacallit, scattered," Sandi stammered as she gathered up her beloved albums. "I'm hearing this one might make it up to category four, and I'm just not going to go through another Katrina."

"I don't blame you," Maura commiserated, remembering her first encounter with this girl at De Lourde's funeral, and the distinct impression that something had seemed slightly "off" about her, slightly edgy. "I promise you I won't keep you more than a minute or so."

"What do you want to know?"

"You were with Mose De Lorde's Yucatan expedition, right? Back in '04?"

"Unfortunately yeah."

"Can you tell me what happened?"

The girl in black shoved the albums into the van, then turned and looked at Maura. "A lot of things happened. What do you want to know about it?"

Maura asked about the hurricane that hit the Yucatan while they were down there.

"Pretty near did us in—Miguel and Michael and me—we were right by his side when it hit."

"By whose side?"

"The professor, De Lourde. Who else?" The goth girl turned and hurried back toward the boarded exterior of her Julia Street row house, and Maura followed along at a skip. A siren pierced the distance. It was starting to spit a little bit, the wind picking up.

"What was the purpose of the trip?" Maura asked.

"The expedition? Who knows?" Sandi circled a

stack of moving boxes that flanked the cracked marble archway, a battered ten-speed bike leaning against one side. Maura helped the goth girl lift one of the bigger boxes, then carry it back across the curb toward the van.

"It was partially funded by the grad school, and by the National Endowment for the Humanities," Sandi Herzog huffed and puffed as she lugged the enormous box across the curb. "Only reason Michael and I went was because they gave us independent study credit. And also because Michael and Moses were, you know, an *item*."

"No, I didn't know that."

"Yeah, you know, obviously it wasn't something they wanted to advertise." She shoved the box into the van. "But God, Moses was like this geriatric Indiana Jones . . . I mean, you should have seen it."

Sandi hustled back toward the doorway.

"What do you mean?" Maura was getting breathless, struggling just to keep up.

"That first day, I thought I was going to pass out. He leads us up the side of this mountain, and there were these dudes from the Bureau of Indigenous Peoples on our ass, and I mean these were serious muchachos, with guns and shit."

"Are you kidding me?"

"I shit you not."

"What was the problem?"

The girl in black grabbed another box, then headed back across the cobblestones. "The problem was Moses De Lourde. I mean, he would never *tell* anybody *anything*. Always really secretive about what he was looking for. I don't blame those guys down there for being suspicious."

"Do *you* know what he was looking for?"

She shrugged as she shoved the box on board the van. "Moses was always real coy about his agenda, and he had all these crackpot theories."

"What kind of theories?"

"I don't know, stuff about the pre-Mayan culture, human sacrifice, hurricanes."

"Hurricanes?"

"Yeah. Something about rituals and hurricanes but don't ask me to explain it. I was his teaching assistant for three years, and I was always the last one to grasp his stuff."

"Did he find what he was looking for?"

The girl in black paused for a moment, breathing hard from all the exertion. Something glinted in her eyes then. Not exactly anger, not exactly contempt, and not exactly bitterness. But maybe a trace of all three. "You're from the press, right?"

"Look, Sandi, I'm not—"

"Is this on the record?"

"Absolutely not."

"But you think the professor was murdered?"

Maura took a deep breath before answering. "I'm helping with an investigation. Unofficially."

"It's for that FBI dude, right? Ulysses Grant?"

"Grove," Maura corrected with a smile. "But this is all off the record."

"Look, I gotta get outta here." Sandi looked over her shoulder then, as though she were being stalked. It was an acquired tic of many New Orleanians lately. As though an entire region were being stalked by nature. "I *will* tell you this though. The people from Tulane that went down to the Yucatan with De Lourde . . . we got more than we bargained for. You understand what

I'm saying? I mean, Michael started to think De Lourde had done some hoodoo down there or something, had somehow *summoned* that fucking hurricane. Look, I gotta go. And if I were you, I'd do the same."

With that, Ms. Sandi Loper-Herzog turned and went to get her bike.

Maura watched, wondering what in God's name she had gotten herself into this time.

"Put this in! Put this in!" Kaminsky's baritone bark penetrated the incredible noise of the vibrating cabin as the Lockheed sliced through the outer bands. The air was popping from the pressure drop. *"Do you hear me, Grove? Put this in now before I lose the stick!"*

Grove tried to see what the big Russian bear was holding in his right hand, but the plane was shaking so furiously now, and the storm was so loud, it was almost impossible to see or hear a thing. In fact, as far as Grove was concerned, the whole gonzo journey into Hurricane Eve had been a complete failure so far. Outside the portal he could see nothing but an opaque moving wall of gray. That was it. He should have known. They were flying through storm clouds, for God's sake. What did he *think* he was going to see? Or feel? Or intuit? *"Whattya got there, Kay? I can't see it!"*

The cabin had blurred in Grove's vision, his hands clamping down on his armrests so tightly they were going numb. His teeth cracked as the craft lurched, and the engines kept singing out in terrific falsetto howls. Outside, beyond Garfield the Cat, a wall of solid steel gray enveloped the fuselage.

"Something to bite down on!" Kaminsky roared. Thunder banged outside the portals, sounding like

somebody firing a twelve-gauge shotgun at the fuselage. The Russian wrestled with the yoke, yanking at the aileron lever, making the plane climb like crazy just to maintain its altitude. "*It is to keep you from biting your tongue when we hit the eye wall!*"

Kaminsky tossed the hard rubber object to Grove, who nearly dropped it.

Grove looked down at the rubber bicycle handlebar grip in his hand, worn down to a gray nub by human teeth. He took a deep breath and stuck it in his mouth. It tasted bitter and gritty like dirty aspirin. Grove braced himself for the piercing of the eye wall, which the Russian had described a few minutes ago as being similar to riding a balsa wood glider over Niagra Falls.

The eye wall is the deadly Minotaur guarding the soft center of a hurricane, the place where the heat exchange reaches its highest velocity. Wind speeds in the eye wall can reach two hundred miles an hour. Rain spins so fast a single drop can cause more damage than a .38-caliber bullet fired in anger. Strangely, Kaminsky never told Grove what was on the *other* side of the eye wall.

The Lockheed convulsed. Kaminsky cursed the plane and jerked the stick, coaxing another horrible aria from the turbines.

Grove clutched at his armrests, his harness digging into his breastbone. He could not breathe properly around the bike handle in his mouth, and he started hyperventilating. For a brief, surreal instant, he imagined what it would feel like for the aircraft to shatter apart as it penetrated the eye wall, vaporizing in midair.

"*A quarter mile now till the eye!*"

A weird sound began rising up outside the plane, in the slipstream of steel gray rushing over its skin, an eldritch whistling noise that signaled the approaching eye wall. Grove's scalp crawled, and the tiny hairs on his arms and neck bristled at the sound. He had never heard anything like it—a wailing locomotive filtered through the longest, narrowest chamber of a great pipe organ. It was a berserk sound, the sound of nature unhinged. The kind of noise that would have driven cavemen deep into their caves.

"*Five hundred yards!*"

The whistling noise rose. Grove's ears popped. Pressure from his waist belt cut into his bladder as the engines shrieked and cried. A ballpoint pen floated up, needles jumping on the indicators. Grove bit into the rubber spike.

"*A hundred yards!*"

The aircraft began to buck and heave and quake, the engines screaming, the dome lights flickering. The shaking got so bad Grove saw double, then triple, and then everything blurred completely like motion-picture film coming off the sprockets. The horrible ululating whistle drowned Kaminsky's frantic pronouncements.

"*Eye wall in five!*"

Grove tried to cry out, but the slab of rubber blocked his voice. It felt as though the floor was about to rip away. Lights flickered off. Grove vomited around the bike handle, thin strings of bile and saliva looping *upward* in the g-forces.

"*Four!*"

Now there was nothing but the dark vibrating blur, and the shrieking death wails of the dragon, and Grove choking on his own bile, spine rigid as an icicle, hands welded like iron talons to the cold leather armrests.

"*Three!*"

Something cracked in the marrow of the plane, the

turbines coughing, failing, the monstrous whistling noise giving way to an impossible all-encompassing chorus of screams engulfing the Lockheed.

"*Two!*"

Grove closed his eyes and prayed and prayed as the plane went into furious paroxysms of shaking.

"*Contact!*"

The nose smashed into a brick wall in the air, Grove biting down hard and lurching forward against the confines of his chest straps.

There was a loud bang, and the aircraft seemed to slam down hard into a trough in the air, and then it found purchase and thumped a couple of times, fishtailing, and then the shaking stopped. Just like that. It simply ceased. The plane was flying steadily again, and the sudden calm was almost as violent as the shaking.

Grove blinked and tried to focus on the cockpit, the console, Kaminsky, *something* to help him get his bearings back. The lights had flickered back on, and the Russian was saying something; his mouth was moving, but Grove could not hear a word. His ears were ringing profusely and for one panicky instant he wondered if his eardrums had exploded in the plummeting air pressure. He smelled vomit, his face wet with upchuck. Finally he realized Kaminsky was pointing at something.

The portal!

Grove looked over at the window and saw that Garfield the Cat still clung by his suction cups to the small lens of triple-layer Plexiglas. But the strange part—the most incongruous, freaky thing about that window—was the sunlight. A bright band of daylight shone across the rim, slicing down on an angle, spreading across the corrugated floor.

At first Grove thought he was seeing things. He thought maybe all the ungodly turbulence had rattled his marbles loose and now he was having some kind of oxygen-starved, high-altitude hallucination. He glanced at the windscreen that wrapped across the front, and he saw blue sky.

Blue sky?

"We made it! We made it!" Kaminsky's voice finally penetrated Grove's ringing ears. "We are in!"

Grove took the handlebar out of his mouth and croaked, "In where?"

The Russian grinned, his nicotine-stained teeth gleaming dully in the sunlight. "Pay attention, Grove! You are not paying attention!"

Crouched in the dark, the Holy Ghost heard the sudden silence fall like an axe, the smell of the kill thick in his nostrils, deep shadows cloaking him.

The sacred space at last!

Outside the shelter, the eye-wall winds faded as though a switch had been thrown, the thunderous churning noise trailing off, the dwindling tympany in synch with his pulse. He huddled there like a spider in the darkness of that old abandoned mill house on the edge of that silver river, surrounded by bodies, dozens of bodies.

The human remains gave off a meaty, protein-rich smell that aroused the Holy Ghost, fueled his ecstasy, galvanized his nervous system. Now, finally, it was time to harvest the ritual blood, to milk the chattel and make the ceremonial dye.

To lure the manhunter once again into the holy circle of vengeance.

The Lockheed went into a steep turn.

Grove gaped at the surrounding clouds.

"Take a good look, my friend!" Kaminsky urged as he canted the control yoke with one hand, his gravelly voice hoarse from screaming over the noise of the storm. The props hummed steadily now as the plane kept banking in one great circular pattern over the tiny fishing village of Ulmer's Folly. The wind had vanished. Streaks of rain were streaming off the outer shell of the aircraft as it kept banking and banking. "This is as close as a man can get, Grove!"

Grove kept gawking at the clouds. He had witnessed so many things in his life, horrible things, stunning things. He had even been lucky enough to observe one or two *miraculous* things—a meteor shower off the coast of Nova Scotia, his wife Hannah's sleeping face in the predawn light—but nothing compared to this. *Nothing.*

He stared and stared at that coliseum of clouds. Somehow, at some point, through some dark magic that Grove would never be able to comprehend, the sky had turned into a stadium. Vast, sweeping vistas of black thunderheads rose up in all directions as far as the human eye could see like raked seating in some celestial temple of the gods. And yet, *and yet*, the sun shone down from overhead, shone down through the eye.

They were *inside* the hurricane. Simultaneously magnificent and menacing, the hole in the storm had a dizzying, claustrophobic effect on Grove, who made a futile attempt to comment: "Gimme a second—I mean I-I-I've never—I'm not sure what—"

"Concentrate, Grove! Concentrate now!" Kaminsky yelled. "I only have enough fuel to make a couple of revolutions—"

"No!" Grove was shaking his head. "Take us down!"

The Russian shot a glance at Grove. "What did you just say!"

Grove pointed at the floor. "Down! Down! Take us down! I need you to land!"

"Are you insane!"

Grove kept shaking his head. "That was the deal! You agreed to get me inside the eye!"

"*You psycho fruitcake case of nuts!—You are inside the stinking eye!*"

"Shit! *Shit!*" Grove tore his gaze from Kaminsky and then peered down through the portal window at the acreage of waterfront land inside the strange, momentary calm.

In the alien daylight a good chunk of Cape Hatteras was visible, a long swath of Pamlico Sound, and many of the cozy little inlets, wetlands, and eddies—all of which lay bathing in the cold rays of the sun with pristine clarity, as though viewed in a dream.

Even a thousand feet up, Grove could see the checkerboard streets of Ulmer's Folly, many of the cobblestone roads flooded from the storm, the gabled rooftops, the steeples, and the tarred-roof warehouses all glistening in the eerie stillness. But he could not make *sense* of anything, could not make any connection to something as banal and ugly as murder.

The plane hit a bump, shuddering for a moment as it flew over a stretch of clear-air turbulence.

Grove bit down hard, cracking his molars, grabbing

his armrests, and tasting the sour metallic taste of fear on the back of his tongue. He swallowed it back down, shoved it down inside himself. The fear was blocking him, scattering his thoughts, and he struggled to stuff it back down his throat. He turned to Kaminsky. "Damn it, Kay, I need to be on the ground if I'm going to ferret this guy out!"

"What is this ferret you are babbling about?"

"Kay!"

The Russian glowered at Grove. "What in the bloody hell are you talking about?"

Grove clutched at his armrests. "Goddamnit, we talked about this! You promised me—"

"You are one dangerous lunatic, Grove!"

"Be that as it may, I still need to get down there so I can lure this guy out!"

"Grove—"

"He wants *me*, Kay! I told you! People are getting killed because of me! I need to be on the ground!"

"That is not going to happen!"

"I will take full responsibility! Now land this piece of shit right now! Please, Kay! *Take us down!*"

Across the cockpit Kaminsky exhaled a puff of breath, glancing down at the instruments, taking inventory of each bouncing needle. "Try to understand something, Grove!" he called out, tapping a gauge with a ragged fingernail. "We only have enough fuel to get this piece of nuts and bolts back to Camp Lejeune! We are going to have to leave the eye now! Do you understand what I am saying!"

Grove let out an exasperated sigh, turning away and staring down through that portal at the brilliant ant farm of streets and buildings caught like bugs in amber. To the north of Ulmer's Folly, just on the edge of visibility, was the Alligator River, snaking through the wetlands like a dirty gray ribbon. Beyond the river, now engulfed by the dark thunderheads, was historic Kitty Hawk, the sacred, desolate grounds of the Wright brothers' miraculous first flights. Beyond that lay the black, slow-moving oblivion of Hurricane Eve.

"Lima Hotel Tower!" The Russian was talking into his headset now, madly flipping switches. The engines were beginning to whine. "This is Three-Delta, do you copy? Over! Lima Hotel Tower, do you copy!"

The air pressure in the cabin had begun to change again, the whistling noise returning. The back of Grove's scalp bristled, and he felt the air becoming agitated, starting to vibrate, the eye closing in around them, the distant freight train roar of the storm wall approaching.

The terror was palpable, a cold, blunt object forcing its way up Grove's esophagus and into his throat. He wanted to scream, but that other part of him was taking over now. *That's what it's all about, isn't it, the terror, the fear?* he thought, addressing that "unknown subject" in his mind, gazing out through the windscreen at that churning wall of wind dead ahead, maybe a quarter mile away, maybe closer. *You're steeped in it, aren't you? That primordial fear, you're soaked in it, baptized in it . . . and these hurricanes are simply fuel, they're fuel for that nourishing fear.*

Kaminsky was yelling again: *"Grove! Put the rubber piece back in! We're thirty seconds from penetration!"*

Grove realized he still had that bike handlebar cover clutched in his sweaty right hand like a charm, like a talisman, and he quickly wedged it back in his mouth. He barely tasted it this time. He was so transfixed by the sight of that dreamlike landscape down there, awash in sunlight, the floodwater shimmering. He stared and stared, and he knew the key to catching the killer was presenting itself.

A burst of garbled voices fizzed out of the console, and Kaminsky shouted into his mike, *"Lima Hotel Tower! This is Three-Delta! Do you copy?"*

Turbulence punched through the floor, tossing the plane sideways as though it were skating on ice, and Kaminsky fought with the yoke and yelled some more into the headset. The light darkened. High-velocity wisps of clouds began streaming past the windscreen, but Grove had stopped paying attention to the aircraft or his own safety. His attention was riveted to the ground now, to that unreal world laid out like a child's toys in the impossible sunlight.

At a thousand feet in the air a person can make out quite a lot on the ground—a missing shingle on a rooftop, a damaged fire hydrant spewing water, a shopping cart floating across a flooded supermarket parking lot. In those last few seconds before thunderclouds once again engulfed the plane, shutting out all the light, Grove saw two things that would stay with him for the rest of his life.

The first item registered in his brain at the precise moment the Lockheed penetrated the inner wall. The plane began to furiously shake, and rain pelted the fuselage with the force of a thousand fire hoses, and Grove had to clench his jaw and tense his body against the seat just to maintain eye contact with the window. But what he saw down there in that brief instant before the gray darkness returned burned an indelible image on the back of his brain, and stayed there, like the afterglow of a photographer's flash. He saw a flock of blackbirds—or maybe they were gulls, Grove wasn't sure; he had never seen black gulls before—*trapped* in the eye.

The birds kept circling the outer boundaries of the eye wall, making soaring leaps, then darting back toward the center, then curling back for another attempt to pierce the rain band. At this distance, they looked like insects caught in a vast, monolithic killing jar.

The Lockheed roared then, and Grove blinked and clenched and then saw the second thing that would forever live in his memory. It registered in his midbrain in the split second before the plane was engulfed in black clouds, but that single instant was all that Grove needed to see it and compute it, and derive a deeper meaning from it.

It first appeared out of the corner of Grove's eye, way up to the north, beyond the village, almost to Kitty Hawk, up there along the northernmost edges of the storm's eye: a vivid streak of color against the silvery gray landscape, glinting in the dying sunlight. And right before the light went away, as the plane lurched and shook and drifted slightly to the northwest, the streak of color came into better focus, and Grove realized it was a deep scarlet.

He swallowed hard and felt his heart rise up in his gorge: The narrow channel of the Alligator River that skirted the northern edge of Ulmer's Folly was now running red with human blood!

The image was gone within a millisecond as the plane plunged back into the vortex of rain and wind, but Grove registered every last detail on his mind screen—the way the river snaked willy-nilly through the ramshackle district of warehouses and foundries, the deep crimson dye clouding the water like ink in swirls and eddies, as though someone had spilled paint at its source. Even the stone banks were stained red at certain points—a stark, ghastly abomination overlaid on this charming little picture-postcard fishing village.

Then the hurricane gobbled all the light, and Grove saw nothing but gray out the window, and Kaminsky rode the bucking bronco screaming and cursing westward toward the safety of Camp Lejeune.

But Grove knew the truth.

He knew it as certainly as he knew his own name.

That river of blood was meant for him.

9

That night, in a brooding, inclement New Orleans, restlessly pacing the cluttered rooms of the late professor's French Quarter apartment, Maura County inadvertently stumbled upon the key to the hurricane killer's identity.

At first, of course, she had no idea what the contents of that mysterious videotape actually meant. The hand-labeled VHS tape was simply one of the many artifacts filed away in the professor's personal archives, and Maura was not exactly comfortable with the prospect of snooping around De Lourde's things. She kept expecting the old coot to jump out of the shadows and play her some Fats Domino on his Rockola, or fire up his old dusty projector with an old Bogart movie. To make matters worse, Hurricane Fiona was looming. Her imminent arrival was constantly being announced on the choruses of gulf winds and rattling shutters.

Most of New Orleans had already evacuated, and forecasters were predicting a storm that could very well rival Katrina. The system had already slammed into the eastern coastline of Mexico, a thousand miles to the south, and was in the process of transforming.

It was happening way up in the troposphere over

South America. Way up in the upper air mass where weather lives. A new high-altitude wind was blowing, spinning the anticyclonic molecules in the same direction as the cyclonic molecules below. Weeks later, weather experts would call this a historically unprecedented event, but right now nobody had any idea what was happening. The cyclonic winds were suddenly fed with a sort of superfuel as the hurricane's engine gathered energy from the vast oceanic area around the storm, pumping it back into the storm's center, and the anticyclone continued to respond, turning faster and faster and faster.

Fiona was experiencing what hurricanologists refer to as "explosive deepening." And she was now heading due north, across the Gulf of Mexico, toward the United States. Most estimates showed her ultimately striking the city of New Orleans sometime within the next twenty four hours. But more importantly, she was the spawn of a monstrous marriage, a marriage of global climactic change and freakish rises in average water temperatures across the Pacific, an epochal period not unlike the one about which Maura County once wrote in *Discover* magazine years ago.

All of which served to make Maura even more jittery, and more awkward and uncomfortable, as she rifled through De Lourde's files.

In those tense hours before she stumbled upon the videotape, she found plenty of tantalizing references to those "crackpot" theories about which Sandi Herzog spoke, references to De Lourde's "little rogue study" and "my notorious project" and then, perhaps most intriguing, repeated references to "the hurricane affair." Like a hound on the scent, Maura began digging deeper and deeper into the professor's journals, unraveling the threads of De Lourde's connection to hurricanes.

Most of the entries were scrawled in haphazard script with grease pencil at high altitudes, others jotted during virtual whiteouts in leaking tents. The gist of the story was this: De Lourde had convinced the British Royal Society of Archaeology to fund a trip to the Yucatan to study unidentified Toltec rituals, the evidence for which had been suggested by fossilized ruins of sacrificial temples found in the mountains of Campeche. De Lourde brought along a ragtag group of grad students and gadflies, including his two best students, Sandi Loper-Herzog and Michael Doerr.

The first week of the trip seemed to go fairly well. De Lourde established a base camp, started a dig, discovered more evidence of sacrificial rites on the mountaintop, and sent back word that he believed now that countless animals such as goats and hares were sacrificed there to the gods of the harvest. But then Hurricane Helena hit the following Monday night, chewing through Cazumel and clawing up the eastern slopes of the Yucatan.

In his diary De Lourde managed to document the terrible grandeur of the storm:

> *It began around suppertime. Since we were so isolated, none of us had heard any forecasts that week. One of our translators said something about a tropical storm brewing out there, but we ignored it, thinking we were high enough, and far enough away from the coast, that it would never reach us. Arrogant stupidity is actually the coin of the realm among my colleagues and me.*
>
> *Anyhow . . . around five o'clock, the rains*

came, and the wind started lashing up the side of the mountain. We tried to batten down the hatches, tried to secure the specimen tables and hunker down in our tents, but the damn bitch just swooped up on us so suddenly. I don't know if the mountain somehow magnified the hurricane, maybe caused some kind of wind tunnel effect, but soon we were in hundred-mile-an-hour winds, and the rains were so hard they were like nail guns. The sky seemed to rage suddenly—a fireworks display of lightning and swirling rainclouds.

Half our camp has been torn away as I write this. Michael went screaming down the side of the mountain an hour ago. I guess the rest of the party made it to the bus, which has apparently either departed or sunk into the mud. Now there's only six of us, and I'm paralyzed here in my sad little tent, waiting out the storm. Miguel told me a few minutes ago that she is now called Hurricane Helena. How rich. The gentile Greek goddess of healing. How perfectly ironic. Now nothing makes sense but my awful little pet hypothesis.

And on and on it went, getting more and more surreal and desperate with each entry. Maura was transfixed by it. She kept running across that strange reference to De Lourde's so-called pet hypothesis.

It was obviously something he had cooked up about the ancient Toltec civilization, and it seemed to somehow embarrass him. But what hypothesis? What was he talking about?

Maura didn't realize it then, but she was very close to learning the answers to all her questions.

The videotape would hold the key.

* * *

At that moment, up in North Carolina, in the foggy darkness, Hurricane Eve would go the way of all tropical storms. She would slam up against an opposing front pushing down off the Chesapeake, and by midnight she would dwindle into a steady gully washer that would dump eighteen inches across the tristate area.

In her wake, flood-ravaged farms and villages from Wilmington to Richmond gasped for air. Half the region lay underwater, powerless, completely dark, the tops of gables and steeples poking out of the black, shimmering waters. Property damage estimates ranged from $750 million to nearly a billion dollars, which bumped the overall damage estimates for the season so far up to almost twenty billion dollars. It would turn out to be the worst hurricane season on record, and it wormed through Grove's soul like a parasitic cancer as he huddled that night in a deserted barracks at Camp Lejeune.

He lay in the darkness, staring at the ceiling, his long body stretched out on a cot that groaned and squeaked with every twitch. Dressed only in his skivvies, his milk-chocolate skin gleaming with a film of sweat, he could feel the humidity oozing from his pores, seeping from every seam and joint in the aging building. The storm season had turned muggy, temperatures creeping into the eighties, even at night.

The Russian lay two cots away, a beached whale, his big nude belly looking like a pale hillock in the darkness. He was snoring as loudly as a cement mixer. Grove closed his eyes and tried to get some much-needed sleep . . . but sleep was far out of reach. His heart thumped. His blood simmered in his veins. He stared at the ceiling fan directly above him, stared at the center of its housing. He stared and stared at that little decorative brass hub.

It looked like an eye.

Grove was becoming aware of something turning inside him, something powerful and electric and primal. He had first become aware of it a year ago, when he had awakened from his ordeal in the cabin with the exorcist, Father Carrigan, his mom, and Professor De Lourde. Whatever Grove had absorbed—back in the aftermath of his confrontation with the murderous Richard Ackerman on that mountainside—it had been expelled from his body in that cabin that day through ancient rituals. It had been purged like a fever or a stomach flu, vomited out in a paroxysm of pain. But something had lingered inside him. A trace element, a residue. Maybe it was something that had been there all along, and the possession had simply *denatured* it.

But whatever it was, it now smoldered in him like a white-hot ember: an almost narcotic need to hunt, to stop the killer, to pierce the eye and track this evil freak down, and then devour him. This compulsion overrode everything else. It was more than vengeance for his friend, more than outrage at the river of blood, more than simple fulfillment of his duty as a criminal profiler. If asked to explain it, to put it into words, to truly articulate it, Grove would be hard pressed. In fact, he was probably reacting precisely the way the perp wanted him to, marching blithely into a trap.

So be it.

So fucking be it.

* * *

Around two o'clock that morning, after a couple of hours of fitful, nightmare-plagued sleep, Maura County climbed out of Professor De Lourde's ornate brass bed and went into the little kitchenette cluttered with spice racks, booze, and well-seasoned gourmet cookware. It was hard to believe the owner of this kitchen no longer existed. In the fridge Maura found lunch meats still in their blister packs, fresh fruit still in the crisper. The old man must have bought these oranges and mangoes the day before he died. Unopened containers of yogurt sat on one shelf, a half-gallon carton of 2-percent still viable inside the door. *To expire before your milk,* Maura thought morosely, *is there a more pathetic reality?*

Her hands shook as she made herself a carafe of chicory coffee in the professor's fancy little coffee press and lit the first Marlboro of the morning. Then she sat at the wrought-iron table next to the French doors and got some welcome nicotine and caffeine into her system.

A few minutes later she went back into the bedroom to look for her cell phone among all the leather-bound diaries tented across the foot of the bed, stacked on the bedside table, arrayed across the floor and under the bed—many of them open to key entries that Maura had flagged with yellow Post-It notes. She found her phone under a notebook and was about to dial Grove's number when she noticed something sticking out of the bottom of a bookshelf that she hadn't noticed before.

She knelt and took a closer look. It was a TDK videotape in a store-bought box with a label on the spine scrawled in De Lourde's flowery cursive hand:

U. GROVE—DEPOSS.—4/28/05—CONFIDENTIAL

Maura's fingertips positively tingled as she turned the videotape over and looked for other markings, other labels, other hints at what it might contain. *U. Grove* had initially caught her eye, but it was the fragment *deposs* that particularly intrigued her. She looked at the date and realized that 4/28/05 was the dreaded weekend immediately following Richard Ackerman's violent demise.

The same weekend during which Ulysses Grove had suffered through a series of torturous exorcism rituals.

The gathering winds moaned outside De Lourde's shuttered windows as Maura carried the videotape out into the living room. The professor owned no TV, but he had an old beat-up VCR wired to his computer, which he used to view taped interviews and academic programs.

Maura loaded the tape, then clicked the little video screen icon on the Mac. Her heart thudded in her chest as she watched the virtual screen fill the monitor. Then she pressed the Play button, and the first jumpy hand-held images of a psychotic, shackled Ulysses Grove appeared on the screen.

For quite a few moments, her gaze riveted, Maura forgot to even breathe.

"Excuse me, folks! FBI! FBI!" Ulysses Grove called out over the dull roar of the early-morning rain and voices, pushing his way through the crowd, holding his ID tag aloft with as much authority as he could muster, his long trench coat billowing in the gusts, his muscles aching from all the excitement of flying into the eye, and then spending a restless night at Camp Lejeune on a bunk that resembled a concrete slab.

He approached an old antebellum wooden footbridge, separating the cordon of gapers from the bloodstained riverbank. The water level was high, only a few feet from the edge of the bridge, the current still hectic and unpredictable. The paramedics looked miserable as they stood thigh-deep on the bank, dressed in hazmat suits, working in the mist, dragging white-swaddled corpses off the police pontoon. The bodies had been collected upriver, a couple tangled in the wreckage of a fishing skiff, a few more in the weeds by the yacht club, several floating helter-skelter around the bends and turns of the silvery Alligator.

"Morning, Deputy," Grove said with a nod as he approached the sheriff's deputy with the Fuller brush mustache and plastic-wrapped Stetson hat. Grove's knees still felt a little watery from all the excitement, his nerves jangled from the lack of antidepressants; he moved with the tentative quality of someone who had just had major surgery. Just for an instant, as he approached the deputy, Grove saw a glint of contempt behind the lawman's blue-gray eyes, a remnant of an Old South that still leered at the presence of an uppity, slick-talking *colored* FBI agent—*colored,* no less—colored and acting all superior. "I'm Special Agent Grove, this is Special Agent Kaminsky," Grove said and jerked a thumb at the hulking Russian, who stood behind him, restlessly smoking a cheroot in his yellow rain slicker. The big man looked more like a drunken whaler than an FBI agent. "Wanted to get a look at the fatality situation," Grove explained, indicating the bloody cocoons coming out of the river.

At this proximity, in the overcast morning light, the

bloody water looked purplish black, as though beets had stewed in it. There was an odor in the misty air that Grove could not identify, a chemical smell like rotten eggs masked by cleanser.

"Well, I'll tell ya," the deputy said and tipped his hat brim toward the flooded river, and the white-clad mummies being lifted out of the fast-moving water. "Seventeen years with the sheriff's police, I ain't never seen nothing like it. Like something outta the goddamn book of Revelation."

"Bad one, huh?" Grove commiserated.

"Ain't just that. We've had plenty of blowers around here before, see a whole slew of 'em every spring. Never saw fatalities like this one though, never. Turned the goddamn river red."

Grove asked where they found these bodies.

"That's just it," the deputy said, wiping moisture from his mustache. "Found a lot of folks upriver, right around the bend at Pickman's Ferry." He shook his head, droplets spraying off his Stetson. "Like they all just collected there."

"Mind if I take a look?" Grove gestured toward the clutch of bodies.

"Help yourself."

The deputy called to a couple of the paramedics who were coming up the adjacent bank, ankle deep in bloody river water, carrying an e-vac gurney. They paused and eased their load to the sodden ground. The white-shrouded body landed with a splat. Grove told Kaminsky to wait there, and the Russian just shrugged noncommittally.

Grove came around the end of the bridge, trundled down the bank, and knelt in the mud by the corpse.

"You got my attention . . . now show me something

I can use," he mumbled under his breath after putting on his rubber gloves—which were still wadded inside his wrinkled Armani sport coat. He peeled back the white plastic fold covering the dead man's face. It was the father of the two teenage boys, the same father who had chased the family dog Mitzie out into the crosshairs of a madman. The man's face was devastated with lacerations, his bloody gums revealing rows of ragged holes where his teeth had once been, his left eye reduced to a gaping black socket full of bloody pulp.

Grove rose, thanked the paramedics, then started north toward the mill house. The rain had momentarily lifted, but the wind gusts were still heavy with brine and metal, and suffused with the reek of ozone. Grove scanned the flooded pea-gravel road for further evidence, further invitations meant only for him, only for his eyes.

He saw constellations of broken glass, random tangles of newspaper, and splinters of wooden siding torn asunder by the hurricane. He saw odd little things, too, like a child's plastic rubber duck floating upside down as though drowned, and a car's rearview mirror lying cracked in the gravel, reflecting the mercurial gray sky. But none of these items resonated for him, and he was about to turn back . . . when he saw the pattern of human by-products arranged in the muck.

He paused suddenly and stared at the teeth and blood and tissues. They had been embedded in the hard-packed mud like a makeshift mosaic, forming a crude design. Grove stared and stared. Thunder rumbled in the distance. The row of teeth led his gaze to a sheltered area behind the corner of the mill house, where more human material was arrayed in a cryptic design on the ground.

Grove went over and inspected the grass.

"Holy Christ," he whispered under his breath as he looked at the display. An untrained eye would have missed it. Storms have a way of depositing things on beaches and riverbanks in strange, Rorschach-like configurations. In 1989, Hurricane Hugo, according to a small sect of local Catholics, stirred the sand into the spitting image of the Virgin Mary. But right now Grove was staring at the work of a highly organized, highly dangerous psychopathic personality—an individual who knew something very personal and very secret about Ulysses Grove.

Grove reached down and parted the saw grass with his rubber-gloved hands.

The ragged little teeth made a huge oval in the weeds, maybe six or eight feet in diameter. A row of human organs, purple and glistening, lay in the center of the oval. A blood-dipped writing instrument—either a palm frond or a finger—had rendered the ancient symbols with astonishing clarity, as though they were traced from a book. A human eyeball lay nestled in its nucleus. Grove recognized the seal as readily as Moses De Lourde had recognized the same symbol on the window of his second-floor bathroom last week in those awful revelatory moments before the rain of Hurricane Cassandra washed it away.

Grove stood up, took a step back, and looked at the whole display.

"Kaminsky!"

The alarm in Grove's voice made the entire clutch of reporters look up in stunned silence.

10

Maura couldn't move, couldn't breathe, couldn't blink. Her eyes could not leave that little square inset on De Lourde's computer screen as it played back a crackling, grainy, shaky, handheld home movie of an exorcism.

The footage showed Ulysses Grove unlike Maura had ever seen him, had ever *conceived* him. Scarred and feverish and wild-eyed in his underwear, he was tied to a padded wooden trundle bed in a knotty-pine cabin somewhere. The image awkwardly zoomed in to a close-up of his contorted face. His jaw kept clenching and seizing up as though electricity were jolting through him, his chapped, blackened lips trembling fitfully. His sputtering voice kept gasping unidentified expletives.

It sounded to Maura like a dead language—Sumerian or Toltec—and it grated at her ears. She had seen films of actual real-life exorcisms on the Learning Channel and in documentaries. She had heard field recordings of missionaries casting out demons in Third World backwaters. She had even written articles on the subject for *Discover.* In fact, she realized now what the abbreviation *"deposs"* stood for: *depossession*. A clinical term used by psychologists for any ritual or ceremony meant to cast out parasitic personalities. Whether or not the psychiatric community believed in the devil was open for discussion. But Maura had never witnessed a friend or loved one in this state. It was beyond excruciating to watch.

On-screen, De Lourde's camera panned suddenly, jerkily, to reveal two other individuals standing over Grove: Father Carrigan and Grove's mother, Vida, whom Maura had met and adored and respected. Vida looked drenched in sweat as she waved a smoking hank of ceremonial wheat over her son and chanted in Swahili: *"Nge—nge!—nge!—NGE!—Nnn!"*

Meanwhile Father Carrigan was murmuring litanies from his dog-eared book of Catholic rites as Grove jerked and jerked and jerked back and forth on the bed as though he were being electrocuted, the padded ropes and creaking bed frame barely containing him, his skivvies ragged with blood and bile. Maura literally jerked backward at the force of Grove's scream, a bloodcurdling wail.

"The Archangel Michael commands you!" Carrigan cried out in a righteous voice. *"Leave this innocent soul this instant!"* The priest suddenly reared back in surprise, his glass vial of holy water flying out of his hand and shattering against the knotty pine wall behind him.

The image on-screen suddenly blurred, violently twisting sideways, as De Lourde's camera slipped from his hands and fell to the floor. The camera landed on the hardwood, and the image came back into focus for a moment—albeit sideways—revealing a surreal moment that Maura would never forget, as long as she lived, an image that would never leave her memory.

Grove's beleaguered body—blackened, scarred, and savaged by demonic possession—had suddenly and spontaneously jerked upward into a semisitting position . . . and then something extraordinary happened. A *second* body—an astral body that appeared initially as pure white light—tore through the flesh of the first like a butterfly ripping out of its chrysalis. It appeared on the sideways video as a glowing, blurry double image.

Then this *second* Grove lurched forward across the foot of the bed and tumbled to the floor. And then, just for an instant, captured forever in that sideways video, bisected down the middle by the cracked lens, there were *two* Groves in that cabin: a blackened husk of the man on the bed, and a glistening, damp, exhausted version sprawled on the warped oak floor, and then, almost instantly, the shell of the man on the bed began to dissolve, literally dissolve, as the sound of an alien wind moaned through the cabin like a dying beast.

The figure blurred and undulated for a moment, like a sculpture made of smoke, then began to whirl off the bed, a column of noxious gas, rising and swirling upward, penetrating the ceiling and then vanishing on a faint, torturous shriek. Thunder rumbled suddenly on the sound track, and in the background, through a window, the gray sky above the treetops was partially visible, roiling like a cauldron, a black whirlpool—as deep and opaque as squid ink—as the black charred air shot upward from the roof of the cabin, darkening the horizon like burned skeletal fingers clawing the heavens.

Lightning crackled and veined the sky, and the rains started. But none of that held Maura's gaze. None of that transfixed her as much as what was visible in the foreground of the video.

In the foreground, Grove lay on the floor, clad only in his boxer shorts and bloody bandages, still semiconscious, and a little delirious, but apparently okay. But he was alive, and he was whole, and he was back. Vida went over to him, and took his battered body in her arms. He closed his eyes and clung to his mother and tried to breathe normally again. Nobody said anything for quite some time as the blessed sound of the rain filled the cabin and the video continued to run—sideways—in the fallen camera.

Maura didn't know it then, but contained within the pixels of that video—the very image of Grove sprawled on the floor of that cabin after his deliverance—was the key to the Holy Ghost's identity. It lay within that shaky, handheld footage of that cabin, visible now for the first time at such a low angle.

The design drawn on the floor in red paint by the priest, the one that circumnavigated the bed within which Grove had writhed and tossed, was known in some religious circles as the Seal of Solomon. To the more outré practitioner, it had come to be known as the Hexagonal Circle. It was made up of two equilateral interlaced triangles within a circle, and was used in binding unwilling spirits in magical ceremonies. This one was unique in that it had another symbol *inside* it—a pentagram—with two points facing upward.

It looked like this:

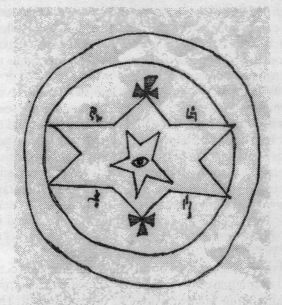

But Maura had no idea what she was looking at here, had no idea that something so significant lay on the periphery of the video. She had a vague memory of studying magical symbols in graduate school while she was working on her master's in anthropology, but could not remember what the pentagram meant with the two points facing upward (as it was in this symbol on the floor of the cabin).

She had forgotten that the two points represented the horns of Satan.

In other words, *pure evil*.

"Pull over here!" Grove ordered from the Jeep's passenger seat. For the last twenty miles or so, they had been heading inland, away from the disaster area along the coast, while Grove sketched on a shopworn spiral-bound notebook the talismanic symbol scrawled in blood and body parts in the weeds along the banks of the Alligator River.

"Where did you say? Here? Into this place!" Ivan Kaminsky, his yellow mack still dripping on the seat, was squinting to see through the fogged windshield as the Jeep thumped along the barren two-lane. They were cruising past a row of roadside businesses outside Greenville, North Carolina, most of the stores still closed down and boarded in the wake of Eve. Distant thunder rumbled on the horizon, the rains intermittent now, the air smelling of metal and rot, still agitated in the shifting storm systems.

"Yes! Here!"

Ivan Kaminsky yanked the wheel, and the Jeep cobbled over a gravel shoulder, then scraped into a narrow parking lot in front of a desolate little strip mall. The Jeep came to an abrupt stop, bumping a cement parking block—the Russian drove as vigorously and hell-bent as he flew—and Kaminsky shoved it into Park, then turned off the engine. In front of them, a neon sign buzzed behind a grimy window, sending a sickly pink hue through the mist around them, painting the windshield with a magenta bruise. It said LIQUOR—BAIT—LOTTO.

"What in the hell are we doing now?"

"Just give me a second," Grove said, finishing his sketch of the shape within a shape.

A few minutes ago he had thrown his raincoat and jacket over the backseat, and now he sat in his shirt-sleeves, his bronze face glistening with sweat. Without his field gear, his cameras and recording devices, he felt naked and amateurish. But this was the only way. Back in Ulmer's Folly, he had been forced to slip away from the suspicious deputy without any pictures or tracings of the bloody display. He didn't want the sheriff's department calling the bureau just yet, or nosy reporters catching wind of foul play going on during a hurricane. And yet, the deputy had still been curious, and kept saying, "You saw somethin' up there, huh? You saw somethin', didn't ya? You saw somethin'?"

Grove had *indeed* seen something, something critical, and he now drew it as best he could on a page of ruled paper in his tattered notebook. Of course, he could easily have drawn the basic shape from memory—the pentagram within a hexagram—which Father Carrigan had painted on the floor of that cabin a year ago. The symbol would forever be burned into Grove's midbrain.

He would never forget waking in his mother's arms in that airless cabin, as limp and damp as a used washrag, feeling as if he had just been underwater, drowning in the deepest part of the ocean, and had struggled back to the surface, inch by inch. He had noticed the mysterious symbol on the floor right before he had broken down into racking sobs in his mother's bosom. Later, Father Carrigan had told Grove that the symbol was ancient, from the gnostic gospels, and very few scholars even knew about it. It represented the symbol of evil contained and neutralized by the larger symbol of good around it.

Kaminsky was gazing down at the sketch, pursing his lips incredulously. "Are you at last going tell me what that is? Or do you insist on keeping me in the darkness?"

Grove told him it was in the weeds next to the old

mill house back in Ulmer's Folly, and chances were good that it was part of the killer's ritual, and it was also why the killer wanted to confront Grove.

Kaminsky made a face. "Does that say 'human eyeball'? Is that what that says, Grove?"

"Yes, Kay, that's what it says."

"Those symbols," Kaminsky said and pointed a big, nicotine-stained finger at the diagram. "Those look Sumerian to me, or possibly Egyptian?"

Grove shook his head. "Old Testament. Hebrew. They have to do with binding spirits."

"Dick Lupoff is the best," Kaminsky said, pulling a Garcia cheroot cigar from his breast pocket. "I would get Dick Lupoff to look at that."

Grove looked at him. "Who?"

"Agent Richard Lupoff down at Quantico, best cryptologoist in the field."

"I don't need a cryptologist, Kay, these symbols are not encrypted. They're from a magical ceremony. The same ceremony my friends conducted to save my life last year."

Kaminsky raised his bushy eyebrow. "You are talking about this nonsense that they did to you on Sun City? This exorcism?"

"That's right."

"How would this suspect know about that?"

Grove shrugged. "That's what I'm going to find out." Then he nodded at the Russian's cigar. "You're not going to light that up, are you?"

"Grove, it is my vehicle. If you want first class, buy a ticket." The Russian pulled out his Zippo, snapped it, and sparked the tip of his cheroot. The cigar crackled and filled the interior with an acrid blue cloud. "What are we doing here, anyway?"

Grove opened his door. "Wait here. I'll be right back." He got out, raised his collar against the wet wind, and hustled across the lot to the liquor store.

Of course it was open. Liquor stores are the cockroaches of retail: Even during the direst emergencies, they are the first to open and the last to close. An electronic doorbell chimed as Grove went in and searched the blazing fluorescent aisles and sticky floor displays for the vodka aisle. He looked for the Stolichnaya, found none, then settled for a bottle of Kettle-One. He also selected a package of smoked almonds, a bottle of water, and an energy bar for himself.

An acne-scarred teenager in a Dave Matthews Band T-shirt bagged his items. Grove asked if there was a bus stop anywhere nearby, and the kid said there *was* one, actually, right at the end of this very strip mall.

When Grove returned to the Jeep with the booze, Kaminsky was on the cell phone.

"And what is the point of impact?" he was saying, looking a little tense now, stroking his scraggly beard. "Yes, the eye, and the P-O-I, tell me *exactly* where it is being forecast." He listened and shook his head. "This is not a good thing . . . and you are certain about this, you are confident about the category rating?" More listening. "What does FEMA say? Have they evacuated?" Listening, head shaking. "This is not a pleasant situation, Joyce." A sigh. "Thank you, Joyce."

He clicked the cell phone off with an exasperated flourish, snubbing out his cheroot.

Grove looked at him. "What?"

"Joyce Melvoin, an old dear friend of mine at the National Weather Service." He looked at Grove. "Your lady friend is down in New Orleans at this present moment in time, is that not correct?"

Grove said she was, and he was planning on joining her as soon as he could get down there.

"I am not so sure that is a good idea, my friend."

"Why not?"

"Because an angry bitch from the Caribbean Sea by the name of Fiona is on her way."

Grove asked the Russian to explain. Kaminsky told Grove all about Hurricane Fiona, and the high probability that she would decimate the city of New Orleans by the following morning.

Grove listened intently, and when the Russian was done, Grove handed the man the bottle of Kettle-One. "I appreciate all your help, Kay, I really do."

Kaminsky looked at the fifth of vodka nestled in his big gnarled hands. "What is this?"

Grove looked at him. "You said the eye is forecast to reach the city sometime around midnight tonight, is that right?"

"That is correct."

Grove nodded. "Then that's where I gotta go."

Kaminsky frowned. "On the ground you are talking about."

"That's right. And I want to thank you, Kay. For everything."

"In the eye of Fiona you think you are going to catch this crazy bastard."

Just for an instant Grove flashed back to those black-birds caught in that horrible vast cage of clouds . . . and the pale, ruined, painted face of Moses De Lourde in his coffin . . . and the bone-white dust devil of his recurring dream. "I told you, Kay, that's where he does his business, in the eye. That's where I've gotta go." Grove gestured to the south, toward the far end of the parking lot. "There's a bus stop right down there. I can catch a Greyhound to Raleigh, then catch a commuter down to Tallahassee or Atlanta. Get into New Orleans through the back door."

Kaminsky looked at the vodka. "I thought I had heard it all, Grove." He opened the vodka, took a lusty sip, grimaced at the wonderful burn, then rolled his window down and tossed the bottle out. It shattered on the rainy pavement. "I truly thought I had heard it all."

"Kay—"

The Russian burned his gaze into Grove. "If you think you are going to waltz right into the worst storm in North America since the nineteenth century without someone with some hurricane expertise, you are not only crazy, Grove, but you are arrogant beyond belief."

"Kay, I—"

"Going down there and getting yourself killed like that . . . giving me all that guilt!" he grumbled as he turned the key, firing up the Jeep. "You would enjoy that, would you not, Grove!"

"Kay—"

"Buckle that seat belt, asshole." He slammed the Jeep into reverse, then tore out of there in a flurry of exhaust and a cloud of mist.

Grove could not suppress his smile. "Kay . . . thanks. That's all. Just . . . thanks."

The Russian was shaking his head as he got back on the highway. "You better call that girlfriend of yours, and tell her to get her head down. That is . . . if she has not already evacuated."

Grove pulled out his phone and quickly dialed Maura's cell number.

11

Maura was driving the rental car down a deserted, windswept St. Charles Avenue, balancing a cup of coffee and a sheet of MapQuest directions on her lap, when the cell phone chirped. She picked it up, thumbed it on, and propped it against her ear. "Ulysses? That you?"

Through the earpiece came a reassuring baritone: "Hey, kiddo."

"Thank God. I was worried you got blown out to sea."

"Still alive and kicking . . . where are you?"

"I'm in the Garden District. I had to get out of that apartment. I was getting cabin fever." There was no humor in her voice. She glanced at her watch. It was nearly 8:00 a.m., and yet the city was practically deserted. She gazed out the window at the gray, misty morning. "I guess I just couldn't stand to be alone in there anymore."

"I don't blame you, kiddo." Grove's voice softened. "Did you spend the night there?"

"Yeah . . . and I saw the video."

"What video?"

Maura sighed. "The one that De Lourde made last year, in the cabin."

There was a pause. "Oh. . . ."

"God, Ulysses."

"I told him to burn that thing."

"I've never seen anything like it," she said, her hands white-knuckle taut on the steering wheel. "I don't know what to say, I just—"

"You don't have to say anything," Grove's voice broke in. "It happened, it's over now. I don't remember much of it."

"I had no idea."

"Maura, listen . . . should you be out and about right now? I understand it's getting pretty dicey down there."

"I thought I'd go see if this kid Michael Doerr was still in town. Remember the kid from the funeral?"

Grove told her he remembered a skinny, shy kid in a tuxedo shirt.

"That's him. And get this. The Herzog girl told me an interesting little fact about this kid. Evidently he and Moses were more than student and teacher."

Another pause. "No kidding. Moses never mentioned it."

"Anyway . . . the Herzog girl gave me his address. I thought I'd ask young Mr. Doerr about the Yucatan fiasco. If he hasn't already evacuated."

"Just be careful, don't get caught in the storm. They're saying this is going to be a bad one, they're saying it's not only worse than Cassandra, but it's going to rival Katrina."

Maura shook her head, gazing with a faint little shudder out the rain-streaked windshield at the bedraggled storefronts and boarded Victorian homes. She could not conceive of a storm the magnitude of Katrina once again assaulting this poor, battered town. It would be like plunging a knife into a barely healed wound.

Before Katrina, St. Charles Avenue was an old, graceful, sprawling divided boulevard with streetcar lines running down its median, flanked by endless rows of live oaks looming over its center like the ancient spirits of Confederate sentries. On any given day, the stately plantation homes that once lined the street would give the neighborhood an air of old southern charm. But not now. Not in this crippled, post-Katrina New Orleans. Now, in the darkening sky, and the ominous cacophony of sirens and Gulf Coast winds, St. Charles exhibited a haunted, sinister quality. Many of the homes were simply gone, their cordoned sites like flooded craters in some wasted landscape of the dead. The ones that still stood wore masks of warped plywood and moldy particleboard, some of the turrets and wings still gashed open or torn away like great broken dollhouses. The trees looked diseased and denuded. Trash tumbled and skittered across the walks. Streetlights cycled ceaselessly, silently, impotently, directing nobody. Every few moments a raincoat-clad person would dart across a storefront or the mouth of an alley, clutching some essential belonging, hurrying to get out of town before this latest dragon arrived.

Maura sighed. "Yeah, I heard something about a storm coming. Are you driving down?"

"Yeah, should be there by early evening, if we can slip through the e-vac cordons."

"Ulysses—"

"My friend Ivan is being foolhardy enough to drive me down there. He's forgotten more about storms than either of us will ever know, and we'll need his expertise if—"

"Ulysses, what are you cooking up in that big brain of yours?"

"What do you mean?"

"C'mon . . . you said you wanted me to help. Okay, I'm helping, but you gotta be honest with me."

"Of course."

"You're waiting for the eye to come, aren't you? That's what you're really hoping for."

After a long pause, Grove's voice returned, dropping an octave, becoming deathly serious. He explained how he had found a symbol at the scene up in North Carolina, a symbol drawn in blood by the killer, a symbol that matched a magical talisman commonly used in exorcisms. "It was used in *my* ceremony, Maura," he said after an awkward pause. "The one last year, the one at Geisel's cabin in Virginia. The same exact symbol."

For a moment, Maura could not speak. The symbol on the floor of that video . . . the pentagram within a hexagram. "Oh my God," she finally uttered. "You're kidding me, you're talking about the one on the floor?"

"Yep."

"Jesus Christ."

Static on the other end. "—Maura?—"

"I'm here, I'm still here," she said, but she felt like slamming on the brakes, turning around, and getting the hell out of there. "I'm just trying to process all this. . . ."

It was as though she were losing her grip on reality, little by little, like a person clinging to an icy precipice. Never mind that creepy home video . . . or her night-mare-ridden sleep. She had been flashing back to her confrontation with the Sun City Killer, more and more often, *during the light of day*. Little things would trigger a memory: slapping a mosquito, seeing a droplet of blood on her arm; glimpsing the ragged, rawboned expression on a homeless person's face; hearing the wind humming through high-tension wires. But despite all this she could not tear herself away from this rotting, sinking ship of a city. As long as there was something left unresolved, undone, something nagging at her—she would stick around in the face of insurmountable odds. Maybe she thought she could still change Grove. *Sure, Maura, and the rich will start paying more taxes, and politicians will start telling the truth, and monkeys will fly out of your ass.*

"I understand what you're saying, kiddo," Grove's voice buzzed in her ear. "And I don't expect you to wait around for us all day. You ought to get your butt out of there as soon as you can."

"Shut up," Maura said with a softness in her voice that surprised even her. "I just said I'm trying to get a handle on all this, I'm not talking about—" All at once Maura saw the littered grounds of Audubon Park looming on her left, the water-stained amphitheater of southern pines and cottonwoods lining the corner of Exposition Boulevard. Across the street rose the massive wrought-iron entrance to Tulane's south campus. Beyond the ivy-clogged archway lay the genteel white columns—now permanently tattooed by mossy flood stains—that bordered the quad. The campus was completely deserted and obscured by veils of mist. "Whoops, there it is," Maura said into her cell.

"There *what* is?"

"My turn."

She reached the corner of Calhoun and St. Charles, turned right on Calhoun, then started up the eastern edge of campus. On her left lay acres of massive old redbrick classroom buildings, many of them still boarded or shrouded with flood plastic, looking ghostly in the silver rain. The school had a decadent Old South feel about it, like a vast crumbling plantation taken over by zombies. "I'll call you back, Ulysses," Maura said into the phone, "give you a progress report."

"Good luck," said the voice, and then with a *click!* the call was disconnected.

The street names in this town had always amused Maura like those of no other city. Some were named for Confederate war heroes, others for obscure Napoleonic victories such as Prytania, Constantinople, or Baronne. Many were unpronounceable to the uninitiated—Tchoupitoulas, Polymnia, Terpsichore. But each one was part of that steaming stew pot of languages and influences that reflected the city's lurid history, as well as its refusal to die.

Michael Doerr lived in a modest little corner of this fermenting cauldron known among Tulane intelligentsia as the "student ghetto"—the six-square-block neighborhood just north of the university that lay completely submerged by floodwaters for more than six months back in late '05 and early '06. Small brick bungalows and shotgun houses sat on narrow cobblestone streets here like the fallen domninoes of old Greek ruins. Ancient, crooked oak trees rose up like syphilitic fingers over wind-damaged tile rooftops.

Maura pulled the rental car onto Freret Street, then slowly drove down the narrow road of cracked herringbone bricks, looking for an address.

The bungalows had a sameness here, an endless row of run-down, charmless, flood-damaged dwellings. Yards cluttered with cast-off furniture, tires, gutter flashing, and shredded shingles. Michael Doerr's place was the last bungalow on the block, a modest one-story box of weathered, eggplant-colored brick nestled in a fringe of newly planted hydrangeas. There was a certain warmth to the house that belied the shabbiness of the rest of the block. An antique hobbyhorse sat on the porch, an old metal milk can filled with cattails and dried flowers next to the door. Freshly painted shutters bordered the windows. All of it very neat, very colorful, very cute. A marked contrast to the storm-trodden neighbors. *This place does not belong to a straight man*, Maura thought wryly as she approached.

She parked in front, and regarded the bungalow for a moment through the blur of slapping wiper blades, trying to assess if anyone was home.

In the rain it was hard to tell. There was no driveway, so looking for a vehicle was out of the question. There seemed to be no lights on inside, behind the windows, although *that* was also difficult to assess since most of the blinds were closed. But Maura got an immediate vibe off the house that somehow encouraged her, and she had another thought: *The owner of this place is not only gay but also a gentle soul. It's in the way the little doodads are displayed, the welcoming feel of the place.*

Maura also had a feeling that *said owner* could tell her a lot more about what had happened in the Yucatan.

She turned the vehicle off and sat there another moment, trying to figure out what to do. Time was a factor here. Thunder rumbled again in the distance, followed by another chorus of civil defense sirens. Maura weighed her options. She could leave a note, but it probably wouldn't be found for days. The young man was probably miles away, waiting out the storm. She could maybe find his number and leave a message. She looked at her watch. Hurricane Fiona would be arriving in fourteen hours.

"Aw, screw it," she muttered, zipping up her raincoat and opening her door.

She got out and hustled up the tidy little stone walk. The rain had picked up to a steady downpour now, the wet morning air smelling of salt and rust. Maura shivered as she hopped up onto the cement porch. She stood under the small overhang, wiping moisture from her face and stomping mud from her Doc Martens. She found a doorbell and rang it.

No answer.

To the right of the front door was a portrait window behind which hardwood venetian blinds hung drawn. Maura noticed a slender gap along the left side of the blinds through which a slice of the living room was visible. She glanced over her shoulder—an instinctive gesture—to see if anyone was watching, across the street or up the block, eavesdropping on her. *As if*, she thought.

She looked in the window.

Once again it was hard to see much of anything in the rainy light, the place was so dark, but she *did* see an antique pine armoire, an Eames chair canted against a hutch, a few Early American quilts on the wall, each of them stained. A braided rug next to a brick hearth. Just as she had suspected, the place exuded a stubborn charm amidst the decay.

Something moved in the shadows.

Maura's heart jumped in her chest. She jerked away from the window as though she'd been burned, and for some reason she glanced again over her shoulder, as though she were doing something naughty. She looked back at the window, and then, almost as abruptly as the shape had darted across the bungalow's rear archway, it revealed itself in a shaft of daylight near the back door.

The massive calico cat was playing with a small stuffed toy, a little gray mouse, tattered from rough use. The cat batted the toy across the front window and back into the shadows, and Maura let out a long breathy sigh of relief. Then she saw the cat cross the rear of the house, then suddenly vanish through a little rubber pet hatch installed in the bottom of the screen door.

Maura rang the bell one more time, then knocked hard on the doorjamb, thinking that maybe Doerr was in there sleeping or something. After all, who would leave their beloved pet cat in the path of a hurricane? Still, nobody answered. Maura stood there for another moment, her hands on her hips. A delicate little *meow* pierced the noise of the rain, and Maura looked down to her left.

The cat was edging its way along the foundation, staying under the eave just enough to avoid the rain. The color of old burlap with splashes of cottony white and charcoal gray in its coat, the cat was so fat its teats wagged as it walked along, its belly scraping the ground like a dust mop. The animal gazed up at Maura with that comical leeriness in its eyes that only a de-fanged domestic animal can summon when its hackles are up—as though it were saying, *Boy, if I were in the wild right now, you would be dead meat. Unfortunately, all I can manage at the moment is an arched back and a few feeble hissing noises.*

"Hello there," Maura cooed, kneeling down by the obese kitty.

The cat hopped up on the porch, purring now, immediately wrapping itself around Maura's shins. Maura stroked its matted fur. The animal seemed ravenous, and maybe even a little weak. Maura picked it up. Stunned at how little it weighed, she kept softly stroking its head, murmuring softly, "Is your master home, sweetie? Huh? Is your master home?" The cat prodded its head amiably against Maura's shoulder. She looked at the animal's collar, and saw that the tag had a registration number and Michael Doerr's name, address, and phone number.

Maura glanced back at the house for a moment, pondering, considering her options.

She could easily get in through the rear screen door, and had a fairly plausible excuse now. She could pose as a concerned neighbor, worried about the imminent hurricane as well as the cat's welfare. If Doerr was in there, and caught her, she could simply say the cat had wandered into her yard or had darted out in front of her car, and she was just making sure the animal was safe.

Taking a deep breath, her decision made, Maura carried the cat around the side of the house, past a bare, soupy patch of mud that looked to have once been a vegetable garden, a plaster Holy Madonna statue sunken in the mire like some relic of a lost civilization. The backyard was mostly mud . . . but still bore signs of a stubborn pride: a newly planted hedge of meticulously trimmed boxwoods, a marble birdbath by the rear door filled with fresh water.

Maura put the cat down, then pushed the tiny rubber pet door open, pressing the side of her face against the door in order to reach inside the darkness. With great, grunting effort she reached up, feeling for a latch or a knob. She had always been fairly flexible, especially as a kid, amazing people in gym class with her twisting pelvis. All at once she felt a button jutting against her index finger, and she poked it repeatedly until it gave. The door clicked suddenly, then gave slightly with a nudge from her shoulder.

The door swung open, and she was inside the kitchen,

the calico curling around her boots like a little, furry motor.

"Hello? Anybody home?"

The house was as still and silent as a tomb, the dust motes hanging in the shafts of gray light shining down onto the kitchen's spotless linoleum floor like pale fire. The air smelled of mold, as did most interiors in this town, but also of cleanser and cinnamon and mint. Maura gave the shelves and sink a cursory glance, astonished at the neatness.

"Hello?"

Only the implacable silence answered, as dead and flat as a cinder block. Maura sniffed the air for a moment, seeking that telltale odor of cat shit. How could this guy have a cat and not have the faintest odor of cat piss or poop in the air? She strode across the tile floor to the adjoining hallway, the skin on the back of her neck prickling with goose bumps. An adjacent door led into a little half bathroom.

Maura peered inside the john, again gazing in awe at the tidiness. Porcelain so clean it was positively luminous. Scented candles on the back of the commode. A lovely little Toulouse Lautrec lithograph on the wall. On the floor, tucked underneath the sink like a dollhouse, was the reason for the shit-free odor of the place: one of those ridiculous little motorized, self-cleaning litter boxes. *For a limited time only*, the late-night infomercial announcer had gushed many times, *you too can own the amazing Miracle-Litter! For three easy payments—a fully automatic cat-dropping disposal system that senses waste and sweeps it away, packaging it in easily removable, sealed Zip-Loc bags!*

Turning away from the bathroom, Maura searched for the cat's feeding bowls. She found two of them on a neat little rubber mat under a butcher block table. One of the stainless steel bowls was licked clean, only a little brown crust of cat food remaining around its rim. The other bowl, presumably the water bowl, was as dry as pumice stone.

Doerr had obviously been away for quite a while. In fact, Maura started wondering if—

Something rattled out in the living room, cutting off her thoughts.

It sounded like a coin tumbling down a slot, or perhaps keys jiggling in a lock—*keys in a lock!* Maura froze then in the chill of her panic, paralyzed with indecision, goose flesh spreading down the backs of her arms and legs. Should she flee or stay and act stupid? Greet Doerr at the door like a nosy neighbor? *Pay no attention to that strange lady in your house, she's just crazy old Mrs. Kravitz.* The jiggling noises stopped almost as abruptly as they started, and Maura began backing toward the rear screen door, each creaking footstep erupting like mortar blasts in her brain.

Maybe it was just a mailman, a delivery boy slipping a package inside the front door. Maura was inches away from the back screen now, her gaze locked on that front hallway, her eyes positively bugging with panic. She reached out blindly behind her for the door handle.

"Hey!"

The sudden cry behind her was accompanied by the sound of the screen door bursting open.

12

Maura instinctively whirled and threw her hands up to shield her face. In doing so, she lost her balance and tumbled backward onto her ass.

The young man lurched into the kitchen with both hands wrapped around the grip of a small black handgun. Dressed in a Tulane sweatshirt, cargo shorts, and sandals, he was soaked to the bone, and shaking so severely it looked as though he might have a neurological disorder.

He pointed the quavering barrel down at Maura and screamed: *"Who are you? What are you doing here? What are you doing in my house!"*

"I—I just—I just wanted to—" Maura stammered there on the linoleum, seeing stars from the fall, mouth dry and dumb from the panic. She tried to formulate her words, but it wasn't easy, she had never looked down the barrel of gun before, especially one gripped in the sweaty hands of someone who looked as though he might shake out of his own skin.

"Who are you? Who are you!" Michael Doerr stabbed the gun barrel at her, shrieking so loudly now the cords in his neck bulged and pulsed with each word. Filmed in sweat, reeking of fear, he wore his

close-cropped spit curls all teased up today, like a club kid or a lost member of Mili Vanilli. Back at the funeral home Maura hadn't noticed the tiny silver stud in his left nostril, or the eyeliner around his soft brown eyes. If he hadn't been holding that gun, Maura probably would have been marveling at how pretty he was.

"I met you at the professor's funeral!" Maura blurted, trying to form some coherent thought, trying to buy time. "Name's Maura County, a friend of Moses!"

Doerr's face twitched at the familiar name. "A friend of *Moses*?"

"I was a friend of Professor De Lourde! From the Sun City case! We met at the funeral!"

"The *funeral*?"

"Yes, we met at the funeral, and I just wanted to talk to you, and I saw your cat outside, and I was worried with the storm coming and everything, so I brought her around back, but I saw . . . um, um . . . I didn't see any . . . she had no water or food, so I just thought I would give her a little water, and I'm sorry, please, please don't shoot, okay? Okay?"

There was a long, agonizing pause then as Doerr held the gun with sweaty, trembling hands and tried to focus through watery eyes at this unexpected intruder on the floor of his kitchen. For an excruciating moment, the silence stretched, neither of them saying a word.

As if on cue, the cat suddenly trundled out from under the kitchen table and trotted toward Doerr, mewling softly, belly swaying.

"*Get outta here! Go on! Git!*"

The cat darted away at the sound of Doerr's angry howl, vanishing into the living room.

On the floor, scalp crawling with terror, Maura looked up into the young man's eyes. She noticed something then, something that she hadn't seen at first. Behind all the fiery rage, behind the bluster, Doerr's eyes were raw with fear.

"I'm a writer, Michael. I'm a journalist, and Professor De Lourde was a friend of mine . . . and, and, and Sandi Loper-Herzog gave me your address, and I just wanted to ask you something about the Yucatan expedition—"

"The *what*? The Yucatan!"

"I swear to you the only reason I came inside was that I saw your cat needed food and water, and please, the gun, could you please not point that gun at me anymore? Please!"

The young man cocked his head at her, still trembling, trying to compute what she was saying, still gripping the gun with both hands. "You came here because you just wanted to ask me about the . . . *Jesus*!" He cringed and stiffened suddenly, as though the mere notion of the Yucatan trip gave him apoplexy. The barrel of the gun wavered, lowering slightly. "You have no *idea*," he snarled at her suddenly. "You have no *idea* what you're dealing with . . . what you're getting yourself into!"

For one awful instant, looking up at the crazed young man, Maura got the impression of a caged animal, a whipped dog forced into a corner, growling and spitting now out of pure terror. But terror of *what*? Maura decided to push her tactic one notch further. "I'm sorry I surprised you," she said as softly and gently as possible. "I can see you're very upset, I'm sorry, but I meant no harm."

Doerr was crying now. Silently. Shoulders trembling, lip quivering. The gun sagged a little farther in his hands, now pointing downward at a forty-five-degree angle somewhere in the vicinity of Maura's Doc Martens. "You have no idea, you have no fucking idea," he uttered under his breath.

Maura rose very cautiously to a kneeling position, holding her hand up. "I'm sorry but it seems like you're frightened by something *other* than me," she said. "Am I right? You can tell me what it is, Michael, this is totally off the record, you can tell me."

Now the gun fell to his side as he wept softly, pathetically, still shaking.

Maura rose. Very carefully. Hands raised in a reassuring gesture. "It's okay. Maybe I can help you. Tell me what's wrong. Maybe I can help."

The gun fell to the floor—the metallic *thunk!* making Maura jump slightly.

"Michael?" She took a cautious step toward him. She could smell his fear like musk. His knees were skinned and lacerated. His long fingernails had grit under them. "What is it? What's going on?"

He looked up at her, his eyes fixing on hers for the first time. "You want to know what's going on?"

"Yes, Michael, I do. Tell me what's going on and maybe I can help."

He rubbed the tears off his face, sniffing back the terror. Then he looked at her. "What's going on is, he's coming here to kill us all."

Maura stared at him. "Who? Who's coming? Are you talking about the hurricane killer?"

Silence.

"Who's coming, Michael?"

The silence deepened.

* * *

By midmorning forecasters at the National Hurricane Center in Coral Gables, Florida, began revising their estimated time of arrival for Fiona. Originally she was moving in a northerly direction across the gulf, a vast, swirling mass of mayhem nearly a thousand miles in diameter, with winds exceeding 190 miles an hour at her core; but she was only moving longitudinally at only about thirty-five knots. Then, around 9:30 a.m. eastern standard time, aircraft reconnaissance reports and satellite images confirmed that the storm had quickened its pace northward to fifty knots, which would move the time of impact up to between ten and eleven o'clock that night.

To make matters worse, experts now agreed that Fiona had not only experienced "explosive deepening," but also was experiencing cycles of "eye wall replacement." This rare phenomenon is seen only in the most intense hurricanes. It meant that Fiona's eye had begun contracting, followed by the formation of a bigger, nastier *outer* eye wall. This new eye would eventually choke out the original inner eye, and the storm would intensify tenfold. Simply put: Fiona's eye would be getting bigger and bigger, and more deadly, as it roared across the gulf toward New Orleans.

Grove and Kaminsky were just outside Augusta, Georgia, on Highway 20, driving through a rain squall, when the first reports of Fiona's amplification came over the air. Grove immediately started calculating how much time they had left. Barring any major traffic tie-ups, they were probably still about nine hours away from New Orleans. That would put them there around seven o'clock that night—only a couple of hours before the anticipated arrival of Fiona.

In the meantime, Kaminsky made a series of cell

phone calls to friends at the NSA, the National Weather Service, and the Hurricane Center. The consensus was, Fiona was shaping up to be a historic event, many times worse than Katrina, which, for many, was beyond comprehension. She would probably be the death knell for the Federal Emergency Management Agency. And most importantly, her eye would likely hit landfall somewhere within a mile or two of Jackson Square.

As the world had learned in 2005, this could very easily mean Armageddon for New Orleans, a town below sea level. The levees—which had protected the city for decades but had collapsed the previous year under the strain of Katrina's catastrophic flood tide— were still being repaired and beefed up. A category-five hurricane now would finish them off once and for all.

But sitting on the passenger side of that tricked-out Jeep Cherokee, bumping along Highway 20, watching the quicksilver rain cocooning the outside of the tinted glass, Grove was starting to make other connections to the apocalypse.

It all started with the exorcism last year, the mysterious symbol that Father Carrigan had drawn on the hardwood-slatted floor of that cabin in red dry-erase ink, then had hurriedly wiped away with a damp towel as soon as the ritual had ended. Days later Grove had asked the priest about the symbol, but the padre had simply shaken his head and said somewhat enigmatically, "The truth is, Ulysses . . . one needs all the help one can get." But now, seeing the same symbol echoed in a madman's carnage, Grove was starting to sense a link to the miseries wrought by a killer hurricane.

Only four people were present inside that rear bedroom during his exorcism: his mother, Carrigan, De

Lourde, and Grove. Or maybe it was five. Perhaps there was a *fifth* individual present that day—albeit invisible to the naked eye. But what exactly happened after that entity inside him—or whatever it was—was cast out? Where does an evil spirit go after being exorcised? Back to hell? To purgatory? To this day, Grove had yet to become a true believer . . . but there was a powerful notion beginning to nag at the back of his mind: Could this killer he was hunting, this lurker in the eye of the storm, could *he* be connected to this entity in some way?

Grove turned to the Russian. "Damn it, Kay, can't you make this crate go any faster!"

"Michael?"

Maura waited patiently, standing in the center of the living room with the tea and honey, as the young grad student sat on the wingback sofa, his face buried in his hands, a mixture of shame, dread, and nervous tension still rocking through him. The living room was a cozy little assortment of secondhand furniture and garage-sale folk art. From the window, the decor looked authentic and antique, but at this close proximity the furnishings were revealed to be thrift shop specials, draped in frayed bedspreads and adorned with tattered throw pillows. Cheap and shopworn, redolent with mold, yet stylishly displayed.

"Michael?"

He was still trembling, his bony brown knees gathered up against his chest, his back slumped over to the point that he had almost assumed a fetal position. He mumbled something into his hands, his voice hoarse with fatigue.

Maura said, "I'm sorry, what was that?"

"I changed my mind about the tea." He nodded at the archway across the room. "Out in the kitchen, in the cabinet above the fridge. There's a bottle of sour mash."

Maura sighed, set the saucer and cup down on a coffee table, and went out to fetch the booze. The liquor cabinet above the refrigerator was well stocked with cheap booze, the no-name off-brand kind of stuff a kid on a grad student's income could afford. The quart of bourbon was half empty.

On her way back into the living room, Maura caught a glimpse of the pistol lying where she had deposited it, on the laminate counter next to the sink, its blue steel gleaming dully in the dim light. It was a .38-caliber Smith & Wesson that Doerr claimed he had bought for self-defense at a flea market in Slidell two months ago when the storm season had started up again. He claimed that he never even discharged the weapon, and wasn't sure if it even worked. However, he had yet to explain to Maura just whom—or *what*—he feared.

"Thanks, thank you," Doerr said when Maura returned with the bottle. He snatched it out of her hands, then took a deep, scalding swig—the kind of gulp one might take before parachuting out of an airplane behind enemy lines or maybe climbing the gallows. He winced at the burning sensation, then took a deep breath. "I'm sorry about the gun, but I thought you might be that *thing*."

"What thing?"

He took another huge, hungry pull off the bottle. "The thing that lives in the wind, the one that's killing people. The same thing that got Moses." The matter-of-fact tone of his voice made the skin tighten on the back

of Maura's neck. Michael looked up at her. "Oh . . . I
know what you're thinking, you're thinking this kid is
nuts, right? A couple of sandwiches short of a picnic?
Elevator don't go all the way to the top? All those colorful euphemisms for bug-fuck loony?"

"Michael, I didn't say—"

"It's okay. I don't blame ya." He took another gulp.
Another shudder, hands still trembling uncontrollably.
"I don't know what it is . . . man, monster, rabid alligator. I don't know. But there's *something* there." He
looked at her again. "In the hurricanes . . . y'all know
it as well as I do. I can tell by the look on your face."

A gust rattled the front shutters, and made Michael
jump. He took another sip and closed his eyes, trying
to breathe as deeply as possible. A tear tracked down
his brown cheek. He reminded Maura of a shell-shocked
GI still hearing the distant thrum of the battlefield.

"I gotta get goin'," he said at last, "get outta here before she hits."

"Michael, um . . . there's something I should tell
you. It's about why I'm here."

The young man looked up at her. His eyes were wet
with terror, his lips still quivering.

Maura told him all about her relationship with
Ulysses Grove, and her work for *Discover* magazine.
But most importantly, she told him that she was now
assisting Grove in an investigation of the hurricane
murders. That's how she came to read De Lourde's
journals. But she could not make much sense of them.
So now, obviously, anything that Doerr might be able
to tell her about the Yucatan, or the significance of the
hurricane that hit down there, or just exactly what this
"thing" that lived in the wind was, or *anything* else,
would be very helpful.

When Maura finished, Doerr looked up at her and said, "You knew that Moses and I were partners, boyfriends . . . right?"

She told him she knew.

"He was a unique person." Doerr chewed his lip to stifle the pain and grief creeping up on him. More tears welled up in his eyes. "He taught me so much. He was a pioneer in the field, did you know that? They laughed at him when he made his presentation to the Royal Academy. That was in the fall, after he came back. They *laughed* at him. Pompous asses."

He shuddered again at the muffled sound of the wind whistling across the tile roof.

Maura sat down beside him on the couch, patted his shoulder, and said, "What happened to you down there in the Yucatan? In his journals, Moses said you ran away."

He looked down into his lap, wringing his hands. Maura noticed his nails had been chewed down to the quick. "I didn't sign up for hurricanes, okay?" His voice was strangled with shame. "I was traveling as a teaching assistant, and a companion, and I wanted to learn about the Toltecs, but I never dreamed that we would—" He bit off the thought, driving it out of this memory. "I basically, like, freaked out." He looked up at her. "Basically I panicked. Okay? I'm not proud of it, but when the hurricane hit I just lost it. I bailed, and hid in the back of a supply van, then rode it back down the mountain, back into Merida. I left the next morning. Soon as I got home, I dropped out. Totally just quit. Been trying to figure out what to do with myself ever since then. Can't sleep, been drinking myself into blackouts." He looked up at her. "But Moses knew what was going on all along. They laughed at him. Now look what's happening."

An anguished pause. Maura watched him. "You're referring to the murders, right? The 'thing' in the eye of the storm?"

Doerr took another gulp of whiskey, then stood up and began pacing nervously across the tiny living room, his eyes shifting across the memories. "Moses believed that the true nature of these Toltec blood sacrifices—the ones we discovered in the fossil record—had to do with *hurricanes*. He believed that there were these 'hurricane cults' that performed human sacrifices in the eyes of storms to appease the angry nature gods."

After a doom-laden pause Maura asked if De Lourde went to the Yucatan to prove this theory.

Doerr looked around the room like a caged animal. "I don't know, I don't know, that whole week is just a blur to me now." Another big gulp of whiskey. He was starting to get woozy, softening his vowels a little. "But I'll tell you this much, the part that got everybody all riled up in the academic community was the part about the present-day cult."

"What do you mean?"

"Moses believed there were members of this cult still active today. He believed that people were still getting sacrificed in the eyes of hurricanes." He paused, wiping his eyes and his face. "Which makes his murder all the more horrible, don't you think? It's like some kind of cruel joke. Like he had to die just to prove his theory."

Another pause.

Maura looked into Doerr's watery eyes. "What happened down there, Michael?"

He looked at her. "What do you mean?"

She asked what it was that had scared him so badly down there.

He swallowed back his tears. "You don't want to know."

Maura stood up, went over to him, and gave his shoulder a tender pat. "It's okay. You can tell me."

He started to silently cry again, and slowly knelt down to the floor as though his body were deflating. Tears beaded on his chin. He put his face in his hands. Then he looked up at her through his tears. "We found a mummy, a child . . . just a little child," he moaned in a strangled voice.

Maura knelt down beside him, put an arm around him, and stared at him, as Michael Doerr slowly, softly recounted the events of March 17, 2004. . . .

Outside on the edge of the cliff, in the rain and the darkness, the sky opening up above him, Michael just stands there, getting soaked, while the others rush for cover, and the lightning stitches across the heavens above him, smelling of ozone and seawater, and he realizes he's going to die if he doesn't run for shelter.

The hurricane slams into the east range below him, sounding like a volley of cannon fire, and he can barely hear Professor De Lourde down there, staggering through the rain a hundred feet below him, with a lantern, screaming: "Michael! Michael, where are you!"

He looks down into the chasm below him, the excavation site barely visible in the blankets of rain. Carved out of the side of the rock face fifty feet down, jutting out on a shelf of sandstone, the site is bordered by rope cordons and marker sticks driven into cracks. It looks like a giant bite taken out of the side of the mountain.

In the shadows of the dig, the tarp covering the find suddenly tears away.

The canvas billows up, peels, and furls into the agi-

tated air, revealing the mummy beneath it. The little
delicate brown boy is curled into the fetal position, still
partially buried in the sediment like a nesting doll. It
looks so sad and lovely lying there in its dusty stasis.
So well preserved its hair and eyes are still intact.
Soon the turbulent rain finds the mummy. Overhead,
the squall rises and rumbles and turns into an angry
whirlwind.

The wind knocks Michael down. Gasping for breath,
he crawls out to the edge of the precipice. De Lourde
has vanished now, taken cover with the rest of them, his
shouts swallowed by the noise. The hurricane's eye
wall is approaching off the coast now like a mad circus
coming to town—the whetstone scream of the inner
winds rising and rising—and Michael has to hold on to
an alpine root, a little knob of petrified wood, in order
to maintain his clinging hold on the cliff's edge. He
peers out over the cropping and gazes down at the
mummified boy.

"He probably dates back to AD 900—a perfect example of Toltec child sacrifice—poor little angel," De
Lourde's voice whispers and echoes in the back cham-
bers of Michael's scrambled memory. Michael has
been close to a full-blown breakdown since he arrived
here in the Yucatan, barely functioning on an overdose
of lithium and Xanax. And now the mummy has opened
the secret wound inside him like a black lance through
his heart.

"Just look at him. The sheer terror on his little face.
The Incas supposedly sacrificed their best and bright-
est children, but they did it very infrequently, only in
the direst of circumstances. And the fossil record shows
us they did it humanely—or at least quickly. The Toltecs
were another story. They buried their children alive to

appease some vague, obscure demigod. Amazing the pain and suffering religion has wrought on the world . . . wouldn't you say, Michael?"

The wind suddenly buffets the precipice, the rain slashing Doerr like cutlasses across his exposed flesh, across his face and his arms. He tries to rise to his feet, tries to run, but another gale knocks him back down. He hears a terrible noise then, an unearthly booming noise from above. He manages to twist around and look up at the night sky.

Something is changing in the black whirlpool above him, a vast hole opening up in the sky. It looks like a great bloody wound gaping open in the dark clouds. And the sound that comes out of it is the worst sound Michael Doerr has ever heard, a sound that begins as an otherworldly vibration, a deep growl, as massive and powerful as an earthquake, but rising up into a monstrous, inhuman voice.

A voice from Michael's past.

"It was my dad's voice," Michael Doerr mewled softly, gasping for air between racking sobs. He was on the floor of his bungalow now, his knees gathered up against his chest. He was hugging himself as though he might fall apart at any minute. "I mean, it was just the wind, I know that now, but it spoke to me in my dad's voice, and it all came back to me."

A tortured pause.

Maura spoke softly. "It's okay, Michael, I mean, you don't have to go any further if you don't want to."

He wiped snot from his face. "Up until then, I had blocked it all out of my mind. You see, I was raised by my mom and my stepdad, and I guess I just stuffed those memories of my biological dad so far down I didn't even know I had them."

"Michael, you don't have to—"

"He used to take me to this place, he called it the whipping post, seriously, he called it that." Doerr cringed at the memory, the physical repulsion contorting his beautiful brown face into a mask of torment and hatred. "This little beat-up shed in the woods. He'd beat the shit outta me. Sometimes he'd do more than that. Sometimes he'd have his cronies join in, and they'd take turns with me."

"Michael—"

"I pushed all those memories so far down, it was like they didn't exist, but then, when I saw that poor little child down there, that mummy, and what they'd done to it, the sacrifice, I felt like I was . . ." He winced suddenly, the tears oozing down his face, dripping off his chin, his trembling chin. He looked like a broken rag doll. Limp, drained, battered, he tried to sit up and catch his breath. "I really need to get out of here, I'm sorry, I need to—"

Outside the front windows, a zephyr of wind had risen suddenly.

Then several things happened all at once, taking Maura by surprise. The wind roared and slapped at the house like a watery cat-o'-nine-tails, whipping the shutters and lashing the roof tiles. At that precise same moment, another chorus of civil defense sirens erupted somewhere close by, the closest clarion call yet, and the two sounds blended like a dissonant symphony punctuating the tension in the room with a sharp, percussive whine. It almost sounded like a gargantuan animal shrieking in pain, and it instantly stiffened Maura's spine, and made her jerk toward the windows.

But at the same time she was aware of something else, out of the corner of her eye, happening almost simultaneously with the noise of sirens and wind: Michael Doerr had started wincing uncontrollably, wincing and cringing. She looked at him. For one wild moment Maura wondered again if Doerr had Tourette's syndrome or some other kind of neurological malady. "Michael? You all right?"

His face had seized up suddenly, twitching with tics and tremors, his eyes fluttering spastically as the storm announced itself outside. His eyes went white. Then he jerked backward, tripping over an ottoman and sprawling to the floor. Something resembling speech yawped out of him, and then he went rigid.

"Michael!"

Maura went over to him, knelt down, and touched his shoulder. His damp, feverish body felt like an engine vibrating. He lay supine on his back, shuddering, tremblers twitching through his nervous system, stiffening his joints, turning his fingers into claws, his hands involuntarily clenching and unclenching.

He was going into seizures.

13

As they raced along the rain-drenched interstate, Kaminsky and Grove weighed their options. Grove wanted to get to New Orleans as soon as humanly possible. He was worried about Maura, and he was concerned that they would not reach the Crescent City before the storm hit. He didn't want to get pinned down somewhere outside of town, and miss the arrival of the eye. The whole point was to catch the eye as it passed over the most populated area, giving Grove his best shot at meeting the killer.

Puffing his nasty cheroot, weaving through traffic, the Russian explained that all this could be academic. New Orleans might not even *exist* by the time they get there. He also reminded Grove that it would be next to impossible to track a killer in the middle of a hurricane's eye. Firstly, there was no guarantee that the eye would pass over the center of town, or anywhere close to a "trackable" area. Secondly, if it did, Grove would still be too petrified of running into the inner eye wall to "track" anybody. Thirdly, it would be very difficult to predict an eye's behavior, no matter how vast and calm it might seem. Kaminsky had witnessed eyes abruptly contracting into nothing with such ferocious suddenness they appeared to have never existed. To think that a manhunt could go down in the middle of an eye struck Kaminsky as the height of lunacy.

"It's not a manhunt," Grove said after a long, pregnant pause. He was gazing out the rain-streaked side window at the flow of traffic moving in the opposite direction, clogging the northbound lanes of the interstate like rats fleeing a sinking ship. About the only other vehicles now occupying the southbound lanes alongside Kaminsky's tricked-out Jeep were military vehicles.

"What do you mean it is not a manhunt? What are we risking our lives for down there?"

Grove looked at him. "I told you, Kay, you don't have to do this, you can bail out at any time."

"What are we doing there if we are not hunting a man?"

Grove thought about it for a moment. "It's more like a fishing expedition."

"A fishing what?"

"A fishing expedition, you know, you got your hook, your bait. You try and catch a fish. That's what we're going to be doing in the eye—*fishing*."

Kaminsky chewed his soggy cheroot for a moment, thinking it over. For the last fifty miles or so, the Russian had refrained from lighting the cigar at Grove's behest. The smoke had gotten to the profiler, and he had begged his old friend to lighten up on the stogies. Now the Russian chewed the cheroot and pondered the steel-gray southern horizon.

They were making good time, despite the horizontal rain hammering them, intensifying with each passing mile. There was less southbound traffic than Kaminsky had expected, and the Jeep was holding up fairly well.

At this rate, if they limited their restroom stops and ate on the road, they might even make New Orleans by six o'clock. That is, if Fiona didn't quicken her pace . . . and if the roadblocks didn't pin them out . . . and if the Louisiana roads didn't flood out on them. *If . . . if . . . if . . .* that was a lot of *if*s.

Finally the big man turned to Grove and said, "I thought it was the killer who was fishing for *you*."

Grove didn't answer.

He just stared at that same swirling black cauldron of a southern sky.

"Michael, what is it? What's wrong!" Maura shook him, felt his pulse racing in his neck, wondering if this was epilepsy, thinking that he might bite his tongue off if she didn't do something quick.

Outside, the winds howled and yammered against the shuttered glass. As if answering it, Doerr went into wilder spasms on the floor, trying to make words come out but merely grunting and groaning inarticulately: *"Rrrrr—hhrrrr—rrrrrrrr! Hhrrrr! Rrrrrrrrrrrrrr!"*

"It's okay, it's okay, it's all right, Michael, I'm here, it's all right," Maura softly reassured him as she stroked his trembling shoulders and tried to figure out what to do, what to do, *what to do.* "We'll get an ambulance, don't worry, you're gonna be fine."

"Rrrrhhhhh—Rrrrrr!"

Maura sprang to her feet and frantically scanned the bungalow for a phone. She saw none in the living room. Michael had gone quiet on the floor next to her. She knelt down again, felt his pulse. His heart thumped irregularly in his chest, his breathing shallow yet steady.

"*Phone, phone, phone, phone, phone.*" Maura rose to her feet again. She saw a wall unit out in the kitchen mounted to the side of a cabinet. She went out there, snatched the phone off its cradle, and dialed 911.

"Shit!"

The recording crackled in her ear: "Due to the high amount of activity, all lines are currently busy. Please try again."

She pulled her cell phone from her pocket, then looked at the tiny liquid crystal display. The indicator told her she had no connection, no cell strength whatsoever.

Something crashed in the backyard, and made her jump and let out a little cry of nervous tension. She searched for the source of the noise. Through the rear window—through a gap in the ruffled curtains—she saw a broken trellis tangled with bougainvillea vines turning cartwheels across the grass in the wind.

The trellis slammed into a tree and shattered.

A sinking feeling gripped her for a moment, weighing down on her, a sense of being trapped. Fiona was breathing down on the city now, and Maura had no idea what to do. She knew she couldn't just leave Doerr here in this condition—whatever that condition might be. Plus, getting back in her car and driving around town, looking for an emergency room, seemed dangerous if not downright insane.

She went back into the living room and checked Doerr's vitals. He seemed okay. Still breathing steadily. But something caught Maura's eye then, something visible beneath Doerr's Tulane sweatshirt that gave her pause.

In all the excitement and writhing and wriggling, the sweatshirt had hiked up a little, exposing a couple of inches of the young man's tummy. A thick scar like a rubber worm peeked out from under the sweatshirt. It was so prominent, so severe, so *ugly*, that Maura instinctively yanked the sweatshirt up over the rest of Doerr's midsection.

"Oh my God."

Maura stared at the scars, not fully comprehending their origin. Were they surgical scars? No. They were too ragged, too imprecise. They were also pink and shiny enough to be inflicted within the last year or two.

They formed a strange topography of slashes like this:

Another noise shook Maura out of her daze. Outside the front shutters, the wind rattled the hedges and roared across the neighborhood, through the high-line wires and treetops. It made a dissonant, whining noise. Rain began lashing the front windows in waves like angry cymbal crashes.

"Okay, okay, okay, okay, okay," she muttered nervously under her breath as she lowered the sweatshirt and weighed her options. If she *had* to, she could stay here and wait out the first wave of the storm. She could at least stay with Doerr until he recovered or until Maura managed to get through to an ambulance—whichever came first. Had she given Grove the address? She couldn't remember.

She looked at her watch.

It was 1:37 p.m.

Less than nine hours now until Fiona was scheduled to arrive in all her horrible glory. It seemed like plenty of time, but it really wasn't. The winds were already making crosstown travel hazardous. Maybe it was time to find a safe place in which to wait things out.

She started searching the bungalow for a crawl space or some kind of reinforced area in which to huddle. She tried to remember if she had seen a storm cellar door outside, maybe along the base of the house in the backyard.

Minutes later she found the secret door embedded in the back wall of the pantry.

The door was locked.

It was ten minutes to two o'clock.

Halfway between Montgomery and Mobile, about two hundred miles northeast of New Orleans, in the billowing sheets of rain, Grove and Kaminsky saw the chaser lights of a state trooper's prowler approaching in the flickering blur behind them. This happened at almost precisely same moment that Maura County was stumbling upon the secret room in Michael Doerr's apartment (at 1:53 p.m. central standard time, to be exact).

At first Grove thought the trooper might be on his way somewhere else, to some storm-related emergency, or to some evacuation center somewhere to provide help with the exodus north. But as the boiling lights bore down on them, Kaminsky said, "Oh hell, Grove, what have you gotten me into now?" The trooper's headlights started flashing, and Kaminsky reluctantly pulled over.

The trooper took his sweet time getting out of his prowler—he was probably running checks on the Russian's federal plates. While they waited, Grove and Kaminsky argued about what they should say or do. They had been tooling along at over ninety miles an hour, so there was a good chance they would simply be given a ticket and be on their way. But Grove suspected there was more to this encounter than a speeding ticket. In fact, he had been having premonitions all day.

Without the buffering effect of his medication, Grove's mind had been seething with dread-saturated noise. Fragmented visions of that eerie white dust devil from the desert kept rearing up in Grove's peripheral vision. Memories of his mother's mystic babbling throughout his childhood echoed in his brain, her tales of apocalyptic angels fighting each other on barren, wasted lands devastated by plague and natural disasters. Grove even remembered one particular story of a river of blood heralding the dark god of the underworld, who had returned to earth to bring about a new age of darkness and misery. Vida Grove's personal cosmos was a mishmash of African tribal lore, Old Testament Catholicism (probably from the missionaries), and her own brand of quirky superstition. But more than anything else, the image that haunted Grove was that single glimpse of a flock of blackbirds madly circling a cage of wind, trapped forever in a moving prison of calm.

At last the trooper emerged from the prowler and splashed through the rain toward the Jeep with his hat down and collar up, his face grim and stony in the shadow of his Stetson's wide brim. Kaminsky rolled down his window, greeted the trooper, and started saying how sorry he was to be going so fast but he and Grove were on a government job and they had to beat Fiona to New Orleans or they were in deep "manure." The trooper listened with monumental patience—especially considering the fact that he was standing in the rain. When Kaminsky was done, the trooper politely ignored it all and said he was going to need to see the Russian's license and registration. Kaminsky complied.

Then the trooper said he was going to need both Kaminsky and Grove to go ahead and get out of the vehicle and come back to the prowler.

Grove and Kaminsky did what they were told. They sat in the rear of the prowler, behind the screened safety partition like two common criminals, wondering what the hell to do now, while the trooper searched the Jeep. Sitting there in the noisy silence of the prowler, the rain a barrage of bullets across the vehicle's roof, Grove asked Kaminsky to let *him*, Grove, do the talking when the trooper returned. The Russian said that was fine with him, and when the trooper did return, Grove launched into a long explanation about being a consultant for the bureau, and being on special assignment. The trooper, ever courteous, ever patient, as unmovable as a granite milestone, listened to it all and then said he was going to need Grove to stop talking for a minute while he asked a few questions.

It turned out that the bureau was the reason that the trooper had stopped the Jeep. Evidently a deputy sheriff from Ulmer's Folly by the name of George Stinson— he of the Fuller brush mustache and racist looks—had called the North Carolina Bureau of Investigation only minutes after Grove and Kaminksy had roared away from Eve's ground zero. Accusations had flown back and forth that Grove was concealing evidence, or something to that effect, and now a bulletin had circulated throughout the Deep South that Grove should be apprehended and brought in for questioning. The trooper explained all this in his courteous monotone, and Grove kept breaking in and saying, "Trooper, I know you're just doing your job, but if you would just please contact a gentleman at bureau headquarters in Quantico named Tom Geisel, a section chief there, he will clear us."

The trooper finally radioed in and asked his dispatcher to get Tom Geisel on the blower. It took a while, but the Alabama State Police finally patched a call through the National Crime Information Center and got Geisel on the phone, and everything was cleared up within minutes. Geisel told them yes, it was true that Grove was affiliated with the bureau, in an *unofficial* capacity now, basically as a consultant, but the Alabama authorities should extend all courtesy to the man and his colleague. The trooper showed very little emotion upon receiving this information, and clicked off the radio with the stoic neutrality of a toll taker. He simply told Grove and Kaminsky that, in the future, they should watch their speed, and they were free to go, and they should have a nice day.

All told, the entire encounter, from beginning to end, took only about twenty-five minutes; but deep down inside his secret thoughts, Grove knew these minutes were critical. Not only because of the imminent storm . . .

. . . but also because Maura County was down there all alone, following leads, putting herself in great jeopardy once again for Grove.

It was sixteen minutes after two o'clock when Kaminsky finally fired the Jeep back up and pulled back out onto the highway.

It wasn't really a *secret* room. The word *secret* implies hidden, inaccessible, known only to a select few. But the door that Maura found in the rear of the walk-in pantry was not exactly camouflaged from view. A person standing in the middle of the kitchen could clearly see into the little six-by-ten-foot alcove next to the refrigerator, past the shelves of Campbell soup cans and cylinders of Jiffy cornmeal flour, to the narrow inner door in back. It was even visible from the east edge of the living room.

Maura had discovered it quite by accident. She had been frantically looking for a flashlight, in case they lost power, and had checked in the pantry. That's when she saw the narrow, burnished pine door embedded in the rear wall. It had a natural blond finish that was so old and chipped it looked like tree bark, and its little stained porcelain doorknob was the color of an old tooth.

Now Maura stood in the pantry, staring at that little door, the distant thunder rumbling so hard it was rattling the contents of the kitchen, dishes and glassware clanking with each volley. The moaning of the wind was omnipresent now, like a gut-shot wolf howling in its death throes. Maura squeezed her way past the bottles of store-brand olive oil, past jars of home-canned peaches and cherry peppers, to the rear of the pantry. She took a deep breath and turned the knob.

Locked.

She turned away and considered giving up, but something stopped her. There was a faint odor hanging near the door like an aura, a chemical smell that tweaked at Maura's curiosity. She searched the pantry for something to use on the lock. Then she remembered the old credit card trick. She didn't have her purse with her, but she saw a thin metal lid on one of the shelves, and she grabbed it.

It took a few tries, jabbing the lid between the lock and the jamb—Maura was not a large woman, and had virtually no upper body strength—but on the third thrust, the old rusty bolt clicked. The door groaned open, sending a plume of dust upward into the light of a bare bulb.

Maura coughed a little, then took a single step inside the hidden chamber.

She couldn't believe what she was looking at.

14

She had to step back in order to take in all the images calling out to her in that cluttered hundred-square-foot room, with its low ceiling of termite-infested wooden joists and exposed fiberglass insulation. Photographs were tacked everywhere, on the drywall panels, on the studs, and on the ceiling. Shelves contained glass containers of unidentified objects, and things dangled from twine and twisted wires hanging off the joists. Maura stood there, frozen, blinking, trying to make sense of the overall impression of chaos that screamed at her.

A cold sensation seeped down through her bowels as she began to identify objects.

A human organ, all gray and pebbly, floated in a beaker filled with yellowish fluid. Another jar held perhaps a kidney or part of a brain. Other jars held other human organs—fingers, eyeballs—some of them modified, pierced with nails or quills, wound with colored yarns. Maura's gaze, now wide and hot, played over the pictures tacked to the walls: grainy, indistinct photographs of monstrous screaming faces, ghastly drawings of demons, people flayed open, disemboweled, their cartoon innards spilling across the ruled notebook pages in scarlet spirals forming crude renderings of aerial hurricane imagery. In fact, every psychotic doodle, every drawing, every feverish diagram emulated that inimitable spiral satellite perspective of a hurricane.

Maura backed farther away.

She now stood out in the pantry, at the threshold of the secret room, holding her hand to her mouth. What she was looking at, the madness of it, had yet to fully compute, had yet to fully register in her brain. But even now, she was beginning to split her traumatized thoughts into two halves. One side silently shrieked in terror and wanted to flee this terrible place while Maura still had a chance. The other side ordered her to shape up: *Look at it! Come on, you're a journalist! Get your ass back in there and look at it and notate it and understand it!*

She forced her legs to move, forced herself to take a step back inside that pungent-smelling insanity. The ceiling seemed lower, the space closing in on her. She took a closer look at some of the images. Most disturbing of all were the close-ups of faces. They were *real.* They were real people captured in their death throes, distorted silent screams . . . torturous, contorted facial expressions. Where in God's name had these faces come from? They looked almost like still frames from some hellish snuff film.

At length, Maura had to look away.

She glanced to her right and saw a long black raincoat, still damp, hanging on a spike. Another nail had ropes and chains with metal hooks dangling off it. Bottles of amber liquid, each one carefully labeled, were lined up along one galvanized metal shelf. Maura forced her legs to move, and she went over to the shelving unit and picked up one of the bottles with a trembling hand. She read its label.

Sodium pentobarbital.

Now both sides of her brain screamed for her to get out of there right away. But she could not tear her gaze away from a bizarre little shrine in one corner of the secret room.

Down on the cracked cement floor lay an old Magnavox VHS recorder, so ancient and greasy with dust it looked as though it were lined with fur. Spaghetti-knotted clumps of old quarter-inch magnetic tape dangled from every corner like shiny brown bouquets, some of the tape charred in ceremonial flames. Broken shards of VHS cassettes were glued to the wall, the front panel of the deck, and across the moldy carpeted floor in lunatic patterns. But the detail that caught Maura's attention and held it was the VHS cassette that lay on a tarnished silver serving dish, congealed in the melted wax of ritual candles: the hand-scrawled label on the spine said: *GROVE EXORCISM—4/28/05.*

Maura County spun toward the gallery of monstrous faces lined up along the opposite wall, and for one terrible moment she could not draw a breath. She realized the photos were indeed close-up frames from a movie—a *home* movie, in fact—but they were not different people. They were all the same person. Captured in bleak, out-of-focus, poorly framed tableaus, they were all close-ups of Ulysses Grove.

A sudden blast of thunder made her jump, her back molars biting down hard enough to crack.

All at once the electricity flickered out, plunging the bungalow into darkness.

* * *

"Damn it to Hades!"

Ivan Kaminsky's heavily accented baritone boomed above the noise of the rain, which was now tommy-gunning across the hood of the Jeep. Over the last half hour, the wind had risen to hurricane-force speeds, and despite the Jeep's heavy undercarriage, the vehicle had begun to hydroplane and pitch and lurch sideways across the fast lane.

"Go around it!" Grove clutched at the upholstered armrest and gazed through the oscillating wiper blades at the roadblock up ahead, about a quarter mile away, clearly visible in the blur of rain. A pair of unmarked vehicles were canted across the right lane near an underpass, a row of flares across the highway like shimmering yellow diamonds in the rain.

"Are you again insane!"

"Trust me on this, Kay, just keep going!"

The Russian grunted something under his breath, tightened his grip on the steering wheel, and chewed his cigar.

As they approached the roadblock Grove realized the two vehicles were Mobile County cars, probably emergency management people, or perhaps Department of Interior folks. That was good, because those guys would never give chase. Hot pursuit was the province of cops, rangers, or state troopers. At most, these guys would shake their fists and jot down Kaminksy's license plate number, and probably forget to even report it.

The Jeep roared past the roadblock on the shoulder, sending up a plume of mist and gravel, kicking up one of the flares, sending it skyward in a shower of sparks and embers.

"Good, good!" Grove looked out at the side mirror, checking to see if they had raised any ire, or even roused the men into a chase. Nothing stirred back there. The cars remained stationary, the flares shimmering. Now Grove wondered if there had even *been* anybody in the vehicles.

The roadblock vanished into the storm behind them. Grove looked at his watch—3:11 p.m. At this rate, they were still a good couple of hours away from New Orleans. Buzzing with anxiety, he refused to get caught outside the city when Fiona hit. He was also worried about Maura—he had been unable to reach her cell phone for over an hour now, and was starting to wish he had told her to wait before she went off and tracked down this Doerr kid. But on another level, he trusted Maura completely. The little fair-haired woman could handle herself in *any* situation. She was a rock.

Besides, what could possibly go wrong in a simple Q-and-A with one of Moses De Lourde's former boy toys?

She fumbled her way out of the secret room and into the pantry, nearly tripping on a sack of potatoes leaning against one of the shelves.

Her eyes had not yet adjusted to the darkness, and yet her other senses were as sharp and sensitive as Geiger counters. She smelled the unsettling mixture of banal food staples—the earthy aroma of root vegetables, grains, and dried spices—and the overpowering odors of formaldehyde and rotting tissue. She felt the cool edges of the galvanized shelves, the grit of spilled cornmeal beneath her Doc Martens. And she tasted the coppery tang of fear on her tongue as though she were sucking dirty pennies. But mostly she heard the bone-shaking mortar fire of thunder, and the lunatic whistle of wind outside the bungalow, as she felt her way out of the pantry.

She reached the kitchen and dug in her pocket for her Bic lighter. It was the only thing she could think of doing—the place was so dark. It made no sense. Her mind raced. The bungalow had been full of gray daylight when she had arrived an hour or so ago. Doerr had turned on a few lights then, but now the place was as dark as a tomb, despite the fact that it was still officially daytime.

Maura sparked her Bic, and the tiny flame flickered for a moment but basically did no good. The kitchen windows gave off a pale gray glow, but much of that room—and most of the living room adjacent to it—lay in utter darkness. "Ouch!" she cried, the hot lighter burning her thumb. She shook it out and put it back in her pocket. Her heart was thumping so rapidly, so fiercely now, that she could feel it in her ears and her neck. She tried to take deep breaths, tried to steady herself and think, think, think—

Thunder crashed, and lightning flickered, and Maura nearly jumped out of her skin. *Stay calm, girlfriend, stay calm*, she admonished herself. *The only way you're going to get out of here alive is to stay calm.*

She found her way over to the back door, and she paused there for a moment, her brain swimming. It was too late to call the police, the lines were down, and anyway, by now, most cops were busy with the evacuation. She pulled her wireless out with a severely shaking hand and looked at the luminous display. Still no signal. And besides, what would Grove be able to do in a car, en route? Sure, he could advise her, tell her how to process the scene, but she was no detective, she was no cop.

What are you waiting for, hotshot? she silently scolded herself. *Get the hell out of this place now!*

Something made her hesitate, something in the back of her mind that hummed like a counterpoint to her frantic internal dialogue. She found herself thinking of the victims—De Lourde lying pasty and painted in his coffin, all the others that had perished for no good reason—and then she found herself thinking of her own kidnapping, and the subsequent ordeal in the back of a panel van a year and a few months ago. Something deep down inside her turned then like a tumbler in a lock. If she left this place now, the man out on the floor of that living room could very easily escape to kill again, to torture and murder and mutilate another innocent person, maybe another woman just like Maura. She could not let that happen, she could not.

The ropes!

All at once a plan formulated in Maura's feverish midbrain. She remembered those ropes dangling in that inner sanctum—the perfect means by which to secure Doerr, to keep him safe and sound until Maura had a chance to get help. A renewed sort of vigor coursed through her then. She was not going to be a victim this time.

She made her way through the gloom of the kitchen to the pantry, slipped between the boxes of powdered mashed potatoes and canisters of pasta shells, and reached the inner door, which still hung open and stank of death and degradation like a coffin liner that had come ajar.

It was absolute blackness in there, and Maura balked for a moment. She did not want to go back in there. She would have rather had hot pokers driven through her eyes than go back in that horrible chamber filled with floating specimens and bloody souvenirs and thousands of contorted faces. But now she could see the faint shimmer of those chains and hooks dangling in there, the ropes hanging right next to them. How perfect and ironic it would be to bind the madman with his own instruments of bondage. Maura's rage seethed in her gut, those old terrible emotions bubbling up to the surface. It never occurred to Maura that Doerr might have a distinct and separate personality, or that Doerr might be catastrophically ill. She simply wanted to hurt him now as harshly and permanently as possible.

She plunged into the room and fumbled around in the darkness for a moment, touching things she would rather have avoided touching, and finally got her shaking fingers around the ropes. They felt rough and hairy in her hands. She pulled them free and then managed her way back out the doorway, through the pantry, and into the kitchen. Her eyes had adjusted enough now to see the pale shadows of the living room. She saw the pine armoire against one wall, the silhouette of the big Eames chair canted against the hutch. She even made out the quilts on the wall.

Her scalp prickled with panic suddenly. She dropped the ropes.

Doerr was gone.

She started simultaneously backing away and turning in little nervous circles, eyes popping wide, scanning every shadow in the kitchen, every dark corner of the hall, every alcove, every nook and cranny. The wind outside bellowed as though feeding off her sudden terror, and lightning flickered again like camera bulbs popping in the windows, illuminating the place with brilliant white light as hot as burning magnesium. Maura made a mad dash for the back door.

A shape lunged at her from behind the fridge, a massive arm swinging up at her face.

"Hhhhumphhh!"

Maura's gasp bleated out of her on impact, her legs buckling, and she went down hard on her tailbone, elbows cracking on the floor of the vestibule inside the back door. It felt as though she had run into an iron bridge span. She writhed on the floor for a moment, trying to scoot backward on her ass, the back screen door so close, within inches, *inches!* But now the monstrous shadow loomed over her.

Lightning arced across the back windows, illuminating the creature standing there, and Maura only had a single moment to look up into his face, only one terrible instant to behold the Holy Ghost in all his grand guignol glory, before his hand came down and pressed the chemical-soaked cotton over Maura's mouth while she coughed and convulsed . . .

. . . and then the world went dark and cold and silent like the deep calm before a storm.

15

Street signs shook and hummed. Sheets of rain billowed on gale-force winds, snapping high-tension wires over the French Quarter in showers of sparks. Ghostly wisps of Spanish moss, uprooted from their parasitic hosts like freed spirits, soared and tossed through the dense air.

By six o'clock, the last glimmers of daylight had been swallowed up by the black storm, and St. Charles Avenue boiled with overflowing culvert grates and robotic yellow lights flashing every half block from Esplanade Avenue to the Huey P. Long Bridge. Up north, along the Pontchartrain Expressway, the thoroughfare already looked like a war zone, replete with overturned, abandoned cars and errant timbers that had blown across the lanes every few hundred feet. Most of the citizens had fled the area, and anybody crazy enough to still be hanging around either worked in emergency services or had a death wish.

The outer bands of Hurricane Fiona were about eighty miles offshore, a little over two hours until impact.

"Stay to the right, stay to the right!" Grove craned his neck to see through the virtual gray-out ahead of them as Kaminsky steered the Jeep through the treacherous obstacle course of Louisiana Interstate 10. "There it is!" Grove shouted above the moaning winds, pointing at the Canal Street exit, which had materialized in the rain a hundred yards away.

They took Canal Street south toward the churning cauldron of the Mississippi. The wide street was deserted and littered with wreckage. Neither man said much as the Jeep charged past boarded strip clubs, flooded parking lots, and dark, barred store windows. They had conquered many impediments in order to beat Fiona to New Orleans, but now they realized that the worst was still ahead of them. Bypassing roadblocks, tap-dancing for state troopers, driving through torrential rains and deadly winds amounted to nothing compared to what they were about to face. They were entering ground zero.

The Quarter felt to Grove like a vast ghost ship. All the deserted, narrow cobblestone alleys sluicing crazily with black water, all the desolate iron-laced balconies obscured by shrouds of rain. The Jeep's high beams sliced through the walls of mist like the twin prows of a ship and, at length, fell on the boarded facade of the Toulouse Luthier Sheet Music Emporium at the corner of Dumaine and Bourbon.

"Pull around back, park in the alley." Grove was already buttoning his raincoat, turning up his collar, and he had to holler just to be heard above the rain. The back of his mind was full of troubling connections sparking like surges of voltage in his brain, the visions of dust devils mingling with that familiar star-within-a-star configured in blood and tissue in the grass outside Ulmer's Folly, and the half-glimpsed images of blackbirds or crows soaring madly to escape the eye wall. But mostly Grove was thinking about Maura County, and hoping against all odds that she was here, safe and dry and waiting for them at De Lourde's apartment.

Kaminsky found a place to park, and then they got out and went up the back stairs to the rear gallery door. Grove still had the key that the professor had given him a year earlier during Grove's first visit. He unlocked the door and they went inside.

No Maura.

Exasperation and a sense of helplessness immediately clouded Grove's thoughts. He figured that Maura was probably still over at this kid Doerr's place in the Garden District. But *where* in the Garden District? And why was she still there? Grove began to pace while the Russian found the bathroom and relieved himself. Lightning zapped outside the drawn shades like a shadow play, and that's when Grove thought of something.

He went over to the computer.

The screen flickered to life and displayed the customary desktop icons—the little hard disk, the trash can, the scattered folders and various program aliases. The background was classic De Lourde—a grainy, garish scene from *The Wizard of Oz*, the one with Dorothy, the Tin Man, the Scarecrow, and the Cowardly Lion, all standing arm in arm, about to jaunt off down the yellow brick road. *This definitely ain't Kansas anymore, old friend*, Grove thought in a brief instant of sorrow.

Grove double-clicked the America On-Line icon—the little concentric O and triangle—and waited for the Web browser to boot up. The browser ran off an old archaic dial-up modem, and the tones and blips and squawks seemed interminable to Grove's ears right now. Grove used PCs exclusively, and always felt slightly maladroit using someone else's Mac, like an American trying to drive on British streets.

At last the Web desktop appeared across the borders of the screen, the multicolored function bar flickering across the top edge, displaying the little mailbox, the globe, the telephone, the calendar, all the little Internet icons. Grove jerked the mouse back and forth, searching for the History button. Although he had used the Mac at Quantico many times, he couldn't remember which part of the Apple desktop provided a summary of recently visited sites.

"What is it you are attempting to do?" Kaminsky's basso profundo voice came from behind Grove, and it made the profiler jump slightly.

"Just trying to find a trail, some bread crumbs left behind."

"Get out of the way."

The Russian pushed Grove aside and leaned over the keyboard, smelling of cigars and garlic. His big gnarled fingernails clicked on the keys, manhandling the little plastic mouse. Finally he located the pull-down menu that displayed the recently visited Web addresses. "Is this what you are looking for?"

Grove told him to click the MapQuest site.

The route to Michael Doerr's place materialized on the screen in meandering veins of red.

The first thing that registered in her sleepy, anesthetized ears was the sound of metallic clicking, like somebody taking apart a pair of skates. She felt no panic, no dread, no awareness of danger, only that slightly dreamy, dissociated feeling of not quite being awake. It was not unlike being in the dentist's chair after oral surgery, and coming back to consciousness in layers. She sensed the cool chemical odor of novocaine, and realized she was covered in gooseflesh, and something was cutting into her wrists, and there was singing, off-key singing, like an elderly woman with senile dementia trying to sing an aria from some forgotten Italian opera, and it was coming from somewhere nearby, but also from far away, maybe from speakers embedded in the ceiling.

Maybe this *was* a dentist's office, and maybe the vague sense of dislocation and terror that began tugging at Maura's thoughts was just a bad dream experienced while one of her root canals was filled, and now she was going to wake back up and everything was going to be okay, and she would soon be joking with her amiable, balding dentist, Dr. Bottman, and would be rinsing and spitting in the little swirling porcelain bowl.

Unfortunately this fleeting scenario of hope swirled away like saliva down a drain as Maura began to register where she was, and what was cutting into her wrists, and who was standing across the kitchen from her.

She feigned unconsciousness for another few moments, letting her head loll back against the tabletop, peering through her squinted, half-closed eyes, trying to gather her thoughts, trying to figure out what to do. Her wrists were rope-bound and tethered to the table's legs. Evidently the power had surged back on, judging by the yellow glow of the bare bulb hanging above her. Less than six feet away stood Michael Doerr, his face downturned, his breathing coming in low, rasping wheezes as he busily threaded a nylon rope through a metal ring.

To say that Doerr had drastically changed would have been an understatement. He no longer wore the collegiate sweatshirt and cargo shorts, but now stood head to toe in filthy black rags and muslin, as if he'd been mummified and then dipped in india ink. A black, pointed cowl draped his head, obscuring his face with ominous shadows. The garb resembled the wardrobe of some kind of religious order or cult. But it was the *face* that truly woke Maura from her narcotic daze. Partially hidden in shadows, Doerr's face had creased and hardened like a brown gourd with the air sucked out of it. His eyes, once soft and full of innocence, had narrowed to the point of looking positively canine. His brows had furrowed and arched into expressions of tormented rage, and his mouth had curled back with the ferocious stupidity of a junkyard dog. The only remnant of his original personality was the little sterling silver stud in his nose.

Maura shut her eyes, and she tried her best to continue faking her nonresponsiveness, waiting for the right moment to move. But now her heart was banging with the volume of a kettledrum as the thing that was once Michael Doerr came over to her. He stood over her, breathing thickly. He smelled feral. There was a muffled clank as Doerr laid a bundle of instruments on the table next to her. Maura was certain that Doerr would notice the goose bumps rashing down her legs and her forearms. Surely he must hear the slamming of her heart. Through her closed eyelids, through her lashes, she dared to peer down at the tabletop next to her.

Her scalp prickled.

The sacrificial blades lay in a neat row on the black cloth like jewels on display. One of them was a petrified black spiral horn from some wild goat or deer, another was a nasty-looking rusted iron spike, another was a huge thorn—six inches long, at least—from some primordial vine or plant, shellacked and honed to a razor point. Maura could not identify the other objects, but by this point she was not thinking straight anyway, the sedative still dragging at her like gauze over her face. But . . . she would not be a victim, goddamnit, she would not.

The monster was whispering very rapidly now, speaking in ancient, dead tongues: *"Si-su-meeru-ee-nu-na-tukum-pa-surru-voventuru—"* Then he picked up a delicate, stainless steel scalpel flaked with dried blood. The blade loomed in Maura's peripheral vision. Then the cold edge of the scalpel brushed the bridge of her nose, on its way to her eye socket. The madman was leaning down close enough now for Maura to smell his rotting breath.

"No!"

She cried out and made her move then—feeble as it was, and without much strategic forethought—yanking her right wrist violently against the ropes. The entire table hopped slightly, the right legs banging on the floor, the sudden movement tossing the bundle of instruments into the air.

Doerr jerked backward, momentarily startled, as metallic blades and animal horns skipped off the edge and clattered to the floor all around him. Maura's heart was jackhammering now as she kept yanking, again and again—*"No, no, no, no!"*—stretching the ropes, harder each time, yanking and yanking, and letting out little grunts of effort on each yank as her brain revved out of control, and her lungs heaved for air. Finally she ran out of strength.

A brief and terrible pause ensued as Doerr stood four and half feet away, breathing heavily, looking down at the fallen blades like a sleepwalker.

At last, he carefully knelt, plucked one of the razors from the floor, and rose back to his feet.

They had been making good progress until they reached Napoleon Avenue. Grove saw the wreckage first. "Hold it, Kay! Hold it! Hold it!" he called out over the storm.

Visibility had worsened noticeably over the last few minutes. The rain was coming down so hard now it was difficult to see a half block in any direction. Kaminsky stomped on the brakes, and the Jeep fishtailed to a stop in a half foot of fast-moving water. The sixty-mile-an-hour winds immediately enveloped the Jeep in white noise.

"Let's try a side street," Grove urged, glancing over his shoulder at the wall of mist billowing off the tops of plantation homes like silver blankets, undulating in the sky, and then whipping down across the deserted Garden District. It was as dark as pitch now, and St. Charles Avenue was almost completely flooded. All along the streetcar line, the live oaks leaned now at distressing angles. Gutters coursed with rapids. Victorian gas lamps jittered and shook, sending nervous light across the roadway. At the intersection of Napoleon and St. Charles, an abandoned streetcar had floated out across the apron and capsized onto its side, blocking the westbound lanes.

Kaminsky flipped on the tungsten searchlight that hung near his side window, grasping the directional handle mounted inside his door. He swept the beam across the street. The dense rain slanted through the shaft of light, swirling in the yellow beam like luminous motes. To the north, General Pershing Boulevard was a tangle of overturned sawhorses and caution lights, the wreckage stuck on top of a drainage grate like a giant child's bath toys left in a draining tub.

To the south, the boulevard looked fairly clear, rapidly flooding, but clear. Kaminsky threw the Jeep into reverse. The rear end lurched backward through standing water. Then he shoved it into drive, and he quickly maneuvered back across the slippery streetcar line.

"Now try taking a right on Loyola." Grove had the Map-Quest printout folded lengthwise in his hands, and it was starting to dampen and wrinkle from all the nervous gripping.

He was starting to wonder why he was endangering himself and Kaminsky just to go see this grad student crony of the professor's, and make sure Maura was okay. Maura could get all the information they needed. As a matter of fact, she had probably already gotten it and was back at the professor's apartment right now.

Grove started thinking about turning back.

Once in a while, during horrible accidents, bar fights, car wrecks, and the like, everything slows down. The passage of time—a single instant, in fact—gets caught in the neurochemical sludge, and all of a sudden that single moment can stretch like taffy.

Maura saw Doerr coming toward her with the blade, and also sensed out of the corner of her eye a single bare lightbulb above her swaying on its frayed cord like Poe's pendulum, slower and slower, the sound of the table creaking faintly under her trembling body, and all at once her mind fixed on a single concept like an alarm bell going off in her head: *The table's old, and wooden, and old wooden tables can be unstable.*

She had no time to think it through, or measure the odds of success, or even make a conscious decision, the moment was so fleeting; all she knew was that her only chance was to put every last ounce of strength she had left into yanking that damn table hard enough to—

Doerr pounced at her, the knife arcing down like a falling star.

Maura yanked the table upward as hard as she could, and there was a loud *crrrreeeeaak!* as the legs slipped suddenly, and the table tipped.

The universe seemed to pitch.

The table landed on its side, and the impact nearly knocked Maura unconscious—the side of her head and the shank of her left shoulder both slamming down hard on the linoleum. Fireworks shot off behind her eyes, and a blast of pain traveled down her spine as she gasped for breath, hands still bound. For a moment, all the pain and disorientation and flashing, flickering, dancing light—the table must have struck the hanging bulb on its way over—created an almost dreamlike sensation of drifting underwater.

Maura lay there for a moment, trying to get her bearings with her face pressed against the cold kitchen tiles, her ragged breathing blowing puffs of dust off the floor. Where was Doerr? Where was he? Maura couldn't see very well now and she felt even more vulnerable wedged between the table and the wall, but the adrenaline kept her sharp enough to sense the killer circling her like a hungry jackal. She began madly working her right hand out of its bonds (the rope had slipped just a bit in the fall, maybe enough to manipulate).

A shadow loomed, only inches away from her head, on the wall, sliding at an odd angle up the plaster like a living ink blot—a perfect silhouette of a man with a blunt instrument, some kind of knife or animal horn. It approached so slowly, so gradually, and with such sinister majesty—the swaying light made it pulsate with mesmerizing power—that Maura could only gape at it for one catatonic instant before she saw something else in her peripheral vision that made all the blood drain out of her face.

The little black Smith & Wesson handgun lay on the floor less than two feet from her bound left hand. It must have fallen behind the table (where she had put it after taking it away from a sniveling Michael Doerr an hour ago). Now the .38 lay almost within her grasp. If she could only work her right hand loose. If only . . . *if only*.

The sweat was helping, the oily perspiration working into the rope, greasing her sore flesh, working it free. Almost, now . . . almost. The shadow loomed on the wall, elongated, distorted, and Maura's right hand was almost out of the knotted rope.

All at once her right hand popped free as the table leaped backward and away from her.

Doerr, standing there, trembling with bloodlust, let out a garbled cry that sounded like something noxious belching out of the earth, something very old and black and rotted by centuries of hate. Maura twisted around and grabbed at the gun. It slipped out of her hand. She made another frantic attempt to grab it, at the same moment Doerr lunged at her, but the table had suddenly shifted between them, and Doerr banged into its corner, letting out a yelp.

Now Maura was dragging the table toward the gun.

The table, which was still affixed to her left wrist, made a wrenching, fingernails-on-a-chalkboard sound as it scudded across the tiles, and the pain was excruciating, but Maura's gaze was fixed on that handgun lying only inches away on the linoleum.

She got a hold of it.

Then two things happened at the exact same moment: Maura spun toward the killer, the gun raised and trembling, her finger on the trigger, ready to blast away, even though she had never fired a gun in her life, and Doerr suddenly squirted something in her face. It came from the slender bottle in his hand that Maura had mistaken for a weapon.

Maura coughed and winced at the stinging sensation in her eyes, the gun still raised and ready, as Doerr whirled, then leaped away, vanishing around the edge of the arched passageway into the living room.

Maura had no idea what had just happened, but she managed to rise to her feet with the gun in one hand and the table still tied to her left. She coughed and coughed, wiping the cool alcohol-smelling fluid from her face, and searched the shadowy living room for Doerr.

"Michael!"

Her cry sounded bizarre to her own ears—a low, distorted baritone version of her own voice, like a tape that had suddenly slowed down—and the table seemed to weigh more now, as though she were dragging a wagonload of sandbags. She managed to hold the gun aloft and keep her finger on the trigger. A shadow moved to her left.

She squeezed the trigger.

The gun barked, and the blast flashed in the gloomy living room, and a chink of plaster blinked across the room. The recoil nearly knocked the gun out of her hand, and the report was so loud it instantly deafened her, starting her ears ringing. The living room started spinning. Maura swallowed back the nausea and dizziness washing over her and screamed: *"Michael, you will not leave this apartment!"*

A noise behind her.

She staggered around and fired wildly into the opposite wall, shattering a framed portrait of Louis Armstrong. Glass erupted, and the picture hopped off the wall, and the blast rang in Maura's ears. The whole living room was tilting on its axis now like a carnival ride, and Maura's vision doubled—quadrupled, actually—and she tried to drag the table toward the front door, because even in her rapidly deteriorating condition she sensed the urgency of protecting the exits. She reached the front door and vomited on the rug.

The bile and the single cup of chicory coffee that she had consumed for breakfast splashed on the floor, and she doubled over for a moment, her stomach cramping, the wooziness tugging her down now, but she could not give up, she *would not* give up, she *would not* be a goddamned victim again and she would not let this killer of innocent people get out of here!

That's when she heard the bang out in the kitchen. She turned and dragged the table toward the archway, her wrist screaming in pain, but the pain was dulled now like radio signals from far away, wavering in and out of audibility. She reached the threshold of the kitchen and collapsed.

She landed awkwardly on her left shoulder and breast, the sudden blunt ache shooting across her sternum. The pain was almost welcome. It woke her up a little, and thank God she was fairly flat-chested—she had never worn a bra above a B-cup—but still, nothing hurt like getting a breast suddenly smashed. It was a radiant pain, like an ankle twist, which was mercifully buffered now by whatever narcotic Doerr had misted in her face.

She looked up.

Something flew past the window, and Maura fired at it, but now the gun was behaving strangely, the report sounding all low and wobbly like that slowed-down recording. The blast, missing the window by a mile, went *splat!* into the refrigerator, almost as if Maura were throwing mud balls, and now Maura heard another noise behind her, out in the living room, a loud click, and she started laughing, or maybe she was crying, it was hard to tell now, the storm was so loud and swirling around the house like the twister in *The Wizard of Oz*, and Maura started dragging the table back toward the living room, thinking—*Auntie Em! Auntie Em! I'm going to blow your friggin' head off, and your little dog Toto, too!*—and now the whole house was spinning and spinning, rising up into the sky toward the Land of Oz, and Maura was still dragging that silly old table, and she was bleeding, the color of her blood all candy-apple red and pretty as a lollipop as it smudged the floor, and now she saw the funny man standing in the front doorway, and she laughed and laughed and shot at him with her pretty little bullets in her funny black gun.

16

"Grove, look out!"

Grove, standing in the bungalow's doorway, ducked down just as the blast rang out, sending a silver plume of fire blossoming across the shadowy living room.

The bullet chewed through the lintel just above the door, sending a puff of plaster particles down on Grove's head, a cloud that immediately dispersed on the roaring wind invading the tiny house.

Kaminsky, who was crouching on the porch behind Grove, yelling again above the noise of the storm: "Get down, get down, get down!"

"It's okay, kid, it's us—it's us!" Grove moved behind the jamb, pressing his back against the door frame, his stomach tight with panic. Lightning zipped across the sky, strobing against the front of the house like a beacon. "It's okay! Maura? Can you hear me!"

Kaminsky was on his belly on the porch, holding his hat over his head, soaking wet and squinting against the rain. "This is the reception you usually get from your girlfriends?"

Grove shushed him and listened. He could hear Maura's crying in there. It was faint, and hard to discern over the locomotive churning of the storm, but he knew it when he heard it. Her sobbing sounded scrambled and hysterical, and maybe even a little drugged up. "Kid!" he yelled. "Can you hear me!"

After a horrible pause, her voice sang out, sounding slurred and intoxicated, "Ulysssssss—"

"That's right, kid, it's me and my friend, Ivan—Ivan Kaminsky. He's a great guy! You'll love him once you get past his cigars! You okay?"

From inside the house: "I'm really, really sleepy."

"Okay, sweetie, we'll fix you a nice bed and you can take a nap."

After another pause: "I'd like that, Uly—Ullllluh—"

"Hey, kiddo, can I ask you a favor?"

"Sss-sure!"

"Can you put the gun down? Maybe stop shooting for a minute?"

"Okay, but . . . but see . . ."

Her words drifted off. Grove sucked the inside of his cheek, trying to think, as the storm swirled through the little vestibule. "Hey, kiddo! You there?"

No reply.

Grove looked over his shoulder at Kaminsky, who was getting soaked. The Russian shrugged and gestured at the thickening black sky behind them.

"Ullleeee . . . ?"

Maura's voice was almost gone. It sounded like the strangled voice of a child.

"I'm still here! How about we come in now? Huh? No more gunplay, whattya say?"

After another tortured pause: "Okay, but . . . there's sssomm . . . something you should know."

"What's that, honey?"

No reply. Another nervous glance between Grove and the Russian. Wind buzzed through the telephone wires above them. Rain slashed at the porch, crawling inside Grove's collar and sleeves and socks. He held his hand up with fingers splayed.

The Russian nodded. He recognized the urgency of the situation, and also Grove's universal gesture of all SWAT teams and paramilitary units. Five fingers splayed open: *Get ready to move.*

Grove then pointed one index finger toward the right side of the vestibule: *You go that way.*

Another nod from Kaminsky.

Grove jerked a thumb, then pointed another index finger to the left: *I'll go this way.*

Kaminsky nodded again.

Three fingers splayed: *On the count of three.*

Grove started counting down, bending each finger over one at a time, when Maura's bleary voice suddenly returned: "H-hhee's still in here sssomewhere!"

Grove and the Russian froze. Grove's hand hung in midair on the count of two.

"Say again, Maura! Not sure I heard you!"

"Heee's still in here! That . . . that guy!"

"Who! *Doerr*? You mean Doerr? What guy?"

A terrible pause: "The guy whooooo's beennn k-killing people in h-hurricanes."

She's delirious, Grove thought to himself in that frenzied instant. *She can't mean that the owner of this house, which looks like it belongs to a little old lady, is the actual hurricane killer, she can't, she's been drugged, she's not thinking right, but wait, wait, wait, wait, the high free-histamine and serotonin levels in the victims' blood also indicated druggings—*

Thunder pealed as Grove swallowed back the nerves and made another gesture at Kaminsky. A wiping motion: *Stand by.* Then Grove pointed at the Jeep Cherokee, which was parked roughly twenty-five feet away, behind the Ford Taurus rental car that Maura had parked next to the curb. He made a little "shooting" gesture, his hand forming a childlike pantomime of a gun.

Kaminsky nodded.

The wind keened as both men whirled and leaped off the porch, shielding their faces as they shambled across the soggy front lawn toward the vehicle. Grove went around back while Kaminsky popped the door locks with his keyless remote. Adrenaline pumping, Grove ducked down low behind the cargo hatch in case he was being watched.

The wind buffeted him as he opened the hatch and dug out his black plastic road case. He worried it open and rooted out the massive onyx-steel revolver that a fellow profiler, the late Terry Zorn, had given him on the Sun City case. The Charter Arms .357 Tracker was a double-action handgun, geared for firefights, no need to cock the hammer, just point and shoot, its hollow-point, liquid-tip bullets ensuring "one shot" stops.

Grove thumbed it open and slammed a speed-loader into its wheel, then ejected six rounds. He stuffed the other speed-loader in his pocket.

Then he made his way back through the rain, crouching, practically duckwalking across the lawn, to the front door where Kaminsky was waiting for him. The Russian held a cut-down twelve-gauge shotgun, the kind with the pistol grip favored by city detectives. Not exactly a subtle firearm but satisfactory for their purposes. The rain dripped off its muzzle as Kaminsky signaled he was ready.

Grove gave him a nod. Then made the splayed-fingers gesture again. Then a fist. Then he yanked it downward: *Go, now.*

Kaminsky kicked open the screen door, the shotgun swinging up in the ready position.

Grove went in first.

His senses hummed as he plunged into that dark living room in the Weaver position, the odors of chemicals and burnt sweat and human terror thick in the air. He scanned the "fire zone" within his field of vision. The layout registered in his mind's eye like an infrared camera marking significant objects. One body—a friendly—lying still in the center of the room. Maybe unconscious now, it was hard to tell in a quick glance. An overturned table behind Maura. Left arm moored to its leg by thick rope.

Nobody else in the immediate vicinity.

Kaminsky moved slowly, cautiously, along the far wall, toward the kitchen pass-through. Grove noted his position. Then noted the position of the windows, as well as the half-open door behind him. He judged it safe to take a closer look at Maura. He went around one side of her so that he had both the kitchen archway and the front door—both forms of egress—in his peripheral vision. Then he knelt and felt her neck for a pulse. It was rapid but strong.

He carefully pried the black .38 Smith & Wesson from her free hand, and checked the breech. The steel was still warm. Maura had fired four times. Grove popped the cylinder and dumped the two remaining slugs on the floor. Picked them up, put them in his pocket. Then shoved the gun behind his belt. Then loosened the rope on her left wrist.

"Maura! Kid! Gotta wake up!" Grove gently held her by the shoulders and shook her. He could see her complexion had turned ashen, with blue circles under her eyes, and her skin felt cold and clammy. Probably very low blood pressure. An instant diagnosis here told Grove she had probably slipped into a narcosis or maybe some kind of anaphylactic shock from a forced overdose, some kind of cheap tranquilizer, chloroform or pentobarbital. He could smell it on her clothes. He knew that she could not sleep this one off.

"The kitchen is clear!"

Kaminsky's voice boomed out in the kitchen, as Grove lifted Maura to her feet. Her legs wobbled. Her arms dangled limply. Grove began "walking" her around the living room as though playing with a rag doll.

"Do a room-to-room, Kay!" Grove yelled out at Kaminsky. "Watch your back! Keep your front sight up around corners, and make sure he's fled the premises!"

Maura moaned. A good sign. Grove walked her a little faster, her legs dragging along as though numb and paralytic. Grove lifted one of her limp arms around his neck for better leverage, raising his voice above the noise of the storm. "Time for school, kiddo, wake up, wake up now!"

A door banged somewhere down the hall, followed by Kaminsky's bellow: "Bedroom is clear!"

"C'mon, c'mon, stay with us, you can do it, girlfriend, c'mon, c'mon."

She murmured something.

"What was that? What did you say, honey?" Grove shook her gently, ushering her briskly around the outer edge of the oval rug. "Say that again, talk to me, c'mon."

Another bang down a hallway. "Bathroom is clear!"

Maura muttering: "Wh-what—toook y-yyoooo—"

"That's it, talk to me, go ahead."

Out in the kitchen, Kaminsky's voice: "The house is empty, Grove!"

Maura slurring: "What—took yy-you sss—"

"That's my girl, keep talking." Grove felt a twinge of emotion in his gut for this amazing little woman in her sweat-damp denim jeans and sleeveless gingham top. She looked like a courageous little punk rocker. It made his eyes well up slightly. "C'mon, say it!"

"What took you sssso long?"

Grove smiled despite his surging emotions. "That's my girl, that's my girl." He hugged her flaccid body. She was shaking slightly in his arms. He felt her arms feebly reach up and wrap around him.

Her irregular breathing filled his ear: "I love you," she whispered.

Grove squeezed her. "Same back at ya, kiddo, same back at ya."

They stood there like that, in each other's arms, for one long moment, as the storm raged against the half-open front door, lightning crackling constantly now, the screen door slapping arrhythmically like Morse code, *S-O-S . . . S-O-S . . . S-O-S,* until Kaminsky's voice rang out again from the kitchen, breaking the spell.

"Sweet Lennon's tomb!"

Grove glanced out through the archway, into the kitchen, and saw the big, hulking Russian filling the pantry door, looking at something in the shadows. "You have *got* to see this, Grove!" the big man announced.

Grove would have given his right arm for a "Pathfinder" print kit with an electrostatic dust lifter and a canister of Luminol to gather fresh latents off the floor and walls. He also could have used a portable Hemident tester with serology ampules in order to obtain a good workable DNA sample. An ultraviolet camera would not have hurt, either, since the inner room was most likely lousy with the victims' secretions, many of them probably smeared and smudged in unpredictable places. Grove could also have put a methane probe to good use since the decay rates on the biosouvenirs in Doerr's little chamber of horrors were probably all over the map. But alas, by that point (a quarter to eight), the closest CSI unit was probably a hundred miles north, settling into storm cellars, starting games of gin rummy, waiting for Fiona to have her way with the coast. As it happened, the only evidence analysis equipment that Grove had at his disposal was out in the back well of the Cherokee.

For nearly an hour, while Kaminsky force-fed strong coffee to Maura in the living room—they had found an unopened canister of Café du Monde chicory in Doerr's pantry—Grove went about the business of documenting the evidence in the secret room as best he could with the equipment at hand. He wore his rubber gloves, and he got as many angles as possible with his digital camera. He documented the human organs in their beakers of formaldehyde, noting the relative freshness of most, guessing they were recently harvested, presumably matching many of the victims, starting with Professor De Lourde's dentures and the delicate root system of his optical nerve.

Grove photographed many of the artifacts and pictures tacked to the walls, instantly making corresponding notes in his spiral-bound notebook. All the drawings of demonic transformations and gruesome carnage coming out of heads suggested to Grove a dissociative mental illness—what the old-timers called a "multiple." The swirling designs and drawings of funnel clouds somehow connected hurricanes to the pathology, although Grove had yet to conclude what those connections actually signified, or how the Yucatan trip figured into the fantasy. Judging from the doctored framed photographs in the little corner video shrine, there were family connections to the disorder, perhaps abuse, the details of which would be relatively easy to gather once the storm had passed and the lines of communication had been reopened.

More significantly, Grove noted without passion or surprise the inclusion of *himself* in the inconographic evidence. He had some difficulty looking at the closeups of his own face during that horrible exorcism ritual last year, but even *those* proved helpful. They began to provide a link—in Grove's mind, at least—between the killer and himself, between the killings and Grove's exorcism, between the ancient symbol drawn on the floor of Geisel's cabin and the markings left at the storm-lashed crime scenes.

But what *was* the link? Judging from the bizarre little shrine in the corner—with its broken cassettes and ribbons of videotape—the Doerr kid had seen De Lourde's home movie of the exorcism. But then what? How did that initial viewing explode into this convoluted pathology? How did this poor, sick kid go from simply seeing a ritual on video to becoming this elaborate, fetishistic, homicidal maniac? Grove felt as though the answers were very close but still just out of reach. Like a word on the tip of his tongue, or a vague melody in the back of his mind that would not go away.

Grove was going through the piles of doctored photographs when a loud crash out in the living room made him jump. He set down his work and made his way out of the secret room, through the pantry, and into the kitchen. He immediately saw the problem. Fiona had arrived.

"Help me open the windows, Grove, come on!" Kaminsky was yelling, struggling with the painted-over old windows along the front of the living room. Evidently a piece of flying aluminum siding had slammed into the front door, shattering the slender pane of window glass near the top.

"What are you doing!" Maura stood behind him with her back pressed against the adjacent wall, eyes wide, almost in a stupor. A bullet hole was visible in the wall only inches away from her head. "We're not waiting the storm out *here!* Not *here!*"

"I am sorry, Miss County!" Kaminsky grunted as he quickly wrestled open a window. "But now I am afraid we have no choice!"

Something thumped across the roof, sifting plaster dust down from the ceiling, as Grove rushed over to a side window and muscled it up. "What are we *opening* windows for?" he hollered at Kaminsky.

The Russian was moving the sofa over to the door, wedging it against the screen. "In order to avoid air pressure blasts!" he explained with a grunt. "She will blow out sealed windows with the greatest of ease!"

Grove helped him. It took both men only a couple of minutes to go through the entire bungalow, lifting double panes, cranking open smaller hinged windows. They worked quickly, without comment, spurred on by that strange, moaning whistle that had been intensifying over the last half hour. There were all styles of windows. The bedroom, for instance, with its tasteful sleigh-back bed and profusion of pillows, had two of those old-fashioned louvered-style windows. Kaminsky flipped them open, letting the wind-driven mist have its way with the room. The bathroom had a narrow screened window above the toilet, which Grove cranked open, and then punched out with a single right jab. The tiny screen pinwheeled into the wind, then vanished in the darkness. Time was ticking away.

A few minutes earlier, Kaminsky had explained that Fiona's outer wind bands were just arriving, and it was only going to get worse now. They needed to find a place to safely sit out the storm, and they needed to pray that the ensuing flood did not reach into the University District before the arrival of the eye.

At last, they got every window open, the rain misting inward now on surges of wind.

Kaminsky ordered everybody out into the living room then, his voice barely audible above the whistling freight train. "Okay, here is the deal! We need to find a spot that is surrounded by a reinforced ceiling and walls!"

"If such a place exists," Grove said, looking around.

Lightning flared again, streaking the darkness outside the front windows.

"There's no crawl space," Maura informed them. "I already checked."

"Foundation's a cement slab," Grove said.

"Goddamned cheap postwar bungalows," Kaminsky growled, tugging at his damp beard, scanning the archway, the hall, the front vestibule.

A massive sonic boom erupted outside, making all three of them jerk. It sounded like an antiaircraft cannon, its echo vibrating the sky before being swallowed by the whistling roar of the wind. The electricity flickered. Lamps fizzled—the power wavering off and back on.

"The hell was that!" Maura said.

"Probably a power station," Kaminsky said.

"Aren't we supposed to sit in the southeast corner?" Grove asked.

"That would be a good idea if this were a tornado, Grove, but this is not a tornado, this is not even remotely a little bit like a tornado!"

Across the front of the bungalow, rain spumed through the gaping windows, beads of moisture already coating the chairs and the rug and the sofa. Grove smelled the cold, wet, briny sea in the air, and he shivered. In minutes the ocean would arrive in New Orleans like an Old Testament God, cleansing the labyrinthine streets of Babylon, washing away hundreds of years of human history.

"Wait a minute!" Kaminsky had become very still, gazing over at the archway into the kitchen. "Wait just one minute!"

Grove was looking at him. "What . . . ?"

Kaminsky lumbered across the room, then ducked into the shadows of the pantry.

"Oh no. No way." Maura looked ill.

"Take it easy, kiddo." Grove went over to her, put his arm around her.

Maura was shaking her head. "No, no, no, no, no . . . I'd rather take my chances under the kitchen table."

Kaminsky emerged from the pantry, his eyes bright with enthusiasm. "Six-inch concrete walls . . . steel-reinforced ceiling. No windows, Grove. It is perfect . . . *perfect*. Come on, help me gather some things."

17

At 9:03 p.m., central standard time, an emissary from hell named Fiona arrived in the darkness—unfurling biblical weather across southeast Louisiana's Brenton Islands, and up through the Atchafalaya Swamp. It was a mortal assault on an already scourged land, and this time, very few people, rich, poor, or otherwise, were around to witness it. Abandoned dinghies and old condemned shrimp boats along the decaying harbors of Terrebone Bay levitated into the air, riding the black waves and slamming into cypress groves and shore stations. Bayous boiled and shifted in the zero-visibility darkness. Tarpaper roofs peeled off buildings and spun into the ether. Miles and miles of shoreline palms and tupelo trees bent over sideways in the savage winds, the torn and shredded fronds and leaves filling the sky like a flurry of birds struggling to escape.

The devil wind pushed north, chewing through the delta, turning the swamp into a witches' cauldron of floodwater and churning, shivering wetlands. Piers buckled and broke apart in the furious gales, tumbling for hundreds of yards into the bogs. Tiny backwoods villages virtually imploded, telephone wires popping, streetlamps exploding like Roman candles.

The official time of impact on the city of New
Orleans that night would be noted in most histories as
9:53 p.m., when Fiona's concentrated winds arrived in
Algiers. At that point, any reckless souls still remaining—hunkered down in their storm cellars or safe
rooms—would have heard that eerie train whistle noise
rising to mind-numbing levels. To human ears, the
sound began to resemble a colossal, insane choir, singing
completely out of tune. The ferocious winds accompanying that sound ripped through the narrow streets,
flaying open buildings with the impassive efficiency of
a giant can opener. The refurbished levees barely held
up in those early hours. Rain strafed the streets, machine-
gunning the sides of buildings with enough force to
leave dimples the size of bullet holes. Live oaks along
the graceful river walks convulsed as if strangled by
unseen assailants. And the huge, black, snaking Mississippi undulated and rose in the darkness to precarious
levels, sending whitecaps over the sides of Tchoupitoulas
and Decatur, drenching the West Bank Bridge.

When this hellish tabernacle finally descended upon
the French Quarter, the area was transformed, the demonic chorus rising into a mad crescendo. It seemed,
at that point, as though the entire Vieux Carré had
begun to vibrate, all the wounded buildings and narrow, litter-strewn alleyways shaking as though in a
great earthquake. Right at that moment, in fact, just
north of St. Louis Cathedral, at the dead end of a deserted side street, under a gentlemen's club identified
only by a broken neon sign that said LIV NUDE IRLS, a
different sort of transformation was taking place.

Down a short flight of steps, behind a storefront
door labeled MADAM TINA'S HOUSE OF CHARMS, a lone
figure huddled in the corner, on the floor. Slender legs

drawn up against his chest, face buried in his hands, he wept uncontrollably as the mad choir rose all around him.

What was he doing here dressed like this? How did he get here, in the middle of another apocalyptic storm? This was once a place of comfort for him, a place he came for solace. The owner, Tina Lucien, was a sweet old Haitian gal who smoked a corncob pipe and played checkers with him. But now everybody was gone, and the world seemed to be turning inside out, and he had no memory of coming here.

The tears poured out of him, streaking his face, dripping off his jutting chin. His skin, the color of café au lait in the dim light of the powerless voodoo shop, was filmed with sweat, and his stubby, gnawed fingers trembled as he hugged his knees against his chest. The long, black, muslin duster that draped his body—as well as the chains and hooks and instruments that dangled off his belt—looked oddly out of proportion to his wiry, brown form . . . like the clothes of a long-dead grown-up, found in an attic, draped over a child playing dress-up. The pointed black cowl on his head looked especially awkward now.

Lightning crackled outside, sending silver tendrils down into the shadows.

In that moment of flashbulb brilliance Michael Doerr noticed a small voodoo doll on the floor a few feet away from him. Made of old cloth, candle wax, and modeling clay, and shaped like a little old lady, her face like a rotten apple core. She had probably fallen during one of the wind tremors. But in that single instant of searchlight brightness, as the winds keened, Doerr sensed something both important and terrible radiating off that little doll, which seemed to be staring up at him with her tiny little metal-button eyes.

Tina Lucien had probably made that little "soul" doll herself, the fabric of its clothes soaked in a mixture of her favorite perfume and her own urine. She'd probably stuffed it with tea leaves and chicken bones and human hair. The lungs were tiny balloons filled with Tina's own breath, the spine a long fishbone. There were secret things in there as well. Magic things.

But more than anything else, the *essence* of it, the *presence* that the doll gave off in that single moment of illumination, those little shimmering eyes staring, waiting, knowing, registered suddenly in Doerr's terror-stricken mind as a clue, a key to his sickness, a window on his fractured soul. The soul doll was created to be a golem—an artificial creature possessed by an elemental spirit.

Was Michael a golem, too?

Throughout his childhood, throughout the years of institutions and medication and group homes, he had heard voices in his head, telling him to do things, things he didn't *want* to do. He had fought to push them away, ignore them, erase them. He had almost succeeded, too. Almost found a way to live a normal life. Made it all the way to Tulane, to grad school, to Moses De Lourde's inner circle. But the memories would always be with him, the voices always inside him like a cancer or a virus that hides in the cells, but no other voice in his head would speak to him as loudly, would penetrate his soul as violently, would fill him with such poison, as the one that came the day Hurricane Katrina blew into town. . . .

Running down Bourbon Street, still clad in his hospital smock, his skinny brown ass hanging out, the winds swirling like mad voices overhead, his wrist still bandaged from his fourth attempt at suicide, Michael Doerr hurls through the rain toward his last salvation: De Lourde's Dumaine Street row house. Michael has nobody else to turn to, no money, no way to get out of town, no hope, nothing. Only Moses De Lourde. Only his old mentor and lover.

He reaches the Dumaine Street gallery house and frantically scales the steps. Bang-bang-bang! Knocking furiously on the back door. No answer. Michael finds the spare key under a flowerpot and goes inside.

Nobody home.

Oh God, what's going to happen to him? With the hurricane closing in, the rain like a machine gun on the glass and the tiles! Michael turns on the lights—thank God the power's still on—and he goes into the living room and he cowers in the corner. He buries his face in his hands, stringers of snot looping off his chin. Pitiful . . . just pitiful. He looks down at his wrist where the jagged vertical gashes have soaked through the bandage, staining the gauze a deep eggplant color. Absolutely pitiful.

He couldn't even kill himself properly . . . and now the chronology of the last couple of years plays through Michael Doerr's brain like an old nickelodeon flicker show: falling so madly in love with the professor, becoming his little bitch boy, his little lapdog, and then following him all the way to the Yucatan. But his relationship with the older man had been doomed from the start. De Lourde had already begun to drift away from the young grad student by the time they embarked on their expedition. Michael felt alienated, unloved, betrayed. And then the debacle in the Yucatan began to unfold.

Getting caught in that hurricane was bad enough, but what really yanked Michael off his spindle was that mummified boy. A victim of savage abuse, Michael had empathized so much with that sad little corpse. Sacrificed to the angry nature gods, discarded like a piece of garbage.

Michael Doerr returned to the States a broken soul. Deep down inside, something had torn away, snapped apart, leaving a gaping hole in its place, a huge empty cavity. But just as water seeks its lowest point, a flayed-open soul hungers for sustenance, hungers for something to fill it. His nights were tormented by dreams.

In his nightmares he saw that little mummified boy, his ancient eyes geeked open in death like petrified white marbles. He saw other things. He saw his abusive father coming for him with empty black eye sockets. The man used to wear these little trademark dark granny glasses, and that affectation got incorporated into Michael's dreams. Michael would awake each morning wanting to tear his own eyes out of his skull. He wanted to burn down buildings, he wanted to cut himself, he wanted to drink drain opener.

Most of all, he wanted to kill.

But somehow, through force of will, through Tina Lucien's healing magic, he fought these powerful impulses. He directed his burgeoning madness inward, directed it toward himself. He drank himself into oblivion, consumed enormous amounts of antidepressants and sedatives and wine and absinthe. He saw visions. Between September of 2004 and August of 2005, he tried to kill himself three times and spent weeks in the psyche ward down at City of Martyrs Hospital in Algiers. But then reports of a major tropical storm out in the Atlantic began filtering through the news chan-

nels, and Michael Doerr sensed a change coming, a reckoning.

Her name was Katrina.

Now, on the night of her arrival, Michael Doerr huddles like a wounded, frightened bird in Moses de Lourde's deserted apartment, just waiting, waiting for death to come and take him into its whirlwind. He has nowhere left to go. He will die in Katrina's hellish embrace, in her violent arms. The building is starting to tremble. Books falling from shelves, power flickering. The sound of a freight train coming across the black gulf filling the air. But Michael doesn't hear it anymore because he sees something then, something that calls out to him.

On the floor, at his feet, a videotape. He saw it once before. De Lourde said something cryptic and mysterious about it, such as, "Oh, that's going to be in my memoirs one day, or at least Ripley's Believe It or Not, but nobody, and I mean nobody, gets to look at that until I'm dead," and now Michael crawls toward it like an animal sniffing the droppings of its prey. He picks it up. Shakes it.

The electrical power is about to sputter out. Quick! Before everything goes dark, look at it! See what that old queen was hiding! See what was so precious to that old faggot! Michael stuffs the videotape into the VCR next to the computer, and he presses Play.

He watches for a moment without even taking a breath. He cannot move. He sees the shaky, handheld image of Ulysses Grove jerking violently, slipping off the edge of his sweat-stained bed, then sprawling to the floor, while a priest and a shaman mutter litanies over him, and the picture goes haywire for a moment.

Michael blinks. His blood freezes in his veins.

Somehow he knows this is important, very important, maybe the most important thing he will ever see in his whole miserable, pathetic life. On the monitor, the thing inside Ulysses Grove has separated from its host like a white membrane separating from an egg yolk, and the second Ulysses Grove flops to the floor like a helpless game fish on the hull of a boat, and then this new Grove turns to the camera, and the thing doesn't look like Ulysses Grove anymore, it looks like a shriveled, blackened, cancerous alien. It trains its jaundiced, hooded, reptilian eyes on the lens. It looks directly at the screen, black lips peeling back away from sharp little yellow fish teeth.

"—Hello, Michael—"

Then everything happens at once, very fast, so fast that Michael isn't sure whether he heard his name being spoken by the creature on the screen or by a voice in his head, but it doesn't matter, because at that exact moment there is a huge crack of thunder outside, and a flash of brilliant magnesium-white light off the computer monitor, and a great eruption of energy plumes off the little screen like a transparent bubble being pressed out of a tube, and it jumps through the air at Michael, and it strikes him dead center between his eyes.

The impact knocks him backward with the force of a battering ram, sending him sprawling to the floor, supine, gasping for breath.

For one horrible frenzied instant Michael Doerr feels as though he is drowning, but not underwater, and not exactly in fluid, but rather in darkness. The texture of it—if asked, he could only describe it as a slimy, dark substance like oil—envelopes his face, oozes down his throat, floods his lungs and his belly and his bowels. He shudders at the impossible voltage running through him, his fingers clenching and his arms jerking with palsy.

The lights go out.

Now Michael lies there in the blackness, the twitching slowly subsiding like the tics of an insect dying on a frying pan, his soul convulsing at the toxic substance spreading through him. Michael grits his teeth so hard now he hears them crack in his ears. It feels as though a pair of great, blackened, papery eyelids are opening in his brain, looking out at the world through the eye holes in his skull. Then the eyelids slowly close. And there is nothing left but the darkness and the great heaving winds of Katrina outside the gallery, shaking the town down to its moorings, whistling through the oaks, the intermittent lightning turning the whole scene into a slow-motion dream.

Somehow Michael manages to crawl across the room to the back door and struggle down the stairs.

He makes his way outside as the first outer bands of Katrina's eye wall reach the West Bank, the rain clawing the side of his face like nails, making his soggy hospital gown flap wildly against his bare ass. He smells the ozone and apocalypse on the wind as he grasps a telephone pole for purchase, the first waves of floodwater shoving across the Quarter. His bandages tear away and fly up into the sky. Fire and brimstone are in the air.

He looks up, and squints at the southern horizon.

He sees it coming on hell winds, illuminated by lightning and thunder as brilliant and deadly as phosphorous. It looms over the world, a great noxious swirling nucleus in the sky, an insult to God and reason. Michael holds on for dear life as it approaches.

He wails, his shriek consumed by the unearthly roar of trumpets and cymbals and broken pipe organs. The hole in the sky approaches, as empty and void of goodness as the stare of an abusive father, or the gaze of the devil.

Katrina's eye.

Now. Tonight. Almost precisely one year later. Michael Doerr found himself curled into a fetal ball on the floor of Madam Tina Lucien's House of Charms, awaiting the arrival of another eye altogether, wanting to die, wanting to finish the job of killing himself, but knowing he was powerless.

For nearly a year, he had been harboring this secret thing inside him, pretending to be normal, even pretending to be getting better, but knowing all along in his secret thoughts that the thing inside would return. It would return as soon as the next hurricane season came, as soon as the next category-four storm descended on the beleaguered Gulf Coast.

The trigger was the wind. Always the wind. The wind was the clarion call that announced the coming of the eye, and the eye was the key. The key that unlocked the door to hell, the window through which evil passed.

It would happen again, tonight, in a matter of minutes. The trigger: the otherworldly sound of the eye wall approaching, like a million runaway freight trains. And then, like a guillotine falling on the land, the abrupt and violent silence. Michael Doerr began to cry, but his tears hardly had time to well up in his eyes before the transformation began once again.

His body stiffened against the display shelf of magic

potions and herbs. A bottle jiggled, then slid off the shelf and fell to the floor. A wheat-colored powder bloomed across the tiles. Michael convulsed. He flopped to the floor and shrank inside himself, and watched his hands and limbs flex and jerk and curl and straighten.

It was like watching a puppeteer jerk his synapses, sending inertia down through his vessels and into his tendons, through his cartilage, and into his marrow and muscle—*twitch-twitch-whirrrrrrrrrrrrrrrrrr*—until the thing inside him spread its black wings and—

Whap! The Holy Ghost suddenly took control, sitting up with a jerk.

Eyes shifting around the darkened shop with insect stealth, ears tuning in the oncoming winds with the sensitivity of a satellite dish, he took in a big, lusty breath, filling his lungs with the delicious smell of must and rot, then rose to his feet. Chains dangling, weapons tucked into inner pockets, long black coat hanging to the floor, he smiled to himself.

It was time.

The eye was approaching, and the manhunter was precisely where the Holy Ghost wanted him.

18

They got situated inside the pantry just in time. It seemed the moment Grove shut the inner door, the entire front half of the bungalow erupted. It sounded as though wild animals had been let loose out there: the muffled zephyr wailing, glass shattering, temblors rocking through the bungalow's foundation. The electricity immediately fizzed out again, and inside the secret room, the specimen jars and picture frames and ritual objects rattled and clanked in the darkness as the threesome crouched down in the far corner where Grove had carefully shoved aside the cadenza and piles of doctored articles and photos. Each person now gazed up at the shadows of exposed ceiling conduit and the trembling, dangling bones, and watched and listened as though the room might collapse at any moment.

They would not know the extent of the damage around them for some time, but it sounded as though anything that wasn't nailed down out in the living room had just bitten the dust. They knew there was a risk of losing the roof—it was now starting to creak and buzz with the sustained chorus of winds—which would probably mean the end of *them*. But the inner room, thank Christ, seemed to be holding up with stubborn integrity. Thank Christ again that Kaminski had had the foresight to retrieve a large battery-powered Coleman camping lantern from the back of his Jeep. He had also brought inside his wireless laptop just in case they got lucky and grabbed hold of an operational satellite cell. He also grabbed a duffel bag full of necessary "survival" items such as cigars, airline-sized bottles of vodka, a box of twelve-gauge shotgun shells, playing cards, condoms, a pair of size-17 Converse high-top tennis shoes, a paperback atlas, an ounce-bag of Maui-Wowie, a hash pipe, a Bic lighter, a half dozen Little Debbie chocolate snack cakes, an iPod digital music player loaded with mostly Frankie Yankavic polka tunes, an eighteen-inch torpedo of hard salami, a couple of XXL T-shirts silk-screened with the National Security Agency logo, a box of waterproof matches, and a battery-operated Bose shortwave radio.

Grove had also gathered as many supplies as possible from the duffel bag he had thrown in the back of the Jeep. He managed to bring in a change of clothes, a toiletry case, his notebooks, and three extra speedloaders filled with .357 hollow-points. He had also found that old two-shot derringer pistol that he kept disassembled in a side pocket of his duffel bag, a nostalgic throwback to the Cold War era. The gun was a gift from a range instructor at Quantico named Hanratty, an old codger who had befriended Grove during his early days at the bureau academy. The derringer was a "last-chance" weapon, the kind of pistol usually taped to shins and the backs of toilets, the kind the cops used to call a "throw-down" gun. Grove wasn't sure how true it fired, but he thought it would at least give Maura an extra layer of confidence.

She had gone through another gruesome ordeal—thankfully not as invasive as the kidnapping a year ago, but horrific nonetheless—and she had done it strictly for Grove. The guilt lying in the pit of Grove's stomach now was overwhelming. He knew Maura was here only out of love and loyalty. He knew she would rather be back in San Francisco, sitting in a coffee shop, sipping an espresso, reading an obscure scientific journal and plotting out her next article. But now it was too late. She had plunged into this nightmare, like Kaminsky, with eyes wide open. The least Grove could do was make sure that she was adequately armed.

All told, with the .38 Smith & Wesson that Doerr had left behind, and Kaminsky's pistol-grip shotgun, they had four firearms and a grand total of thirty-eight rounds of ammunition. Not exactly a well-stocked armory but probably enough to bring down an ordinary man.

Of course, calling Doerr "ordinary" was probably akin to calling Fiona a little passing sprinkle. From all indications, the student was in the grips of an off-the-scale dissociative fugue state, a true psychotic break, which had its own set of rules. Over the course of his career, Grove had made it a point to familiarize himself with these rules. But now, with the tantalizing clues in the secret room—not to mention the connection between the subject and Grove, which, for the moment, remained just out of Grove's reach—the rule book now seemed superfluous.

"I am getting something, hold on a moment!" Kaminsky blurted from the corner, his face owlish in the light of the lantern. He sat Indian-style next to the cadenza, his big barrel of a belly jutting out over his belt. He wore one of the NSA T-shirts (while his damp coat and shirt hung on a nail across the room, drying). He held the small shortwave in his lap, an earphone jacked into it. "Quiet please!" He listened some more, the faint static audible above the muffled winds. "Some news here."

"What is it?" Maura was shivering against the wall with her knees pulled up against her slender body, her arms wrapped around herself.

Kaminsky listened some more. "She has unfortunately just been upgraded once again."

"Upgraded?" Grove stood up and gazed around the narrow chamber. The ceiling was so low, with so many obstacles, Grove had to slump to avoid rubbing the top of his head on the mobiles of human bones. He too wore one of Kaminsky's XXL T-shirts while his clothes dried out. "I thought she was already at category five. Doesn't that top her out at—"

Kaminsky raised a hand to cut him off, then listened some more. "Her winds, I am afraid, according to the NWS, have already passed the two-hundred mark, which makes her officially anomalous."

Maura looked confused. "Anomalous?"

The Russian looked at her. His gravelly voice softened. "It means *bad*, Miss County, I am afraid, far worse than Katrina. Only two others on record that I know of."

"Jesus, *Jesus* . . . what are we *doing*? What if the floods make it up here?"

"We'll have to cross that bridge when we get there," Grove said, only half joking, hands thrust in his pockets now. The walls seemed closer.

"If there *is* a bridge left," she commented. "God, I need a cigarette."

"Are you out?" Grove asked her.

"Ran out on the way over here." She gave him a defeated shake of her head.

The Russian was listening to the shortwave more intently now, pressing a finger against the earphone. The faint sizzle of static came out of it.

Grove gave Maura a wink. "You can always smoke one of Kaminsky's wretched cigars."

She looked over at the pack of Antonio Varga cigarillos lying on the floor next to the Russian. "You know something, that might not be a bad idea."

"Are you serious!"

She scooped up the box. "It'll mask the smell in here, which is about to make me puke."

"God help us," Grove murmured, then glanced at the opposite wall, now draped in a sheet, behind which sat rows of macabre specimens in their fluid-filled jars. Grove had covered much of the ghastly evidence with linens that he had found in the hall closet. He used duct tape, and had covered as much of it as possible so that Maura would not have to look at it, or dwell on it. But now he almost missed having it all within his field of view. He almost relished the smell. This was his habit, his drug. The hunt. And the odor of hard evidence—no matter how gruesome—was now almost Pavlovian to Grove.

"The eye is currently twenty-five miles offshore," Kaminsky announced. "Which means she is less than sixty miles away from us."

"ETA.?" Grove asked.

"I would say about an hour to forty-five minutes, plus or minus."

Maura lit one of the cigars with the Bic and coughed around a mouthful of smoke. The roaring white noise continued all around them, rattling the foundation, vibrating the walls. It seemed impossible that the storm would continue to worsen, but so it was. "You're not still thinking of going out there, are you?" Maura said, looking at Grove.

Grove didn't say anything.

Maura grimaced at the smell of the cigar. The smoke, as thick and acrid as that of a burning tire, filled the room. "Ivan, let me ask you a question."

The Russian took the earphone out of his ear. He grabbed the box of cigars, lit up one for himself, and savored the smoke. "Yes, Miss County, go ahead."

"First of all, call me Maura. Okay?"

"Yes, Maura, of course."

"Second of all, is it even *possible* for a man to just wander outside in the middle of the eye of a hurricane?"

"Well, the truth is—"

"I know you just flew an aircraft into one, but is it actually possible to do it on the ground, like it's just some peaceful summer night, and a man's just gonna go out and catch a bad guy during a commercial break in the action?"

Grove broke in. "I know where you're going with this, Maura, and you can just—"

"To answer the question for the lady," Kaminsky asserted, "I would say that it is possible but not probable. Considering the behavior of the eye."

"I don't follow."

Grove and Kaminsky exchanged a glance. Kaminsky let out a sigh and began rummaging through his duffel bag. He had a fleck of ash in his beard. "Think of it this way, Miss Coun—I am sorry—*Maura*. Think of it this way. It is like trying to thread a needle while skating on thin ice, if I may mix some more metaphors with my clumsy way of English."

Maura stared for a moment. Grove watched her. She touched her lips, then said very softly, "So what's the worst-case scenario?"

"The *probable* scenario, even if our courageous Agent Grove can stay in the path of the eye, is that it will close on him in the heat of battle."

"And?"

"And . . . then poof! No more good guy *or* bad guy," Kaminsky said, pulling the tube of sausage out of his bag. "Salami, anyone?"

Scholarly studies, many of them published in the wake of congressional emergency management reform, could only speculate on the number of living human souls remaining within the New Orleans city limits that night between the hours of 10:00 p.m. and midnight—despite all the ghostly reminders of Katrina still hanging over the place.

Many of those officially declared as "missing" were most likely carried out to sea, lost in the currents of the swelling Mississippi, or washed away in the ensuing floods. The following day, survivors were found all across the city in air pockets within capsized vehicles, floating on wreckage, or perched on rooftops or high ground waving makeshift flags made of torn clothing and rags. But for the most part, authorities acknowledged how the scope of the previous week's evacuation had saved millions of lives.

That night, by eleven o'clock, central standard time, the town's population had been reduced to only a few hundred people—and most of those hearty souls were safely tucked away "uptown" (far to the west, in newly established hurricane shelters). The only stragglers remaining within the confines of the French Quarter were the mad, the lost, the homeless, the forgotten, and the foolhardy. At 11:04 p.m., as the inner eye wall pushed into town, and the angry surge reached its apex twenty-five feet over the awnings of the marketplace, crashing through the air like a great fragment bomb, inundating Jackson Square, tearing through the park, ripping bronze statues from their pedestals: Sixteen transients lurked in the moldering nooks and crannies around St. Louis Cathedral. Seven of these were women—prostitutes all—most of whom now huddled, terrified, inside the basement of the free clinic on Chartres Street. The other nine ranged in ages from seventeen to sixty-three.

They were each about to learn that the hurricane was the least of their problems.

A Haitian gentleman with graying tufts of hair and wild eyes by the name of Charles Petiere—street name Carpet Man, due to his propensity to acquire rancid carpet remnants—was the first to see the devil himself materialize out of the storm. Petiere had been clinging to a padlocked door inside one of the cathedral's portals, clutching at the bars like a gargoyle, while the horizontal rain tried to claw him into oblivion. When the levees finally began to fail, the first black waves crashed over the square, the furious river slamming up against the stones of the cathedral like an invading army.

Petiere lost his grip then, and went careening into the floodwater now devouring St. Ann Street, floodwater that had already risen to nearly four feet and was traveling inland with the speed and intensity of a rapid-moving river. Madly flailing his arms, his garbled, watery cries inaudible in the din, the Haitian coursed westward like a leaf tossing on the rapids, careening across Canal Street, then into the Warehouse District, before getting tangled in a fallen traffic signal. His head tagged the iron wreckage hard enough to knock him senseless, and he gasped for air for a moment as he instinctively held on to the mangled metal post.

Before passing out, he managed to look up at the wind-torn surface of the water before him.

The figure rose out of the black currents like some kind of fabled sea monster, moored to the street-grating by strong nylon ropes and anchors. Black cape flagging crazily in the hellish wind, his narrow dark face creased with evil and madness, the devil growled something inaudible at Petiere—the screaming heavens drowning out all sound but the storm. Then, moving with cobralike speed, the devil lashed out at the Haitian, the barbed chain sinking into Petiere's jugular. The homeless man's blood mist and scream both vanished instantly in the wind.

It was the first harvest of the evening, but it would not be the last.

"Jesus Christ, look!"

Maura was pointing at the floor near the sealed pantry door, and all eyes turned toward the door. Grove saw it next. In the dim light of the lantern, a thin, gray tongue of dirty water shimmered and seeped under the door. All three of them stood up. The noise of the storm was so intense by that point, it was making Grove's ears pop and ring. It sounded as though a herd of elephants were stampeding across their roof.

"Shit!" Grove said.

"This is precisely what I expected," Kaminsky commented dryly, glowering down at the moisture.

Maura looked nauseated. "The whole place is flooded, goddamnit, which means—"

"The levees have already gone south," Grove interrupted. "C'mon, help me get some towels over there."

They had collected a bundle of towels from the linen closet for this very purpose, and Grove and Maura hurried them over to the door, stuffing them against the gap at the bottom, while Kaminsky puffed his stogie and watched. The muffled jet-engine noise of the storm had changed over the last few minutes, like a giant blender rising up through its highest speeds, indicating the advent of the eye. The fastest winds mauled the Garden District now with ferocious bloodlust, the intermittent spasms jolting through the bungalow's foundation. Every few seconds, another distant, sickly cracking noise would rise above the atonal symphony, or a sharp crash of broken glass would ring out across the neighborhood, signaling the demise of another vehicle or building. It sounded as though the grand refurbished New Orleans was falling apart like a house of cards.

"Oh my God, there's something I forgot to tell you about that."

"What . . . ?" Grove turned away from the door, and saw that Maura was pointing at his spiral notebook, which now sat open on the cadenza. The sketch of the bloody hand-drawn characters and ritual placement of organs left at the Ulmer's Folly scene was clearly visible in the lantern light.

"That symbol," Maura said, turning her nose up at the drawing as though it had a smell.

Across the room, Kaminsky put the earphone back

in his ear and listened to the faint crackling of the National Weather Service.

Grove came over and looked down at the notebook. "What about it?"

Maura looked into his eyes. "This is on his chest."

Grove stared at her. "What?"

She explained how she had accidentally discovered the strange scars on Doerr's midsection, and how they had matched up perfectly with Grove's sketch. It was as though Grove had literally *traced* the wormy, ropy tissue snaking between Doerr's nipples.

While Maura spoke, Grove felt that tight, cold pinch in his gut that always happens when the windows open up on a case, when the sources of psychopathology begin to reveal themselves. The kid had not only *seen* the exorcism, but had also *seen* the symbol on the floor, and had become obsessed enough to make shrines and even carve the symbol into his chest. Doerr was a lunatic. Sure. But now Grove was realizing that Doerr was *more* than a crazy person. Grove's heart rate began to quicken. Like Ackerman in the previous case, Michael Doerr had taken on the same parasitic personality.

Icy dread trickled through Grove's midsection. "Doerr wasn't the one who carved that symbol on his chest," he said in a low, grave tone.

Maura looked at him. "What are you talking about, Ulysses?"

Grove gently took the spiral notebook back from Maura. He closed it and dropped it on the cadenza. "According to the padre, that star within a star is like a nuclear reactor for spirits, a giant black hole."

Maura was shaking her head. "Now you lost me."

"The eye just hit the Mississippi," Kaminsky announced, nervously chewing his cigar. "It will be right on top of us in a matter of minutes."

Grove said to Maura, "It's back, kiddo."

"What's back?"

"The thing in Ackerman."

A stunned pause. "Gimme a break, Ulysses."

Grove didn't say anything, just turned away from her, reached over, and felt the collar of his Armani sport coat, which hung on a nail by the corner of the shelving unit. "There's a point in every case," he said as he quickly slipped out of his NSA T-shirt, "a point where evidence analysis evolves into something else, and I think we've reached that point."

"What are you doing, Ulysses?"

"My job." He slipped on a fresh oxford dress shirt. It was slightly wrinkled but blazing white. He buttoned the sleeves, then tucked it into his slacks, which also looked brand-new. He began buttoning his shirt. He needed to straighten himself out. This was *his* ritual. He was a professional, and he required neatness. "We've reached the takedown phase," he murmured then, "and that's what I'm going to do—I'm going to take this individual down. Whatever it is. Evil spirit. Schizophrenic. Whatever."

"Any minute now!" Kaminsky called out, his finger pressing against the earphone.

Maura was wringing her hands. "Ulysses, I know what you're planning to do . . . and I'm gonna ask you one last time, wait till morning. At least wait until morning."

Buttoning his shirt, Grove saw something for a moment in his mind's eye: a flash of those damned blackbirds madly flapping their wings, trying to penetrate a wall of wind. "The eye is the key," he said then to

Maura. "He wants me in the eye. But he's vulnerable there, too, because the eye is the prison he's made for himself."

"Oh, that is such voodoo profiler bullshit!"

"Maura—"

"C'mon, Ulysses, listen to that storm! That storm is real! That's not some abstraction out of your diagnostic manual. You think it's going to help matters for you to go out there in that shit and get yourself killed? You think that's going to slay this dragon?"

Grove reached into his knapsack and pulled a worn shoulder harness out. He slipped it on. The muffled shrieking of the storm kicked up yet another notch. It now seemed to squeeze down on them like a gargantuan vise. Grove stepped into a pair of hiking boots that he had brought in from the back of the Jeep. Rubber-soled and treated, they were affectionately known as "duck boots" among the bureau guys. "I'm not going to get myself killed," Grove said above the noise, tying the boot strings, ears popping. "I'm going to get *Doerr* killed."

"So now you're judge, jury, and executioner?"

Grove didn't answer but instead adjusted the harness, buckling it, paying close attention to the way it hugged his ribs and looped over his shoulders. He adjusted his collar. Everything had to look impeccable, lean and streamlined. He pulled the Charter Arms .357 from the pack. He snapped open the cylinder and checked the six rounds already seated there. The storm wailed.

Grove clicked the cylinder shut.

Up until the Sun City case a year ago, Grove, a one-time shooting champion back in the military, had grown a tad rusty with the old handguns. Profilers had very little call to fire weapons in the field. But in recent months, in the wake of all the insomnia, therapy, medication, and just general paranoia, he had become a regular at the shooting range. His weekly target practice sessions had become another security blanket, just like the medication. By the spring of this year, he had gotten back his old reptilian calm, his facility with the speed-loader, and his eye. His sighting eye.

"Listen to me, Ulysses, listen. Doerr's probably halfway to East Texas by now!"

Grove slipped on his spare Armani jacket, shot the sleeves, and brushed off the shoulders. He could see his reflection in the broken glass of a picture frame. He looked ready. He looked like an African-American senator about to go out onto the floor for a crucial vote, or maybe a dapper assassin. The latter was probably more appropriate.

"Listen to the nice lady, Grove," Kaminsky piped in. "What she is saying is correct."

"He's waiting for me, and he—*it*—is not gonna flee until one of us is dead." Grove's voice was flat and cruel in his own ears as he pulled on his street-length black overcoat. He had already gone some place else. Some place deep inside himself. He was no longer a member of any established agency or law enforcement bureau. He was a practitioner of an *older* system of justice now. "I'm the last piece of the puzzle."

Grove found the speed-loaders and dropped them into the overcoat pockets.

"We'll get a goddamned exorcist to help us," Maura panted, "a witch doctor, a voodoo priest, *whatever*— just don't do this.*"* She was clenching her fists. She looked beautiful to Grove right at that moment. Her gray-green eyes on fire, her translucent skin blushed with emotion. Would this be the last time he would drink in those features? Almost as an answer to Grove's silent question, the storm wailed overhead, louder than ever. It sounded like the sky peeling open.

The room quaked then, something slamming down on the bungalow's roof, a tree perhaps. Grove buttoned his overcoat up to the neck, turning up his collar. Then he tightened the Velcro on his sleeves, putting on his fingerless, leather Carnaby gloves. The shooting gloves were gifts from his late wife, Hannah, and they had taken on almost talismanic power over the years. "I'm the exorcist now," he said with a terse nod, flexing his fingers. "I'm going to cleanse the situation once and for all."

Another barrage of wind assaulted the bungalow, this one stronger yet, rattling the structure down to its core. The floor trembled. The inner eye-wall winds had reached their zenith, tearing and rasping through the district.

"I give up!" Maura shouted, backing into a corner and hugging herself nervously. "What are we supposed to do while you're out there getting yourself killed?"

"You two stay put," Grove said, straining his voice to be heard above the noise, reaching into his knapsack for one last item: a pair of night-vision goggles. He quickly looped them around his neck. "If I'm not back before the other side of the eye arrives, seal yourself in and wait out the storm!"

"Grove, listen to me!" Kaminsky had dug into his own pile of gear, and now stood in front of Grove holding one end of a massive coil of salmon-colored nylon mountaineering rope. The noise and pressure of the storm had risen to unbearable levels, so intense now it felt like Grove's eardrums were going to explode in his head.

"What the hell is that?" Grove indicated the rope.

"Take it, and tie it off to your waist!"

"Are you crazy!" Dizziness swam through Grove's brain, toying with his balance. He fought it, biting down hard enough to crack his jaw.

"Pay attention, Grove, for once in your life!"

"I gotta be able to move out there!"

"This line is nearly a thousand feet long, which is almost a quarter mile!"

"I don't need it!"

"Goddamn you, Grove, you will do this if you want any chance of survival!"

"Why is this fucking rope so important?"

"Because the eye is not only the most dangerous place in the world, it is also the most unpredictable!"

"Warning noted!"

"Listen to you, listen to you! 'Warning noted'! You are truly an arrogant piece of a job!"

"Goddamnit, Kay—!"

"I am trying to tell you that if the eye closes on you, you will be blind!"

"What do you mean?"

"Two-hundred-plus-mile-an-hour winds behind the rain is a complete gray-out!"

"How much time do I have?"

"It is impossible to predict, it could stall over land, sure, for ten or fifteen minutes—"

"That's all the time I need!"

"You are not listening! It could just as easily pass through in a matter of seconds!"

"I'll take that chance!"

"If you do not tie this rope to your belt right now I

will shoot you in the head with my shotgun until you are dead!"

Maura screamed: "Tie the fucking rope to your belt, Ulysses!"

"Jesus Christ, okay!"

The beast outside roared its primal roar, as Grove snatched the end of the rope out of Kaminsky's hands, then threaded it inside his belt, securing it to a loop, then slinging the heavy coil over his shoulder. The inner eye wall was right on top of them, the towels on the floor near the door completely soaked through, the long gray tongue of water reaching across the floor, the tremors constant now, making it feel as though the foundation was about to cave in.

"Goddamnit, Ulysses! You want me to beg, I'll beg—please, please, *please* don't go out there!" Maura backed into the corner, her tiny hands balled into tight little white fists. She burned her gaze into him.

"Shut up, Maura! Just shut up! *Just shut up and let it go!*"

Grove's outburst, driven by an unmooring of his grief and pent-up rage and raw emotions, was almost immediately drowned by the deafening peal of the storm, which now had reached a thunderous crescendo. The closest analogy would be an immense, celestial engine revving so furiously and uncontrollably that it flies off its own bearings in a fiery metallic eruption. The final booming report was so loud and so palpable it seemed to crash down on the little bungalow with the force of a wrecking ball. Maura slammed her hands over her ears—to block out either the storm or Grove's bellowing anger—and Kaminsky staggered back against the wall, knocking several gruesome artifacts to the floor, while Grove, standing alone in the center of the room, suddenly fell to his knees and covered his ears. The pandemonium seemed to collapse suddenly, caving in under its own weight, a great paroxysm of air pressure sucking the volume out of the wind, and then there was nothing but swirling white noise, and then . . . a sudden and unexpected silence.

They each froze there for an infinitesimal moment of pure shock before realizing what the silence meant.

The eye had arrived.

PART III

Revelations

On that day all the fountains of the great deep burst forth, and the windows of the heavens were open.

—Genesis 7:11

19

Grove paused at the front door, breathing in the eerie stillness outside. It was like snorting a pinch of smelling salts. The air prickled with static electricity.

The front door squeaked as he pushed it open and stepped out into the night.

For a brief moment, he paused on the front porch, gathering his bearings, ankle-deep in standing water. He barely felt the heavy coil of rope digging into his shoulder, its tail snaking back behind him and into the shadows of the house. The rope was designed to be lightweight for mountaineering purposes, but still must have weighed forty or fifty pounds. Complicating matters was the fact that the other end was tied off to *Kaminsky*. (This was a decision made after a frantic debate on the safest way to anchor it. Kaminsky thought that tying it to the house—no matter how stable or strong the object—was risky since the house could literally not be there when Grove returned).

The screen door slammed behind him, making a strange, flat, echoless bang—the sound of a door slamming in a recording studio. The air outside the bungalow was cool and dank and malodorous like the air in a basement. A dog barked somewhere in the black distance.

The neighborhood had flooded. The new, improved levees had already given out. That was one of the first things that registered in Grove's brain, which was working feverishly now, a clockwork mechanism absorbing every detail in his field of vision, processing all the sensory input flowing into him. Freret Street had become a canal. The tops of cars rose out of the lazily moving water like little, square, metal islands. The lawns lay under two to three feet of water, which rippled in the gentle wind. That was another thing that occurred to Grove in those early moments, a detail he hadn't noticed on board the plane: *There's wind inside the eye.* It was a subtle little breeze of maybe ten to fifteen miles an hour, hardly noticeable, but it was there.

He descended the steps, letting out the rope as he went, then quickly waded through the brackish water of the lawn.

Moonlight shone down on the flooded street. That was the next thing Grove noticed. With dreamlike clarity it glimmered like luminous ribbons across the surface of the water. Tree debris floated hear and there. Downed telephone poles drifted calmly across a surface hectic with shards of wood, litter, and broken glass glistening like diamonds.

It didn't occur to Grove to look up just yet. He was too busy listening and smelling and absorbing every last sensory detail: the distant moaning of the eye-wall winds, the sulfurous stench of the stirred-up river, the prickling sensation on the back of his neck. He could feel a pair of feverishly attentive eyes behind him, tracking his every move from inside the darkness of the bungalow. He had convinced Maura and Kaminsky to stay inside the inner room for the duration, but Grove knew they couldn't resist peering out of the pantry, watching through the jagged, damaged front windows.

Grove paused and reached inside his coat. He pulled the Tracker from its holster. The gun felt cold and reassuring in his hand. His nerves were wired to its grip, to its hammer, to its long barrel and its front site. And he realized suddenly—maybe subconsciously, maybe consciously—he was here in this hellish place to do a job that no one else was willing or able to do. This was his destiny . . . and all those years of studying and collating off-the-scale mental cases, years of getting inside the criminal mind, and getting that old empathy going for these pathetic individuals—all of it—now seemed like lies to Grove. They seemed like a part of the *old* Grove, a skin that he had shed—a veneer of civilized behavior that had been sandblasted away in the crucible of this hurricane.

Perhaps *this* was the secret meaning within the visions that had been plaguing Grove all his life, the very simple kernel of truth inside all the mumbo jumbo his mother had visited upon him over the years: "You are chosen, Mwana, chosen for something real, something big, it is written in the bones, in the words of the 'seer.'" Grove realized what it was now: The gods simply needed a garbage collector. They simply wanted somebody to periodically come along and take these assholes out, thin the herd, shore up the accounting. And after all the ponderous analysis, and profiling on the fly, Grove realized he felt no sympathy for this damaged young man named Michael Doerr. He made no allowances for the probability of abuse in Doerr's past. At that moment, Grove could not have cared less about Doerr's scars, both psychic and literal, or the profound anguish Doerr must have experienced for most of his wretched life. There was nothing to learn from Doerr. There was nothing to learn from *any* of the homicidal maniacs whom Grove had hunted. They were mutations—created by nature, and nurtured by the brutality of cruel caretakers, and very possibly hosts to a single parasite, *whatever it was*. . . .

Grove took a deep breath and then waded across the street, letting the rope uncoil off his shoulder as he moved, grasping the gun tightly with his right hand. He moved with a purpose. Not hurriedly . . . but *purposeful*.

He knew he only had a few minutes to get the job done.

And he would do just that: *get the job done . . . or die trying*.

"Can you see him anymore?" Maura was leaning against the doorjamb outside the pantry, still feeling the sting of Grove's outburst, trying to see through the gaping windows in the living room, where the outer world was obscured by jagged puzzle pieces of broken glass, most of them beaded with condensation, and fogged almost to the point of being opaque.

"No, regrettably, he has just passed behind the Jeep." Kaminsky stood just inside the kitchen archway, the rope looped around his massive girth and tied off on a metal carabineer.

"Jesus Christ, what is that noise?" Maura leaned back against one side of the pantry, accidentally knocking a box of instant grits to the puddled floor. The two inches of standing water in the pantry was littered with soggy spilled cereal and pasta. It smelled like moldy dog fur in there. Roaches floated like bloated raisins in the puddles.

"That noise is the eye wall," Kaminsky informed her. The big man came back into the pantry, dragging the rope like a tail, and plucked the shotgun from the shelf. He started clicking shells into the breech as he talked, the snap of each shell punctuating his deep, gravel baritone. "It is not cooperating." *Snap!* "To be perfectly frank with you." *Snap!*

"What do you mean?"

"It has doubled over the last few hours." *Snap!* "Which means it is big, and will take a while to pass through." *Snap!*

"What's wrong with that? That doesn't sound so bad. It'll give Ulysses more time. Right? *Right?*"

The Russian looked at her. "That is true, Maura, but unfortunately when the eye *does* finally pass through, and the other side of the eye wall returns, it will be worse than ever." *Snap!* "Perhaps the worst we have ever seen." *Snap!* "And Grove will be stuck."

"God *damn*, that noise is driving me batty." Maura put her hands over her ears and slid down the shelf until her rear end plopped down into the water, soaking through immediately. She didn't care anymore. She didn't care about anything anymore, except Grove's chance of survival, which right now seemed to be diminishing faster than Maura's resolve.

The water rose to his knees now, and the moaning noise was changing, rising, getting closer, but he kept on. He kept on wading through the muck toward St. Charles Avenue, which lay in the tomblike stillness several blocks away. He had no idea if the rope would reach, but he had to try. Doerr *had* to be in this general vicinity. Considering the intensity of the storm, the young man would have gotten pinned down shortly after he had fled the bungalow. Clinically possessed or not, no human being could negotiate those eye-wall winds.

Only a few seconds had passed since Grove had emerged from that bungalow, but already he was becoming attuned to the strange universe inside the eye. He could hear his own heartbeat in his ears, which were still ringing. The lapping sounds of the thigh-high water sent gooseflesh down his back, and the eerie moaning of the wind wall—judging from its constant, plaintive wailing, it lay a quarter mile or so off in all directions—began to resemble a vast armature, as though Grove were trapped inside a giant turbine. Finally he paused, and he looked up at the sky.

Directly overhead, as though through the open roof of an indoor stadium, the clear black heavens were visible, rich with stars, a brilliant moon shining down. It seemed impossible, but there it was, like a proscenium portal in the middle of a boiling, milky, time-lapse sky. Grove gaped up at it, enthralled, paralyzed with the simian fascination of a caveman staring at fire.

A noise to his left.

He spun toward the sound and aimed the gun, and almost squeezed off a shot, but something told him to wait, *don't shoot, don't give your position away, not yet, not yet.* He pointed the gun at a cluster of loblollies in a flooded lawn across the street. In the moonlight, a leprous snout poked out of the water near a phalanx of stumps. Opening and closing convulsively, revealing dull yellow fangs, the snout belonged to an injured alligator, evidently in its death throes. A dark cloud of blood stewed in the floodwater around it.

The gator had somehow tumbled across the lawn in the storm and gotten itself impaled.

Another noise rattled across the street and Grove whirled. Stuck the gun out. Bit down hard. Held his breath. An icy needle of panic pierced him as he scanned the shadows of a deserted parking lot. Nothing moved at first. Only the lazy drifting of debris across the surface of the flooded lot. A boarded storefront lay just beyond the lot, the moonlight painting it silver. But no movement. No shadows. Then another noise gurgled to Grove's immediate left.

The gun swung over, Grove's hot gaze locking onto bubbles, *bubbles*, coming up from beneath the surface. In that one feverish instant before the source of the bubbles made itself known, Grove figured it might be another alligator. He pointed the gun at the disturbance on the water.

The corpse bobbed to the surface as though making an entrance in a carefully choreographed play. Grove grew very still. The body was male, dark-skinned and elderly, with graying tufts of hair, and it floated a few feet away from Grove, the gentle currents caressing it as though it were anchored there. The old man had sustained massive lacerations to the jugular, and had already started to bloat in the water. His wrinkled face was caved in on one side, his mouth a bloody, toothless divot, his left eye an empty black crater of glistening tissue. Deep arterial blood blossomed around the cadaver like an inky penumbra in the moonlight.

More noises clicked and burbled all around Grove now, and he began breathing through his nostrils in long, regular, rhythmic beats, shrugging off the coil of rope, the coil splashing in the water. He cupped the gun in both hands, assuming the Weaver position, fixing the front sight on the shadows behind the adjacent trees and buildings. He held his breath then, reaching down inside himself for that snaky calm he needed to take the target down, because he saw more bodies in his peripheral field of vision.

They bobbed to the surface in the middle distance, one after another, each in more putrefied stages of mutilation. They were connected somehow—both literally, through guide wires or cables or ropes, and figuratively, through some insane logic that Grove would have to collate at a later time—and they were meant for Grove's eyes only. And also maybe God's eyes. They had turned the moonlit water scarlet black, forming a familiar pattern that Grove was just beginning to recognize when another noise yanked his attention to a parallel rooftop.

A dark figure crouched up there—on top of an old, stately, Italianate mansion—perched on the steep pitch of its gable like an enormous owl.

For one slim instant, Grove hesitated. He had a clean kill shot—maybe forty yards, fifty at the most; a completely acceptable range for the weapon—but something stopped him. Something made him stare at this creature that used to be called Michael Doerr.

At this distance Grove could just barely make out the expression on the figure's face beneath that weird black cowl of a headpiece—leathery skin the color of cowhide, sunken eyes, a giant crevice of a mouth. The mouth widened until it practically split the face apart, peeling away from dull white teeth. At first Grove thought the thing was grinning. But soon it became clear the rictus on that ravaged face was a look of pure hate.

"*Whoever you are! Whatever you are!*" Grove called out, his voice shattering the tenuous silence of the eye. "*It ends tonight!*"

The killer cocked his head to one side like a dog hearing a high-pitched whistle.

He seemed to be savoring the moment.

The Holy Ghost gazed down upon the flooded street, memorizing every last detail of the tall African-American standing down there with the weapon. The true nature of this "FBI" man's spirit registered in the deepest recesses of the entity's core like a spotlight flaring on, illuminating the darkest corners of its being with cleansing light.

Electric heat began to bolt up the entity's spine, something as pure as liquid sunlight, crashing in his brain, resonating through him in the darkness like a tuning fork being struck: The final rite, the last part of the ritual, the sacred sacrifice was about to commence!

In that radiant instant, the Holy Ghost felt the rage crackle in his nervous system.

This was anger dating back centuries, anger worse than the bloodiest of tribal feuds, anger predating the modern world. This was anger formed over the centuries, fired in the furnace of eternal hellish misery. Like a lump of coal transformed into a diamond, this rage was cast under tremendous pressure and heat, a crystallization of pain into the sharpest, most brilliant, most deadly of all emotions: the need for revenge. It had survived the great Mayan rulers, the Toltec civilizations, the brutal Aztec empire, the Colonial periods, the wars, the Indian dictators, Pancho Villa, Zapata, earthquakes, floods, and year after year of hurricanes. And now, tonight, this instant, it had denatured into a single glimpse of a caramel-skinned man aiming a gun in the eye of a storm.

This was the one. The manhunter. The shaman. The mourning spirit.

The one who must be destroyed.

Grove got very still, standing thigh-deep in the mire, both hands on the Tracker, his body frozen in the tripod position. He now could see the shimmering length of chain up there, dangling from Doerr's hand, terminating in a long, curved, razor-edge sickle. The death grimace on Doerr's face widened, as though he had come to some arcane conclusion. Tremors shivered through Doerr's upper body, making the terrible chain jangle.

In that single instant, a sense of imminent violence bristled in the air like a magnetic field, and Grove got the distinct impression that this showdown would become the centerpiece of the ritual.

Suddenly, almost in response to Grove's thought pattern, the creature tossed its head back, then began to hiss a rapid sequence of sibilant foreign phrases and words that Grove could not begin to identify. The chain began to slowly rotate, the killing blade gently orbiting like a slow-motion lariat.

Grove felt the cold tableau, the bloodshed forthcoming, like a clammy breath on the back of his neck. *"Go ahead! Go ahead and do it! Do it!"*

The chain bull-whipped suddenly as Grove's gun came up in one fluid—perhaps involuntary—motion of the arm.

The muzzle roared.

The blast lit up the night air, and the chain soared through the darkness, a silver bird of prey swooping down on Grove. The two equal and opposite actions glittered for an instant in the mist.

The curved blade struck Grove's right arm, slicing through his raincoat and tearing a bite out of his upper biceps. It gashed him down to the bone before bouncing off and skipping into the water, but Grove barely felt anything, his blood now boiling with so many neurochemicals it was almost humming.

On the roof Michael Doerr was reeling at the impact of the blast. The bullet had grazed him, chewing a gob of tissue from his left shoulder, and sending him slamming backward against the steep tile pitch.

Down on the street, in a cloud of blood mist and cordite, Grove struggled to stay on his feet, awash in adrenaline, eyes going out of focus, brain swimming. The pistol slipped out of his hand, plopping into the water and sinking out of sight. He immediately crouched down and fished around for the weapon.

Up on the roof the maniac that used to be Michael Doerr had vanished.

Grove did not panic. He finally got his greasy fingers around the gun. Now time was critical. The eye wall was closing fast.

He didn't know it then, but the ritual had just begun.

20

In all the postmortems of that horrible, deadly night, the single detail that remained fairly consistent was the estimated span of time it took Fiona's eye to travel across central New Orleans. The FBI's 243-page *Report to the Director on the Events of 23 September 2006* listed the elapsed time it took the eye to pass through the area at a mere fourteen minutes. The transcript of the Orleans Parish district attorney's *Inquest on the United States versus Michael Doerr* clocked it at only twelve minutes and thirty seconds. The National Weather Service, not to be outdone in the exactitude department, posted the official time at thirteen minutes, eleven seconds.

In any case, it was generally agreed that the eye crossed the city in an amazingly short amount of time. The heart of New Orleans comprises a roughly nine-square-kilometer area, which includes the French Quarter, the Garden District, and the Downtown area, and features all manner of restoration and architectural renewal, from the funky galleries of the Quarter, to the soaring church steeples and high-rises of the Central Business District, to the massive, stately plantation homes along St. Charles Avenue. The city had done such a splendid job of rebuilding itself in the twelve months since Katrina's floods, it was heartbreaking to see the tender wounds of this grand old town torn asunder once again by the angry winds.

But very few citizens knew of the secret, epochal battle that was also unfolding in that brief period of time.

In the FBI's *Report to the Director*, investigators managed to find a single eyewitness, a surgical orderly named Andy Drood, who happened to be barricaded inside a top floor of St. Charles General Hospital during the worst of the storm. When the eye wall hit, and the sudden calm was broken by the sound of Grove's gun, Drood ran to the north windows—many of which had been broken out—and gazed down at St. Charles Avenue. He recounted later, in a sworn affidavit:

. . . a few blocks west of the hospital I saw this figure leaping from rooftop to rooftop. I mean, I just couldn't believe my eyes. This guy was dressed all in black, and he vaults off the roof of a house and lands in the water at the corner of General Pershing and St. Charles. Then I realize there's another guy chasing him with a gun. I saw a flash, and I . . . I heard a shot. I couldn't believe it. But then this guy in black climbs on top of a stalled streetcar, which is obviously swamped in the floodwater, and he starts running across the roof of the train! He's heading northeast toward the French Quarter, leaping from car to car. Unbe-lievable! Then I saw something even more bizarre. This other guy, the one with the gun, he tries to follow the guy onto the streetcar, tries to hop on back of the caboose, but just as he's about

*jump onto the traincar, something yanks him
backward. I mean, it was like whiplash, man, it
was like somebody grabbed him by the neck and
jerked him backward, and he fell into the water. . . .*

At that moment—which official records pinpoint at
10:05 p.m.—Ulysses Grove was completely submerged, stricken senseless in the black, cold, moving
floodwater. Everything was utterly silent and dark, and
he flailed and gasped and swallowed a mouthful of
water, and he struggled to see, struggled to get his
bearings, to grab hold of something. Had somebody
ambushed him? He felt an iron grip clutching at his
belt. His mind raced. He finally burst back to the surface, coughing for air, spitting salt water and blood.

He glanced around for the source of his fall and realized instantly what had happened.

The guide rope had reached the end of its length. It
was no good to him now.

He quickly wrestled it off the belt, unsnapping the
metal carabineer that the Russian had used to secure
the rope. The gouge in Grove's arm had opened farther,
and now it burned, but he put it out of his mind.

He searched for something to which he could attach
the rope. He chose a fire hydrant a half block north, a
rusty little iron plug embedded in the sidewalk, pocked
with peeling red paint. Grove hastily looped the rope
around it, then tied the loose end in a square knot.

It had taken roughly thirty seconds to do all this, but
thirty seconds was forever inside the eye. Like a
dream, time had no meaning here. Thirty seconds was
a blink and was also a thousand years.

Wading back toward the streetcar, Grove felt as
though he were trapped inside the dislocated, surreal

futility of a nightmare. His strides were inhibited by
the water, slowed down to a syrupy trudge, and the
harder he tried to charge toward that derailed streetcar
the more difficult it became. But worse than that, he
could hear the ululating moan that had risen now to the
level of a shriek. The eye was on the move. How long
had he been outside in it? Three minutes? Five? Soon
the town would be plunged back into chaos . . . and
there would be refuge for neither good *nor* evil.

Grove reached the downed streetcar, then climbed
onto the rear step rail with his Tracker still gripped in
his frozen-wet hand. He scaled the back of the train,
which was treacherous with oily, rain-slick surfaces,
and then climbed onto the roof.

He started creeping across the top of the trolley as
swiftly as possible without slipping—side-stepping the
vent stacks and the low-hanging power cables, which
were as tangled and crisscrossed as giant steel spider-
webs—searching the distance for Doerr.

The dark figure was visible seven or eight cars away,
his black coattails furling in the wind. Grove cocked
the gun and hurried after the killer. The first leap between train cars was nearly his last.

He slipped twice: once while launching himself off
the greasy caboose (when he didn't get the lift he
needed) and a second time as he landed on the next car.
His knees slammed the door's glass lintel, cracking the
pane and sending him over the top, sprawling across
the car's roof.

He slid headfirst into an exhaust stack, skyrockets
bursting across his field of vision. He nearly dropped
the Tracker again. Gasping for breath, shaking off the
pain, he rose to kneeling position.

Grove swallowed his dizziness and wiped the moisture from his face. The wind had kicked up again, tossling Grove's long coat: Gusts of maybe forty miles an hour now—maybe even fifty or sixty—threatening to buffet Grove off the top of the train. And that horrible, moaning jackal howl, growing louder and louder, tearing open the sky.

Panic slithered through Grove's gut like a cold snake. He refused to allow Doerr to flee. He shoved the gun inside his coat, down into his harness holster, which was sticky and cold with his blood.

Then he grasped the night-vision goggles. Raised them to his eyes. Yanked the rubber strap to secure them. He flipped them on.

Luminous green silhouettes materialized before him. Buildings became glowing monoliths. Broken telephone poles became radiant green stalagmites. Lightning became phosphorous tongues of emerald fire. The French Quarter, whose border lay only a few blocks away, was transformed into a flickering video game.

Grove's pulse thumped in his neck as he rose and started across the train's roof. Blocks rushed by.

In the chartreuse distance, a little glowing figure climbed the side of a dilapidated row house on Julia Street.

When Grove was a kid, he used to climb the tallest trees in his Northside Chicago neighborhood in seconds flat like a little lemur. He just had a knack for it. A skinny kid, nimble and light on his feet, he grew into a natural athlete. While at the academy, he blew his fellow bureau cadets off the obstacle course. But now, decades later, hindered by extra pounds, and a gun clutched in

his hand, and a fresh wound still bleeding under his
sleeve, he moved like an old man.

Making matters worse was the dizzying disorientation caused by the goggles. It was like trying to run
through a deadly pop-up book full of nasty booby traps
using only a tiny telescope for guidance. Depth percep-
tion had gone all to hell. The moonlight put a halo
around everything like a frozen photographic negative.
Grove couldn't see his feet, or the power lines dangling
willy-nilly across the top of the train, now registering
as thin silken lines across the green view-screen.

Two blocks ahead of him, the luminous figure
vaulted through the air and landed batlike on the back
of an abandoned semi trailer lying cold and dark in the
water near Lafayette Square. From this distance, the
truck looked like something prehistoric lying there in
the moon shadows.

Doerr was getting away.

At the bottom of Canal Street the Holy Ghost abruptly
changed course and headed northwest, backtracking
through the moonbeams, in synch with the moving
eye. Silently, almost gracefully, he crossed the dark
landscape, leaping from rooftop to car top, splashing
through floodwater, his entire being vibrating with ancient emotions.

It took Grove less than a minute to reach the top of the
Highway 90 overpass, but in the fifty seconds or so that
it took to scale the ladder, the atmosphere across the
French Quarter and the Warehouse District had changed
significantly.

The air pressure had dropped ruthlessly, enough to make the hairs on Grove's neck and arms bristle again, and the moonlight had faded, as the inner eye-wall clouds began churning counterclockwise over the riverfront like a vast dilating pupil. The levees began hemorrhaging tidewaters again, and the howling winds closed in, the locomotive roar returning on a wave of high-pitched screams.

Grove tore the goggles off his face, tossing them over the side of the overpass. He had no use for them anymore. In the transition winds, he would be able to see better with his naked eyes. He gazed off to the west. He could see St. Charles Avenue stretching ribbon-like into the Garden District a half mile away.

He had started toward the ladder when he saw something out of the corner of his eye that made him abruptly stop.

Despite the fact that every second counted now, and despite the fact that he was close to collapse—he had already lost an alarming amount of blood—he still paused there for a moment, gaping down at the black night-scape to the west. Just beyond the Warehouse District, where the tight little storefront shops and flickering sodium lights gave way to the massive shadows of live oaks and plantation homes, Grove could see the boulevard down which he had just come.

He swallowed hard. He could not believe what he was seeing. It simply would not compute in his mind. And for a long moment—and this was a critical time for Grove, a life-and-death stretch of time—he stood there thinking he *must* be seeing things. It must be a trick of the light, an artifact of all the adrenaline and exhaust. But the more he gazed out over the rooftops and tangled power lines, the more he realized that what he was looking at was real.

It stretched from Coliseum Square to Audubon Park, the entire length of the flooded, storm-ravaged Garden District. From this distance, in the moonlight, Doerr's victims, most of which floated along the central avenue, anchored to the rails of the median, looked like rubbery, fleshy buoys, each one highlighted by a corona of bloody water as dark as India ink. But it was the big picture seen from Grove's proximity on the overpass that gave the seemingly cryptic placement of victims its true meaning: a vast constellation of victims, the corners joined by deeper shadowed tributaries of inky black blood, a perfect terrestrial rendering of a five-pointed star.

A pentagram.

With two points facing north like horns.

For the first seventeen minutes of the arduous trek back to the bungalow, Grove made good progress. He found enough footholds along the tops of swamped cars and vans and low-hanging awnings and barricades sticking out of the water to get from the Pontchartrain Bridge all the way to the St. Charles General Hospital—a total of fifteen blocks—without breaking his stride more than a couple of times. During this period of time, the moon was swallowed by boiling clouds, and the night darkened, and the rain started back up. But the worsening atmosphere merely spurred Grove on.

He got into a rhythm of running, jumping, running, and jumping some more, while the eye-wall winds bore down on him in frightening stages, each one more violent and treacherous than the last.

He faltered once at Felicity Street where he ran into a swirling whirlpool of broken glass—with nary a car roof or wall on which to jump. At that point he dove in without hesitation, and swam, freestyle, churning his arms and legs, through the glistening soup of jagged glass diamonds and twisted car fenders, nearly a block and a half, past floating mannequins and bobbing street signs and colorful gobs of torn haute couture like shredded seaweed.

Then the eye wall arrived.

It came on a freight train chorus of wailing winds, and Grove instinctively held on to a telephone pole still rooted in the pavement as the tide crashed across the district. Like a great, black, phosphorescent blanket unfurling over flooded streets, the Mississippi went rampaging northward. From Grove's position in front of the hospital—which unbelievably still had some lights on inside some of the windows—it was like watching the very ground billow in great undulating waves.

The first wave carried with it scores of wrecked cars and fragments of buildings. Grove clung to the telephone pole as the water surged around him, cold and salty and greasy, enveloping him with the g-forces of a nosedive. A series of magnificent crashes in every direction put the final kibosh on his hearing—a plume of sparks going up near the hospital as a lighted sign ripped free, a sonic boom as a bus careened into the side of a building. Grove's ears rang fiercely now.

Then came the ultimate winds—the inner wall—and everything slashed sideways as though the earth had just turned on its axis.

Debris whipped past Grove with the speed of major league fastballs. Any one of these projectiles could have instantly killed him. It was a miracle he wasn't brained by a flying hubcap or impaled on a hurling fence picket. Something drove him onward, onward toward the safety of Doerr's bungalow, onward toward that infernal fire hydrant at the corner of Calhoun and St. Charles.

The next leg of the journey passed in that maddening dreamtime for Grove.

Trudging through a horizontal wall of rain, lurching from handhold to handhold, he somehow managed to cross at least eight blocks amidst the worst winds in recorded history, and it only took him—according to the clock, at least—something like twenty minutes. His saving grace was the streetcar, which had blown over onto its side in the second surge. Grove was able to use the knotted power lines along its mangled roof as handholds.

By the time he reached the fire hydrant at Calhoun, the little rusted plug was underwater. He had to dive down to its base in the pitch-dark, fighting frenzied currents, in order to feel for the rope.

Sadly, the rope was not there anymore. All Grove could feel was the scabrous surface of the iron hydrant. Then, all at once, the frayed end of the rope brushed his hand, and he grasped it. He had some difficulty untying it, but finally managed to loosen it.

He burst to the surface sucking air, the mountaineering rope firmly clenched in his hand.

The rain slashed his face, nearly drowning him, and he gasped for air. It was dark as pitch now, the moon gone, his goggles gone, his long coat torn and flagging in ragged strips. The wind was a constant deadly foe now. Like a billion fire hoses strafing the street from the south, driving the floodwater into the heart of the city.

Grove only had moments to get inside. The next wave could easily do him in. He couldn't feel his right arm. His lungs burned, and he couldn't hear a thing, but he began blindly tugging himself north along the channel where Calhoun used to be, using only the rope for purchase.

The bungalow was now only about six or seven hundred feet away—a couple hundred yards at the most. Grove starting pulling himself through the black void, the rapids curling around his waist. It was not unlike pulling himself upstream, waist-deep and hurting in the world's fastest-moving river. The rope was taut one moment, then slack the next, then taut as it caught up on wreckage, then slack again as it slipped free.

The only thing that kept Grove going was the fact that Kaminsky was attached to the other end, safely ensconced inside the bungalow on Freret Street, three short blocks away. At this very moment, in fact, the Russian was most likely wedging himself against a stationary object inside the house like a doorjamb or a wall strut as the rope's tension waxed and waned. Grove could just see the big man hunkering in that dark bungalow, grumbling obscenities at the violent give and take on his fat belly, as Grove reeled himself in.

Not much farther now. Maybe a hundred yards. Not much more than the length of a single football field. But it might as well have been a million miles because the storm had risen to the level of an unadulterated blackout.

Grove dipped down until he was practically underwater as he pulled himself across the flooded lawn of an adjacent row house. His ears filled with white noise as he closed in on the bungalow, the rain whipping the side of his face. His buttons had torn off, and now his coat flapped furiously behind him. He could barely see his hand in front of his face—the only illumination coming from a flickering gas lamp on the corner still feebly sending a nimbus of dirty light across the block.

So close now. So close. He was going to make it! Goddamnit, he was going to make it!

He pulled on the rope as hard as he could, when all of a sudden, without warning, the rope gave—and the sudden slack sent him careening backward.

He splashed into the rapids, nearly dropping the rope. He flailed for a moment, then got back on his feet and got a hold of the rope, which was now a limp noodle in his hands.

He started frantically reeling in the loose rope, his heart racing, his mind swimming with panic. He reeled and reeled, as the winds spun around him like a great jet engine revving out of control, churning gravel and shards across his face. It felt like barbed wire scourging his flesh.

Blinking away the pain and disorientation, and the moisture stinging his eyes, he reached the end of the rope, pulled it out of the water, and looked down at it. In the flickering light, he gaped at the frayed end. His heart rose into his throat. His testicles shrank up into his body.

The end of the rope was soaked in blood.

21

Grove made it to the front porch just as an ancient oak was rent apart behind him, just off the southeast corner of the house, the cracking noise penetrating his deafened ears.

The tree crashed down on the lawn with an immense, booming splash, carving a boulder-sized divot out of the back of Kaminsky's Jeep.

Grove didn't even hesitate. He lurched through the bungalow's gaping entranceway where the screen door hung off its hinges by a thread, banging in the wind. The inside of the flooded living room was dark and painted with darker stains, the wind swirling through it like an insult. Grove stood there for a frenzied instant fighting the dizziness and panic, gazing hotly around the empty room.

Many things registered simultaneously in Grove's sputtering consciousness.

One: The dark stains were blood, and they were profuse and hectic. Some of them were smudges, most likely indicating a struggle, others were spray patterns indicating open arteries. It looked like a war had taken place in there, and it looked as though it had taken place recently.

Two: Despite the constant, excruciating noise of the storm, and the mad winds blowing rain into the bungalow, the place felt empty, or at least lifeless, which made Grove's gut pinch with monkey-brain panic. It felt like a trap. He reached into his torn coat and removed his .357—

—because he was also registering at that point a *third* realization: The dark lump lying in the corner near the overturned couch, just under the florette of plasma decorating the wall, was Ivan Kaminsky.

Grove assumed the tripod stance—more out of instinct now than anything else—and began sidestepping across the sodden living room, his Tracker raised and ready to talk, his jerky, paramilitary movements kicking up six-inch bursts of water that instantly diffused in the unstable air. He reached the body and, keeping the gun raised, allowed himself a single moment to look down at the remains.

He saw that the Russian had sustained major injuries to the trunk and upper body. His throat was gashed so deeply a white knuckle of trachea was visible. A wide dark pool of sticky, drying blood spread beneath his skull. Kaminsky's eyes were still open, a frozen stare.

Grove knelt and blinked. Emotion tried to push through the back of his heart, but he stuffed it back down, swallowed it like a stony pit in his throat. His eyes watered with anguish. He wiped his face with the back of his arm. His gun still gripped in both hands, he glanced away and saw something else across the room that caught his attention for just a moment.

Above the archway into the kitchen, a jagged, charred hole, fringed in pockmarks, marred the wainscotting. It looked fresh, and just about the size of a twelve-gauge wad cutter at close range. Grove looked back at Kaminsky. "You tried, Old Hoss. . . ." Grove's broken, crestfallen utterance was drowned by the atmospheric din. "I'll get him. I promise you, Kay."

Right then, almost on cue, punctuated by a surge of wind that sounded like the sky shearing apart, Grove thought of Maura, and a fresh jolt of adrenaline streamed through his limbs, driving him back to his feet. He spun and aimed the Tracker at the shadow-draped far corner. Had something moved? His eyes were playing tricks again.

He started sidestepping his way into the kitchen, which was now littered with pots and pans and overturned chairs and Rorschach patterns of spilled cereals. More signs of struggle. No sign of Maura, though, no sign of a second body anywhere, thank God, thank God. Grove whirled back toward the archway when a small black lump flew across the room at him.

The sap tagged him square on the forehead right above the bridge of his nose.

The impact was so well placed and well timed, it knocked Grove backward with the force of a battering ram, sending off skyrockets in his eyes. He staggered against the wall, managing to stay on his feet for several seconds, completely dumbstruck. The pistol slipped from his grip and clattered to the floor. And for one sick instant Grove thought the storm had kicked something off a shelf at him.

Then the blackjack arced out at him again for one last finishing blow.

This time the heft struck him right on the pivot point of his jaw. Firecrackers popped behind his eyes, and the lights flickered off, and he folded to the floor with a gentle sag. He landed on his back.

It was as though a shade were drawing over him as he struggled to move. The last thing he saw was the thing that was once Michael Doerr, outlined in lightning, stepping into view, soaked and breathing hard and holding a homemade sap filled with steel slugs.

Then everything went black and silent.

He saw a wall of gauzy white, and felt himself being lifted, lifted, lifted up into the air, and he blinked and gasped for breath, his first breaths, and he felt the cold hands of the tabibu midwife hoisting him high above the swaddling bed, high enough to see the landscape around the village. The ramshackle huts and shacks were barely visible in the dust storm. In the distance beyond the village, the mompambo plains boiled with sand clouds.

He cried out, a primal squeal of shock and terror at the harsh, unwelcoming world into which he had emerged, and he felt the pinch of the tabibu fingers on his tiny rump, and he squalled and squalled, but he could not stop gazing out into the distant barrens with his infant eyes.

A great pale whirlwind had appeared out there. It rose off the undulating sands, swirling and twisting toward the village, gobbling every baobab tree and scrub brush in its path, and sending shards of timber and weed up into the air like a brown fountain. This was Vida's dust devil, now glimpsed by her newborn baby, coming faster and faster, like a monster, coming straight for the infant son, who stared, transfixed by the twister, as it began to transform, like an impossible moving sand sculpture, melting and reforming, metamorphosing, elongating into a dark, hard, shiny object roaring around the outskirts of the little village.

Somehow, even in this elemental, nearly embryonic state, the baby—that is, Grove—recognized this object as being the true object behind the ghostly dust devil: a truck. *A very menacing black pickup truck kicking up a swirling cloud of dust. The truck had a painter's ladder hanging off one side of its whiskey-pocked quarter panel, and big broken searchlights like bugging eye-balls on its roof. The truck slammed to a stop in front of the midwife's hut, raising a thunderhead, and a tall, light-skinned black man emerged from the cab.*

Danger radiated off this man in the faded jeans, sweaty, sleeveless T-shirt, and rippling muscles, as he ambled up the path toward the midwife's door. The wind swirled around him like ghostly accompaniment. The dust clouds seemed to follow him like a pack of hounds. He approached the door through which the midwife had already carried Vida and the newborn Ulysses, and he kicked it in with a pointed cowboy boot.

Squeeeeeeeak! Bam!

The door jerked open on rusty hinges, then slammed back shut. The man was enraged, his white-hot anger seeming to spur the dust storm behind him and above him, which was now swirling around the hut. It moaned and whined as the man screamed at Vida in Swahili, "Ngozi ya mnyama mtoto mchanga!" *("You hide my own baby from me!") And again, the man thrust a boot against the battered screen door.*

Squeeeeeeeak! Bam!

The storm rose in answer to the jerking door, and the man screamed and threatened and menaced, and Vida screamed and sobbed, and the baby shrieked, and the wind wailed, and this was the true storm into which Grove was born—a terrible, chaotic home punctuated now by that slamming door.

Squeeeeeeeak! Bam!
Squeeeeeeeak! Bam!
Squeeeeeeeak! Bam!
Squeeeeeeeak! Bam!
Squeeeeeeeak! Bam!
Squeeeeeeeak! Bam!

Wwwwooosh! Thump!

Coming awake in stages, groggy and confused and hurt, Grove felt the rain on his face, his arms tied and raised over his head. For an unknown amount of time he had been wavering in and out of consciousness, incorporating the strange, watery wooshing-thumping noise from the darkness around him into his fever dream—or vision, or primal memory, or whatever it was—of his volatile biological father kicking in that door.

Wwwwwoooooooosh! Thump!

Grove looked around, swallowing back the panic. He couldn't feel his legs, and for quite a few frantic moments he could not see very well, his skull panging with agony, his throat burning with a cold, dry, narcotic rawness so painful he could hardly swallow. His wounded right arm was as numb and cold as a block of ice. But worse than that, far worse, was the fact that he had begun to understand, little by little, just exactly where he was, and what was happening to him.

Wwwwwwwwwwwwoooooooosshh! Thump!

The strange, gurgling, thumping noise blended with the moaning, echoing storm in the distance, which told Grove that he had been dragged back outdoors, perhaps back into Fiona's eye. Somehow he had the feeling that he had been unconscious only for a few

minutes—ten, twenty at the most. The rhythmic tugging on his arms, wedged and bound painfully above
his head, told him he was lying supine and being
dragged along some rough-hewn, bumpy surface—an
ungroomed path or some sort of trail—his lower body
submerged in water from the waist down.

*Wwwwwwwwwwwoooooooooooooooosssssshhhh!
Thump!* What the hell was that noise? What *was* it!

With great, agonizing effort Grove managed to twist
around and crane his neck upward enough to see just
exactly what was making that sound. He blinked
woozily, trying his best to focus, upside down, through
the misty darkness, until he finally saw the strange contraption that was dragging him along, and the dark figure commandeering it.

For a moment, Grove could not make sense of what
he was seeing. Granted, he was looking upside down at
it, and the sodium pentobarbital was still working on
Grove's scrambled brain, but it just looked so comical
and surreal: an old, leprous, iron railroad handcar,
squeaking along a length of deserted, submerged
railroad tracks in the middle of nowhere, with a madman at the controls, dragging Grove like a sack of tin
cans.

Michael Doerr, who stood on the leading edge of
the handcar, slowly and steadily pumping the massive
handlebar up and down, up and down, was evidently
unaware that Grove had stirred awake. Perhaps Doerr
was too busy muscling the handcar through the brackish water—hence the whooshing-thumping noises—
sending out a wake in the black floodwater that bubbled
and simmered like a kettle on a stove. His face was
deeply creased, contorted with fury. In the dim moonlight it resembled a rotting pumpkin. The black divot of

a mouth was working busily, softly reciting some archaic litany.

Was Grove still dreaming? The pain throbbing behind the bridge of his nose was real enough, and when he looked back down at his own body, submerged up to his midriff in black ooze, he realized that it wasn't just the cold that was penetrating and seizing up his joints. It was the residual effects of the same sodium pentobarbital that Doerr had most likely administered after knocking Grove cold.

A shiver of panic crawled up Grove's back because he heard those telltale lunatic winds moaning and wailing in the near distance behind him—he had no concept of direction—and he realized now what Doerr had done: *He had followed the eye.* God only knew why. Or for what psychotic purpose. Or where the hell they were. From the look of the riotous, swaying shadows of thick foliage, they were probably in some remote, forsaken corner of the bayou.

That was the direction in which the eye had been moving . . . toward the bayous to the west. Or maybe it was toward the lake. Which was it? Goddamnit, Grove could not remember. His mind would not cooperate. It kept sending fiery little sparks of emotion across his synapses, down through his nervous system, jamming his logic center, sabotaging his rational thought—a megawatt alternating current of rage and hatred. He needed to destroy this freak Michael Doerr more than anything he had ever needed to do in his life. And maybe, just maybe, if he played dead . . .

The handcar squeaked to a halt. They had reached a natural clearing, and now Doerr climbed off the contraption. His chains and weapons, still dangling from the inner loops of his coat, jangled in the unsettled breezes as he moved around the car through the knee-deep mire. Grove shot a quick, furtive glance at the tree line to his left.

They had stopped on the edge of some sort of long-forgotten Cajun cemetery.

In the blustering darkness, just for an instant, Grove saw the aboveground stone crypts, many of them cracked and ruined with age, stretching into the distance in all directions. The walkways, fossilized and embedded in the soggy earth, were all underwater. But the steepled and gabled rooftops of the tombs were visible like rows of wormy gray archipelagos. It was a vast necropolis, deserted by the ages, haunted by overgrown cypress and long, ragged chandeliers of Spanish moss hanging down and swaying in the eye winds with eerie nervousness.

Grove kept his eyes closed, his wrists screaming in pain from the ropes. He could smell the killer looming closer. It was a skunky, rank odor—like rotting meat left in a root cellar for years and years. He felt his upper body being jostled, the bonds loosening around his wrists. He felt his shoulders slip free of the handcar.

He fell with a thump—still feigning unconsciousness—down onto the fossilized rail bed. He saw stars. He felt his wrists screaming with pain, as they were once again yanked over his head. The rain had picked up. Grove could feel it on his face. It braced him and gave him strength to wait for the right moment . . . before the ropes were tied to the track . . . before this went too far . . . the element of surprise . . . the right moment to strike.

Now he could hear Doerr fiddling with something metallic. It sounded like knives and forks clanking in a metal container. Grove very cautiously cracked open on eye and peered up to his right. He saw an upside-down Michael Doerr assembling instruments. He had a pair of delicate, stainless steel, bird-beak pliers—a dental extractor used to pull teeth—and a six-inch surgical scalpel with a spoon-shaped blade. At a glance the latter instrument looked like a small ice cream scoop. It took Grove a moment to figure out its purpose.

Grove decided it was time to strike. He suddenly yanked with all his might on the loose wrist ropes, and at the same time kicked out at Doerr's legs—

—and nothing happened.

Nothing whatsoever happened because Grove was almost completely paralyzed by the aftereffects of the drug, and all he had done was let out a little gasp of effort, which merely alerted Doerr to the fact that Grove was conscious now. The killer froze for a moment, gazing down at Grove with those rotting pumpkin eyes. Doerr's black rictus of a mouth spread into either a smile or a grimace—it was impossible to tell anymore—as he selected the scoop-shaped scalpel. Grove looked up at the scalpel, then up into the rheumy, red eyes of the psychopath. "Go to hell," Grove said then in a flat, resolved tone.

Five hundred yards to the south, the windwall moaned balefully . . .

. . . as the creature that was once called Michael Doerr began removing Grove's eyeball.

22

The human eye, oddly enough, is an incredibly tough organ—not unlike the stalk of an ironweed—and the Holy Ghost had to resort to pressing a boot down against the man's chest for leverage, as though worrying a recalcitrant root out of the ground. It took quite a while just to work the razor-sharp edge of the scalpel down into the gap between the skull and the eyelid. The FBI man wailed a watery, strangled cry in the darkness that sounded like a spring calf being slaughtered—the anesthesia almost completely worn off by that point—and blood streaked down the man's face in dark rivulets.

The sound of the man's cry energized the Holy Ghost. Even in the midst of the closing eye wall, it was almost sensual, the way the scream worked on the entity's central nervous system, despite the laborious aspect to this part of the ritual. Older folks gave up eyes much easier. A middle-aged man like this still had a lot of bone density and tissue. Extracting *this* eye would be a chore, but the Holy Ghost was more than willing to do the work. This was his finest hour. After *millennia*, he would finally complete his righteous mission.

A tiny ejaculate of blood spurted across the FBI

man's open lips as he wailed and wailed. And the man's ragged scream was instantly drowned by the mounting winds. The rain was coming down in sheets now, immediately washing away the stringers of blood and pink, foamy drool from the wriggling man's face into the black floodwater of the burial ground.

The Holy Ghost paused for a moment, then began hissing the holiest of holy invocations: "*Si-su-meeru-ee-nu-na-tukum-pa-surru-voventuru—*"

"F-ff-fuck—yyou!" the FBI man spat suddenly at the Holy Ghost; bloody, garbled words that had no meaning whatsoever. The Holy Ghost slapped the man.

Zzzzzzzzing!

An unbidden image flickered suddenly in the mind of the Holy Ghost, a mosaic of broken memories like shards of glass, a dual image: a Toltec priest on the side of a mountain, dressed in a black gown and hood, with chains of hammered bronze hanging off his shoulders, slashing his ceremonial knife across the throat of an innocent child, and overlaying this image like a double exposure, a modern man in a sweat-stained cowboy hat, a Tony the Tiger tattoo on the inside of his hairy brown forearm, hurling a young Michael Doerr across the bedroom of a remote cabin in the woods.

In the vision the boy slammed into the knob of a brass bedpost, the impact injuring his eye, knocking half his teeth out of his mouth, the tiny teeth tumbling across his floor like minuscule little dice! The boy looked down at the teeth, then up at the face of pure cruelty, the man with no eyes, the little silver granny sunglasses reflecting the child's terrified face—

In the here and now, the Holy Ghost suddenly reared back with a jerk, startled by the power and horrible symmetry of the vision.

*—as another face superimposed itself over the face
of Michael Doerr's father like a ghostly afterimage:
the blood-streaked, insolent, dying face of the FBI profiler named Ulysses Grove. The two handsome faces so
similar in appearance. The same butterscotch cream
skin tone, the same long, almost feminine lashes, the
same high, regal cheekbones. It was uncanny. And it
was without a doubt a message from the elder gods:
These were the faces of the enemy—the central figures
toward whom the Holy Ghost must focus his ultimate,
ceremonial powers—and the two enemies jibed so perfectly. The enemy of an ancient spirit, the enemy of an
abused child—*

A tormented pause here.

Closing his eyes, turning away from the subject,
trembling with chaotic emotions, the Holy Ghost
dropped the ritual scalpel onto the pile of instruments,
which were now coated with blood as black as tar. He
would extract the eyeball and the rest of the teeth later.
He would prepare the subject in due course. Now it
was time for the most important part of the process,
and the furious sky, churning overhead, called it out to
the Holy Ghost like a clarion. Vengeance!

The word, the idea, the very concept of it, called out
from the black tide coming across the swamp now,
from the walls of wind that were closing in, from the
black beating heart of the storm itself: *Vengeance!*

Yes, he was ready. He would close the circle. He
would fulfill his destiny. He would use the holiest of
holy knives, and he would open a vein, and he would
bleed the swine to death. And he would feel the life-
blood drain out of the guilty one now because that's
what the elder gods wanted. *Sacred vengeance.* That's
what the angry sky and the sea and the very air itself

wanted now: sacred vengeance on all the parents of the world. For all the suffering and agony visited upon the innocent children of Meridia. For the abused, and the wounded. For all the helpless lambs led to slaughter.

"Vengeance!"

The word came out of the Holy Ghost in an alien voice, garbled by emotion, thick with mucus, but loud enough to pierce the coming winds. Tears welled in the holy one's eyes and scattered in the wind. Something inside him began to contract like a flower blooming in reverse, shrinking, dilating down into a hard, black, little seed inside him. What was happening? He felt his entire being begin to shake, his body going weak, limp, palsied.

"*Vengeance!*"

He was sobbing now and didn't even realize it. He was a terrified little boy hiding under a bed as big work boots probed the floor only inches away. He was weeping uncontrollably now, a lost child in the whirlwind. "Vengeance, v-vengeance, v-vennnn—vennj—"

In his hand now was a long, honed, sacrificial ram's horn with a razor tip, which he had begun to raise with both hands, hovering it over the FBI agent.

Over the man's throat, over his jugular.

Over the cruel father's jugular.

"You put that knife down this instant or I will tan your hide, boy! You hear me!"

It took everything Grove had left, every ounce of strength that wasn't already completely sapped by the pounding agony behind his mangled left eye, just to yell loud enough to be heard.

It also took everything Grove knew about the psychopathic mind, every last shred of intuition about Doerr, every half-formed hunch he'd been developing about what had happened in the Yucatan, and the abusive childhood endured by Doerr, and even the doorway through which the alter personality had invaded Doerr's soul. It also took a significant amount of luck. Grove was betting on the fact that Doerr's original personality was deep down inside Doerr somewhere, lurking there full of pain and fear. It was a long shot, but Grove had no other options. No other plan. No other hope in those tenuous milliseconds before the blubbering killer brought the knife down.

"I will make you sorry you were ever born, boy, if you don't put that knife down this instant!"

Grove's bawling, booming cry was hoarse and broken, barely audible over the rising wall of wind, his words impeded by the searing pain in his eye, which was still oozing blood down the side of his face. Although his eyeball was still intact—the scalpel had apparently only dislodged it slightly, severing arteries and tissue inside the top of the lid—Grove was completely blind now in the offended eye. And the pain was excruciating, a cold steel sword stabbing through the top of his skull. But he ignored it. He ignored it and gave the ruse his all.

And it seemed to be working. For the moment, at least. Doerr had frozen midstrike, the ritual knife stalled in midair, its gleaming point at its apex. In the unstable darkness, as the rising wind bull-whipped ribbons of rain across the graveyard and the bayou beyond it, and lightning slithered snakelike through the screens of rain to the south, Doerr looked like a mannequin from some macabre house of wax, a weeping executioner caught in a terrible tableau, as rain beaded on his chiseled face and arms.

Grove's own seething, tormented rage helped. It fed his barrage of patriarchal ravings: *"You hear me, boy! You hear me! You put that knife down this instant!"*

Something changed then on Doerr's face, a deepening and narrowing of the eyes, a furrowing of the wrinkled, maplike forehead. His lips curled back, and rows of white teeth shone in the flickering ambient glow of oncoming lightning. The look of hate that crossed his features then was unlike anything Grove had ever seen, or ever *would* see, or ever *wanted* to see again. It mingled the anguished pain of an abused little boy with the otherworldly fury of an ancient dark god, a dark god driven by endless vengeance. It looked like a face that had turned itself inside out, a face that had rotted from *within*. It was so horrible that Grove—partially blind, seeing in the tunnel vision of a single eye—found himself transfixed, his angry gambit faltering like an engine that had abruptly died.

Doerr wailed an unearthly howl like a metal blade scraping flint and then he stabbed the pointed horn down hard toward Grove's neck—

—but Grove managed to yank himself a few inches to the right just as the weapon pierced his flesh!

A sharp needle of pain stitched across the side of his face as the wind crashed down on the trees, and there was an enormous cracking sound as the atmosphere shifted suddenly, and a gust slammed into Doerr, a sheet of rain as deadly as a spray of bullets, making the back of Doerr's long black coat flap and twist so noisily it sounded like a drumroll.

Another gust hit them full-bore, throwing Doerr

across the train tracks. He sprawled to the ground, still gripping the weapon.

The feeling was coming back into Grove's arms now in prickling stages, and he flailed and strained against the bonds, the left side of his face throbbing with cold wet pain, his wrists on fire. The eye wall loomed. The noise drowned out all other sound. The trees jittered crazily, great tumbleweeds of Spanish moss spinning through the air.

Doerr was screaming something, but none of it reached Grove's battered eardrums. All Grove heard now was the eye wall, its dragon roar like a billion angry voices. The rain had become a spinning dynamo around the boneyard, blurring the night, pounding the land, engulfing them in layers of misery. Grove cried out with equal parts rage and agony when he saw Doerr climbing back to his feet and coming for him with the razor-tipped horn gripped in white knuckles.

This was the end. Grove sensed it. So did Doerr. The pointed horn would finish Grove now, and then the storm would wipe Doerr off the face of the earth, and nobody would be left to tell the tale.

Doerr lunged.

Something popped in the air.

It happened right before the knife had a chance to reach Grove, and Doerr jerked backward suddenly, startled, like a man who had just stumbled into a cobweb. He blinked and blinked and coughed once and looked around the sheets of churning gray for the source of the noise.

Grove lay there for a moment, nearly blind, skull throbbing, blood salty in his mouth, body as tense as a spring, his breath stuck in his throat. What the hell had just happened? Over the clamor of the hurricane, it had sounded like a small balloon had popped, but there was something else that had accompanied it, almost in unison with the popping noise: *A spark had jumped off the rail!*

Everything seemed to seize up then like clockwork jamming as both men gazed off the south, an almost comical double take, both of them glancing up at the crumbling brick rampart that ran along the lower edge of the cemetery beyond the railroad tracks, veiled in billowing blankets of rain.

The figure was barely visible down there.

She looked like a ghost.

A fading ghost.

It was a miracle she was still standing, considering her injuries and the proximity of the inner eye wall a hundred yards behind her. It was also a miracle that she had placed her first shot so close to the killer—considering the fact that she had never fired a gun in her life.

The little .38-caliber ninety-grain load had skipped off the iron only inches from Doerr's right leg.

Now only one round remained, and she stood there wavering in the fierce slashes of lightning and killer rain on top of those ancient paving stones, one hand clutching the slippery, scabrous cast-iron gatepost, the other hand shakily aiming the tiny two-shot derringer pistol at the two men on the ground by the railroad tracks.

She could not see very well—her swollen right eye had already closed up, the salt spray stinging her left—and her body had already begun to shut down from the exhaustion and hypothermia and wounds. Each injury told the story of her flight.

The deep gash running down the length of her left thigh had resulted from the leap out the back of the bungalow as Kaminsky valiantly held the killer at bay. The broken ribs, the sprained wrist, and the bruises over 90 percent of her body had occurred during her death-defying circumnavigation of New Orleans on floating wreckage. As Fiona's eye wall had rampaged its way north across the Central Business District, and then slammed into the neighboring bayou, Maura had followed a hunch: She kept up with Doerr by remaining *inside* the eye.

But now all the sprains and fractures and gashes— and all the cuts and scrapes from wrestling through saw grass and hurling across ancient railroad trestles— were about to pay off. Especially if she managed to put her last remaining bullet through one or more of Doerr's vital organs.

The trouble was, like Grove, she found her vision was almost gone, and she couldn't hold the gun steady, and she really had no idea what she was doing. But she aimed the little thing anyway, feeling puny and impotent in the vortex of the coming winds, and trying to scream above the impossible racket: "Get away from him or I will put the next one into your head!"

In the gray distance Maura saw the faintest outline of Michael Doerr standing up and facing her, gunslinger style, as if they were in a dream or an old western movie. Grove, on the ground beneath him, face coated with blood, screamed something inaudible, looking like he was just about to chew his arm off in order to help her. Maura held her breath and aimed the gun at Doerr.

She had never intended to let him live. She had planned on killing him all along. She just wanted one single thing from God or the Fates or Lady Luck or whoever it was that granted such things: *one clean shot*.

Thirty yards away, Doerr began swinging a long chain with a sickle blade on the end. It swung and swung in the rain, almost hypnotically. Maura began squeezing the trigger.

But she stopped suddenly.

Doerr stopped, too.

It was the sound.

23

It was a sound unlike anything they had heard yet, a sound that heralded something deep and inexorable and maybe even biblical, and for one incredible moment Doerr and Grove just stared up at the thing that was coming off the southern horizon. Maura finally looked over her shoulder.

Her gasp was vanquished by an unearthly thunder, not from above but from *below*.

At first it appeared as though the very land were rising up into the air, like a vast hydraulic hoist raising the swamp, lifting it up over the cemetery. Maura had only enough time to drop the gun and grab the wrought-iron post, clinging to it with simian panic as the black tsunami finally crashed down, dumping a trillion cubic feet of ocean on the world.

The wave obliterated everything in its path as it unrolled across the cemetery on the force of the eye-wall winds. Tombs peeled away like papier-mâché toys. Stone walls tumbled like dominoes. Jumbled knots and bundles of something that looked like twisted tree branches took flight. Counterwaves crashed in the air like the rearing heads of white dragons, tossing and vaporizing in the black tumult, then slamming down and dispersing across the flooding land in vast, agitated sheets of foam.

Maura watched in mute horror.

The entire quadrant of swamp—from the railroad tracks to the heart of the piney woods to the north—flooded almost instantly, as though a glistening blanket of oily black ocean had unrolled across the land. Some of the smaller marsh trees along the boundaries of the graveyard were ripped from their moorings and sent spinning. Thousands of granite markers tore loose and went careening on the currents.

Lightning cracked the sky once again, flickering mercury-vapor brilliance down on the apocalyptic scene.

A sharp dagger of horror and repulsion stabbed through Maura's guts as she realized that the jumbled, knotted bundles of tree branches—many of them now tossing on the floodwater—were not what she thought they were. They were *people*. Bones and shrunken, emaciated corpses. Human remains draped in rags of burial garb, many of them twisted and pretzled into un-recognizable shapes. Maura had to turn her rain-lashed face away from the scene for a moment.

Now the waterline had reached six feet over most of the graveyard.

Beyond the trees, almost a mile out, a monstrous gray thunderhead of debris—mostly shards of foliage and earth—had billowed up into the air. The swamp was being transformed, and it was exceedingly difficult to see now, the atmosphere so dense with rain shears and sea foam.

Maura had to squint just to see out into the far reaches of the cemetery, which were vanishing now—thousands and thousands of salt-gray sand castles dis-solving in the breakers. At last her gaze found the faint silhouette of one of the two living souls still in the graveyard.

The last thing Maura saw before all of it turned to floodwater was Michael Doerr flailing and writhing in the frenzied white water, tangled in his own chains and cables, his own instruments of destruction. The water finally punched through him and covered him.

And then he was gone.

Maura had no idea what happened to Grove.

The strangest thing was the silence. It was so abrupt and unexpected, so cold and black and stunning, that he lay there for several moments, completely still, holding his breath, trying to get his bearings in the darkness.

He knew several things. He knew he was underwater now, and he knew he had to hold his breath for as long as possible if he wanted to survive.

But he also had no idea how he was going to do that because his arms were still wrenched over his head, still bound to the rails.

The muffled pounding of the storm came from above, penetrating the water like dull depth charges, but it did little to rattle him. Grove knew he had to remain as calm as possible. He knew that panicking meant death. Panic would squeeze the air from his lungs, from his blood.

Panic would kill him.

He felt his untethered lower body slowly levitating, his legs drifting, swaying upward with increasing buoyancy, twisting him into awkward postures. He tested the bonds by yanking his wrists gently against the rusted metal. They slid a little bit, making a weird scraping noise, but were still secure around the rails. *Damn it! Think! Think, asshole!*

The thudding noises reverberated down through the water, reaching his ringing ears, and his chest tightened and his throat closed down and his flesh crawled with the first stages of oxygen starvation. He had only a couple of minutes left—three at the most.

Something brushed across his shin, a branch or an errant fragment of dirt.

Lightning veined the black surface above him, flickering down through the water.

Human skeletons loomed in the darkness all around him, reflecting the silver light. Grove saw them in the tunnel vision of a single eye. In various stages of decay, visible only during intermittent flashes of lightning, they assumed all conceivable postures. Some of them, completely intact, as immaculate as laboratory specimens, stood erect in the soupy brine. Others, as black and leprous as tree bark, fringed in rotted burial attire and leathery shreds of mortified flesh, floated upside down, legless, headless. Empty black eye sockets stared at Grove. Disembodied arms and fingers softly caressed his extremities.

He felt something shift behind him, in the storm, and then he felt the rail jerk.

He realized Fiona was having her way with the cemetery, but that did little to help Grove. Surrounded by the dead, alone and helpless, he was about to run out of air. He felt his one good eyeball bulging with the pressure, an elephant standing on his chest now. His lungs had caught fire. The burning sensation stole his ability to think. Slimy seawater enveloped him in deathly cold. He was about to drown.

When he was a kid he used to read about the great

escape artist, Harry Houdini, and all the amazing tales of Houdini's exploits. One particular trick that had always fascinated Grove was the "Water Cell Torture" escape. In this trick Houdini was shackled with iron handcuffs, then hung upside down, completely immersed, in a water-filled cell, the door of the cell securely padlocked.

Houdini reportedly had an almost superhuman lung capacity. He could hold his breath for nearly five minutes. Which is approximately how long it usually took him to wriggle his way out of the cuffs and then pick the outer lock of the cell, ultimately bursting out of the top of the cell, dramatically gasping for air, resurrecting himself from the jaws of death in full view of the amazed and appreciative Victorian audience.

The memory of this heroic escape taunted Grove, tapped into his rage, stoked his burning lungs, pounded in his skull. The fire raged out of control. The flames bloomed and spread through his body, blazed through his bloodstream, made every cell, every last drop of hemoglobin scream for oxygen.

He roared with anger, his cry coming out in a muffled wail of bubbles in the darkness, streams of bubbles that nudged the skeletons, and he silently cursed all the twisted freaks like Doerr who had led him here to this awful place to die, and the lightning flickered again almost in answer to his outburst, slicing down through the dark water, illuminating the stoic staring faces of the dead, and he started shaking and flailing his legs and furiously yanking on the ropes, and he had lost all control now, and he would die now . . .

. . . except . . .

. . . *except!* . . .

In his convulsions, the ropes on his wrist had

slipped a little farther, not much, but far enough down the greasy rail to alert him of something important, something that just might save his life. His heart was about to explode in his chest, but somehow, *somehow*, with his last soupçon of strength, he managed to wrench himself around so that his belly was on the rail, and he stared up at his bound hands, and he saw over the space of a single instant, with his one good eye, his last chance of survival.

The rail to which he was bound had somehow been damaged in the flood, and now it buckled upward like a great crescent sticking out of the moving water.

Grove started climbing the rail, sliding his bound wrists along the bent metal, using the frayed rope for purchase as a mountain climber might shimmy up a cable, although he was never really conscious of what he was doing.

The maelstrom consumed his body as he slipped backward every few inches on the slimy iron, but he kept a tight noose around the metal, getting into a rhythm of yanking, slipping, clutching, then yanking, slipping, and clutching again. The flames chewed up his esophagus, searing his veins.

Only ten more feet to go, as lightning strobed through the filthy currents.

At a certain point, only inches away from the surface, Grove nearly slipped off the rail when the entire track shuddered suddenly, nudged by the storm, but somehow, through a simple, mindless stubbornness that was almost involuntary now, Grove managed to hold on.

Then he made last grunting lurch to the surface in an almost stupefied trance.

24

Grove burst out of the water and gasped and gasped for air but found none in all the pandemonium near the surface.

Waves sloshed against him. Debris swirled and clawed across the back of his head, and he clutched at that greasy rail as best he could for fear of being blown to smithereens. He sucked dry steel-wool rasps into his raw throat, but still no air would come. It felt as though someone had plunged a fist down his gullet and lodged it in his airway.

He noticed very little of the surreal wreckage or macabre debris hurling through the air at that point. He noticed nothing but his flaming lungs.

He was beginning to lose consciousness, his vision going completely dark as the freight train winds shook him and lashed him and pitched ribbons of torn funeral clothing and cypress bark through the air all around him—viewed in his failing single eye as a slow-motion flicker film—until he finally hunched forward and heaved up a lungful of water.

His vomit—mostly muddy salt water—roared out of him, instantly diffusing into the wind, then blowing back at him in a frothy spray that mingled with the blood on his face. Coughing and hacking, he clutched at the rail and tried frantically to get his senses back. The world around him blurred in his right eye, becoming a noisy cubist canvas of fractured glistening violence. The din was so deafening now he could only hear a tinnitic white noise in his ears.

At length Grove got his air back and started breathing regular gulping breaths.

Now all he could do was wait and hold on, turning his face away from the chaotic winds, and hope that nothing bigger than a branch decided to strike his exposed head. It almost seemed as though the hurricane had stalled over the graveyard, although Grove knew that Fiona was moving inland, as all hurricanes ultimately do, and soon the eye-wall winds—the worst of them, at least—would pass through.

But the assault seemed to go on forever.

Clinging to that damaged train rail, Grove found himself doing something that he hadn't done since the worst days of the Sun City case—*he prayed*. He prayed to his own private conglomerate of a god: part African deity, part descendent of Abraham, part secular higher power. Trapped in that envelope of deadly wind, barely conscious, Grove prayed that the storm would pass soon, and he prayed that Maura would survive the initial wave, and he prayed that he would be spared. But he added a *caveat* to the latter: *Take me, if you have to, Lord, but please, please, please let Maura live.*

How long did he hang there a mere inches above those roiling whitecaps? It was impossible for Grove to judge the passage of time. His blind left eye had gone numb, and his body was nearly paralyzed. Every few seconds a wave would slam into him, coating him with black foam, threatening to drown him. Debris grazed the top of his head more than once. There were stones, shards of bark, old fossilized bone chips, even dead birds pinwheeling through the air like ragged black meteorites strafing the earth. Grove kept his head down, his face averted, and his numb hands welded to the rail.

At last the noise and pressure subsided—just a little, just enough—so that Grove was able to look up without getting tagged in the forehead by a rock or drowned by a fire-hose stream of horizontal rain. It was still nearly impossible to see a thing in the steady deluge, but the silhouettes of objects had returned in the shimmering dark, just barely, materializing in Grove's field of vision.

He ignored his exhaustion and creeping hypothermia. He could see that his own flesh was the color of ash now, and judging from the bleary vision in his one good eye, as well as the profuse shivering and incessant dizziness, he was most likely flirting with the advanced stages of hypothermia.

Grove knew all about hypothermia. He had experienced it on Mount Cairn a year ago, chasing the thing that was once Richard Ackerman into the upper altitudes. Hypothermia occurs when the internal temperature of the body dips below 95 degrees Fahrenheit, and it wreaks havoc with bodily functions. Without immediate treatment it can plunge a victim into unconsciousness, cardiac arrest, or coma. Grove could feel all the telltale symptoms. Each breath was a labor, and his muscles were as stiff as old rusted bolts. He felt almost narcoleptic, he was so dizzy. He also had to pee with a fierce urgency.

He was just starting to relieve himself, the warmth of the urine cloud strangely comforting as it engulfed his midsection, when he saw the figure ten feet away.

The figure was visible in a strobelike flash of lightning that only lasted a few seconds, but it was enough time for Grove to see the mangled body of Michael Doerr.

Grove figured it all out later: Evidently the railroad track had buckled so severely down the middle it had snapped, the two separate ends sticking up into the air like the bent tines of a monolithic fork. Somehow, in the initial tumult of the flood wave, Doerr had been thrown backward almost directly onto the jagged point of the broken rail. The rail had been driven like a stake through Doerr's upper body, presumably piercing his heart and a number of other vital organs and arteries in the bargain. The rail was nearly eight inches wide and would have killed him instantly. His brain might have lingered for a few agonizing moments, projecting God only knew what onto his mind-screen, before he quietly expired.

Which was precisely the state Doerr was in right now, Grove realized, squinting through the veil of rain at the body. To paraphrase Dickens, the boy was as dead as a doornail. Which made Grove feel . . . *what*?

That was a central question throbbing through Grove's feverish mind now as he looked for a way to cross the gap of rapidly churning water in order to get to Doerr's body. He never asked himself that question at the terminal point of a killer's life. He usually felt nothing but a vague sense of disappointment: The chase was over, and in a way, so was Grove's passion. So why all the complex emotions now? What was prodding the back of Grove's mind?

What *did* he feel?

He took a deep breath into his sore lungs and dove into the water.

It took some effort but Grove managed to half swim, half lunge across the ten-foot gap of rapids until he was able to get his cold fingers around the other side of the broken rail, five feet or so below Doerr's body. Grove managed to tread water there for a moment, holding on to the blood-spackled rail, panting and coughing, his joints aching, full of ground glass.

He looked up through one eye.

Doerr hung above him, as bloodless as a scarecrow, skewered on that upward loop of rail in some corrupt parody of the Crucifixion. The man's feet were bare and dangling limply, his boots getting knocked off at some point in his demise. His black coattails flagged crazily in the winds. His face, marbled in blood, hung downward, void of expression. He almost looked peaceful in his waxen stasis.

The thing inside him was gone.

Grove noticed a jagged piece of cross-tie still attached to the rail only inches below Doerr's feet. It stuck out like a massive step, shivering in the wind. Grove stared at it and felt a strange compulsion cross his mind—all the contrary emotions swelling within him like a dissonant chord—the contempt, the pity, the hate, the empathy. He pulled himself up onto that cross-tie.

Then Grove did something highly unprofessional that surprised even himself.

He braced himself on the cross-tie, the wood creaking faintly, then lifted himself up so that he was face-to-face with Michael Doerr.

It was so bizarre, perched on the rail like that, clutching that rusted iron bar and staring into a dead man's downturned face. Grove was close enough to kiss the young man. The coppery odor of entrails was strong, and Grove had to consciously keep his eye averted from the exit wound where the massive rail, still caked with gore, had impaled Doerr's left pectoral.

Grove felt that inscrutable rush of emotion again. It was inchoate, dark, and tangled, from the deepest recesses of his soul. He wanted to whisper something hateful into Doerr's ear. He wanted to spit on him. Finally he leaned forward and uttered under the sound of the wind so that nobody but Doerr could have heard it: *"I'm not your abuser. Okay? You got that?"*

Lightning crackled in the mist, making this strange tableau glow and flicker like a surreal diorama in some nightmarish exhibit. Grove sensed the swamp coming back to life all around him, ravaged by the inner winds of less than an hour ago. Cypress groves looked like battlefields of broken kindling, their razed bald peaks sticking out of the floodwater. The area that was once the cemetery was now a single square mile of flooded granite wreckage, many of the battered coffins still floating away into the distance.

Grove looked at the dead man and continued whispering with great scorn, *"You killed my friend. You getting this, Doerr? You killed my ff—"*

On the word "friend" a pair of icy hands shot out and grabbed Grove by the throat.

Grove's one good eye popped wide as Doerr's head came back up on its own power.

A sound came out of Doerr's mouth that was neither human speech nor animal growl.

And Grove looked into the eyes of the abyss.

25

Grove's hands, moving on pure instinct now, reached up and found *Doerr's* throat, one nanosecond before the entity had a chance to ooze from one host to another. *No, you don't!* Grove's hysterical inner voice demurred. *Not this time! Not this time! NOT THIS TIME!*

The two men hung there in the wind for one insane moment, clutching each other's throats in a state of mutually assured destruction, staring into each other's eyes, into each other's souls.

Grove could not breathe, could not utter a sound now, but the adrenaline-fueled rage pulsed in his veins and gave him superhuman strength and made his hands tighten like vises around the killer's throat—and for one fraction of a second, in that shimmering darkness, Grove's senses absorbed everything about Doerr.

The killer's eyes resembled highly polished onyx ball bearings placed into the head of a doll or an automaton. His teeth, exposed now in his death throes, looked like the yellowed, burnished fangs of a deformed jungle predator, a creature in a carnival freak show. His breath penetrated even Grove's strangled olfactory organs, and smelled of ammonia, of things under a rock, of rancid proteins gone so bad they had changed their chemical structure.

Many things happened over the space of that single terrible instant.

With his heart and lungs threatening to erupt in his chest, and his good eyeball threatening to pop out of his skull, Grove saw entire worlds pass across Doerr's tortured brown features, the horrors of human sacrifice, the destruction of entire villages, the pain and agony and sheer terror of an innocent child drawn into deadly dark machinery. Doerr's face was a death mask of metaphysical hate, quaking and shivering and rippling as Grove strangled the last spark of life out of it. A weird hissing noise issued from Doerr's throat.

"Aaacccchhh—"

Grove tightened his grip on the killer's throat, his thumbs pressing down so hard they were nearly buried in the man's tendons, and Doerr's hands did likewise, tightening their python stranglehold, and although he could not see his own face, Grove felt his features contorting, his lips flaying back, teeth clenching so tightly they were starting to crack, forming a grimace of utter hellish rage.

In this state Grove managed to let out a barely audible grunt in Doerr's face.

"Y-you—"

The first word came out in a strangled gasp, registering in Doerr's sharklike eyes as a tiny cinder of heat, a crimson spark. And Grove strained and strained and strained to get the other words out before fainting dead away and slipping off the rail and plummeting into the water: Sisyphus dragging the eternal stone toward inevitable doom, a man completely torn free of the moorings of sanity.

"—are—"

The second word, although following close on the heels of the first, barely escaped Grove's crimped airways, and he began to convulse in Doerr's deadly mechanical vise, and the pain only fanned the flames of madness blazing out of control inside Grove, as he let out a garbled wail that fed his grip on Doerr's throat one last surge of pressure, one last furious cry in the darkness of the storm.

"—finished!"

Grove put everything he had into a final, violent, and very abrupt twist of Doerr's neck.

Ironically this little trick was taught to Grove when he was back in the army's crack CID training unit as a young MP candidate, learning paramilitary assault techniques. They had taught Grove all the spooky fast-kill tricks such as plunging knives into major organs, or striking instant shut-down blows to a combatant's skull, all of which Grove had promptly managed to forget. But *this* one—the sudden dislocation of the upper cervical vertebra, resulting in a swift paralysis or, in many cases, death on arrival—had come back to Grove tonight at the precise moment he was beginning to lose consciousness himself. But the result of this killing move—albeit a precursor to the inevitable shutting down of Doerr's stubborn, insectlike bodily functions—was not what Grove had expected. The result was something else entirely.

It was like watching a chrysalis melting and reforming, as Doerr's head lolled forward, all the demonic anger melting away like a fogged pane of glass suddenly clearing. His hands instantly loosened their grip on Grove's throat, then slipped away, dangling lifelessly, and Grove reared back, coughing and hacking and drawing in great heaving gouts of air, nearly falling off the rail. He held on to the iron with one hand, the other going instinctively up to his own injured neck and trachea as he sucked in huge unobstructed breaths.

But Grove's gaze never left Doerr, because Doerr was changing before his very eyes.

The ravages of mental illness seemed to evaporate from the young man's face as though the wind were sweeping it all away. His eyes cleared, returning to their original chestnut-brown color, filling with innocent awe, the creases around his mouth vanishing. By all medical accounts, he should have expired by then, but he hung on, he hung on for many incredible moments, while Grove watched, transfixed. The expression of rage on Doerr's face melded into one of pure, unadulterated anguish, the anguish of a frightened child. It wasn't just the realization of the searing pain and agony knifing through his organs.

Michael Doerr had transformed back to Michael Doerr.

Grove shuddered. Something deep in the pit of his being clenched up suddenly as he gazed at the dying killer and felt the pain and sorrow radiating off that face, that heartbreaking face. Tears shone in Doerr's eyes as he tried to speak, tried to say something. Of course, he couldn't. He was breathing his last breaths, and he could only stare in his final moments at Grove. He could only stare at the profiler while his sad face collapsed like a little boy who never had a chance to live a normal life.

A little boy lost and alone in thousands of years of darkness.

Grove suddenly hugged Doerr to his chest, hugged him tightly, even tenderly.

It was a ridiculous gesture, something that would haunt Grove for a long time, something that he would ponder for weeks and months and even years. This was not what criminologists did—even rogues like Grove. This was unprofessional, ludicrous, and offensive. But Grove didn't care. At that moment, he only wanted to give the little boy inside the monster one last moment of peace before he left this life. So Grove held the frightened child and stroked the back of his head, and whispered that it was okay to die now, and he would go to heaven, and he would be with God, and he wouldn't have to be afraid anymore, and nobody would hurt him anymore.

Doerr heard very little of it, Grove realized later, because the young man had already died.

Fiona did not go quietly into that particular dark night. After savaging the wetlands west of town, she changed course and curled back up over Lake Pontchartrain, dumping four feet of tidewater over the Black Pearl River, and pounding communities northeast of New Orleans like Slidell and Bay Saint Louis, Mississippi—communities that had only recently begun to recover from last year's apocalypse called Katrina, not to mention, most recently, Cassandra.

By the time dawn came, the worst of it had passed through Louisiana. The state licked its salted wounds in a series of stunning bulletins in every medium. Newsradio anchors droned grimly on about death tolls and property damage, and the irony of the Second Coming of Killer Hurricanes. TV units set up remotes on the outskirts of a ravaged New Orleans, emoting dramatically over the wind in their modulated voices about starting all over again, and rebuilding the already rebuilt, and tsk-tsking about how much these tough southerners could take. Mercifully, the newly remodeled infrastructure of New Orleans seemed to have survived by the skin of its teeth, the recently installed pump stations already draining the mess.

It seemed as though New Orleans would rise again from this calamity.

But this did little to appease Grove, who sat on the passenger seat of a rattling swamp boat that was making its way up the misty green reaches of the Atchafalaya River. A blood-spotted bandage patched Grove's injured left eye. The boat's driver, a stoic deputy from the Assumption Parish Sheriff's Department, kept his square head and thick eyeglasses fixed on the foggy horizon.

The sky had begun to lighten.

"Sun's comin' up," the deputy commented over the whine of the big stern-fan. His name was Prudhome, and he had hardly said two words since Grove had dropped in unannounced at the Pierre Cane Sheriff's office a mile north of the bayou cemetery an hour earlier, his left eye completely hemorrhaged out, his face maplike with splattered blood, begging somebody to help search for Maura County.

"So it is." Grove gave a little downtrodden nod, shivering in his still-soaked and torn overcoat. He had received rudimentary medical attention at the Pierre Cane Hospital emergency room—first aid applied to his eye, the gash in his arm dressed, stitches, plasma and antibiotics administered—but the night resident had issued stern warnings that he was still in shock, and probably suffering from both hypothermia and a concussion, and he would most likely lose his left eye if he didn't get some treatment from a major trauma center as soon as possible.

"I know she made it, I *know* she did," Grove murmured, lying to himself. "Gotta keep circling, keep looking."

A wall of tangled cypress passed on either side. Debris floated in their wake, bumping the hull every few seconds. Clouds of mosquitoes brushed past Grove's face. The early dawn made the swamp look eerily luminous, as though the netting of air moss and cobwebs and thick tangles of palmetto were phosphorescent in the magic-hour light. It made the bayou look beautiful, but dawn was a milestone for which Grove had not yet prepared. It signified the futility of his search.

"One place I'm thinkin' we should check," the deputy commented suddenly. He leaned on the stick, and the prop boat pitched to the right, throwing a three-foot curl as it turned down a tributary choked with vines and saw grass.

"What's this?"

"This here's the Chitimacha Indian Reservation." The deputy nodded at the broken-down row of docks in the distant shadows. One of the storm-battered boats looked official, like some kind of police boat with some sort of seal or coat of arms just above its keel. Prudhome threw the swamp boat into low gear, the engine grinding, the craft lurching as it slowed. "Tribal police department's right up yonder."

They drifted through a narrow channel of storm wreckage up to the rotting pier, came to a bumpy stop, and docked the boat. Grove had no expectations, no hope, no enthusiasm whatsoever as he climbed out of the boat, hopped onto the creaking dock, and followed the laconic deputy into the encampment of buildings.

The tribal police department was situated at the end of the promenade.

"This here fella's a G-man, worried he lost one o' his best folks last night," Prudhome announced to the plump little Native American matron sitting at a desk just inside the door, a dispatcher's headset perched on her oily black bouffant.

"Hold your horses, HQ," she said into the headset, while holding up one plump index finger, tipped with a long pink press-on fingernail. Then she looked at Grove and jerked a thumb. "Is that gal in there yours, honey?"

Grove's heart hopped as he pushed his way past the cluttered desk, past the watercooler and file cabinets and other desks, and then into the inner office.

She was huddled in the corner, her hair still matted to her head, her shivering body covered with a police-issue woolen blanket, the kind they put over horses. Her lips were nearly blue. She looked up at Grove without comprehending what she was seeing.

"Thank Christ," Grove uttered, pausing in the doorway, paralyzed with emotion.

He couldn't move. He couldn't smile or wave or wink at her or do any of those things that men do to break the ice with women. He could only stand there, staring at her, feeling his spirit rise out of his body. For one brief instant, he shot his cuffs and smoothed his wrinkled lapel.

"Oh my God," she said at last, suddenly seeming to recognize him like an old friend or a loved one she hadn't seen in many years. She looked thunderstruck. "You're crying," she said. "I've never seen you cry."

Grove looked down at his hands, which were shaking now, and he felt the wetness on his face, a tear tracking down from his good right eye. "So I am," he said.

Maura rose and went over to him.

Another pause.

Then they hugged, and Ulysses began to sob.

EPILOGUE:
Legacies

Learn what you are and be such.

—Pindar, *Odes*

That autumn's hurricane season would live in the annals of meteorological lore as the worst on record, far worse than the previously year's deadly spate. In the weeks after Fiona, five more category-three storms battered the Gulf Coast, albeit none of them remotely as powerful as the Big One that swept through New Orleans that dark night in September. Damage estimates for Fiona alone were in excess of $75 billion making it the single-most expensive natural disaster in the history of the United States.

The only silver lining to Fiona's perilous sky was the relatively low death toll, and the fact that the Louisiana Office of Emergency Preparedness, in the aftermath of Katrina, had drilled such a wide-ranging evacuation plan into the state's media. In those critical days during which Fiona lurked out in the gulf, bloating to unprecedented levels, moving ever closer to the Big Easy, the citizenry reacted with stunning immediacy. All told, only forty-eight deaths were attributed directly to Fiona, bringing the grand total of hurricane-related deaths that season to 279.

Of course, one of these deaths, which was first directly linked to the hurricane, was later ascribed to an even *more* unnatural cause.

In his haste to find Maura, Grove had simply left Michael Doerr's body mounted there on that jagged rail, abandoned in the rain in that flooded graveyard. The Assumption Parish Fire Department finally stumbled upon the body in the wee hours, got it down, and had it shipped off to the morgue in Napoleonville. It took nearly a week for the body to be released to the FBI for autopsy and DNA tests.

In the meantime, Grove had already given both oral and written statements to the bureau's Department of Professional Standards, including a fairly detailed time line reaching all the way back to the mysterious phone call a week and a half earlier from Moses De Lourde. It wasn't until the middle of December, however, a full month after Fiona had vanished into the history books, that the Central Crime Lab and Index at Quantico released positive matches on Doerr's blood type and DNA with trace tissue found on three of the victims, including a single hair found underneath Professor De Lourde's right index fingernail, an artifact that continued to haunt Grove. How much did De Lourde know back then on that blustery night he had made his desperate cell phone call? Had he tangled already with Doerr's alter ego? Had he seen that mysterious symbol—a star within a star—scrawled in human blood on his window? The answers would forever be buried in LaFayette Cemetery Number one.

Despite all the physical evidence, though, Grove found himself embroiled in a series of contentious disputes between the bureau, the Justice Department, and the Louisiana State Police Investigative Unit. Evidently, rogue FBI agents were not tolerated well in this post 9/11, post-Katrina world. Never mind that Grove hunted down and caught one of the strangest and most elusive serial killers in the history of law enforcement—he'd done it without proper documentation. Plus, he got Ivan Kaminsky killed in the bargain.

The Russian's memorial service was held in October on Kitty Hawk Island, not far from the weather station in which he had spent his latter years staring at screens, exiled from civilization by the National Security Agency. Kaminsky had been an atheist, and had left strict instructions that he was to be cremated, and his ashes were to be spread over the sea, and people were to get together afterward and drink enough vodka to, in the words of his last will and testament, "properly become so inebriated as to forget not only their own troubles but the reason they had gathered in the first place."

Covered in bandages, walking with a cane, and now sporting a rakish black eye patch, Grove complied with Kaminsky's last wishes as best he could. Grove's poison was single malt scotch, but he drank nearly half a fifth of vodka that day.

After the ceremony, Grove and Maura County stood arm in arm on a rocky outcropping, under an overcast sky, toasting Kaminsky, laughing at his antics. Afterward they threw two unopened bottles of Stolichnaya into the ocean. They figured the Russian would appreciate the extra supplies.

Then they walked back to the little Point Harbor bed-and-breakfast in which they were staying—not far from the banks of the Alligator River, where Grove had first seen that arcane hexagonal symbol slashed in blood on the grass. The inn was a quaint little two-story clapboard, with a butter churn on the porch, and a four-poster bed that squeaked noisily with the slightest movement. Grove had convinced Maura to stay there with him that night, although they had yet to resolve their future together.

Around ten o'clock that night, woozy from all the booze, they decided to turn in. Grove decided to sleep on the davenport out in the living room by the fire—as usual—and Maura would sleep in the bedroom on the four-poster. But before retiring, she came out of the bathroom in an oversized San Francisco 49ers sweatshirt and fuzzy slippers.

"I need to know something," she said, standing in the bathroom doorway, the single incandescent bulb behind her putting a halo on her dishwater-blond hair and revealing the silhouette of her nude hips.

"This sounds serious," Grove murmured, rising from the couch. Still dressed in his jeans and velour shirt, he stood in his stocking feet across the room, staring at her, waiting. The pause stretched.

"Grove, I need to know if you're sleeping out here on the couch because you think it's what *I* want."

After a long pause, he told her yes, that was probably the case.

She took a step closer. "Well then . . . maybe you should check with me first."

Grove swallowed hard. Her words had that intense slur of a tipsy person finding courage, expressing some painful truth. Finally Grove said, "You're right. When you're right, you're right."

She took another couple of steps toward him until he could smell her powdery scent, and could see the gold flecks in her green eyes. She looked up at him. "So then . . . tell me why the hell I'm sleeping alone in the bedroom."

Grove smiled. "That's an excellent question."

She had to stand on the tips of her toes in order to kiss him on the lips.

Grove took her in his arms.

Time came crashing to a halt as they tasted each other, as they consummated their desire in one great, moist, seething kiss that carried them backward like a warm tide to the sofa. And they lowered themselves to the sounds of the light rain tapping at the building's roof, and they urged each other's clothes off in the flickering light of the fireplace. She was careful around Grove's wounds, lightly brushing her fingers across his bandages as she flicked her tongue here and there. She wore nothing under the sweatshirt, and Grove's hands were everywhere, sampling every curve of her thin, wan body. She found his erection and fell back against the armrest and guided him into her, and they made love in convulsive, desperate gasps, and there was a hint of blessed release beneath the passion, and even traces of sorrow, sorrow that brought tears to Grove's eyes as he thrust softly into her, clinging to her, holding on for dear life.

In late January, two individuals came forward during the roughest part of the bureau's internal hearings to vouch for Grove.

Grove's old friend, mentor, and section chief, Tom Geisel, made a surprise appearance one morning, showing up in a crisp white linen suit that made him look like a southern dandy who had just walked off the pages of a Carson McCullers novel. Instantly taking charge of the proceedings, Geisel angrily testified that Ulysses Grove had *always* been a rogue on some level, and that this very same rebellious nature was what made him such a valuable member of the Behavioral Science Unit. "You people ought to be pinning a medal on this guy, for Chrissake," Geisel snarled to the panel before storming out. Oddly, Grove could not find the man after the proceedings. Tom Geisel had simply vanished without a word, flying back to his Virginia farm, leaving Grove's future with the bureau as mysterious and unresolved as Geisel's appearance.

The second person who figured prominently in Grove's defense was a slight, olive-skinned Bulgarian woman who appeared before the dais wrapped in a shawl and scarf, looking like a refugee from some forgotten war. In broken English, she related how her ex-husband had loved adventure, and also had loved Ulysses Grove. And according to this little woman from another time and another world, if Ivan Kaminsky could have chosen the circumstances of his own death, they would be "fighting some son of the bitch by the side of Mr. Ulysses."

By mid-February, most of the bureaucratic tortures had been administered, and Grove had ultimately been cleared of all complaints brought against him by Professional Standards. The hard truth was, Grove had brought a mass murderer down with extreme prejudice, and that, in the end, was exactly what Joe Citizen wanted from his investigative agencies. The fact that Grove was working essentially under the radar—and stepping on the toes of law enforcement people in five states—none of this mattered to old John Q. Public.

During his final days in the wounded, moldering city of New Orleans, Grove visited the professor's old haunts one last time, and spent time with his cronies. He drank absinthe at Poppy Brite's, and heard the Joe Crown

Quintet play at Tipitina's. He also dined at Antoine's with Miguel Lafountant, Delilah Debuke, and Sandi Loper-Herzog, and he answered all their questions about the dreadful business with the Doerr boy. They could not conceive how such a sweet and adorable kid such as Michael Doerr could do all those hideous things, especially to poor Moses. Grove agreed with them, concurring that a normal, healthy human mind had difficulty finding purchase on such a slippery slope.

"But what about *you*?" Delilah blurted at one point in the evening, fixing his painted eyes on Grove. "*You* seem to be able to conceive of such things."

Everybody was drunk by that point, and Miguel shushed the drag queen from across the table.

Grove waved it off, and said, "It's okay. She's right. You're right, Delilah. It's what I'm good at. It's what I do." Then he allowed himself a faint, exhausted smile. "I guess somebody's got to do it."

The moment passed, and they kept drinking and talking about everything *other* than murder, and the evening dissolved away like the sugar cubes in their chartreuse cocktails. But hours later, after they all had said their tearful good-byes, and Grove had started back to his hotel, the accusation continued to reverberate in his brain. Why *did* he have a hunger to hunt? Why *him*? He thought of his mother, and he thought of his birth amid that terrible dream-storm. He thought of his biological father—the angry, volatile presence in the heart of that hallucination. The truth was, the only storm that day was the storm kicked up by his father's rage. Everything flowed from there. Everything. For better or worse.

That night he dreamed of that same Kenyan village

in which he was born, but this time he was alone, the sky overhead a blank gray shroud.

As silent and still as a tomb.

The day after the final hearing, Grove was in his hotel room packing for the trip back to Virginia, when his phone rang. It was Maura. She was down in the lobby, which made no sense whatsoever, since he had put her on an airplane less than a week ago. He had not expected to see her until the following week when he was scheduled to take a holiday in San Francisco.

Grove was nonplussed, but also delighted that she had caught him, and told her he was just checking out and he'd be right down. He quickly finished his packing and then checked himself in the mirror.

His injuries were still apparent. A slender pucker marred his brow above his left eye where the stitches had come out a week earlier. His eye patch now was the sporty black velvet model worn over the years by such fashion plates as Moshe Dian and Yule Brenner. Some of his bruises had yellowed, and some showed as dark patches on his brown skin. But other than that, he had cleaned up fairly well. He looked at his reflection, and checked his suit, an Armani double-breasted number the color of toasted coconut. Underneath he wore an eggshell button-down oxford, open at the collar.

The old Grove stared out from the mirror.

With a nod, Grove turned away, grabbed his suitcase, and strode out of the room.

He took the elevator down to the lobby, and found Maura waiting for him by the bar. "What are *you* doing here?" he said, putting down his suitcase and pulling her into a hug. "I thought we were meeting in Frisco next week?"

"That's a fine greeting," she said, embracing him with an almost aggressive warmth and affection. She smelled of chewing gum and the stale air of a jet cabin. She wore a black, spandex tank top, and had her milkweed-blond hair pulled back in a no-nonsense ponytail.

Grove was vexed. "I'm sorry, kiddo, I'm just a little . . . Did I miss something?"

"We need to talk," she said, her gray-green eyes shining with emotion. The ebullient, almost earnest look on her face told Grove something new had developed here. He couldn't put his finger on it, but he could tell immediately—*something* was going on.

Maura was looking around the bustling lobby for a quiet corner in which to talk, but the place was teeming with activity. The Philippe de Champaigne was one of the first hotels to reopen after the second year in a row of disaster relief and cleanup, and today its bellhops scurried to and fro while guests marshaled their luggage past the ornate brass fixtures and marble colonnades and jungles of fichus and fern plants.

"Why don't we take a walk?" she said at last, indicating the glass doors.

Grove stashed his luggage behind the concierge desk, and they took their leave into the sultry afternoon.

It was already edging toward ninety degrees as they started toward Canal Street, sidestepping street musicians and panhandlers. New Orleans had risen from its watery grave once again, and was almost back to business as usual.

The heat seemed to lie on top of the city like a veil, and Grove instantly perspired through his shirt. He shrugged off his coat and carried it on his arm as they talked about minor things for a few minutes, travel plans, the results of the hearings. Finally Grove said, "You gonna tell me what's going on or what?"

"First let me ask you a question."

"Fire away."

"Do you love me?"

"What? Yes."

"It's not a trick question, Ulysses."

"Yes, Christ. Yes. I do. I love the hell outta you, Maura." He put his arm around her. "I really do. You're it, kiddo. For the duration."

She nodded, satisfied. Like it was a test, and Grove had just passed.

They were walking south on Canal toward the Mississippi. The streetcars clanged past them, the pale sky low and heavy with humidity. The air smelled of wood smoke and rotting fish and diesel fumes. Signs of the flood were everywhere. Most storefronts were still boarded, and river scum still clung to the sides of buildings twenty feet above ground level. Construction equipment and roadblocks choked the streets. But things were getting better every day.

"Hold on a second, stop, stop!" Grove stepped in front of her as they approached Riverfront Park. The shipyard behind him boomed and wheezed with activity, the ravages of the second killer hurricane still visible in the piles of wreckage. He took Maura by the arms. "What's the matter?"

"Nothing's the matter, Ulysses. There's some news, is all."

He looked at her, his heart beginning to thump. The look in her eye made him nervous all of a sudden. "Wait a minute," he uttered.

She was grinning, her eyes going liquid all of a sudden. "I wanted to tell you in person. As soon as I found out. I'm eating for two, Uly."

He looked into her shimmering green eyes, and he felt the world tilt slightly. He couldn't move. A pelican shrilled in the distance. He felt his face flush hot with blood, then break out into the stupidest smile in recorded history. "You are not," he murmured.

"Yep, sure am." Maura's smile lit up her face, and she put her arms around him. "You're gonna be a daddy, Ulysses."

He hugged her tightly, and he tried to say something intelligent, but the lump in his throat would not let him. His eyes were stinging now, watering, and he wiped them with the back of his hand. At last he looked at her and said, "If you start smoking again I will shoot you."

She laughed. "C'mon. I'm starved. Did that place that serves alligator reopen yet?"

They turned and walked back up Canal Street, hand in hand, until they vanished into the heat rays of people and machinery and a city rebuilding once again.

Afterword

The parade of souls is marching across the sky
Their heat and their light bathed in blue as they
   march by
The All Stars play "When the Saints Go Marching
   In"
A second line forms and they wave white hankies
   in the wind.

—Mary Gauthier, "Wheel Inside the Wheel"

In these final pages, which are usually reserved for the requisite thank-yous and smoke blowing, I would like to dispense with customary protocol and extend my love, best wishes, and deep gratitude to an entire city.

I confess I am merely a tourist, a distant admirer of the great New Orleans, but this book not only owes its existence to this amazing town, it also merely skims the surface of New Orleans's greatness. Notwithstanding the strange confluence of events that occurred during the writing of this book—an example of life imitating . . . *something* . . . maybe art, maybe simple fate—I would like to pay tribute to the town that existed before Hurricane Katrina and will exist long after we all go to that parade of souls in the sky. Thanks to all the parishes that welcomed me during my visits and opened their funky-big hearts to me—especially Orleans, Jefferson, St. Tammany, St. Bernard, and St. Charles.

Thanks to the people of the French Quarter, with their patina of grace and soulfulness, the street musicians like Glen Andrews and the Lazy 6, and the guys down at the Louisiana Music Factory, 210 Decatur Street, for keeping the local music scene alive (www.louisiana musicfactory.com). Thanks to Joe Crown, and Papa John Gros, and Grayson Capps (you always get back up), and the great eateries of the Quarter like Dickie Brennan's and K-Paul's. And especially Antoine's, 713 St. Louis Street, for keeping the incredible cuisine alive (I had oysters Rockefeller number 4,010,763). Thanks to the caretakers and stewards of the great cities of the dead, such as Lafayette Number 1, where Professor De Lourde was put to rest, and the St. Louises, established in 1789, a true community of spirits. Thanks to the fascinating Historic Voodoo Museum on Dumaine, and the beautiful Tulane campus, and the magnificent Audubon Park. And these are just an apéritif of all that the city has to offer.

Enormous gratitude and affection goes out to all the generations of artists, thinkers, and eccentrics who have populated this spectacular gumbo of culture and history called New Orleans (and who have inspired me). To Marie Laveau, the Mardis Gras Indians, Buddy Bolden, Tennessee Williams, Louis Armstrong, Anne Rice, Jelly Roll Morton, William Faulkner, Professor Longhair, Clarence Gatemouth Brown (R.I.P.), Dr. John, and many many many more. And last but not least, thank you to those who risked life and limb in August of '05 to save the town and the people from the lethal floodwater: the first responders, the firefighters, the NOPD, and the American Red Cross.

The Red Cross, in fact, is still, at press time, taking donations to help the ongoing relief efforts across the gulf and around the world. You can reach them at www.RedCross.org. Please give until it hurts. New Orleans is a living museum, a treasure, a national heirloom. It is where popular American music was born. It is the true literary Mecca of the country. We must preserve it, celebrate it, move to it, visit it, and always, always, always remember it.